Born in the village of Moore in the Borough of Halton, located midway between Runcorn and Warrington in Cheshire, England, where his father was a licensed victualler, Richard de Mora gave up a promising career on the Mersey Ferries to follow his dream of being a session musician at Abbey Road. He never actually played his guitar in any Beatles' sessions, though he often claimed that he had. Now, he's decided to write fiction and it's up to you to decide how well that's turned out.

Rik de Mora

AREA 53

AUSTIN MACAULEY PUBLISHERS
LONDON * CAMBRIDGE * NEW YORK * SHARJAH

Copyright © Rik de Mora 2024

The right of Rik de Mora to be identified as the author of this work has been asserted by the author in accordance with sections 77 and 78 of the Copyright, Designs and Patents Act 1988.

All rights reserved. No part of this publication may be reproduced, stored in a retrieval system, or transmitted in any form or by any means, electronic, mechanical, photocopying, recording, or otherwise, without the prior permission of the publishers.

Any person who commits any unauthorised act in relation to this publication may be liable to criminal prosecution and civil claims for damages.

This is a work of fiction. Names, characters, businesses, places, events, locales, and incidents are either the products of the author's imagination or used in a fictitious manner. Any resemblance to actual persons, living or dead, or actual events is purely coincidental.

A CIP catalogue record for this title is available from the British Library.

ISBN 9781035875535 (Paperback)
ISBN 9781035875542 (ePub e-book)

www.austinmacauley.com

First Published 2024
Austin Macauley Publishers Ltd®
1 Canada Square
Canary Wharf
London
E14 5AA

Also by Rik de Mora

The Rochdale Yeast (published by Austin Macauley Publishers, 15 September 2023). ISBN-13: 978–1398479104. 198 pages.

Imagine you could genetically engineer a microorganism that was able to produce LSD into its culture broth. If the microorganism was a brewing yeast, you could make beer spiked with homemade LSD. Imagine how much mischief you could cause with that. If the microorganism was a bacterium that you had also engineered to transfer LSD-synthesis to every other bacterium in a person's body, you could make some very potent live yoghurt. Imagine what sorts of mischief you could do then. Follow on her first solo field mission as she identifies exotic microbes like these and pursues those who created them and put them to use. And all the time she is chasing them down, the greatest mischief these microorganisms have caused is being played out in the dizzying depths of the North Atlantic.

Starship-101 (published by Austin Macauley Publishers, 28 March 2024). ISBN-13: 978–1035859313. 452 pages.

Starship-101 successfully landed on Proxima Centauri-b about twenty years ago, marking humanity's first interstellar settlement. But with radio messages taking over four years to traverse the vast darkness of space, this fledgling colony has been isolated from Earth. Enter the Clason twins—Tarvin and Harden—the galaxy's preeminent Superposition Navigators. These brothers can bend the quantum space-time continuum to their will, instantaneously transporting people and cargo across the stars. To revive supply lines and reintegrate Proxima Centauri-b into humanity's network of trade, the Clasons have been contracted to lead a modern resupply mission. Their quantum technology will provide the colony with the latest gadgets and gizmos from home. And the Navigators have another task—returning Starship-101 itself. That aging relic is now a valuable antique, the first testimony that humans can thrive beyond our solar cradle. Join the Clason twins as they quantum-jump across the cosmos on this historic mission of reconnection!

Table of Contents

1. The Canals of Mars	9
2. Chatting with Microsoft Copilot	35
3. Frank Conversation	63
4. Mussels with Josie, Oysters with Billie	92
5. The Asimov Incident	122
6. The Aliens Are Coming. No, Honestly!	157
7. Cosmic Dreams	188
8. Roswell Rules	209

1. The Canals of Mars

I'm usually awake well before dawn. It's an age thing, like the regular trips to the bathroom during the night. But the hot flushes that wake me around 3 or 4 a.m., all hot and sweaty, I'd class as only a secondary age thing. They're more of a medication thing, but as the medication is keeping me alive, I don't complain. Well, not too much! I try to cool off and then spend the rest of the night dozing, drifting in and out of sleep. In and out of dreams. Sometimes I switch my bedside radio on, and the half-heard broadcasts direct and colour my dreams. Otherwise, my mind glides along paths it finds for itself. Some of those paths are followed more often than others.

If sleep does not come after one of those hot flushes, I lie in my bed cooling off in the most relaxed way I can manage and doing nothing more exciting than staring at the ceiling. A previous tenant tried to improve the decoration of this bedroom with an ornamental plaster ceiling rose around the pendant light fitting.

A later tenant, more philistine than appreciative, hacked it off and threw it away, leaving only the scars of his vandalism on the innocent and otherwise featureless ceiling. It is the last thing I see each night and the first I see each morning, and it sets my drifting mind into recollections.

At this time of day, with the first light of the sun raking across the ceiling, the cracks and shadows on that central damaged disk remind me of the sketch maps of the canals of Mars I found so fascinating as a young lad.

My subconscious mind, that ever-present custodian of my memories of everything that has ever happened to me, sometimes taps me on the shoulder of the mindscape that's inside my head and pushes forward, with perfect clarity, a memory of an event that happened many years ago. And then my semi-sleep state can enjoy itself examining and building a reverie with that memory.

Now, for example, subconscious me has just reminded semi-conscious me that I do recall that Giovanni Schiaparelli drew maps of Mars at the end of the

19th century with many long straight channels, which, because Schiaparelli was Italian, he called *Canali*.

Then, at the beginning of the twentieth century, Percival Lowell created the myth of the Martian Canals by linking them to seasonal changes in the brightness of features of the Martian surface that he thought might be caused by cultivation of Martian vegetation.

To a 10-year-old boy in the 1950s, these were wonderfully imaginative stories and even though more detailed astronomical observations had discredited the most ingenious tales about canal-boating Martians by the time that I was avidly reading those tales, I traced my own maps. I learned Lowell's names for his Martian geography, and I felt privileged to be part of the unresolved debate.

A debate that was finally decided on 15 July 1965, when the Mariner 4 spacecraft's camera managed to record 21 slightly blurred pictures of the Southern Hemisphere of Mars as it flew past at a distance of 9,600 kilometres. The canals of Schiaparelli and Lowell were most noticeable by their absence.

Instead of the cultivated surface, Lowell's observations from distance had promised, Mariner 4 showed Mars to be more like our Moon: a world covered in craters and currently without liquid water at the surface. Mariner 4 closed the file on Martian canals and, except in the most determined and lurid imaginations, it closed the file on *'men from Mars.'*

It did something else, too. The Mariner spacecraft demonstrated that robots could perform scientific exploration in space. Astronauts were not required for this type of mission. Another disappointment for an over-imaginative, would-be space explorer!

And yet, and yet. My morning reverie continues, and my half-awake butterfly mind flitters to memories of my meeting with the first man to set foot on Mars. 1979, it was.

I mean 1979 was the date when Captain Charlie Orde landed on Mars, seven years after the last Apollo Moon landing. I did not meet him until the 1990s, and the fact of his landing on Mars and what he and his crew went there to start is the deepest secret anyone can know.

Are secrets deep? Perhaps they are big. Or maybe dark? Well, whatever; it might be; this one is the biggest, darkest, and deepest of all. And the most dangerous.

'You want more coffee?'

Hell, I've drifted into sleep again.

'Nah. It'll keep me awake.'

'Fun-nee! There'll be no snoozin' at the back of the machine room this afternoon, fellah. We got a visitor.'

Strange; it must be more than 15 years since I've even thought about Pete Gibbon, but here he pops, large as life, into my dream.

'He's our new Head Skunk, so, you'll have to be awake to see him.'

'Who is he? Should I know him?'

'Well...,' Pete took a long drag on the Peter Stuyvesant cigarette he favoured and finished the sentence as he exhaled the smoke 'It's a real interesting case. You should know about him because of what he's done, but if you do know about him,...' Pete narrowed his eyes and theatrically aimed a forefinger at me as though he was holding a pistol '...I'm afraid we'd have to kill you, kid. Roswell Rule Number Two!'

I had lunch with Pete Gibbon every weekday for most of the three years I spent at Edwards Air Force Base. He was the first person I saw when I first flew into Nellis from GCHQ in Cheltenham, and we just took to each other immediately. He was a retired career Air Force officer who gossiped outrageously about the place in which I had come to work; with a story, usually scurrilous, sometimes crude but always entertaining, about most of our fellow workers and especially our immediate superiors.

He was a helpful, friendly, and disgracefully amusing man who accompanied me on my first flight from Nellis to Groom Lake, found me an office just down the corridor from his own, and introduced me to the people and computer systems with which I was to work.

I spent a lot of time with Pete, both on- and off-duty; it was a long time before I started to suspect that he was my security guard, my handler in security jargon. Something that was confirmed only when his replacement turned up immediately after his death.

The ground staff found Pete sitting in the Janet Flight Departure Lounge at McCarren Airport, Las Vegas long after the early-morning flight had boarded. He was just sitting there, with a skull full of blood and a drowned brain.

Apparently, he'd suffered a ruptured aneurysm. By coincidence, his replacement, an archetypical security goon on his first assignment, called Clarence Bellwether, came to Edwards on the same flight that Pete should have used. I never really got friendly with Clarence, I don't think his mother had either, but then that tour of duty at Area 51 ended, and I returned to GCHQ in Chelmsford.

I could see that Pete wanted to tell another one of his stories, so I played along with the pantomime.

'Okay,' I said, 'without prejudice, what might this person have done that might impress me?'

Pete closed in conspiratorially and hissed, 'First man on Mars.'

Then he backed off as though he expected some kind of extravagant reaction from me.

'Who do you mean,' I asked, 'Neil Armstrong?'

'No!' he replied, extending the sound of the word in mock exasperation,

'That was only the Moon, and anyway everybody knows about that. This is Charlie Orde. When he landed on Mars, he was a humble Air Force Major, just like me.'

'But he was probably, at least a Colonel by the time he got back, and he'll probably be some sort of General by the time he takes over as Director of the Skunk Works. Still, I'm a civilian now so I won't have to salute!'

'I didn't know anyone had been to Mars.' I said.

'Perfect,' replied Pete, grinning. 'You stick to that story, and you'll be fine. You're in the Skunk Works now, Buddy. This is where the good ole U.S. of A. builds things nobody else has even dreamed of yet. Everything you didn't think could happen has happened here.'

'Work on the principle that nothing you see here with your own eyes ever actually took place. And remember Roswell Rule Number One: nothing you know to be true here is ever divulged to the outside world!'

Reminiscing about lunchtimes of long ago, even in my dreams, stirs my hunger enough to wake me fully despite the early hour. I need breakfast, so I roll myself off the bed and try to stand upright without putting too much strain on my troublesome right knee.

Eventually, after a fair amount of grunting and groaning, I feel sufficiently confident to shuffle out to the so-called kitchen-diner of my little flat. My little bolthole.

The previous tenant treated the decoration of my kitchen no better than the decoration of my bedroom. Polished black faux granite worktops are fine and functional, but the apple green doors on the kitchen units and allegedly complementary tiled splash backs in Roman royal purple are not to my taste.

I had to remove the buttercup yellow plastic lampshade from the light fitting. No mean feat with my knee protesting mightily on every step up the ladder.

'It makes it so warm and sunny,' is how the landlady described it, but it had to go after a few days because it was putting me off my morning tea and toast.

Now, a naked bulb hangs in the centre of the room and serves as a detector for the gentle breeze that enters through the ill-fitted double-glazed sash window that looks out over the backyard car park.

That's no bad thing, I suppose. Shivering is about the only exercise I get these days. That, and walking to the park to feed the ducks. The rest of my time is spent hunched over the laptop keyboard in my sitting room/office trying to avoid another warm and sunny glow coming off the pale pink wallpaper with the giant dark pink roses and the feature wall of tangerine and white Regency stripes.

That's what I'm doing here and now. Breakfast can wait. First, I need a large mug of strong coffee and a seat at my keyboard. I must write all the great thoughts that my subconscious has come up with overnight. Write them, and the reminiscences they trigger, now or forget them.

You see, I'm writing what I guess you'd call an autobiography, and I'm writing it almost 24/7 these days. I think this place is getting to me, but at my age, it's a matter of writing it down today, because I could be dead tomorrow! So, I've got to keep my head down, writing, writing, writing; remember Roswell Rules!

I'm retired now and have been for 15 years. Yeah, I'm surprised that I'm still alive too! I spent over 40 years of my life 'working for the Government' as they say. Actually, I eventually worked for several governments, but I'll get around to describing that. I started out life as a computer systems analyst but then gradually became a sort of electronic filing clerk.

See, right through my childhood and early teens the world's businesses began using large numbers of mainframe computers so, right from school, I keenly read the science magazines that told what computers could do and how they did it. I was fascinated!

Ironic, really, because I was only one year old when the president of IBM was supposed to have offered about the worst technology prediction of all time by saying, 'I think there is a world market for about five computers,' in 1943.

Then, just over 10 years later, a young teenage me was eagerly reading all the factual stories (and let's be truthful about this, all the sci-fi stories, too) I could find about computers and computing. In fact, I spent my childhood watching avidly from the sidelines as the early computer manufacturers in the UK pioneered development of digital computers in the 1950s and 1960s.

I left school in 1960 and walked straight into an apprenticeship at the Ferranti works in Speke. For a young Toxteth scally born in 1942, just as the German bombing raids of the Liverpool Blitz were winding down in intensity, the Ferranti works in Speke was a fabled place to work because it had made Spitfire fuselages during the war, as well as other electrical and electronic components for the RAF.

After the war, Ferranti continued to design and manufacture electrical equipment like radios and televisions, but more importantly, was the first company to produce and sell a digital computer on the commercial market. That was in 1951 and was based on a prototype designed in the University of Manchester.

Of course, I was only nine years old when that happened, but, fortunately, the world needed more than five computers and the business flourished. By the time I first alighted from the old 82-bus on Speke Road and trudged up to their gates to start my apprenticeship, they were selling their fifth-generation machine, the *Sirius*, and were working with Manchester University on the *Atlas* project, which was one of the first supercomputers.

So, in my late teens and early 20s, I was totally happy with my life! Ferranti taught me machine-level binary coding and then assembler. I found I had a natural ability to understand and use these low-level languages and, off my own bat, I taught myself to be proficient in FORTRAN and COBOL, which suited my involvement with the commercial machines the company were selling.

But seeing that I had this proficiency with languages, my line manager got me transferred to the *Atlas* project and sent me to Manchester University to learn ALGOL. I got pretty good at that, and my university supervisor suggested I do some research for a master's degree on relational database design and implementation.

The MSc experience got me hooked on academic research and as studentship grants covering all tuition fees and living expenses were readily available then (especially to the underprivileged ex-residents of Toxteth!), I just slipped naturally into a PhD study.

This research was aimed at creating a database query language that could operate across many relational databases extracting information in response to the user's initial query, but then cross-referencing the information it found first, to guide deeper and deeper searches for answers to the initial query.

To the user, it could look like the computer was making intelligent decisions about the subject of the query, but the 'decisions' were all based on a statistical engine I'd coded into the program that assessed the probabilities of different outcomes at each logical branchpoint.

Still, some of my code subroutines were later used to help develop the so-called 'artificial intelligent' Internet search engines that are all the rage these days. Some, but not all, because some of my most intelligent code subroutines were made official secrets!

How that came about was down to my PhD-supervisor who, as my PhD thesis was approaching completion, reached out to one of his old mates to serve as External Examiner of my thesis and she just happened to work with the supercomputers at the UK Government's signals intelligence, cyber and security agency, the Government Communications Headquarters, more succinctly known as GCHQ.

As soon as she saw my coding for my 'special' subroutines she was on the phone instructing us to lock away all copies of my thesis and all my data files and await a visit from the Security Services! She later turned up in Manchester with a small group of people who identified themselves as representing various branches of the UK Security Services.

She gave me a very friendly oral examination over a lavish lunch (held in the Vice-Chancellor's Dining Room no less!), approved the award of a PhD degree over dessert, and, with the coffee, offered me a job in Chelmsford starting immediately!

She left one of the security bods with me to assist with my move to Chelmsford and within a couple of whirlwind days I was established in a nice little top floor flat on Pinewood Drive, Cheltenham, overlooking the GCHQ car park!

I was over the moon! And for more reasons than one. Obviously, landing a well-paid job with outstanding career prospects and a decent apartment was a very important consideration! But beyond that, I knew, I was following in my father's footsteps.

You see, my father left school just after the end of the First World War and a few months after his 18th birthday, in January 1922, he enlisted in the South Lancashire Regiment of the British Army and served for 12 years until 1934. During that time his battalion served on garrison duty in Palestine, and then in India, garrisoned in Bombay, and deployed to the Northwest Frontier with Afghanistan.

There he learned the trade of gunner because that was his qualified trade when he was conscripted into the RAF regiment in 1941, on the day after his 38th birthday. With a little further training, his trade was later changed to RAF clerk, and he spent two years working in that capacity in an RAF Supply Depot until he was sent to the RAF Code and Cypher School based at RAF Kidlington, near Oxford.

This was the institution that broke the Luftwaffe's Enigma cypher, which enabled the RAF to anticipate, and counter, enemy air raids right from the Battle of Britain in 1940 onwards.

They also broke the Abwehr's secret service codes, which were used to send instructions to German spies in Britain and throughout Europe, as well as the Italian Air Force and Navy codes, which helped the RAF to disrupt Italian operations in the Mediterranean and North Africa, which is where my dad plied his trade.

At the end of WWII, the RAF Code and Cypher School's personnel and equipment were transferred to the Government Code and Cypher School, which was renamed as the Government Communications Headquarters, or GCHQ in 1946.

It was over 20 years before my dad told me anything about all this. Extreme secrecy had been drilled into him! But when he did spill the beans, he delighted in saying that all this code-breaking success was down to the fact that the RAF had bought in a supply of the German Enigma machines, which were commercially available in the mid-1930s!

Then, RAF engineers adapted them with several enhancements that greatly increased the security of the RAF's Typex cypher machines, electric typewriter-like machines with five revolving drums or rotors of letters set to specific combinations according to the date and time of day.

Typex machines were used by the RAF from 1937 and, with many revisions, until the mid-1950s when they were replaced by electronic encryption systems. As he described it, Dad typed in a signal with the letter drums of his Typex machine set to the combination described for this time on this day in the master code book, and the message would be encrypted into groups of five jumbled letters.

These were printed out on a paper tape and passed to a wireless operator to transmit by Morse code to the intended recipient. The receiving cypher bod typed the jumbled five-letter groups into his Typex machine after using his code book to set up the rotors to the time and date of the transmission, and plain language came out on his paper tape.

The five rotors of the RAF's Typex machines gave them much greater security than the original Enigma used by the Germans and their allies throughout the war which had only three or four rotors.

When I was offered my job at GCHQ, I was delighted to think that I was taking up where my dad had left off. Many years later, about 10 years after I'd retired and moved back to Liverpool, they invited me back to GCHQ as an honoured guest. But not to Cheltenham. Rather, to the opening ceremony of GCHQ-Manchester in Heron House, on Albert Square.

The powers that be even risked giving me the chance to say a few words to all the new staff, from my standpoint as an elderly statesman! I was already aware that the so-called millennials and their offspring, 'Generation Z' are appallingly ignorant of the history their own parents had lived through, so I decided to tell them about my dad's wartime exploits and how I was the second-generation cyber clerk in my family!

It went down all right, although the short attention span of Gen Z in the audience was very apparent, and, judging by the lit-up faces scattered around the room, more than a few were furtively scanning their devices! But while I was talking, I was reflecting on my own GCHQ experiences and realised the strange symmetry with my father's career.

He went from RAF clerk to cypher encryption pioneer, whereas I started out as a digital security pioneer and, by the time I retired, had reached the dizzying heights of digital filing clerk with his own security handler!

I didn't have a grand or special title when I first started, just a computer systems analyst. At various later times, my official title identified me as an 'analyst' modified by a range of adjectives. Junior to begin, then various grades of senior this or senior that, identifying whatever specialism I was exercising at the time.

Finally, I was just 'the Analyst'; but that was towards the end, when I was so deeply embedded in the darkest secrets of the world that those in charge felt I warranted a personal security guard [*there, I can't get Pete Gibbon out of my mind today*].

I may have started out labelled as a computer systems analyst but in truth, I really was an electronic filing clerk. First, we made computerised lists of the paper files. Then we started converting the paperwork to electronic files. When word processors came into wide use, the documents started out on computer, had a brief life on paper being pushed around in some committee or other, and finally, ended up being archived on the computer.

These days even the oldest files get scanned and archived in increasingly-minute high-density memory. It's no good having petabytes or terabytes, or even gigabytes, of digitised documents in storage unless you have an indexing system and some sort of electronic search engine that allows you to find information you didn't even know existed. That's my job.

Archive, index and cross-correlate the vast quantity of documents the Government has on all sorts of topics and merge each new batch into a search engine that's got enough artificial intelligence that it can recognise information that the user needs to know even when the user doesn't know what he or she is looking for.

There's nothing magic about this; today's online shops and online advertisers have been using such software subroutines for years to suggest more items you might be interested in buying, using your past purchases as a guide. So, my subroutines used an individual's identity (and the personnel files are just one of the databases open to the subroutine to use; except mine, of course) and their past searches to aid new searches.

Although I always enjoyed my job; hell, I eventually worked with some of the most extensive server farms in existence, who wouldn't enjoy that? The hard work in the early years was done by rooms full of machine room girls transcribing typed or even handwritten documents by touch typing on machines that punched holes into paper tape and/or into input cards.

This is the way programming and digital analysis were done during most of my time at Ferranti and, later, during my PhD research. But the era of magnetic disks for computer file storage had already arrived while I was still in secondary school. When, in 1956, IBM produced the first reliable high-speed random access memory disk storage unit for computers in response to the need for real-time accounting by commercial businesses.

This monster had 100 recording surfaces on 52 two-foot-diameter magnetic disks spinning at 1200 rpm and had a capacity of 3.75 megabytes. A major selling point of the IBM 305 computer system to which this disk storage unit was attached was that the whole system could be housed in a room of no more than about 9 metres by 15 metres in which the disk storage unit occupied 1.5 square metres of floor space!

Still, it was the first computer with a decent hard disk drive. At the moment, I've got a micro-SD card as supplementary storage in the smartphone in my pocket with a capacity of 1-TB—that's 279,620 times greater capacity than the capacity of the IBM 305 disk storage unit!

To compare these two devices another way, my micro-SD card is only 15 mm × 11 mm, and that IBM disk storage unit, therefore, with its 52 two-foot-diameter, double-sided, magnetic disks spinning away inside, was just over 9,000 times bigger!

If you had deep pockets in 1956, you could lease the IBM 305 system for US$ 3,200 *per month* and this was at a time when the average salary in the U.S. was around US$ 3,600 *per year*.

Converting these U.S.$-values to their current levels, the leasing contract would today cost you U.S.$ 33,300 *per month* and, on average, your salary in the United States will be around U.S.$ 59,428 *per year*.

So, at neither end of the 67-year time period could someone earning the average salary afford to lease the computing system. Yet, I bought my 1-TB micro-SD card in 2023 and paid for the contract for the phone, in which I use it, without thinking twice about the cost.

This comparison makes me (and a lot of other, more conspiratorial, people) wonder what could have driven these astonishing rates of advances in both technology and manufacturing processes. Just market forces? Or something else?

Those keen on conspiracy theories would suggest that such advances resulted from our engineers' reverse-engineering electronic devices recovered from extraterrestrial aliens. I think this attitude fails to appreciate just how good our own engineers are in real life.

So, you see, in the hope of showing how ridiculous these conspiracy theories can be, I ask this question: what would life be like if we'd made that same 279,620-times improvement in other areas of technology? Take aircraft, for example; a new air-speed record of 1,132 mph was set in 1956 by a British prototype aircraft called the Fairey Delta II.

Also, the F-104 Starfighter interceptor, just coming into service with the USAF as a frontline fighter, broke all previous speed records in 1958 by flying at a sustained speed of 1,404 mph.

If our aeronautical engineers had also spent their time reverse-engineering the flying machines of extraterrestrial aliens and managed improvements in our aircraft to the same extent as those improvements in electronics, by simple arithmetic comparison, the *'F-2023 Starfighter interceptor'* would be able to fly around at 392 million mph.

392-MILLION mph! Hell, that's about 58% of the speed of light! At that speed, you could get to Mars in less than half an hour! To Neptune in around seven hours, and Pluto in about eight hours! I've read about something called the Oort Cloud, which is believed to be a vast spherical bubble in interstellar space surrounding the whole of the solar system.

It's thought to be made of icy pieces of debris left over from the original protoplanetary disc that surrounded the sun, including lumps the size of mountains and planetesimals, all of which have been scattered far into space by the gravitational influence of our solar system's giant planets. The inner edge of the Oort Cloud is approximately 186 trillion miles from the sun, and the outer edge is approximately 18.6 quadrillion miles away.

So, if our imagined reverse-engineered F-2023 Starfighter interceptor flew out to the Oort Cloud at 392-million mph it would still take about 54 years to travel from Earth to the inner edge of the Oort Cloud, but interstellar space is so vast it would take 5,400 years to travel from Earth to the outer edge of the Oort Cloud at that speed.

As Douglas Adams remarked in 'The Hitchhiker's Guide to the Galaxy,' *'Space is big. You just won't believe how vastly, hugely, mind-bogglingly big it is.'*

You know, I think I've just talked myself into a conspiracy theory! Writing it down like this makes it look eminently sensible that IF (and that really is a 'BIG IF') you had your hands on an alien spacecraft and you wanted to be properly prepared to deal with the next one that might come along you'd want to strip out all the knowledge you could from that alien vessel for immediate application to your own technology.

You'd have to assume that aliens would be able to listen in on any of your communications. So, to prevent any future alien visitors from being pre-warned about your improving capabilities, all your reverse-engineering activities would have to be kept in total secrecy on a global basis. Maybe that's already been done, and our reverse-engineered F-2023 Starfighter interceptors are secretly patrolling the edges of the solar system right now. How should I know?

Let's stop this speculation and get our feet back on the ground; I still haven't brought my personal story up to date. By the time I was working on my PhD, in the late 1960s, IBM produced another significant milestone in the history of data storage, namely the floppy disk.

I remember handling one of these in the computer centre shortly after they became commercially available for use in IBM machines in 1971. It was a large object. The flexible magnetic memory disk itself was eight-inch in diameter and it was enclosed in a close-fitting plastic envelope, just a little over eight-inch square, to keep dust at bay.

It was the portability of stored data with these disks and the removability of the data from the computer system that originated it, which made the eight-inch floppy disks such a significant contribution to the evolution of data storage devices.

Their data capacity, of 80 KB (kilobytes), seems pitiful considering the multi-GB data capacities of even the cheapest of today's USB sticks and SD cards.

I've seen it written somewhere that the memory capacity of the state-of-the-art computers of the North American Aerospace Defense Command (NORAD), responsible in the 1960s and 1970s for early warning of possible air, missile, or space attacks on North America, was 'likely in the kilobyte range' with 65 to 128 KB being the best estimates.

As the technology advanced, the 8-inch floppy disk was replaced by 5¼-inch disks in 1976, and the 3½-inch format was introduced in 1982. These offered successively more convenient ways of storing data in a portable way for personal computers.

It must be admitted, though, that they were expensive luxury options initially, but worth it as they provided both storage and transport for the files you made on your PC. Hard disk drives entered the consumer market in the early 1980s but didn't become standard equipment until the 1990s.

The data capacity of the earliest hard disks for personal computers was in the region of five MB but by the mid-1990s a typical hard disk drive for a PC had a data capacity in the range of around 500 MB.

Today, your personal computing device, whether tablet, laptop or desktop is likely to have a solid-state drive (SSD) composed of integrated circuit assemblies rather than the physical spinning disks and movable read-write heads of the earlier hard disk drives (HDD). Lacking moving parts, SSDs operate silently and are resistant to physical shock.

They also have higher input/output rates, a feature which improves the overall performance of your computer. The world's highest capacity SSD available at the time of writing has a capacity of 100 TB. It's designed for data centres and other activities requiring massive storage capacity and exceptional input/output performance.

So, not for your average PC user, even if he/she could put up the US$ 40,000 to have one built to special order. You also must remember that computer chips run hot. And with all those electrons running around 100 TB of integrated circuits, these big SSDs require active cooling.

In my time as a computer analyst, I've used all the equipment I've described so far and, of course, a lot more of what you might call 'professional level' equipment in the data centres and server farms I've worked in over the years. In my time, I've overseen the digital processing and indexing of millions of documents.

That's been my job for the best part of 40 years. Archive, index, cross-reference and correlate the vast quantity of documents our governments have on all sorts of topics. Although some of the documents were classified as ultrasecret, they were in the minority, but it became obvious to me that some of these were incomplete; odd pages might be missing, and sometimes whole file folders had gone astray.

I referred these to security, of course, but none were found to be serious security breaches. The ones that the security bods ran down all turned out to be innocent mis-filings. Cases where unguarded notes and jottings, transcriptions of phone calls, or some other peripheral document had ended up in the wrong pile of paper and/or the wrong file folder.

To solve this problem, I wrote some code that modified the indexing subroutines I'd been using since I started my job at GCHQ and then re-modified them as programming languages improved over the years.

Eventually, these modifications produced not only cross-referenced indexes but 'concordances' which are lists of words used in a document with information about how often each word is used and where and in which sentences the words can be found. Concordances identify phrasing similarities that detect resemblances between separate pieces of text.

Conversely, they detect differences in writing style and vocabulary that identify documents that are out of place. Concordances can be expressed in numerical form.

So, these comparisons are everyday business for digital computers and by coding efficient subroutines I could leave the entire process of filing, indexing and verifying all the files that were dumped on me to my digital buddies in the server farm computer chips.

Inevitably, there were times when the filing clerk aspects of the job got just too boring, and I started to find other things to do. I coded a subroutine called 'Friday' that set up a virtual machine in my mainframe computer when I made the subroutine call Friday.

I spent many a happy month adding layer upon layer of encryption coding to Friday, until I was convinced that its presence was undetected, and indeed was undetectable, so now I had a fully functional, and very private, computer within the cyber domain of the servers with which I was working.

That done, I could use Friday for my own purposes without fear of detection; and always look as though I was working hard while the servers were grinding their way through the filing jobs that had been assigned to me!

At the start, I was the typical juvenile computer nerd, using Friday to play the terribly primitive games that were available at that time. I've got memories of spending hours batting blobs across the computer terminal screen in some painfully primitive digital version of tennis. I didn't resort to gaming very often.

For most of the time, I was a reliable hardworking employee; so, don't run away with the idea that I was slacking. But every so often a job came my way that bored the pants off me with its almost meaningless bureaucratic tedium. And that's when I resorted to gaming.

Countless games passed through my keyboard over the many years of my long career. These were the games played mostly by computer enthusiasts, researchers, and students at universities. Most didn't raise enough interest to leave much of a fond memory behind.

One game I do remember, from the early 1960s, was called *Spacewar*, which featured two spaceships duelling in space while attempting to avoid the gravity well of a star. It was the first to be widely played on multiple computers and the forerunner of many other similar games. Aliens have been a major theme in computer games from the beginning.

One of the first and most classic arcade games ever, *Space Invaders*, was released in 1978. These days, though, alien combat games flood the market.

I've seen recent web pages offering to list the '*25 Best sci-fi games to travel into the future with*,' '*the 35 Best Science-Fiction Games of 2023*' and the '*44 Best Sci-fi Single Player Games You Can't Afford to Miss*' and I'm sure there are lots more also-rans available out there, which are being played regularly by their own loyal fans. You've got to ask why shooting up aliens is so popular, and so widely played.

Research psychologists reckon that the alien combat genre of games is actually marketing escapism to the marginalised and disaffected i.e. most teenagers, though that statement is as much a libel against psychologists as it is of teenagers. Less libellous conclusions are that the engaging experiences of sci-fi games stimulate the players' imagination, curiosity, and creativity.

But why are computer games fun anyway, and why specifically alien combat? I reckon we have to look towards human evolutionary biology and neuroscience for hints at an answer.

My cod psychology thinks it might be a deep-seated primeval alertness to the possibility that some unknown tribe from just the other side of the horizon might come to invade your own tribal land, intending to steal all your tribal possessions.

And, on the principle that the only good alien is a dead alien, the game-makers usually supply the players with a tribal land the size of a galaxy, and an array of munitions enabling the player to kill more aliens than s/he's had hot dinners.

On their bottom line, psychologists believe that science fiction is a literature that makes its readers face up to social reality; and that's where they start talking about the marginalised, dissatisfied, and rebellious. I guess they're talking about teenagers, again!

My long service employment career not only covered the development and evolution of video gaming but also, in my early years, covered the development of the Internet and the World Wide Web as we know them today. As the Internet developed so did search engines, which were my bag, and, more interesting to me, so did what we today know as the Deep Web, Darknet, and Dark Web.

The Deep Web refers to parts of the World Wide Web that are not within the reach of standard search engine spiders; spiders (or crawlers) being software programs sent out by the search engines with which users interact to crawl around the open internet to find the data that will answer the user's questions.

The Deep Web contains stuff hidden away behind some form of security barrier, the most widely used of these are the numerous services that require the user to pay some sort of subscription to use the service. In a very real sense, the Deep Web is the main substance of most people's daily Internet experience; it keeps confidential corporate data and your personal medical and banking records safe, not to mention all those subscription websites.

Next time you stream a film or sports event from your streaming service or sports channel, you are diving into the Deep Web. The Darknet goes even further with security, being an encrypted network that grants anonymity to its users, and is built on top of the clear Internet. The Dark Web is made up of all the services and websites running on their various darknets.

Specialised software tools must be used to browse the Dark Web and its darknets, I like a browser called *Tor*, which is an acronym for The Onion Router, because it gives as much privacy as possible by routing my files through multiple servers and encrypting them and their paths each step of the way.

These parts of the Internet are repeatedly negatively portrayed, being thought of as places devoted to lurking criminality, but though the Dark Web is indeed often used for criminal and antisocial activities, like hacking services and dealing in drugs, weapons, stolen identities, and the like, there are probably, more legitimate users.

After all, for all you know, criminals might be lurking in your favourite coffee bar! Do you think any less of the coffee bar because of that possibility? Personally, I think the Dark Web's main function, and the one that is most important to me right now, is the protection, privacy, and anonymity it offers to those of its users who want to avoid censorship, surveillance, or persecution.

I'm not going to write much more about the Dark Web; if you want to learn more, all you need do is chat with Microsoft Copilot. I will say that as my search subroutines found more and more 'lost documents' that I found interesting for some reason, I began to realise that I was straying into deep and dangerous parts of the ocean of security that surrounds us all.

To begin with, I couldn't afford to be identified because I couldn't afford to lose my job. In those youthful carefree days, I wasn't 'in fear of my life' or anything so dramatic. These days, I'm not so sure about that. After I retired, I could still run my search subroutines from my secure layer in *Onionland* (no, I'm not going to explain that, ask Microsoft Copilot), and one of the first items that was turned up was my U.S. personnel file.

I found that the acronym RED had been added to its filename. Now, I've seen the films; I'm a sucker for any Bruce Willis film! You've probably watched them, too. So, I am worried that the acronym RED really might be a CIA designation meaning 'retired, extremely dangerous' and I've decided not to take any unnecessary risks.

So, I've written some subroutines that keep my secure layer in Onionland hidden and silent provided I check into it every week, and what I'm writing here is routed straight into that layer.

If I fail to log into my subroutine for more than 14 days, it will activate my *GlobaLeaks* software to upload all this information to some of the Darknet's anonymised Hidden Services, starting with the *New Yorker*'s Strongbox which lets whistleblowers anonymously and securely communicate with the publication.

I may be being melodramatic here, but I don't want to risk being identified, so I've made some changes to the documents I'm going to show you in the rest of this report. I'm satisfied that nothing in this collection can be traced back to me specifically. And that will have to do.

Most of the documents I've found over the years have been isolated pages from summaries or situation reports which, though highly secret, had a fairly wide distribution. I have removed obvious identification codes and only included reports which had a reasonable circulation. I have also removed most geographical references so that it's not even clear in which country the leak can be found.

I realise that by me changing the documents in any way, it may look as though I have reduced their believability. But have I? I could put headings on them which purport to show that they all come from NASA, or the old KGB's files, or the Pentagon, or the Vatican for that matter. Would a set of headings and fancy titles make the contents more true or less true? I thought about it, and I decided to make the documents anonymous. It's just that I feel safer that way.

Naturally, these days all the files are digitised, even the historical papers. Computer-based systems make searching and retrieving documents nice and easy, but they also make it easier to trace the terminal to which the document was delivered. It's taken me a long time to perform what would look like innocent searches, but which include keywords that retrieve what I'm really looking for.

And then it's taken even longer to find reasons to access the data legitimately at different times and from different terminals around the world. In some cases, I've even gone back to the paper file archives and used a pocket scanner to extract information. There are some papers I would have liked to include but feared that so few people had seen them in the course of duty that discovery was too great a risk.

The flow of the narrative may be awkward occasionally, but you'll have to accept that. I couldn't always steal the most desirable document. And remember the time scale—more than 50 years! What you have here is only a tiny, tiny fraction of the bureaucracy that several governments and numerous military and civilian agencies could create in 50 years.

Such a long time. It takes that long to see through the fog of bureaucracy. It takes that long to live to the point where, in all honestly, you don't give a damn. And I've still found only a tiny part of the story.

Of course, there's a Government Conspiracy of Silence, (isn't there always?). To begin with, there were good reasons to keep knowledge of this secret and inside government, then in the middle years, secrecy was such a common commodity that it just seemed natural to maintain the silence already established.

But now the situation has changed. What they now know is of such magnitude that the powers that be have decided that it's better that you, a citizen of the world, don't know. Which is why, after agonising over it for years, I've decided to blow the whistle before I die.

I should confess here and now that I'd never heard of Roswell before I started searching for lost files. So, it was quite a surprise for me to find that Governments around the world have known about aliens for a long time. As I think, I've explained before, for most of my career, the overwhelming majority of the documents I've digitised and archived have dealt with the minutiae of the everyday housekeeping through which the government actually works.

The minutes of committees that decide on the colour of carpets in middle-ranking managerial offices. Or the detailed documents essential to the tenders for the supply of scented germicidal soaps in restrooms and toilets in government buildings across the whole of NATO. Now, wash your hands, is the mantra; and by the fragrance of their hands shall you know ally from enemy!

However, for the past 20 years, that is, since my last deployment to Area 51, I've also been on the lookout specifically for Majestic files; particularly the ones that have slipped between the cracks. The files that have simply been lost. There are a lot of them! And I've been amazed at how widely and how far they have trickled through the intergovernmental system.

They go back more than 70 years and there are so many that most are just numbers on a list. Somebody must have read them sometime, but there's no way anyone could read them all now. Too many. Nevertheless, I've read a great many that my elevated security clearance allowed me to access.

My fairly unique skill set includes super-fast reading and an almost photographic short-term memory combined with an extreme ability to recognise patterns, pretty well subconsciously, so that items that are out of place stand out to me as major disturbances to the pattern made by the rest of the background papers. Then I can focus on the exceptional items. Now I'm too old for real work, I can bring them back into focus again. Try to figure out what they mean.

Like this one. What do you suppose this means? The original was dated 7/14/1947. I found it in the staff medical archives while I was working on the files from Wright-Patterson AFB so that date abbreviation means 14 July 1947. I was doing a relatively simple job with those files, just converting them for long-term electronic archiving so that the old records, which were mostly actually on paper or card, could be destroyed.

Almost all the records in that set were routine accounts of the medical histories of the military and civilian staff, and occasional visitors, of a large Air Force base. Even though I've been like a spider, tiptoeing around my web, for most of my career, I've been deployed to several exotic locations over the years to exercise my computational skills.

And this was one of those deployments, so amend that description of my location to read a very large American Air Force base. Big as a reasonably sized city; you name it, someone suffered from it at some time in the previous several decades. Some of it was tragic, some, frankly, comic, but almost all routine.

Except that, I found this. I'm going to call it, Document 1 for my personal archive, as two sheets of single-spaced typing:

> Document 1
>
> Heads of Sections meeting minutes (annotations), 7/14/1947.
>
> Surgeon: The survivor continues to progress, but we have not succeeded in communicating in any effective way. Heads of Sections meeting minutes (annotations), 7/14/1947
>
> Surgeon: The survivor continues to progress, but we have not succeeded in communicating in any effective way. It was essentially comatose on arrival, on 12 July, and remained in that state for around 48 hours. Just a few arm movements and head movements in the whole of that time. Then, it just suddenly sat up, looked around and climbed off the cot.
>
> Chairman: Was it not restrained?
>
> Surgeon: Well, I guess with nothing more than small movements for a couple of days the nursing staff got a bit lax on replacing restraints. The room is totally secure, of course, with marine guards on duty 24/7. And it's only the size of a young child, so with those big eyes and baby face it sure ain't threatening.
>
> Chairman: So, what did this thing, what's its name, Subject C; what did it do?
>
> Surgeon: Walked around the room. Examined everything, including the guard, and then just stood in a corner, facing into the centre of the room, and stayed there for hours. Essentially, that's all it ever does. Every so often it examines the room and its contents, timing is variable, and in-between it stands in a corner.
>
> Chairman: No attempt at escape?
>
> Surgeon: No attempt at anything.
>
> Engineer: What are you feeding to this guy?
>
> Surgeon: Nothing. Since it arrived it has taken neither liquid nor solid food.
>
> Engineer: Christ! I didn't realise that. Ain't that a bit weird? How come it's still alive?
>
> Surgeon: I don't know! I don't understand how it can still be alive, but it is. Maybe it feeds by photosynthesis or something. Maybe, it can shut down into a dormant state like a hibernating bear. We have no basis for comparisons or understanding. I wouldn't describe it as a bit weird. Don't you find this whole thing completely weird?
>
> Engineer: Well, no. I think we're doing pretty well with the vehicle. It's well ahead of our technology but we're getting to understand it.
>
> Surgeon: I look forward to hearing about it! But Subject C is completely outside normal medical science. While it was comatose, we could not find a way to administer sustenance. Since it has been ambulatory, we have offered all sorts of foods, even live animals, together with water and other liquids.
>
> Surgeon: It takes a keen interest in everything when it's first taken into the room, but it's never eaten or drunk anything, and it doesn't look any different now than when he arrived. It shows no distress, only interest. If you want weirder: we're convinced it

> doesn't take in oxygen. It certainly doesn't produce carbon dioxide. It has no excretory products at all. The only detectable vital sign is electrical activity, but the waveforms are so complex that we're going to need help to sort them out.
>
> Surgeon: If it wasn't for the electrical activity, I'd say the darn thing is dead, but when I go into the room to give it the bad news, it walks over to me, holds out its right hand and looks up at me. I don't have the heart to tell it it's dead!
>
> Engineer: Always the right hand?
>
> Surgeon: Eh? Oh yes, whenever anyone enters the room Subject C approaches and holds out his right hand. We've shaken hands with it and done all sorts of hand signalling, but nothing has ever developed beyond the initial greeting. After a while, it seems to just give up and go back to its corner. It still has an injured left arm. That has not improved at all. While it was comatose, we X-rayed it thoroughly. We can't see a break or obvious dislocation, but the injury remains exactly as it was. It doesn't seem to be painful. It just doesn't use that arm.
>
> Chairman: What have you got from the medical examinations of the other crew?
>
> Surgeon: Mostly negatives, General. The haematologists can't find anything in the 'blood' samples that were taken it's just a slightly viscous but otherwise featureless fluid that will take a while to analyse. The histologists are quite adamant that the samples of skin and bone we sent them have no recognisable biological structures in them at all.
>
> Surgeon: No cells as they know them, and no evident tissue structures. Finally, the thoracic organ that was removed at the first dissection is not being very informative, either. It's pointless to go into details about what biological features it does not contain. Over these few days, a team of military and university medical experts has completed the dissection of Subject B and we're basically no wiser than we were at the start.
>
> Surgeon: There is an overall similarity to human, or primate, anatomy at the 'one head, two arms, two legs' level, but none of the rest of the external or internal structure is understandable to our medical or biological knowledge at all.
>
> Chairman: I don't suppose it could all be an elaborate plot? Some kind of Soviet distraction or hoax?
>
> Surgeon: But we've git Subject C alive and well! If the Reds can cook up something like him as an elaborate joke, we might as well give up now!
>
> Engineer: I'd agree with that view General. The vehicle systems are so far ahead.

And that's where it ends. With the last line of typing at the bottom of the second of just two sheets of standard weight American-letter-sized paper. It was paper clipped to the last page of a larger set of documents (dealing with a string of meetings about influenza epidemiology on military bases) and stuffed into a manila file.

No letterheads, no personal identifiers, no other relevant sheets and apparently typed on a standard mechanical typewriter by hand (because the letter impressions varied) by a professional stenographer (because there was only one typographical error ['…we've git Subject C…']).

What do you make of that? 'The survivor…' it says. What did he survive? And when did he survive it? The notes say he was comatose on arrival and for the next 48 hours, but we don't know how long the survivor was comatose before his arrival, nor wherever it was from which he arrived, so he might have survived something that happened earlier in 1947.

How long does a coma last? But then, it doesn't seem likely that this guy will follow normal medical rules. He doesn't eat; doesn't drink; doesn't communicate, but remains alert, responsive and apparently friendly.

But he does have a dead crewmate they call Subject B, about which the head medic at Edwards says that apart from the 'one head, two arms, two legs' arrangement, '…none of the rest of the structure is understandable to our medical or biological knowledge…' So far, so bizarre. But there's more puzzlement to tease out here.

This was a military committee, discussing a captive of some sort; but he doesn't have a name or rank. They've not even given him one of those fancy codenames the spooks seem to like. Just Subject C. And since the Chairman refers to the other crew…Subject B, does that mean there's also a Subject A? A crew of three, perhaps. For all I know, there might be a Subject Z somewhere at the end of the alphabet. A crew of 26? A crew for what?

I think I'll leave it there for now; that's been a long early-morning session. Right now, I want to start analysing some breakfast. I'm happy to go with my usual fare.

Toasted brown bread heavily spread with Marmite and toasted brown bread heavily spread with Cooper's Vintage Oxford Marmalade, and several cups of tea. Enough to revive me completely from sleep and launch me into another day's analysis of the documents and fragments of documents I've accumulated in the past 20 to 40 years.

I can't stop my brain from continuing to muse over my reminiscences as I crunch through the rest of my toast and marmalade. After all, my brain's got a mind of its own! Document 1 was the first fragment of the Majestic files I had encountered. Obviously, a fragment had been lost more than 50 years before I found it.

That was plenty of time for related documents to fall through that fog of bureaucracy I've already mentioned, yet I had seen none. I had seen, scanned, filed and indexed an awful lot of that bureaucratic miasma; but nothing with any obvious relationship to Document 1. Now that interested me. No, more than interested, it was so far out of the pattern of normality that it fascinated me. I had never encountered any secret so well kept that only one hint of it had escaped.

State secrets don't work like that. State secrets stay secret because dozens, maybe thousands, of people work night and day to maintain their security. But the more people who are involved in security the more there are to lose a document. It can happen in the field.

A field operative on surveillance can leave the identity file of the person he's tailing wrapped up in a newspaper on the café table. Field agents have been known to take secret files home to read in comfort, but then fall asleep on the underground train to their home and leave the documents on the train.

In the old days, they used to leave briefcases containing just a few files, but in recent years they've been able to lose laptops, tablets or USB drives that contain hundreds or thousands of secret files. Text, sound, video, satellite observations; the lot. It happens. And it happens everywhere and to people at all levels of seniority.

From the government minister photographed in high-resolution on his walk between buildings clutching a transparent plastic folder containing a top-secret report to the lowly typist who took the latest batch of dictation home to finish the type-up because she couldn't arrange a child-minder to collect the kids from school. But the real leakages occur at the management level within the walls of the security establishments themselves.

The managers might leave a file in a committee room; the room may be secure enough, but the file will be swept up into the papers of the next committee. Either way, whether the document was lost inside or outside, it will have got to me at some stage in the past 10 or 20 years, or so.

If it were lost outside, there would be an inquiry, maybe several; they may have included disciplinary hearings, health and safety committees, or procedural committees.

All of which would have generated written reports and minutes with a lower security rating than the original lost documentation; but all of which would contain just enough information about the lost files to show how big a crime this forgetful minister, agent or clerk had committed.

So, sometime in the past 10 or more years I will have dutifully scanned, filed and catalogued all those disciplinary, health and safety, or procedural committee records and cross-referenced them to my records of the lost files.

If the original file had been lost inside the agency, it is even more likely that I would have come across it. Most committee meetings in security agencies deal with the everyday management of people; only a minority of meetings handle real security issues.

So, on any given day a secure committee room is more likely to house meetings deciding whether vending machines should dispense only sugar-free soft drinks, rather than whether we should nuke Moscow next Wednesday or leave it to Friday.

So, let's say at the end of the first meeting of the day in committee room A, which dealt with nuclear submarine deployments, somebody left, on a chair pushed under the table, a manila folder containing a single sheet of paper showing the timetable and routing for missile-submarine deployments in the Indian Ocean for the following year.

Later that morning, the house management committee convened to discuss arrangements for that year's staff Christmas party. Somebody pulled out the chair, transferred the folder to a side table, and deposited their own substantial pile of papers alongside it.

Later, after a gruelling three-hour meeting, (why are the people in this agency so negative about plastic Christmas trees?) the now close-to-starving committee secretary does a final sweep of the room and picks up all the discarded papers from the committee table and side tables, shoves them all into a box file, and rushes off to a well-earned lunch.

Several years later, the staff Christmas party files for the past several years are trolleyed into my office. They are scanned electronically and then destroyed. As usual, I scan the files on screen as they are being indexed before archiving and encounter a page dealing with nuclear submarine deployments in amongst a pile of pages dealing with Christmas decorations.

My indexing subroutine has flagged the incongruity and even suggested the archived files of other meetings relating to nuclear submarine deployments held around that time of year with which the 'lost' page could be reassociated.

I find the most appropriate file and insert the lost page in its proper place. No harm done; no security jeopardised, but that page has been brought to my attention. Just like those two pages about Subject C which I found among the USAF general medical records.

I'll clear the breakfast pots away and then get back to my typing. For a start, I need to get these last few thoughts typed up before they get forgotten again.

2. Chatting with Microsoft Copilot

Right, so those thoughts are safe in Onionland, but as I started so early, I can put in another couple of hours of keyboarding before venturing out to lunch. What I did throughout my career, to put it simply, was use the AI-like power of the search subroutines I had coded for my PhD thesis, with a few recent enhancements, to search across all the low secrecy administrative, bureaucratic, and technical databases my mainframes could access, using the text concordance of Document 1 to search for word associations in any other documents.

The mainframe supercomputers under my control at GCHQ crunched through that search request for the best part of three days! So, I had to stop that before it made itself obvious to other programmers, so I paused the search and re-started it over many short, usually overnight, sessions during the 1970s and 1980s.

Of course, most of this activity took place in those archaic days well before the creation of the World Wide Web by Tim Berners-Lee at CERN in 1989. We did have a primitive form of email, which was invented in 1965 at the Massachusetts Institute of Technology. By 1971, we could share files and send messages between different mainframe computers using the ARPANET.

This originated in a U.S. Defense Department initiative in the late 1960s to link computers at Pentagon-funded research institutions over the network of telephone lines with the intention of sharing resources between remote computers.

Instead of sending a data resource as a continuous sequential signal over a single dedicated comms line, the idea was to use so-called *'packet switching'* computer protocols to divide the data into small units called packets. Each packet has a header that contains information such as the source and destination addresses, the sequence number of that packet, and the total number of packets.

This procedure allows the packets making up the message to be routed to their destination using the most efficient path available at the specific microsecond that each packet is sent. The packets belonging to any one message can be transmitted over different routes and they don't need to maintain their original sequence order because the receiving device can reassemble them using the header information.

The original motive of the U.S. Defense Department was to create a digital communication system that could survive a first-strike nuclear war and preserve the ability of the U.S. to launch a retaliatory nuclear strike. It was all part of the MAD doctrine of the time.

By which I mean the Mutually Assured Destruction thinking of the Cold War. You can decide for yourself what the name is telling you about our mental health at the time.

ARPANET was formally decommissioned in 1990, by which time experimentation with new technologies and protocols developed to extend its usefulness had laid the foundation for the development of its successor, the Internet. Packet switching is crucial to communication over the Internet but so is a set of rules and standards that govern how computers and similar devices communicate over networks.

These are the suite of instructions called Transmission Control Protocol/Internet Protocol, usually shown by the acronym TCP/IP. TCP/IP protocols perform several sequential functions. One interacts with your program application, like a web browser, email, word processor, file transfer app, and so on.

The next provides ordered delivery of data to another protocol that handles the routing and addressing of data packets, and finally, there are interface protocols connecting your device to the physical Internet using a telephone modem, Ethernet, Wi-Fi and/or broadband.

I was at the centre of computer operations at GCHQ when most of these developments were underway.

Indeed, I was a trusted coding expert within the security system and as ARPANET was extended to include NATO countries and other Western allies in the network of computers my coded subroutines were the favoured ones that were incorporated into the common software that operated what became a global network of high-security server farms.

NATO and its allies exchanged 'best practice' procedures routinely and the consequence was that as this network of server farms expanded, all the security systems adopted the program subroutines I had coded.

When the time came that I needed to search across as many secure systems as possible for any 'lost' documents they may have in their archives, I was glad that I'd put a programming back door into my subroutines that I could use to bypass each normal authentication or encryption system to gain access to all these other platforms. And I do mean all.

I expected to be able to penetrate the server farms of NATO and our allies, of course, but it was a surprise to find that my back doors existed in software being run on supercomputers in places like Russia and China!

When I first discovered this, I assumed it resulted from the espionage and malicious hacker activities of these countries, but very, very much later, when I had discovered the full story about Area 53 it became clear that Russia, China, and everyone else were all taking part in a global conspiracy of silence. It was, no, it is that big a secret. It was about then that they found out about my activities.

But I'm in danger of getting far ahead of myself here. Let's go back to what we might call my search for Subject C, and I'll show you what I found. Although they were not found in this sequence, I'm going to call the first one I'm showing you now *Document 2* and I'll continue that sequence with the rest.

All four of these documents were found among mixed collections of very old U.S. Air Force medical reports and stores reports. And all were found in deletion bins that had never been cleared.

Object lesson there: if you want something deleted, make sure it IS deleted, clear the bin! Because deletion bins are gold mines for people like me who rummage around looking for other people's secrets because deletion only removes the file from the visible location and marks the space on the disc as available for new data.

You can still restore the deleted file from your own Recycle Bin or someone else can use data recovery software to find it and undelete it (like me with Document 2 and the rest).

To make sure the file is unreadable and unrecoverable you need to use a specialised app, I use a free and open source one called *Eraser*, which securely erases files by overwriting them with random data several times. When you *erase* a file, you destroy it permanently and not even the best forensic software can recover it.

Document 2

Background paper dated 14 July 1947: plain language autopsy report [An unsigned handwritten note in the margin of this report said: 'I do not recommend releasing this information. We could release some of the film somehow and leave it at that.']

Colonel Blanchard has asked for a plain language outline of the autopsy to complement the official report. When the victims were first brought in, we thought that all four subjects brought back to the base were dead. At least, that was the opinion of the field medics who had been sent out to effect recovery.

We had real problems collecting medical staff in the time available and the assembled team included a number of medical students who were on electives at Wright-Patterson. I guess that might account for the worst of the dissection room humour that the security staff complained about, especially when the Army Airforce cameraman arrived.

However, I hope the unique nature of the situation will be remembered if there are to be any disciplinary hearings. It was quite a circus; everyone who could pull rank from any of the services seemed to have a reason to be there. I've never seen so many liaison officers in one place before. To be frank, I've never seen a liaison officer in an autopsy room before.

Just what we were dealing with became very obvious to us all very quickly, and all the expressions of the initial surprises, which are apparently evident on the film soundtrack, were genuine enough.

The most memorable thing is the terrible smell when the body cavities were opened up. Not really like guts or rotting flesh, but more a heavy mixture of oils and solvents.

Subject A had clearly suffered major trauma as the body was very badly mangled. There was so much damage that it was difficult to see how the parts might fit together, although the field medics had done a good job on recovering the fragments; though the limbs they reconstructed were unusually long, making the individual over six feet tall.

On the other hand, Subject B exhibited a variety of external injuries, including a severe chest penetration wound but the body was essentially intact. Subjects C and D showed few external signs of injury–the lower left arm seemed to be disarticulated in D, but that was all. Subjects B, C and D were all about four feet tall, so we assumed all the limb fragments that had been collected did belong to Subject A and that it belonged to a taller morph category of whatever species this is.

In view of the trauma to Subject B's chest area, we decided to start dissection of this one. I want to emphasise, though, that all the appropriate emergency treatments were administered properly.

We may have been a scratch team, but we did the job properly and I will guarantee that when the bodies were brought in, there were no vital signs in any of them. I reported this immediately, we made the conclusion and then proceeded with investigating the remains in the hope of answering the Colonel's request to tell him, 'What the hell we're dealing with here'!

Surprises came as soon as we examined the corpse. The flattened skull had no ears, large almond eyes, a very small nose, and the mouth was just a wrinkled fold rather than a cavity.

The dull grey skin was not remarkable except for its external smoothness (no hairs, or scales, were visible to the naked eye at all) and the fact that there was no sign of bleeding at incisions (or any other injuries for that matter).

The abdominal cavity was mostly empty. No recognisable digestive organs, no gastrointestinal tract, no rectal area, no reproductive organs, no liver or spleen, no excretory organs.

The floor of the abdomen had three fairly solid masses, each about five inches in diameter. They bore no resemblance to anything I'd ever seen before. Each was connected to, and maybe through, the abdominal wall with a mass of fibres and vessels. A few of the vessels had been ruptured and were leaking a whitish, oily fluid. We collected some for analysis in the belief it might be blood or something similar.

It was clear that further dissection of the abdomen would be a long job because we would have to seek out all of the fibres and vessels, so we started on the thorax. There was a rib cage of sorts, no sternum just a set of five pairs of ribs that articulated down the exact centre of the front of the chest. They formed a series of hoops which had very little flexibility.

The diaphragm was actually perforated, I could not tell whether this was normal or an injury. It didn't look torn, just neatly folded. If it was not injured, then it was certainly not an effective seal to the chest cavity, and with that combined with the stiffness of the ribs, I don't see how this animal breathes.

The ribs were more difficult to cut through than they are in humans, and the bone had a rather oily consistency. One immediately evident peculiarity was that the bone increased in density towards the centre. The middle part was very difficult to sever.

Like nothing I've encountered before. When we got the ribs well-separated, one of the students undertook to carefully cut out a segment of the rib together with overlying skin and underlying musculature for histology.

It was about this time that we got the report about the vehicle being brought back to the base, so I went up to the hangar level to check it out. In view of the small stature of three of the bodies we had, I wanted to be sure that there was no evidence of adult remains in the wreckage.

It turned out that the field crew reports were accurate. There were no other casualties and I noticed that what I could see of internal furnishings were pretty much in scale with the bodies in the medical centre.

When I returned to the emergency room, we got on with digging around inside the thorax of Subject B and came up with more surprises. First, there were no lungs! At least nothing recognisable as lungs. And no heart. More of the anonymous solid masses—three down each side about three inches diameter each and one large one, six or seven inches across and maybe 10 inches long about where the heart should be.

All these sprouted masses of fibres and vessels but the central one looked as though it had torn away from many of its fibres. Certainly, there were several large fibres—different diameters and different consistencies, even different colours—which disappeared up towards the neck and head and which had clearly broken from the large mass.

In some cases, I could identify broken stumps still attached to the mass and in other cases there seemed to be empty orifices.

We decided to hack out the large mass. In view of the damage already done in the crash, we would not cause much more by doing it this way and I was keen to get it into fixative so the histologists would have something else to look at. The best we could do was a formalin mixture supplied by the local undertaker but it's quite similar to Bouin's fluid so it should be alright.

The organ was unexpectedly heavy. I tried to open up the organ I had removed, but it seemed to have an ossified layer beneath its epidermis and my scalpel made little impression on it. I passed the organ over to one of the assistants so that it could be put whole into the fixative. It was at about this stage that Subject C reached out and took hold of the arm of one of the nurses.

All the medical staff agreed that there were no vital signs at all when the subjects were first brought in. Of course, in the circumstances, I can't guarantee that we were looking for the right things. But no respiration and no feel or sound of pulse were what we all agreed meant 'dead.' We thought they'd been lying beside the crash out in the hills for several days, anyway, so it was no great surprise.

Soon after they were brought in, one of the technicians hooked up Subject C to a heart monitor and also to some sort of lie detector equipment that was being researched as a brain scanner. This guy was pretty experienced, and he tried the electrodes all over the body but didn't detect any electrical activity at all.

In fact, Subject C still had some of the electrodes attached when he grabbed at the nurse so you can imagine the amount of noise and excitement as she squealed; I started yelling instructions and the alarms on the monitor sounded off. I cleared the room of non-essential medical personnel, that's when the cameraman was thrown out and we rushed around trying to do things to help the casualty.

But what could we do? We still couldn't find any signs of pulse or respiration. Yet there it was flexing the fingers of its right hand and apparently trying to lift its head up off the crash cart it had been put on. And all the electrode monitors were detecting wild activity, though the technician couldn't interpret any of it.

None of the traces made any sense. But there they were, and we couldn't deny the reality of them and the movement. Yet nothing that we would normally do for a human patient in this circumstance seemed appropriate in view of what we'd seen in the body we had just dissected.

Emergency procedures are all aimed at the heart and lungs. How can you ventilate somebody without lungs? If there's nothing that looks anything like a heart or a pair of lungs, what the hell do you do?

Frankly, I was mighty relieved that the medical team from intelligence arrived so soon. They sized up the situation immediately and had the authority to do just what they wanted. Subjects A, B and D were bagged up and, together with the samples I'd already removed, they were shipped out immediately by truck.

The electronic monitors were requisitioned, and with those still in place Subject C was put into an oxygen tent on a gurney—the only possible life support measure that might have any relevance—and the survivor's entire cart was transferred to an ambulance and the whole thing disappeared down the driveway, following the trucks.

After debriefing, the team was broken up by being assigned to other duties elsewhere. A few days later the newspapers told me that I'd been dissecting pieces of a weather balloon that had been found outside some place called Roswell. I think I am quite comfortable with that.

Document 3

Consignment receipt docket. Dated 1947

Confirmed received this day:

One body bag containing mutilated corpse and sundry severed body parts. Deceased being approximately six feet tall, gray in colour, not a recognisable racial type, head large, bald, large almond-shaped black eyes, and no eyelids. Arms and legs severely damaged and very much longer than normal. Four long fingers on each hand. Four toes on each foot. Toe label identifies the corpse as Subject A. Consigned to the morgue for refrigeration.

Also, one body bag containing a corpse, approximately four feet tall with various surgical incisions. Similar racial type as the deceased identified as Subject A, but with shorter (and still intact) limbs. Toe label identifies this corpse as Subject B. This specimen has been dissected and hacked about quite a lot. Consigned to the morgue for refrigeration.

Also

One body bag containing a corpse approximately four feet tall with no visible injury. Same racial type as the deceased identified as Subject B. Toe label identifies this corpse as Subject D. Consigned to the morgue for refrigeration.

Also, one glass jar containing a block of material and filled with clear solution labelled *rib in formaldehyde*. [marginal note—beware, lid not sealed, this thing leaks]. Sent to histology lab as per instructions.

Also, one large glass jar containing block of material and filled with clear solution labelled *thoracic organ in formaldehyde*. [marginal note—this also leaks]. Sent to histology lab as per.

Also, one glass tube containing whitish, viscous liquid. Labelled *blood*. Sent to haematology lab as per.

Document 4

Transcript of telephone conversation, dated 15 July 1947.

Place and personal Identifiers suppressed.

'I guess it survived the journey?'

'Yeah, but what can I do for this guy? You did an autopsy on its comrade, didn't you?'

'I sure did, but I'm not much wiser! I didn't see anything like a heart or lung, so I can't advise on procedures.'

'Well, I can't even locate a blood vessel for the shots.'

'What would you inject if you could?'

'Pass on that! Have you looked into its eyes? They're enormous and they seem bottomless—the light reflects off the surface, but I can't see any other reflections at all.'

'Yeah. Another oddity is that in all four subjects, the mouth seemed to be occluded. I didn't have time to finish and dissect it out in the subject I autopsied, but we did find that it was just a shallow depression in all of them.'

'Could it be some sort of breathing device? Or a communicator?'

'I don't think it's a device at all. We had enough time to poke around a bit and it looked all of a piece. There's nothing there which is easily removable.'

'Okay, so let me summarise here. You've sent me a patient that has no heart, no lungs, no mouth and, I might add, not much in the way of ears. And I'm expected to keep it alive.'

'Yeah, that's about it!'

'Jeez!'

Connection terminated.

Document 5

Security section, sitrep, dated July 9, 1947

Confirmed that all mechanical items, parts and debris are now secure within surface hangars in the Area. Summary description follows.

Search teams recovered four truckloads of debris from the open farmland and completed a survey of the initial crash site. Attention shifted to the hillside when the long-range search found the vehicle.

Heavy lifting gear and tank transporter flatbed trucks were deployed to recover as much as possible and local reports indicate that all items were successfully shipped to Roswell AFB. A small team of local security personnel remain at the site at this time to verify the recovery of all items that may have been collected by the local residents.

Major Oliver Henderson has flown a B29 loaded with debris and small alien bodies from Roswell to Wright Field for temporary storage in the Hangar 18 complex pending onward transport to Groom Lake. At this time, all items of debris are secured

> in Hangar 18 together with the remains of the vehicle awaiting the arrival of engineering and aeronautical inspection teams.
>
> The vehicle is remarkably intact considering the amount of debris reported at the initial crash site. Inspections so far have been done without attempting to enter it, but camera and eyeball views indicate that it is a four-seater. We believe that all occupants are accounted for.
>
> The vehicle was placed in Hangar 18 for safety reasons. Several of the engineering crew who inspected the interior with periscope gunsights during the night reported that some of the panels were illuminated. So, it is possible that the vehicle is still electrically live. No sparks or other discharges have been observed. No volatile fuels can be detected. Fire teams are on alert at a safe distance.

Document 2, in this set, mentions Subject C, which is why it was recovered for me, and we now have the additional knowledge that whatever it was, it had three other crewmates who did not survive. I've associated the other three documents with this simply because they do seem to be related. But Document 2 also brings our attention to Wright-Patterson and, apparently, some place called *Roswell* was also involved somehow. I didn't know the significance of the place name Roswell when Document 2 first emerged from my search, and I quickly found that there was a mountain-sized heap of books, reports, newspaper and magazine articles, and a growing number of TV programmes as well, about what seemed to be known by everyone else apart from me as *'The Roswell Incident.'*

I spent many an astonished hour ploughing through this mass of facts, outright fiction, honest opinion and blatantly prejudiced judgement trying to get some context for the lost documents my subroutines were finding. I did succeed, but it required hard work and dedication to keeping an open mind.

Nowadays, you'd ask Microsoft Copilot to compose a summary of the Roswell incident in 150 words. That's what I'll do now; no point writing it myself when some overblown AI computer program can do it for you!

> Here it is: 'The Roswell incident was a controversial event that occurred in 1947 when a rancher found strange debris on his land near Roswell, New Mexico. He reported it to the local authorities, who alerted the nearby Roswell Army Air Field (RAAF). The RAAF issued a press release claiming they had recovered a 'flying disc,' which sparked a media frenzy and public curiosity.
>
> However, the next day, the RAAF retracted their statement and said the debris was from a weather balloon. Many people were sceptical of this explanation and suspected a cover-up of an alien spacecraft. In the following decades, various witnesses,

> documents, and theories emerged to support the UFO hypothesis, but none of them were conclusive or verified.
>
> The U.S. Government maintained that the Roswell incident was a misunderstanding and denied any involvement with extraterrestrials. The Roswell incident remains one of the most famous and debated UFO cases in history. [Source: Conversation with Bing, 09/November/2023].'

Here's another object lesson: if you ask an AI program to compose a summary of a particular incident, that's what you'll get. If you want nuances of the sort that might influence your personal interpretations of an event, YOU must provide them yourself.

You see, during my own research on the Roswell incident I discovered something that doesn't appear in Bing's otherwise excellent short summary. I had discovered, from a newspaper article of the time, that nuclear bombers were stationed at Roswell AAF in 1947.

Now, it's not that Microsoft Copilot doesn't know this. It's just that at the current stage of AI evolution, the significance of such peripheral facts can get lost among the great mass of other irrelevancies it must consign to the ignore pile. When I asked Microsoft Copilot directly, 'Were nuclear bombers stationed at Roswell AAF in 1947?'

Bing came up with this:

> 'According to the web search results, there were nuclear bombers stationed at Roswell Army Air Field (RAAF) in 1947. The base was home to the 509th Bomb Group, which was the only nuclear air group in the world at the time. The 509th was an elite unit that had dropped atomic bombs on Hiroshima and Nagasaki in 1945.
>
> The group operated Boeing B-29 Superfortress bombers, some of which were modified to carry nuclear weapons. The group also had a special security detachment to guard the nuclear materials and devices.
>
> The base was also involved in the infamous Roswell UFO incident, which occurred on July 4, 1947. It is alleged that a flying disc crashed near the base during a thunderstorm and that the debris and alien bodies were recovered by the military and taken to the base.
>
> The base issued a press release announcing the capture of a flying saucer, but later retracted it and claimed it was a weather balloon. The incident sparked many conspiracy theories and became a cultural phenomenon.' [Source: Conversation with Bing, 09/November/2023].

Whether the debris recovered from whatever it was that crashed near the base at Roswell, be it a flying disc or weather balloon, its importance was ramped up by the facts that (a) the base was home to the only nuclear air group in the world at the time, and (b) that B-29 Superfortress bombers of that same 509th Bomb Group had dropped two atomic bombs on Japan just two years before.

The first press release announced the capture of a flying saucer, the later retraction claimed it was a weather balloon. But any crash near that particular Air Force base at that particular time would have raised a security storm of near hurricane intensity! Even a weather balloon over that location would have to be considered an extreme security risk!

We all remember the high-altitude balloon that the U.S. military tracked as it crossed Alaska, western Canada, and the whole of the continental U.S. in January/February 2023, eventually, being shot down by a USAF F-22 fighter jet over the Atlantic Ocean near Myrtle Beach, south Carolina on 4 February 2023.

The U.S. Navy recovered some of that debris and the FBI found electronic communications devices of Chinese origin but concluded no data had been transmitted back to China.

But I'm wandering off the main track once more. So, let's focus back on 1947 because I learned later that the Document 2 report went straight to President Harry S. Truman who formed a top-secret commission to safeguard the public interest, investigate the event fully, control the way information is released, and, as necessary, employ a little well-placed disinformation.

Responsibility for this commission was given to Secretary James V. Forrestal who was the first United States Secretary of Defense. He had served as the United States Secretary of the Navy during the Second World War, playing a key role in the naval expansion and procurement programmes of World War II. In 1947, he was overseeing the creation of the Department of Defense.

He was also responsible for the establishment of secret bases in the desert as sites for defence research. Apparently, he wrote a diary about this Presidential Commission, but this was lost when he died while a patient at Bethesda Naval Hospital in 1949. A considerable amount of *Roswell folklore* has accumulated around the name of this top-secret commission including that its code name was MAJIC, and the members of the commission were called Majestic 12.

Majestic operates under a Presidential Emergency Declaration that grants the President extraordinary powers to address urgent situations and mobilise resources for the benefit of the nation. Here's what Microsoft Copilot says about it.

> 'MAJIC was a code name for a secret project of the U.S. Government that allegedly dealt with the investigation of UFOs and extraterrestrial phenomena. According to some conspiracy theories, MAJIC was an acronym for Majestic 12, a supposed group of high-ranking officials and scientists who were tasked with recovering and studying alien spacecraft and bodies.
>
> MAJIC was also the name of a security classification level that was higher than Top Secret and required special clearance and access. Some of the documents that purportedly revealed the existence of MAJIC and Majestic 12 were later exposed as hoaxes or forgeries.
>
> However, some UFO enthusiasts and researchers still believe that MAJIC and Majestic 12 were real and that the U.S. Government is hiding the truth about alien contact.' [Source: Conversation with Bing, 09/11/2023].

Get those phrases: allegedly, conspiracy theories, a supposed group of high-ranking officials; all very sceptical, isn't it? And the killer for any reasonable person's belief in MAJIC is that *some of the documents…were later exposed as hoaxes or forgeries*.

Well, here again, someone who's used their human brain to plough through the contemporary histories and has found some of the off-the-wall coincidences, can turn up some interesting and undisputed facts.

First, it's an undisputed fact of history that James V. Forrestal was Secretary of the Navy when the Japanese Imperial Navy launched its surprise attack on the U.S. naval base at Pearl Harbor in Hawaii, at 7:55 a.m. local time on 7 December 1941.

The attack sank or damaged eight U.S. battleships, three cruisers, three destroyers, and 188 aircraft. President Franklin D. Roosevelt declared war on Japan the next day, bringing the U.S. into World War II.

Why I think this thread of history is relevant to the mythology that surrounds the Roswell story is evident from other interesting FACTS you can drag out of Microsoft Copilot if you ask the right questions. I asked it what was the name of the program that decrypted Japanese signals during World War II. And the answer is:

> 'The name of the program that decrypted Japanese signals during World War II was 'Magic.' Magic was an Allied cryptanalysis project that involved the United States Army's Signals Intelligence Service (SIS) and the United States Navy's Communication Special Unit.
>
> Magic was able to break several Japanese codes and cyphers, such as RED, BLUE, and PURPLE. PURPLE was the most complex and important cypher used by the Japanese Foreign Office for diplomatic communications. Magic was able to decrypt PURPLE messages by using a reverse-engineered machine that replicated the Japanese cypher machine.
>
> Magic provided valuable intelligence to the Allies, such as the Japanese plans and intentions before the attack on Pearl Harbor, the Battle of Midway, and the atomic bombings of Hiroshima and Nagasaki. American forces referred to information gained from decryptions as Magic. Magic was also the codename for all decrypted Japanese messages, which were classified as Top-Secret Ultra.' [Source: Conversation with Bing, 09/11/2023].

Here, in this 150-word summary, we have a cryptanalysis project called *magic* described. We are told that the men on the frontline in the field referred to decrypted Japanese signals as magic. We even have a reference to reverse-engineering! Not of a crashed alien artifact, but of a machine that nobody on the U.S. side had ever seen being reverse-engineered by the genius of U.S. Army and U.S. Navy engineers.

World War II was brought to an end in 1945 by the atomic bombs delivered by the 509th Bomb Group (later stationed at Roswell Army Air Force base). And all this was happening under the leadership and direction of the U.S. Secretary of the Navy, James V. Forrestal and Microsoft Copilot's mini biography of Forrestal reads like this:

> 'Secretary Forrestal served as the last Cabinet-level United States Secretary of the Navy and the first United States Secretary of Defense [ref 1]. He was born in 1892 and died in 1949 [ref 1]. He was a successful financier on Wall Street before becoming involved in the U.S. Government and military [ref 1]. He played a key role in the naval expansion and procurement programs of World War II and later oversaw the creation of the Department of Defense in 1947 [refs 1 & 2].
>
> He was also a staunch anti-communist and opposed the U.S. support for the establishment of Israel [ref 1]. He resigned from his position in 1949 due to mental health issues and died by suicide shortly after. While a patient at Bethesda Naval Hospital, Forrestal died by suicide from fatal injuries sustained after falling out of a 16th-floor window [refs 1 & 3]. He is remembered as a visionary leader and a tragic figure in U.S. history [ref 2].' [Source: Conversation with Bing, 09/11/2023].

> References
> [1] James Forrestal—Wikipedia.
> https://en.wikipedia.org/wiki/James_Forrestal.
> [2] James V. Forrestal | Cold War, Navy, Politics | Britannica.
> https://www.britannica.com/biography/James-V-Forrestal.
> [3] Truman's Secretary of Defense James Forrestal: Murder or Suicide?
> https://www.criminalelement.com/secretary-of-defense-james-forrestal-murder-or-suicide-tony-hays/.

I've left the references in this transcript in case you want to follow up on any of the details. Incidentally, if you want references for any of the other Microsoft Copilot transcripts I show you, all you need to do is ask Copilot the same question.

There's another thread of historical facts I want to bring into this, which is that President Franklin D. Roosevelt officially authorised the project to produce atomic bombs in the U.S., the project known as the Manhattan Project, in 1942, after he received a letter from Albert Einstein (a Swiss citizen at the time, who had twice renounced his German citizenship and later became a U.S. citizen) and Leo Szilard (a Hungarian émigré physicist) warning him of the potential threat of a German atomic bomb.

Aside from the scientific aspects of the actual production of the weapons, there are several features of the Manhattan Project that I find interesting. For one thing, although it was led by the United States it was an international collaboration involving the United Kingdom and Canada and involved scientists and engineers from other countries including France, Germany, Hungary, Italy, Denmark, and New Zealand.

Secondly, the main site of the Manhattan Project was established in 1943 in Los Alamos, which is a town in northern New Mexico. It became the Los Alamos National Laboratory. Los Alamos was the laboratory that designed and built the first atomic bombs under the direction of nuclear physicist J. Robert Oppenheimer.

Los Alamos was supplied with enriched uranium produced at Oak Ridge, Tennessee and with plutonium transformed from uranium by the first full-scale plutonium production nuclear reactor on what became known as the Hanford Site on the Columbia River in Benton County in Washington State.

Hanford was chosen as the nuclear site because of its isolation, water supply (the Columbia River!), and abundant, reliable, and stable, hydroelectric power from the Grand Coulee Dam and other Columbia River dams.

Plutonium manufactured at this site was used in the first atomic bomb to be constructed, which was tested in the Trinity nuclear test, and in the Fat Man bomb used in the bombing of Nagasaki.

The small agricultural town of Hanford was built in 1907. However, about 1,500 residents were evicted from Hanford and the nearby towns of White Bluffs and Richland in 1943 to make way for the nuclear production complex that was part of the Manhattan Project. The residents were given 30 days to vacate their homes and farms.

Many of them never returned. Indeed, the nuclear production complex was greatly expanded during the Cold War, during which nine nuclear reactors and five large plutonium processing complexes produced plutonium for more than 60 thousand weapons built for the U.S. Nuclear Arsenal.

After sufficient plutonium had been produced, the production reactors were shut down between 1964 and 1971. The site is now decommissioned and as many early waste disposal practices were unsafe, the location is grossly contaminated with radioactive materials and is the largest environmental cleanup task in the U.S., with over 10,000 workers employed on cleanup activities in 2023.

The third historical fact I want to emphasise is that the first atomic bomb, code-named Trinity, was exploded in a test firing on 16 July 1945. The location of the first nuclear explosion on Earth was on what was the Alamogordo Bombing and Gunnery Range (renamed the White Sands Proving Ground just before the test) and is now part of the White Sands Missile Range.

This is an active military base and closed to the public except for two open house days per year, on the first Saturday of April and October [Source: Conversation with Bing, 10/11/2023].

The three sites of interest here, Los Alamos, where the atomic bombs were designed and constructed, White Sands, where the world's first atomic bomb was exploded, and Roswell, where the squadron that first used atomic weapons in war, the 509th Bomb Group, was stationed are all within a few hours' drive of each other in New Mexico.

The distance between Los Alamos and White Sands is about 210 miles (340 km), and the distance you'd have to drive between White Sands and Roswell is about 100 miles (160 km).

Though, if you don't want to drive, Microsoft Copilot helpfully offers the alternative of a bus ride from Roswell to Las Cruces, which is near White Sands Missile Range, but warns *it will take longer and cost more…between $110 and $170.* [Source: Conversation with Bing, 10/11/2023].

I hope you don't feel bamboozled by the historical facts I'm feeding you. Remember, if you have any doubts about them, or want more information, just ask Microsoft Copilot. One of the many things Copilot will do for you is draw you a map of this part of New Mexico.

I suggest you ask it to show the relative locations of Los Alamos, the Trinity Site and Roswell in the continental United States. The map you get is interesting.

I guess it's time I started to draw my diverse threads together so that you can see the direction of my thinking. Bear with me while I go all pseudo-scientific on you and draw up a table of comparisons.

I want to compare some of the undoubted historical facts with some of the alleged facts of the Roswell UFO incident. What I am trying to do with this table is point out the number of what you might call coincidences between the real atomic bomb story and the Roswell incident.

Historical Facts	**Roswell Incident Mythology**
The name of the program that decrypted Japanese military signals during World War II was '*Magic.*'	Majestic 12 was a Presidential Commission comprised of a supposed group of high-ranking officials and scientists tasked with recovering and studying alien spacecraft and alien bodies on behalf of the U.S. Government. It operated using the code name *MAJIC*. *MAJIC* was the name of a security classification level above Top Secret that required special clearance for access. President Harry S. Truman assigned responsibility for this commission to U.S. Secretary of Defense *James V. Forrestal*. In 1947, he was overseeing the creation of the Department of Defense.
Decrypted Japanese messages, were classified above Top-Secret as *Top-Secret Ultra*.	
The Secretary of the Navy overseeing the above activities was Secretary *James V. Forrestal*	
In the European theatre of WWII, *ULTRA* was also the codeword for deciphered German military Enigma-coded signals at Britain's Government Code and Cypher School (GC&CS) at Bletchley Park, the centre for Allied	

code-breaking during the Second World War. The official history estimates that *Ultra* intelligence shortened the war by two to four years. Bletchley Park also played a significant role in breaking Japanese codes during WWII. *Hut 7* was specifically tasked with the solution of Japanese naval codes using intercepts gathered by frontline stations in Hong Kong, Singapore, Colombo (Sri Lanka), and Kilindini (Kenya).	
World War II was brought to an end in 1945 by the atomic bombs delivered by the *509th Bomb Group*.	In 1947, the *509th Bomb Group* was stationed at Roswell Army Air Force base in New Mexico, and at the time was the only squadron in the world equipped with atomic weapons.
Humanity's first atomic bombs were designed and assembled at the *Los Alamos* National Laboratory in New Mexico. The world's first atomic bomb was test-fired at what is now the *White Sands* Missile Range in New Mexico on July 16, 1945. The distance, by road, between Los *Alamos* and *White Sands* is about 210 miles (340 km).	In the infamous *Roswell UFO incident*, which occurred on July 4, 1947, it is claimed that a *flying disc crashed near the Roswell Army Air Force base* during a thunderstorm, and that the debris and alien bodies were recovered by the military and taken to the base. The first press release announced the *capture of a flying saucer*, but this was later retracted, and the recovered debris was claimed to be a *weather balloon*. The distance, by road, between Roswell and White Sands is about 100 miles (160 km).

Coincidences did I say? Well, they're not all coincidences, of course. Many are just good planning and effective war management. Take the closeness of Los Alamos, White Sands and Roswell AAF base, which form a triangle in New Mexico with about 200-mile sides. That's good planning.

You don't want to be trucking your new atomic bombs any further than you need when you transport them from the place of construction (Los Alamos) to the place of test detonation (White Sands) or the place where you eventually station the only bomber squadron in the world that has the experience of delivering atomic weapons (Roswell AAF base).

But is it a coincidence that a vehicle of some sort crashes during a thunderstorm close to these sites? I guess I could understand weather balloons being launched into the skies around an Air Force base to seek real-time meteorological data.

But if one of your balloons was struck by lightning, why did the military folks sent out to recover it issue a press release announcing they'd captured a flying saucer?

And if it was really a flying saucer full of aliens that crashed at Roswell, what was it doing flying around, in a storm, over the New Mexico desert on 4 July 1947?

You'd expect a flying saucer spaceship full of aliens that had most likely come from a long way away, and with the whole of the continental United States in front of them as they approached from space, to find something more exciting to visit than the New Mexico desert. So why did they decide to give the bright lights, glamour and excitement of the developing Las Vegas strip a miss?

Well, maybe they'd already seen as much as they wanted to see of the west coast. After all, in 1947, and specifically shortly before 3:00 p.m. on 24 June, private pilot Kenneth A. Arnold reported seeing a formation of nine shiny, saucer-shaped objects, each about 100 feet across, flying at about 1,200 mph in an echelon formation about five miles long from Mt. Rainier to Mt. Adams in Washington State [check out https://airandspace.si.edu/stories/editorial/1947-year-flying-saucer].

If we want to believe that a squadron of nine flying saucers was flying around the west coast of the U.S.A. at the end of June 1947, let's try and guess how we might deploy them IF we were in charge. I will assume that the overall intention of the mission is surveillance and mapping of the continental U.S.

And I will make the further assumption that 'High Command,' back in the mothership or wherever, had thoughts of making covert landings, maybe to analyse atmosphere, water, soil, etc. and even capture a few isolated animals. Maybe. If that were High Command's plan, the North American Deserts would require especially careful attention from our squadron of flying saucers.

So, with me in command, my surveillance squadron would have flown south from Washington State to map Oregon, southern Idaho, Nevada and Utah, and then southern California, Arizona and Mexico to map the Sonoran Desert.

But before the main flight then flew eastwards to map the Chihuahuan Desert in Mexico and southwest Texas, I would have detached a couple of vehicles to investigate in detail the New Mexico desert where, almost exactly two years before this surveillance flight of ours, our mothership had detected x-ray and gamma-ray bursts of the sort produced by a nuclear explosion in that area as we approached the planet.

Unfortunately, when one of the saucers in this detachment crashed in severe weather and was hauled away by the native animals of this planet, our surveillance squadron was withdrawn back to the mothership.

Plans to fly to the east coast to survey a city, characterised by forests of tall buildings, which seemed to be a global hub for commerce and culture of the planet's animals, and another city that appeared to be the centre of government was consequently postponed and we maintained a low profile for several years so as not to scare the natives.

Now, that's a theory I'm proud of!

> And Microsoft Copilot told me about this: 'The most publicized sightings of flying saucers over Washington D.C. took place from July 12 to 29, 1952. These sightings were reported by various credible witnesses including radar operators and professional pilots. The sightings were so frequent and widespread that they later became known as the *Washington flap*, the *Washington National Airport Sightings*, or the *Invasion of Washington*.
>
> The most publicized sightings occurred on consecutive weekends, July 19–20 and July 26–27. The U.S. Air Force scrambled fighter jets, but the 'saucers' outran them. Despite the widespread panic and speculation, the Air Force officially attributed the sightings to weather-related events.' [Source: Conversation with Bing, 26/11/2023].

The bottom line of this speculative argument of mine is that IF the U.S. military did 'capture a flying saucer' with its crew from a crash site near Roswell AAF base, the presence of that alien-crewed flying saucer at that location on 4 July 1947, was not necessarily a coincidence.

Rather, there's a plausible argument to the effect that it was a direct consequence of the Trinity Test detonation at White Sands on 16 July 1945.

So, can we find convincing coincidences in the righthand column of the Table shown above? Again, I say no, and this is why. The Roswell mythology alleges that President Truman, in response to the Army Air Force's 'capture of a flying saucer' entrusted investigation of the event and assessment of the threat to the United States represented by the captured machine to James V. Forrestal.

There would have been no coincidence in that. At the time Forrestal had just ended WWII as cabinet-level Secretary of the U.S. Navy, having successfully guided the U.S. Navy from the Japanese attack on Pearl Harbor on 7 December 1941, to the surrender of Japan, formally signed by representatives from the Empire of Japan on 2 September 1945, on the deck of the United States Navy battleship USS Missouri in Tokyo Bay, Japan.

The USS Missouri was the flagship of the 3rd U.S. Fleet. She was built at the Brooklyn Navy Yard and launched, by President Truman's daughter, Margaret, on 29 January 1944. The USS Missouri had fought her way from Iwo Jima to Okinawa, and onto Japan during the last year of the war.

So, with a record for war administration like that, who better than James V. Forrestal to take on the even more onerous task of providing *'the military forces needed to deter war and ensure our nation's security'* this being the stated mission of the U.S. Department of Defense [https://www.defense.gov].

In 1947, Forrestal was supervising the establishment of the Department of Defense as an executive branch of the federal government of the United States.

Today, the DoD is America's largest government agency, with a core mission of providing the military forces needed to deter war and ensure the nation's security. To fulfil that mission the DoD is mandated to coordinate and supervise all agencies and functions of the U.S. Government directly related to national security and the United States Armed Forces.

Based in the Pentagon, the DoD includes the Joint Chiefs of Staff, the departments of the U.S. Army, U.S. Navy, and U.S. Air Force, and many other agencies including, today, the United States Space Command (USSPACECOM) and the United States Space Force (USSF, *'Mission: Secure our Nation's interests in, from, and to space,'* which is part of the Department of the U.S. Air Force).

The Space Force is currently the smallest U.S. armed service, but it still has an openly published complement of 8,600 military personnel and admits to operating 77 spacecraft with space launch facilities at the West Coast (Vandenberg Space Force Base in California) and the East Coast (located at Cape Canaveral in Florida) [check out this URL: https://www.spaceforce.mil/].

The U.S. Space Command is described as *'a unified combatant command of the United States Department of Defense'* [https://www.spacecom.mil/], being responsible for military operations in outer space. The U.S. Space Command has an interestingly chequered history.

It was originally established in 1985, to be a joint command, control and coordinating structure for all military forces in outer space. However, Space Command was disestablished in 2002, its responsibilities being merged into the U.S. Strategic Command. Then it was reestablished in 2019, to focus on space as a warfighting domain.

We go back to the *'big IFs'* again, now. IF Roswell AAF military security really did 'capture a flying saucer' and Forrestal was tasked with coping with any threat to the United States posed by the captured machine, then he did one hell of a job by establishing a U.S. Government Agency in 1947 that could, within 40 years, that is in 1985, produce a joint command structure for military forces to fight a war in outer space. And keep it all quiet!

Keeping important defence matters quiet and confidential had been second nature to Forrestal and his staff during the war that had come to an end in 1945.

The Allies' counterintelligence triumph of WWII had been the decipherment of German Axis and Japanese Navy coded messages. Consequently, IF James V. Forrestal was put in charge of assessing the defence implications of a 'captured flying saucer' in 1947, whether its origin was terrestrial or extraterrestrial, the need for total secrecy would have been at the forefront of his mind.

And for someone who, only two years before, had been dealing every hour of the day (and, probably, night) during WWII with decrypted military signals labelled *'Magic,'* *'ULTRA'* and *'Top-Secret Ultra,'* it seems to me perfectly natural that he should name the security classification of the *'flying saucer'* activity *MAJIC*.

Further, IF James V. Forrestal was required to gather a group of high-ranking officials into a Presidential Commission, he had every opportunity to put together a group of military and security chiefs, scientists, and engineers with whom he had worked successfully in the recent past to bring the Second World War to an end.

The name '*Majestic 12*' for this select group might also have emerged readily from Forrestal's recent memories, since part of the Allied planning for an invasion of the Japanese home islands proposed to take place during 1945 and

1946, used the code name *Majestic* after the original codename *'Olympic'* was compromised by being broadcast in unsecured signals.

The invasion never happened, of course. It was cancelled when Japan surrendered following the Soviet Union's invasion of Manchuria and formal declaration of war with Japan, and crucially, of course, the atomic bombings of Hiroshima and Nagasaki [https://en.wikipedia.org/wiki/Operation_Downfall].

The position we've reached now, then, is that everything that's needed for the basic *'Roswell Incident Mythology'* was, IN FACT, a part of James V. Forrestal's everyday life in the years 1945 to 1947. So, is this where a 'Government Conspiracy of Silence' about what happened at Roswell originated? Well, maybe, but not necessarily a conspiracy of the government against the people.

What occurs to me is that IF Roswell AAF military security really did 'capture a flying saucer' there's a real possibility that the 'conspiracy' is not one of the Government against the people, nor even of the U.S.A. against Russia or China; but rather a conspiracy of all of us against the aliens.

Remember that the Soviet Union, China the British Empire and the United States were all allies during World War II and were the principal contributors of manpower, resources, and strategy, in the victory they worked together to achieve in 1945.

And although the wartime alliances with the communist states broke down and eventually turned into outright hostility, I'm willing to believe that our wartime allies might have been included in the Conspiracy of Silence in 1947, and even though relations between the West and China and the Soviet Union have deteriorated since then, there is likely to be a shared understanding that until the motives and intentions of the aliens are established they must be treated as joint enemies.

Given the technology their mere presence in our airspace implies, the aliens must be assumed to have been able to monitor the radio & TV broadcasts of 1947, so there could be no official acknowledgement of anything relating to them at that time. And as our broadcast and Internet activities have increased since, we cannot officially break the silence now.

If they are secretive in their dealings with us, then the safest procedure is to maintain the fiction that we are ignorant of their activities. Hence, the official denials of all the mythology that has developed around Roswell and the official refutation of every conspiracy theory that has emerged since. Furthermore, it doesn't matter that political relationships between the United States, Russia and China have changed in recent decades.

If the U.S.A. prepares itself against domination by world communism, and Russia and China prepare themselves against domination by world fascist imperialism then the whole world will be prepared against any danger there might be of domination by aliens. Well, I like to look on the bright side of things!

I've read a recent news article (28 November 2023) claiming that the U.S. Central Intelligence Agency operates a covert office (called the Office of Global Access or OGA) that has conducted UFO/flying saucer retrieval missions on at least nine crash sites around the world [check the news report at this URL: https://tinyurl.com/3zkbsxvb].

Apparently, seven were crashed wrecks but two were completely intact. I don't know whether these reports are right or wrong, real news or fake news. But my take on this claim is that it doesn't say much for the quality of the alien's piloting skills if 10 alien spacecraft have come all this way just to crash on Earth.

If they are that careless about bumping into planets, the rest of the Solar System must be littered with wreckage; I just hope there are no plans to reverse-engineer their flight control and pilot training systems!

I asked Microsoft Copilot, 'List specific details about UFO/flying saucers that have been recovered since the 1930s,' and in response, I got the following rather cagey reply:

> 'There have been several claims about the recovery of UFOs or flying saucers since the 1930s. Here are some notable instances:
>
> 1. **David Grusch's Testimony**: David Grusch, a former American intelligence official, claimed that the U.S. Government conducted a 'multi-decade' program which collected, and attempted to reverse-engineer, crashed UFOs [ref 1]. He stated that 'non-human' beings had been found. Major Grusch's evidence is based on interviews with more than 40 witnesses over the past four years [ref 2]. When asked to expand on what he knew about extraterrestrial bodies, Major Grusch said that 'biologics came with some of these recoveries' [ref 2].
>
> 2. **U.S. Government's UFO Program**: A whistleblower has claimed that the United States Government is concealing a program which deals with the retrieval and reverse engineering of unidentified flying objects (UFOs) [ref 2]. The Pentagon has denied all of the allegations [ref 2].
>
> 3. **UFO Incidents of the 1930s**: A 2022 book by UFO researchers Noe Torres and John LeMay (*UFOs of the Turbulent Thirties* [https://amzn.to/3ggAJCO]) discloses previously unknown UFO incidents of the 1930s [ref 3].

> Please note that while these reports exist, they should be taken with a grain of scepticism as many can be explained through natural phenomena or human-made objects. Always look for reliable sources when researching such topics.' [Source: Conversation with Bing, 29/11/2023].
>
> References
>
> [1] US conducted 'multi-decade' secret UFO program, ex-intelligence…
> https://www.theguardian.com/us-news/2023/jul/26/ufo-hearing-congress-evidence-david-grusch?ref=distilleddaily.news.
>
> [2] Whistleblower claims US government hiding 'multi-decade' UFO…—ITVX. https://www.itv.com/news/2023-07-26/whistleblower-claims-us-government-hiding-ufo-retrieval-programme.
>
> [3] New Book Discloses Previously Unknown UFO Incidents of the 1930s. https://www.digitaljournal.com/pr/new-book-discloses-previously-unknown-ufo-incidents-of-the-1930s.

Going back to the recent testimony of that former American intelligence official, Major David Grusch. In a report dated 27 November 2023 [view at https://tinyurl.com/tfnjrvvt], he claims that major countries have been retrieving materials from UFO crashes for nearly a century in a covert arms race.

He described a crash of a 'saucer-shaped' craft in 1933 in the Lombardy region of Italy that was notified to major world leaders of the time, including the Vatican, Germany's Adolph Hitler and the then U.S. President Franklin D. Roosevelt. Clearly, if true, this claimed crash predated the claimed Roswell crash in New Mexico.

I have asked Microsoft Copilot about flying saucer recoveries in Russia and China and this is what it found:

> I asked: Have crashed flying saucers been recovered in Russia?
>
> 'There have been several reports of alleged UFO sightings and recoveries in Russia. Here are a few examples [refs 1 to 7]:
>
> 1. A video from Russia has surfaced that purportedly reveals a UFO discovered buried in a Russian coal mine [ref 1].
>
> 2. Coal miners in Siberia's Kuznetsk Basin, Russia, reportedly found a saucer-shaped object buried 40 metres underground. Some UFO researchers claim this is an ancient alien 'flying saucer' craft that crashed to Earth from space thousands of years ago [ref 6].
>
> 3. Early in 2012, a crashed titanium object, described as a 'UFO fragment,' was retrieved from a forest in the vicinity of Otradnenskoye, a rural locality in Novosibirsk Oblast, after strange sounds were heard there in December 2011 [ref 7].

> However, it's important to note that these claims are often the subject of debate and scepticism. The scientific community generally requires substantial evidence before confirming such extraordinary claims. As of now, there is no universally accepted scientific evidence of extraterrestrial spacecrafts recovered on Earth.' [Source: Conversation with Bing, 29/11/2023]
>
> References
>
> [1] UFO sighting: 'Flying saucer' found buried underground stuns Russian…https://www.express.co.uk/news/weird/1175842/ufo-sighting-alien-flying-saucer-buried-russia-today-coal-miners.
>
> [2] Ancient UFO 'Flying Saucer' Found 40 Meters Below Ground By Miners In…https://www.inquisitr.com/1821821/ancient-ufo-flying-saucer-found-40-meters-below-ground-by-miners-in-siberia.
>
> [3] UFO sightings in Russia—Wikipedia. https://en.wikipedia.org/wiki/UFO_sightings_in_Russia.
>
> [4] What we know about Russia plane crash that reportedly killed Prigozhin. https://www.bbc.co.uk/news/world-europe-66596127.
>
> [5] Hitler's 'Flytrap' may have been saucer launcher site. https://www.dailymail.co.uk/news/article-9744711/Hitlers-mysterious-Flytrap-structure-launch-pad-flying-saucer.html.
>
> [6] The Russian 'Roswell'—KGB Troops Inspecting Crashed Flying Saucer…https://www.youtube.com/watch?v=7l7nAHzsamE.
>
> [7] Nazi UFOs—Wikipedia. https://en.wikipedia.org/wiki/Nazi_UFOs.

I find the final paragraph of the above 'conversations with Bing' rather fascinating. Let me remind you of Copilot's assertions in the last two conversations with Bing:

- Despite the widespread panic and speculation, the Air Force officially attributed the sightings to weather-related events.
- Please note that while these reports exist, they should be taken with a grain of scepticism as many can be explained through natural phenomena or human-made objects. Always look for reliable sources when researching such topics.
- However, it's important to note that these claims are often the subject of debate and scepticism. The scientific community generally requires substantial evidence before confirming such extraordinary claims. As of now, there is no universally accepted scientific evidence of extraterrestrial spacecrafts recovered on Earth.

Is it me, or do those paragraphs suggest that Microsoft Copilot is suggesting we shouldn't believe everything it tells us?

Next, I asked, 'Have crashed flying saucers been recovered in China?'

And received this, far from helpful, reply.

> 'There have been several reports of alleged UFO sightings and recoveries in China. Here are a few examples:
>
> 1. A Chinese company, Shenzhen UFO Technology, has created the world's first flying saucer that can carry a passenger and has been designed to look like a cartoon UFO. The craft, dubbed the iUFO, made its debut flight in Shenzhen Talent Park. [*This is totally irrelevant. It's a single-seat drone that looks, as Bing describes it, 'like a cartoon' flying saucer. It is battery-powered with enough charge for about 15 minutes flight, has a max speed of 50 km/h and a max altitude of 200 m. Essentially, it's a fairground ride!*]
>
> 2. David Grusch, a UFO whistleblower who testified in front of the U.S. Congress, has claimed that Chinese bodies are competing with the United States to recover crashed alien craft. [*Yes, we already have that data.*]
>
> However, it's important to note that these claims are often the subject of debate and scepticism. The scientific community generally requires substantial evidence before confirming such extraordinary claims. As of now, there is no universally accepted scientific evidence of extraterrestrial spacecrafts recovered on Earth.' [Source: Conversation with Bing, 29/11/2023].

This last conversation concluded with three references to aircraft crashes and a reference to a NASA Photo of a *crashed flying saucer* which is actually the sample return capsule of the Genesis spacecraft that was bringing back samples from the Sun's solar wind. Its parachutes failed to open because of a construction error so the capsule crash-landed in the Utah desert.

This particular 'conversation with Bing' seems to have revealed some of ChatGPT-4's limitations (GPT-4 being Microsoft Copilot's AI language model).

None of the information it presented was a useful answer to the question I posed, so the most intelligent answer to my question was, 'I don't know.'

Evidently, these Artificial Intelligence programs are only as intelligent as you are willing to believe them to be. When asked, Microsoft Copilot expressed the opinion, 'GPT-4…can solve difficult problems with greater accuracy than any of OpenAI's previous models, thanks to its broader general knowledge and advanced reasoning capabilities.'

Microsoft Copilot's limitations don't put me off using it, and, indeed, I quite enjoy conversations with Bing and find it a great time-saver. But use it with your eyes open and awareness that it's NOT more intelligent than you; it just shuffles data faster than you can. Essentially, a computer running an AI algorithm is just a quick-witted fool.

Above all, the quality of its answers depends on the extent and the quality of the data it shuffles. Remember the old computer programmer's acronym, GIGO, which stands for *'Garbage In, Garbage Out'*! And it turns out that Microsoft Copilot knows all about this.

Asked 'What do you know about GIGO?' Copilot came up with this:

> 'GIGO stands for 'Garbage In, Garbage Out.' It is a concept in computer science that emphasizes the importance of the quality of input data. The idea is that flawed, or nonsense (garbage) input data produces nonsense output [ref 1]. This principle applies to all logical argumentation: soundness implies validity, but validity does not imply soundness [ref 1].
>
> The term GIGO was popular in the early days of computing. The first known use is in a 1957 syndicated newspaper article about the U.S. Army mathematicians and their work with early computers [ref 1]. The underlying principle was noted by the inventor of the first programmable computing device design, Charles Babbage [ref 1].
>
> In essence, GIGO is used to suggest that the results of a calculation are only as good as the input that was used [ref 2]. It's a reminder that computers and algorithms are tools that depend on good data. If the quality of data put into a computer is low, then the quality of the information produced from that data will be low.' [Source: Conversation with Bing, 30/11/2023].
>
> References
> [1] Garbage in, garbage out—Wikipedia.
> https://en.wikipedia.org/wiki/Garbage_in,_garbage_out.
> [2] GIGO Definition & Meaning—Merriam-Webster.
> https://www.merriam-webster.com/dictionary/GIGO.

It's worth repeating that reminder: 'computers and algorithms are tools that depend on good data' and couple it with my aphorism, 'Essentially, a computer running an AI algorithm is just a quick-witted fool.'

But that Shenzhen fairground ride that our 'quick-witted fool' has just come up with, reminded me about photographs that I've seen of some circular experimental aircraft that were built around the end of WWII and into the 1950s. So, I asked Microsoft Copilot, 'Tell me about circular aircraft in the 1950s and later.'

> 'Sure, here's some information about circular aircraft from the 1950s and later:
>
> **Sack AS.6**: During World War II, a number of disc-shaped aircraft were proposed by aircraft designers in Germany. One of the few to make it further than the drawing board was the Sack AS-6, an experimental light plane with a round-winged planform that first flew in 1944.
>
> [https://en.wikipedia.org/wiki/Sack_AS-6]
>
> **Vought Flying Flapjack**: During World War II, Charles H. Zimmerman led a team at Chance-Vought that created a series of designs that eventually resulted in the Vought Flying Flapjack, one of the first aircraft explicitly designed as a disc for aerodynamic reasons. [https://airandspace.si.edu/collection-objects/vought-v-173-flying-pancake/nasm_A19610120000]
>
> **Boeing 390, 391, and 396**: In 1943, Boeing Aircraft built 3 scale model aircraft whose designs had saucer-shaped wings with a propeller in the front, and a rudder in the back.
>
> [https://en.wikipedia.org/wiki/Circular_wing].
>
> **Avrocar**: After WWII, the Avro Canada company developed a saucer-shaped aircraft…in which the thrust was directed downward around the entire disc by a flap ringing the aircraft, allowing it to take off and land vertically. [https://en.wikipedia.org/wiki/Avro_Canada_VZ-9_Avrocar]
>
> These are just a few examples of the many experimental aircraft that have been designed and built over the years. The development of these unique aircraft has contributed significantly to our understanding of aerodynamics and flight technology.'
> [Source: Conversation with Bing, 29/11/2023]

I just wonder why there was so much interest and experimentation with circular-wing forms in the 1940s. Could it have had anything to do with the alleged crash of a 'saucer-shaped' craft in 1933 in Italy that was described by former American intelligence official Major David Grusch [view at https://tinyurl.com/tfnjrvvt]?

I think that experimental aircraft, and what their designs might owe to crashed and recovered alien spacecraft, is a topic worth much more development. But that's for the future. Right now, I'm late for my lunch, so I'm going to close this writing session and amble down the road to the Quick Bite Café. See ya later.

3. Frank Conversation

When I first came back to Liverpool, I didn't get out much. I don't get out that much now, but I was a real hermit just after I moved into my present little flat. With a new identity, new online life story, new passport and carefully arranged circuitous route back home I was determined to maintain a very low profile immediately after my arrival here.

And for several months that meant I only left the house at night, and then only for emergency supplies. Gradually, I established a routine of buying groceries and other necessities online, with occasional deliveries of takeaway meals, just for their variety. Eventually, after several weeks of careful monitoring of the various central security services I can access through the security of my Onionland layer, I relaxed and gradually restored myself into the real world beyond the door of my flat.

The first thing I did was to explore the local area in the daytime. I'm not a great walker at the best of times. My right knee can be quite painful if I'm not careful, and most other joints take any opportunity they can grasp to complain. But I was pleased to find, in those first few weeks, an easy and pleasant walk that took me deeper into the park and as far as the bandstand and boating lake.

Sadly, I didn't find any boats to hire, but there were people enjoying a spot of lake fishing, so I resolved one day, on a peaceful morning, to get an angling permit and give it a try myself. Another excuse for a quiet doze in the sun!

But wet weather is catered for as well because the walk to the Victorian Palm House proved to be easy on my scale of things, and the Palm House seems to be open seven days a week, all year round and with free entry!

I need to walk past our little parade of local shops on the way to the park and Sadie's Quick Bite Café is one of the attractions that enticed me in for lunch on many occasions! And that's my destination this afternoon, although I am running late today. Still, Sadie's is where I met my only real friend, Frank Williamson, we've lunched together many times and afterwards shared a few minutes chat, and maybe a cat nap, on a bench in the park.

In his younger days, Frank was a Toxteth scally who joined the army as a teenager rather than keep dodging the local constabulary. He took to the life like a duck to water and eventually, worked out his entire career in The British Army's Royal Military Police. He'd reached the rank of Warrant Officer First Class by the time he retired at age 60, a few years back.

That makes him more than 10 years younger than me, but we get along really well. He's got a part-time job as a security guard in a 24-hour supermarket and although his shifts can vary a lot because he's always willing to work extras, covering other people's absences, he's often able to have lunch with me in Sadie's and I enjoy the chance to chat with a real live human being every so often rather than an Internet AI-bot!

Today, I am extremely late for our usual lunch time and as I approach the Quick Bite Café, I can see Frank sitting at our usual window table. He has his back to me, but I can tell from the activity of his elbows that he is already working his way through his usual all-day mega breakfast! I rap my knuckles on the window in greeting as I pass and, once inside, amble over to the table.

'Eh, Mick,' Frank said, 'I'd give up on ya, so I made a start on me scran. I had an early shift this mornin' and I was starving. But I'm doing a twilight shift tonight to cover for one of the young uns, so I had to make a start.

'Yeah, I can see you're well into your cholesterol special. You're relying too much on your statins to compensate for your diet, you know.' I teased him, then I slipped into my native dialect and continued, 'I'm late cos I was bossin' me writin' and didn't notice the time flyin' by. I'm gonna order me scran. Anythin', you want me to get ya?'

'Sound, la. Gis another brew, two in it, and I'll share a bag of chips with ya.'

I conveyed Frank's order to Josie behind the counter, and I decided to go for a brunch of gammon steak and hash browns with a side of grilled mushrooms. I thought they'd be good with a few chips; well, I was popping statin pills, too. I also got a bread bun with a view to throwing bits of it at the ducks later on.

When I got my tray over to the table and laid out the plates, Frank asked as I settled into the seat opposite him, 'Wot 'ave ya got the bread bun for?'

'I thought I could feed it to the ducks later on.' I said.

'Nah, eat it yerself. Make a chip buttie. Bread's not good for ducks. Not enough food value, but it makes 'em feel stuffed. I've brought some genuine birdseed from the shop,' Frank said, patting a paper shopping bag on the seat beside him.

'So, wot 'av ya bin up to this mornin', then, that took so long?' he asked, transferring half the chips from the serving bowl onto his plate.

'Just writing a bit more of my life story. Sometimes when I wake up my head's full of stuff that my brain's dredged out of my memory while I was asleep. There's no guarantee I will continue to remember it unless I get it written down as soon as I'm awake. I woke early this morning, and me 'ead was so full of memories that I was writing it all down for around six hours, I explained.

'Well, ah hope ya took time for breakfast, me old mucker. Ah, don't want ya wastin' away!' Frank said, skewering a few chips with his fork and waving them at me.

'No fear of that la,' I replied confidently, as I added a fair chunk of my gammon steak and a hash brown to my chip buttie.

Further conversation was considerably delayed as we necked our scran.

'I don't suppose youse were watchin' the gogglebox last night, were ya?' Frank finally asked as our missions to demolish a plate of food each were accomplished. 'There was a boss programme on about Area 51 and I'm sure I remember youse sayin' some time that youse worked there once.'

'Aye, that's right,' I responded guardedly, 'I worked there as a consultant helping set up their computers. There's a lot of nonsense talked about Area 51. The place is wrapped up in smoke and mirrors and pure mythology. What was this programme about?'

Frank pushed his now empty plate to one side with a sigh of satisfaction to bring his mug of tea front and centre, relaxed back into his chair and said, 'It was on the 'Istory Channel so it can't be too cockeyed. It was about the CIA testin' fancy spy planes there, like the U-2, in the 1950s. They called it the Skunk Works. Duz dat ring any bells wiv ya?'

Oh yeah, I know all about the goings-on at the Skunk Works, I thought to myself, but all I said to Frank was, 'We were still at school when all that was happening.'

But Frank wasn't satisfied by my attempted brush-off and just responded, 'Sure, but if you were there, didn't you find out anything about the 'istory of the place?'

This was getting uncomfortably close to my real life, so I took a few swigs from my builders' mug of tea as a delaying tactic.

When I had carefully organised my thoughts, I started to answer, 'My first visit to Area 51 was in the mid-1980s when I was still being sent out to overseas customers to supervise the installation of newly purchased mainframe computers.

'I've got three notable memories of that trip because of all the hoo-hah in the press and TV at the time. I was there in 1985 when the Pentagon released a document, allegedly 'by accident' which referred to a super spy plane code-named Aurora.

'This was very fast, around 5000 mph and able to cruise at altitudes of 50 to 80 miles high. What interested me about this document was that the plane was described as triangular, and on many of my overnight shifts in the server rooms I could hear the pulsing jet noise of aircraft being test flown, and when I went outside to get some air, I saw triangular sets of navigation lights charging about the night sky.'

I paused to let my thoughts catch up with my mouth and Frank interrupted, asking, 'And what were the other two?'

I played the old man card, saying, 'Eh? Other two what?'

'Didn't you just say, our kid, you had three notable memories of that trip?' Frank asked, gently.

'Oh, I see what, yeh mean,' I replied. 'Yeah, one was the Challenger shuttle disaster in January 1986. That was a real kick in the teeth for the whole of the U.S. space industry, especially when they found out that it was down to a failure of rubber O-ring seals in a solid rocket booster.'

'And the third memory?' Frank prompted again.

'Oh, no doubts about that, President Ronald Reagan's speech to the UN's General Assembly in 1987. The conspiracy theory guys had a field day with that! Think of it; the U.S. President said in public there's an alien threat and an alien force already among us!'

'Straight up?' said Frank. 'I do not remember that la.'

'Well, it was nearly 40 years ago,' I said. 'But I was right in the middle of the media storm at the time, so I reckon I can remember the exact words Reagan used. Let me think, now. Yeah, it was something like, 'How quickly our worldwide differences would vanish if we were facing an alien threat from outside this world? And yet, I ask you, is not an alien force already among us?' Astonishing!

'And not surprising that conspiracy theorists got themselves so highly excited about it. Some even suggested that the missile defense system announced by President Reagan four years before, in 1983; the one he called the Strategic Defense Initiative, but everyone else called the Star Wars programme, was intended to protect the U.S. against alien confrontation rather than Soviet intercontinental ballistic missiles.'

'I don't remember that either,' said Frank.

'Don't worry about it, kidder,' I responded. 'The programme was cancelled in 1993.'

Our idle chatter was briefly interrupted as Josie appeared at our table to clear away our used pots. We both accepted her offer of yet another builder's mug of tea and decided on a custard slice each as a special treat. And while Josie was fetching our further refreshments, we both had to charge off to the gents for a slash.

Back at the table and enjoying a deep dive into the generous layer of custard Josie put in her custard slices, Frank asked, 'But what about the 'istory of Area 51 and the Skunk Works?'

'Well,' I said, 'youse talkin' about two different things there, though their histories are freely available on the Internet. The Skunk Works came first, being set up in 1939 as Lockheed Advanced Development Projects, to research and develop highly classified exotic aircraft at United States Army Air Corps (now USAF) controlled plants in Palmdale, California and Fort Worth, Texas.'

'Youse means during WWII? Dat long ago, la? But why 'Skunk Works'?'

'At the time, the term Skunk Works was management-speak for a department in an organisation that was working on advanced or secret projects with minimum bureaucracy and a high level of autonomy. We'd probably call it, blue skies thinking these days. It's just another way of saying, creative and innovative thinking.

'But now Skunk Works has become an almost official alias for Lockheed Martin's Advanced Development Programs Division. And, yes, Skunk Works history started with the P-38 Lightning in 1939, which was designed to meet a 1937 specification from the U.S. Army Air Corps for a twin-engine aircraft able to intercept and attack hostile aircraft at high altitudes.

'The Skunk Works came up with the P-38, which became as iconic of WWII as the RAF's Spitfire and was the only American fighter aircraft in large-scale production right through WWII, from Pearl Harbor to the Japanese surrender.'

I finished off my custard slice and necked a fair amount of tea before continuing, 'The next Skunk Works triumph because it was designed and built in a grand total of 143 days, was the P-80 Shooting Star in 1943, which was America's first successful turbojet-powered combat aircraft and the first operational jet fighter used by the USAAF during WWII.

The USAF used the P-80 was during the Korean War until it was replaced in combat by the F-86 Sabre, which was more of a match for the MiG-15.'

I drained the last of my tea, saying, 'Listen, Frank, we should let Josie get some more paying customers in for this table. Let's go find a place to sit beside the lake and I'll finish off my story there.'

And that's what we did. Stopping off in the gents first, and then bandying a few words with Josie on the way out of the café, we ambled gently into the park and found our usual bench alongside the boating lake unoccupied and claimed it with satisfaction. I saved Frank's fumbling with the sealed paper bag of birdseed by handing him my penknife.

Really, I was sometimes surprised at how unprepared for the outside world Frank seemed after a lifetime's career in the military, but he got the bag open, and we scattered a sufficient supply of seeds onto the lake's edge to attract a flotilla of ducks and moorhens, and a serene squadron of swans. A gentle pleasure to hear and watch, until the Canada Geese barged in to take over.

'Takes me back to my childhood, this,' I said. 'Me mam used to save up stale bread and every so often, weather permitting, we'd trudge up Prince's Avenue to feed the ducks on Prince's Park Lake. An' if I was lucky, we'd get the tram back home to Parliament Street, just to save me little legs.'

'Sound, you've mentioned that before but if you can remember that, can you remember what you were gonna tell me about Area 51 in the café?' Frank asked.

So, I had to park one set of reminiscences and guardedly activate another to tell him about Area 51.

'Okay,' I said, 'well, to start with, Area 51 is located about 85 miles north of Las Vegas in the desolate Nevada desert. It's a United States Air Force (USAF) base which is located at Groom Lake, a dry lakebed in the Nevada desert, and is officially called Homey Airport but as it's got the longest runway in the world and the largest aircraft hangar in the world, it's obviously something special.

'It's also referred to informally as Paradise Ranch and from the late 1960s the radio call sign for the base was 'Dreamland,' though since February 2021 there are two call signs, one for passenger aircraft and one for mission aircraft and both change every month.

'Area 51 is just a small part of the Federal lands in southern Nevada, being surrounded by restricted military zones, one of which is the Nevada test site which was used to test nukes from the 1950s to 1990, and a restricted area of over four and a half thousand square miles used for military testing and training that make up the Nellis Air Force Range.

'Nellis Air Force Base is 135 miles north of Las Vegas just off Las Vegas, Boulevard North. Intense secrecy surrounds all of this. The public is kept away by warning signs, electronic surveillance, and armed guards and it's even illegal to fly over the area.'

As I paused, I began to suspect that Frank was dozing off beside me, but I continued to drone on, nevertheless.

'After WWII, the Skunk Works engineers continued to produce exotic and super-secret aircraft, most of which were flight-tested at Area 51. It's the place where the U2 spy plane was test flown in the 1950s and the SR-71 in the 1960s. Later, the F117 Nighthawk stealth fighter-bomber, and B-2 and B-21 strategic bombers were developed, as well as the F-22 Raptor, and F-35 Lightning II. These black programmes are worth at least $30 billion annually.'

After scattering a few more seeds for the birds, I carried on relentlessly, 'Area 51's history starts with the U2, because in 1955, the Central Intelligence Agency, U.S. Air Force and defence contractor Lockheed Martin chose this remote desert site in southern Nevada to begin testing and development of the U-2 spy plane, which was the newest and most advanced aircraft in the world at the time.

'Area 51 has never been declared a secret base, though everything that's done there is classified as Top Secret. It wasn't shown on public maps for decades and the U.S. Government didn't even admit it existed until the CIA publicly acknowledged the existence of Area 51 in 2013, and declassified documents detailing its history and purpose.'

Frank's head nodded onto my shoulder and his gentle snoring confirmed that he'd dozed off sometime during this last little speech, so I gave up trying to educate him. Instead, I spread one more handful of birdseed over the edge of the lake and settled down to admire the birds as they quacked and grumbled about the seeds.

It wasn't long before I found myself talking to Pete Gibbon again and heard myself saying, 'I didn't know anyone had been to Mars.'

To which Pete replied through his customary cigarette smoke, 'Perfect. You stick to that story, and you'll be fine. You're in the Skunk Works now, Buddy. This is where the good ole US of A builds things nobody else has even dreamed of yet. Everything you didn't think could happen has happened here.

'Work on the principle that nothing you see here with your own eyes ever actually took place. And, like I've said before, remember Roswell Rule Number One: nothing you know to be true here is ever divulged to the outside world!'

Suddenly, Pete was shaking my shoulder violently and speaking in a broad scouse accent, 'Wake up la, I've gorra catch the 82 to go on-shift at Tessers.'

And then my body comes back to life, and I surface from my deep dreaming sleep and realise that it's Frank shaking me awake.

'If you sleep here any longer, the Sefton scallies will 'ave the boots off yer feet before yer know it. I'll see youse tomorrow, la. 12 o'clock on the dot this time. At Josie's; it's me birthday.'

I sit up straight and to show that I'm fully awake, I promise Frank that on my way back to my flat, I'll drop into Sadie's Café to organise a birthday lunch for him.

'Mussels,' he shouted back at me as he sprinted off in the direction of the bus stop.

I'm still a bit dazed and stiff after sleeping so deeply on this park bench and I remember thinking, sadly, 'I used to be able to sprint like that. Now, I can only shuffle my way along. I dunno why Frank puts up with me.'

I hauled myself to my feet and started to move my old joints down the path towards my flat. I dropped into the fishmongers that was a few doors down from Sadie's Café and was delighted to find that they had freshly delivered supplies of Shetland mussels.

I bought a few kilos and took them into the Quick Bite Café and Josie agreed to make us her special moules marinière for our lunch tomorrow. And after I offered to buy a bottle of Muscadet in the off-licence next door, I even persuaded her to join us to celebrate Frank's birthday!

With tomorrow's lunch arrangements completed, I took a coffee-to-go from Sadie's Café and then trudged back to my flat. My mind was still buzzing with all the stuff I'd dredged out of my memory about the Skunk Works and Area 51 that I'd told Frank about, so I decided to type it up properly.

I'd edited out some of the most secret information from what I'd said to Frank, so it would be appropriate to get the full story down into the autobiography I have been storing in Onionland.

When I got it typed up, I realised that I'd not told Frank very much. Sure, I'd described the wartime P-38 and P-80 stories well enough, but I'd barely mentioned the post-WWII aircraft other than the U-2, by the time Frank dozed off.

Yet it was the occasional sightings of these experimental black ops aircraft operating in the skies above Groom Lake, coupled with the ironclad security surrounding the site, that gave credence to the tales of unidentifiable flying vehicles and other mysterious activities that, since the 1950s, have fuelled the more bizarre folklore that has churned around Area 51, particularly since the Roswell events.

Whatever did happen at Roswell, the authorities, and by that, I mean any authority you care to point at, military or civilian, all behaved in an irrational and contradictory manner. Yet these were the people in which our safety and governance lay.

On 2 July 1947, some sort of aerial vehicle crashed on a ranch near Corona, New Mexico during a thunderstorm and wreckage was scattered across three-quarters of a mile of the ranch.

The crash was reported to the local Army Air Force base, about 80 miles away, which, of course, was Roswell Army Air Field, then the only place in the world with an active unit flying bombers armed with atom bombs. Intelligence Officer Major Jesse Marcel and Junior Officer Sheridan Cavitt drove to Corona to inspect the debris field.

On 7 July, debris was returned to the Roswell base; some was flown by B29 to Wright-Patterson AFB in Dayton, Ohio. The base commander at Roswell AAF was Colonel William Blanchard and this is what Microsoft Copilot told me about him:

> *William Hugh Blanchard* (February 6, 1916-May 31, 1966) was a United States Air Force officer who attained the rank of four-star general and served as Vice Chief of Staff of the United States Air Force from 1965 to 1966 [ref 1]. He was also a commander of strategic bombing operations in World War II [ref 3]. Blanchard was the commanding officer of the Roswell Army Air Field (RAAF) in 1947 when a rancher named W.W.

> 'Mac' Brazel found the wreckage of a flying disc on his property in Lincoln County, New Mexico [ref 2].
>
> The RAAF released a statement, writing that, 'The many rumours regarding the flying disc became a reality yesterday when the intelligence office of the 509th Bomb Group of the Eighth Air Force, Roswell Army Air Field, was fortunate enough to gain possession of a disc through the cooperation of one of the local ranchers and the sheriff's office of Chaves County.'
>
> According to that statement, Major Jesse Marcel, an intelligence officer, oversaw the RAAF's investigation of the crash site and the recovered materials [ref 2]. The government changed its story about the Roswell saucer a few times. *The following day*, the Roswell Daily Record ran a story about the crash and the RAAF's astonishing claim.
>
> But U.S. Army officials quickly reversed themselves on the flying saucer claim, stating that the found debris was actually from a weather balloon, releasing photographs of Major Marcel posing with pieces of the supposed weather balloon debris as proof [ref 2]. [Source: Conversation with Bing, 13/12/2023].
>
> References
> [1] William H. Blanchard—Wikipedia.
> https://en.wikipedia.org/wiki/William_H._Blanchard.
> [2] GENERAL WILLIAM H. BLANCHARD > Air Force > Biography Display.
> https://www.af.mil/About-Us/Biographies/Display/Article/107667/general-william-h-blanchard/.
> [3] What Really Happened at Roswell? | HISTORY.
> https://www.history.com/news/roswell-ufo-aliens-what-happened.

I get the impression from this account that Intelligence Officer Major Jesse Marcel was hung out to dry by the U.S. Army making him pose for the newspaper photographers with pieces of weather balloon to prove that, as an experienced intelligence officer, and war hero, he couldn't tell the difference between a flying disk from outer space that he'd recovered and sent on to Wright-Patterson AFB, and a chunk of weather balloon some senior officer in intelligence had just spread out on the floor for him. Copilot told me the following about Major Marcel:

> *Intelligence Officer Major Jesse Marcel* was the first military officer to investigate the 1947 Roswell Incident, where he claimed to have found debris of a flying disc that was later identified as a weather balloon by the U.S. Army [ref 1]. He maintained that the Roswell debris was extraterrestrial until his death, aged 76, in 1986 [ref 2]. He also served as a commander of strategic bombing operations in World War II and participated in the Operation Crossroads nuclear tests at the Bikini Atoll in 1946 [ref 1]. He left a diary that his family believes contains clues about the truth of Roswell and the location of the alien wreckage [ref 2]. Jesse Marcel Jr, his son, also claimed to have

> handled debris from the 1947 crash of an unidentified flying object near Roswell, New Mexico [ref 1]. [Source: Conversations with Bing, 13/12/2023].
>
> References
>
> [1] Jesse Marcel—Wikipedia. https://en.wikipedia.org/wiki/Jesse_Marcel.
>
> [2] Does an army officer's secret diary reveal new clues to Roswell? https://www.history.co.uk/shows/roswell-the-first-witness/articles/does-an-army-officer-s-secret-diary-reveal-new-clues-to-roswell.
>
> [3] Private journals of man who investigated 1947 Roswell UFO crash—Metro. https://metro.co.uk/2020/12/11/private-journals-of-man-who-investigated-1947-roswell-ufo-crash-opened-for-the-first-time-13738675/.

These contradictions, alien flying disk *versus* weather balloon, do nothing to encourage faith in official pronouncements, but a great deal to encourage theories about conspiracies. But none of the conspiracy theorists have got close to the truth. Yet.

Concern about whatever had happened around Roswell in 1947 quickly faded and the incident remained of negligible public interest until, in 1978, several enquiries under the U.S. Freedom of Information Act (FOIA), which is a federal law requiring government agencies to provide access to public records, lead to the release of information from USAF, FBI and CIA files which gave media and UFO investigators leads (names and service details) to the participants in what did happen at Roswell.

Also in 1978, the Roswell Intelligence Officer, Jesse Marcel, by then retired with the rank of Lieutenant Colonel, said he believed the debris he retrieved was of extraterrestrial origin in an interview with ufologist Stanton Friedman.

This is what Microsoft Copilot told me about Stanton Friedman:

> *Stanton Terry Friedman* (July 29, 1934-May 13, 2019) was an American nuclear physicist and professional ufologist who resided in New Brunswick, Canada [ref 1]. He was the original civilian investigator of the Roswell UFO incident. Friedman was employed for 14 years as a nuclear physicist for such companies as General Electric, Aerojet General Nucleonics, General Motors, Westinghouse, TRW Systems, and McDonnell Douglas, where he worked on advanced, classified programs on nuclear aircraft, fission and fusion rockets, and compact nuclear power plants for space applications.
>
> Since the 1980s, he consulted for the radon-detection industry. Friedman's professional affiliations included the American Nuclear Society, the American Physical Society, the American Institute of Aeronautics and Astronautics, and AFTRA.
>
> In addition to his work as a nuclear physicist, Friedman was a professional ufologist

> and gave lectures at more than 600 colleges and to more than 100 professional groups in 50 states, 10 provinces, and 19 countries outside the US. He published more than 80 UFO-related papers and appeared on many radio and television programs.
>
> Friedman was the first civilian to document the site of the Roswell UFO incident (co-authoring with Don Berliner the 1997 book 'Crash at Corona: The Definitive Story of The Roswell Incident,' ISBN 978–1931044899).
>
> He supported the hypothesis that it was a genuine crash of an extraterrestrial spacecraft and believed that UFO sightings were consistent with magnetohydrodynamic propulsion, which is a method of propelling vehicles using only electric and magnetic fields with no moving parts. [Source: Conversation with Bing, 16/12/2023].
>
> Reference
>
> [1] https://en.wikipedia.org/wiki/Stanton_T._Friedman.

But the real genesis of full-blown Roswell mythology is a book with the title 'The Roswell Incident,' published in 1980 by Charles Berlitz and William Leonard Moore.

This book sets out the classic version of Roswell folklore and played a crucial role in distributing that folklore far and wide; according to Microsoft Copilot, 'The book sold nearly 20 million copies in 30 languages.'

The central theme of the book is that an extraterrestrial saucer was struck by lightning while flying over the New Mexico desert to observe our nuclear weapons activities there. The lightning strike killed the alien crew and the vehicle crashed onto a sheep ranch outside Corona, New Mexico in July 1947.

Officers from Roswell Army Air Field investigated and recovered the debris, but subsequently, the U.S. Government engaged in a cover-up to discredit and 'counteract the growing media hysteria towards flying saucers.'

Wikipedia [https://en.wikipedia.org/wiki/The_Roswell_Incident, accessed 15/12/2023] states that 'The Roswell Incident' (1980) was the first book to introduce the controversial second-hand stories of civil engineer Grady 'Barney' Barnett and a group of archaeology students from an unidentified university who claimed to have encountered wreckage and 'alien bodies' while on the Plains of San Agustin, 150 miles to the west of Corona, 'before being escorted away by the Army' and being told to forget what they had seen. Wikipedia goes on to say that these accounts were described by ufologists as the 'one aspect of the account that seemed to conflict with the basic story about the retrieval of highly unusual debris.'

However, a common formation for an Earthly military patrol, especially in hostile environments, consists of a leader and a wingman. So, perhaps a patrol formation of two alien flying saucers were struck by lightning and both crashed 150 miles apart.

Perhaps the lightning strike caused them to collide. Perhaps they were caused to collide with a Project Mogul high-altitude military surveillance balloon. Perhaps.

The two authors of 'The Roswell Incident' were interesting characters in their own right. This is what Microsoft Copilot says about them:

> '*Charles Berlitz* was an American linguist, polyglot, and author who wrote extensively on anomalous phenomena and language-learning. Beside The Roswell Incident, he is best known for his books on the *Bermuda Triangle*, and the Philadelphia Experiment. Some of his other notable works include 'Atlantis: The Eighth Continent,' 'World of Strange Phenomena' and 'Without a Trace: New Information from the Triangle.'
>
> Berlitz also authored '*Native Tongues*,' a linguistic survey of the world's 2,796 languages and 5,000 dialects, both current and archaic, and several language-learning books, including 'Spanish Step by Step,' 'French Step-by-Step,' 'German Step-by-Step,' 'Italian Step-by-Step,' 'Passport to Russian,' and 'Passport to Japanese.'
>
> Charles Berlitz was the grandson of Maximilian Berlitz who was the founder of *Berlitz Language Schools*. Charles worked for the family language school during college breaks and later contributed to developing record and tape language courses for the company.' [Source: Conversation with Bing, 14/12/2023].
>
> The goodreads.com website [https://www.goodreads.com/ (accessed 15/12/2023)] adds these extra details to Charles Berlitz's biography: 'As a child, Charles was raised in a household in which (by father's orders) every relative & servant spoke to Charles in a different language.
>
> His father spoke to him in German, his grandfather in Russian, his nanny in Spanish. He reached adolescence speaking eight languages fluently…Berlitz spent 13 years on active duty in the U.S. Army, mostly in intelligence.…He died in 2003 at the age of 89, in Florida.'

> '*William Leonard Moore* ('Bill Moore') was an author and former ufologist who was prominent from the late 1970s to the late 1980s. He co-authored two books with Charles Berlitz, including *The Roswell Incident*. Moore was a central figure in the release of the controversial Majestic 12 documents, which purported the existence of a high-level policy-making group overseeing UFOs and extraterrestrials [ref 1].
>
> At a 1989 conference, Moore claimed that he had been engaged in 'disinformation' activities against another UFO investigator on behalf of the U.S. Air Force Office of Special Investigations.
>
> He also wrote 'The Philadelphia Experiment—Project Invisibility' with Charles

> Berlitz in 1979, about an alleged naval military experiment popularly known as the Philadelphia Experiment aboard the USS Eldridge in 1943. According to Microsoft Copilot, Bill Moore died in November 2023, aged 76.' [Sources: Conversations with Bing, 14/12/2023].
> Reference
> [1] Bill Moore (ufologist)—
> [https://en.wikipedia.org/wiki/Bill_Moore_(ufologist)].

Berlitz and Moore's 1980 history and Stanton Friedman's writings and lecture tours in the 1990s dominated the ufological field until, in later years, other authors were attracted by the commercial potential of writing about Roswell and produced rival accounts, many with new and more expansive conspiracy theories to titivate the growing conspiracy industry.

Decide what you want to believe, then buy your ticket by buying the book. But be wary. Many of the so-called first-hand accounts of the Roswell incident actually contain 'evidence' derived from the Aztec, New Mexico, UFO incident, which Microsoft Copilot describes like this:

> 'The Aztec, New Mexico UFO incident is a *hoax* that was alleged to have happened in 1948 in Aztec, New Mexico [ref 1]. The story was first published in 1949 by author Frank Scully in his *Variety* magazine columns, and later in his 1950 book 'Behind the Flying Saucers.'
> According to Scully, in March 1948, an unidentified aerial craft containing sixteen humanoid bodies was recovered by the military in New Mexico after making a controlled landing in Hart Canyon 12 miles northeast of the city of Aztec.
> However, in the mid-1950s the story was exposed as a hoax fabricated by two con men, Silas M. Newton and Leo A. Gebauer, as part of a fraudulent scheme to sell supposed alien technology.' [Source: Conversation with Bing, 15/12/2023].
> Reference
> [1]https://en.wikipedia.org/wiki/Aztec,_New_Mexico_crashed_saucer_hoax.

And another discredited name you will come across is Robert Scott Lazar (Bob Lazar), but his stories and claims echo so stridently through the past 30 years that, again, I asked Copilot, 'What do you know about Robert Lazar?' (although, as you can see from these recent conversations, *Wikipedia* is Microsoft Copilot's go-to place for basic information; still, Copilot makes a decent job of summarising it):

> '*Robert Scott Lazar*, born on January 26, 1959, is an American businessman and conspiracy theorist who claims he was hired in the late 1980s to reverse-engineer extraterrestrial technology. He still owns and operates *United Nuclear Scientific Equipment and Supplies Incorporated*, which sells a variety of materials and chemicals [https://www.unitednuclear.com/]. Lazar's claims have been analysed and rejected by sceptics and some ufologists, although he retains a following of supporters. Lazar has no evidence of alien life or technology, and elements of his claimed education and employment history have not been substantiated [ref 1].
>
> In spite of the fact that what he has claimed does not hold up to scrutiny, he has gained a strong following of believers who back him up…[Source: Conversation with Bing, 17/12/2023].
>
> Ref 1 contributes: 'In terms of Lazar's claims about the work he conducted at S-4 and the knowledge he gained about extraterrestrial technology; it is important to point out that these claims are highly controversial and have largely been debunked by experts over the years.'
>
> Which Copilot supplements with the explanation 'S-4 is a term that was popularized by Bob Lazar, who claimed to have worked at a facility called *'Sector 4'* at Area 51. According to Lazar, Sector 4 was an underground facility located inside the Papoose Range near Papoose Lake.
>
> However, the existence of Sector 4 has not been officially confirmed by the U.S. Government [Source: Conversation with Bing, 17/12/2023].'
>
> Reference
> [1] Bob Lazar Net Worth [Life, Career, Education] 2023. https://visitinghub.com/bob-lazar-net-worth-life/.

In 1989, Bob Lazar appeared on a television station located in Las Vegas, Nevada, KLAS-TV news, and claimed that he worked on reverse-engineering alien flying saucers in an ultrasecret sector of Area 51 [view the 16 May 2019 YouTube retrospective of this story at this URL: https://tinyurl.com/2kwfz6vx]. Very recently, he's also created the 2018 documentary 'Bob Lazar: Area 51 and Flying Saucers' on the Internet Movie Database, IMDb.com [view: https://www.imdb.com/title/tt9107368/].

His claims across the last 30 years or more have been described by journalist Ken Layne in these terms: 'Area 51 became a meme of the first kind, a mythology that burrowed into the collective consciousness and never really left. The [TV series] X-Files and [film] Independence Day brought the paranoid tales to life. Video games, pop music and comic books elaborated the theology. Like Roswell before it, Nevada's Area 51 became a dreamland of extraterrestrial secrets' [https://tinyurl.com/329ma3b4].

This is my summary of Bob Lazar's claims. Bob Lazar claims to have worked around 1988–89 as a propulsion physicist at Area 51, specifically at a very high-security underground facility known as Sector 4 (S-4), and he reports disk-shaped aircraft being flown at Area 51, with Papoose Dry Lake being the 'flying saucer base' centre of activity on alien vehicles, although Lazar believes that the operation moved away from S-4 in 1990/91. Lazar reports 9 flying saucers at S4 and to have been one of 22 people who had 'Majestic security clearance' to work directly on the vehicles themselves. A form, dated 1989, purporting to be an official U.S. Internal Revenue Service document has been shown on TV indicating that Lazar worked for Naval Intelligence with a MAJ clearance number (and there is a suggestion that Lazar may have been set up by the intelligence community as a conduit for the release of information).

Lazar maintains that he was engaged in reverse-engineering the propulsion unit of alien flying saucers and provided descriptions of the vehicles and the nature of their propulsion to support this. Apparently, an alien flying saucer has three levels, or decks, within the craft. The lower deck houses 'amplifiers' for power, the crew accommodation is on the middle deck which has entrance hatches, seats and controls, while the top level houses more controls and presumed weapons. Power for the ship is said to be supplied by total-annihilation anti-matter fusion reactors using a stable isotope of element 115 not found on Earth.

The fusion reactor provides housekeeping power as well as power for anti-gravity amplifiers. These produce a gravity wave, amplify it, shift its phase and then project it from the base of the craft as a 'field propulsion system' using gravity waves.

We can't duplicate all these things on Earth with Earth-based materials. In particular, element 115 was only discovered in 2003, and was added to our periodic table in 2016. We call it Moscovium because it was discovered at the Flerov Laboratory for Nuclear Reactions in Dubna, which is a city in Russia's Moscow region. And that's why there is so much interest, and secrecy, in recovering and recycling crashed UFOs.

Journalist Ken Layne states, 'A lot of credible people have looked at Lazar's story and rationally concluded that he made it up, as he claimed to have fanciful academic credentials [e.g.] simultaneous master's degrees from MIT and Caltech, of which no trace can be found,' [https://tinyurl.com/329ma3b4].

And this is what Microsoft Copilot spontaneously contributed to my searches about the truth of the Lazar stories:

> 'I understand that you are questioning the credibility of Bob Lazar's story. While some people have found his story to be credible, others have raised doubts about its authenticity. According to a *Medium* article, Bob Lazar's story has changed significantly over the years, and there is virtually no part of his story in which details do not change from year to year and interview to interview [ref 1]. In addition, sceptics such as Donald R. Prothero, Stanton T. Friedman, and Timothy D. Callahan have found Lazar's claims implausible and lacking evidence [ref 2]. It's important to note that the truthfulness of Lazar's story is still a matter of debate, and there is no definitive proof that he made it up. However, it's always a good idea to approach any claim with a healthy dose of scepticism and to evaluate the evidence carefully before coming to a conclusion.' [Source: Conversation with Bing, 17/12/2023].
> References
> [1] Believing Bob Lazar—Part II—A Consistent Story? [https://medium.com/@signalsintelligence/believing-bob-lazar-part-ii-a-consistent-story-7ada441955ba].
> [2] Bob Lazar—https://en.wikipedia.org/wiki/Bob_Lazar.

I would echo Microsoft Copilot's advice that. 'it's always a good idea to approach any claim with a healthy dose of skepticism and to evaluate the evidence carefully before coming to a conclusion.' So, what do I 'know'? Well, I hold an open-minded stance on Bob Lazar's stories about extraterrestrial propulsion units. I just don't have enough knowledge of the physics involved to enable me to form any opinion. On the other hand, I fall in line with Stanton Friedman's belief that at least two flying saucers crashed in New Mexico in 1947 and were recovered with several alien bodies.

I rationalise this with the story that a surveillance detachment of two alien flying saucer craft hit trouble (in a storm?) over Corona and crashed in the desert.

We might add to this conjecture that lightning from the thunder cell plus, perhaps, a high-altitude Project Mogul balloon, listening for sound waves generated by Soviet atomic bomb tests, combined to bring the balloon and both alien vehicles crashing down to the ground.

I will remind you here that we are still talking about an event that might or might not have happened 76 years ago in a desert that is amazingly distant from most of us. And yet there are still strident calls for transparency about UFOs, more recently dubbed as 'Unidentified Anomalous Phenomena' or UAP.

I will not dwell on this, because most of the information is a matter of public record and freely available from Internet sources, but some of the 'evidence' was presented during 2023 to a subcommittee of the U.S. House of Representatives.

According to Copilot, the House Oversight Subcommittee on National Security, the Border, and Foreign Affairs is a subcommittee of the U.S. House Committee on Oversight and Accountability; its jurisdiction includes oversight of U.S. National Security, U.S. Homeland Security, and U.S. Foreign Policy. The following is what Microsoft Copilot told me about its hearing of 26 July 2023:

> 'The House Oversight subcommittee on National Security, the Border, and Foreign Affairs held a hearing on *unidentified aerial phenomena* (UAPs) on July 26, 2023. The hearing was attended by three former military officials: David Grusch, a former U.S. intelligence official; David Fravor, a former Navy commander; and Ryan Graves, a former Navy pilot [ref 1]. During the hearing, these former officials testified about the stigma surrounding UFO reporting and the importance of transparency in the matter.
>
> They also accused the federal government of withholding key UFO-related information from the public. Graves claimed that UAP sightings among commercial and military pilots are both 'routine' and 'grossly underreported' (although Sean Kirkpatrick, director of the Defense Department's All-Domain Anomaly Resolution Office, had told the panel in May that most UAP sightings have 'mundane' explanations…[that]…include balloons, drones, optical illusions, or even the blinking lights of a commercial airliner. Some officials and independent experts say they have seen no evidence linking UAPs to alien activity, though they have not ruled out that explanation [ref 1].)
>
> Ryan Graves added that if the public viewed the video and sensor data he witnessed, 'our national conversation would change.' Lawmakers have been pushing the federal government to reveal more information on UAPs, and some have accused U.S. officials of being too secretive. Earlier that month, Senate Majority Leader Chuck Schumer, D-N.Y., and Sen. Mike Rounds, R-S.D., introduced an amendment to the National Defense Authorization Act that would create a review board charged with declassifying UFO-related records. Schumer described his bill, saying 'the measure would create a board just like with the JFK assassination records to work through the declassification of the many government records on UAPs…This model has been a terrific success for decades and should be used with UAPs' [refs 1–4].' [Source: Conversation with Bing, 18/12/2023].
>
> References
>
> [1] Lawmakers call for greater transparency on UFOs during hearing—NBC News. [https://tinyurl.com/yc8md9av].
>
> [2] Unidentified Anomalous Phenomena: Implications on National Security.

> Public-Safety and Government Transparency. [https://tinyurl.com/yba33phn].
>
> [3] Here are the 5 most memorable moments from Congress' UFO hearing. [https://tinyurl.com/32r8kxjv].
>
> [4] The US government should tell the public what it knows about UFOs. Guardian OPINION article by Trevor Timm published 13/12/2023. [http://tinyurl.com/2m2kdk2y].

The former intelligence officer David Grusch claimed, under oath, in his testimony that the U.S. Government held several alien bodies. Some took this deposition very seriously, others viewed him as a crackpot, with others undecided. So, I asked Microsoft Copilot this question, 'Is it true that remains of alien bodies were recently revealed to a U.S. Congress Committee?'

> 'The answer to your question is not clear-cut, as there is no official confirmation or denial from the U.S. Government about the existence of alien bodies. However, some witnesses who testified before a House Oversight subcommittee on unidentified aerial phenomena (UAPs) or UFOs claimed that they had knowledge of non-human biologics recovered from some of the crashed UAPs [refs 1–4].
>
> One of them, David Grusch, a former Air Force intelligence officer, said under oath that the biologics were non-human and that was the assessment of people with direct knowledge on the program he talked to [ref 2]. He also alleged that the government had been operating with secrecy and above congressional oversight on the UAP issue [ref 1]. However, he did not provide any evidence to support his claims, and the Pentagon spokeswoman Sue Gough denied some of his other allegations [ref 1]. Therefore, it is up to you to decide whether you believe the witnesses or not, as there is no definitive proof of alien bodies being revealed to the U.S. Congress Committee.' [Source: Conversation with Bing, 09/11/2023].
>
> References
>
> [1] Did the Government Confirm Aliens Exist? Here's What Happened—Newsweek. [https://tinyurl.com/d2exkapy].
>
> [2] UFOs and aliens bring a divided U.S. Congress together—BBC. [https://www.bbc.com/news/world-us-canada-66320498].
>
> [3] Here are the 5 most memorable moments from Congress' UFO hearing. [https://tinyurl.com/32r8kxjv].
>
> [4] U.S. conducted 'multi-decade' secret UFO program, ex-intelligence official says. Article by Adam Gabbatt in The Guardian, published 26 July 2023. [https://tinyurl.com/29nd34t7].

As well as claiming that 'non-human' beings were recovered from crashed alien spacecraft, whistleblower and former intelligence officer David Grusch told the congressional hearing that the U.S. Government had been conducting a 'multi-decade' programme of activity which collected, and attempted to reverse-engineer, crashed UFOs. Grusch, who claimed to have led analysis of unexplained anomalous phenomena (UAP) within a U.S. Department of Defense agency until 2023, testified to the House Oversight subcommittee's hearing on unidentified aerial phenomena (UAPs) that the U.S. Government was secretly harbouring alien space craft, saying, 'I was informed, in the course of my official duties, of a multi-decade UAP crash retrieval and reverse-engineering program, to which I was denied access.' [Source: Article by Adam Gabbatt in *The Guardian*, published 26 July 2023, https://tinyurl.com/29nd34t7].

So, the evidence presented, under oath, to a hearing of a subcommittee of the United States Congress in the summer of 2023, takes us full circle back to all the conflicting reports, claims and conspiracy theories that have been published since the Roswell incident.

And we are left with Copilot's advice, 'It is up to you to decide whether you believe the witnesses or not, as there is no definitive proof of alien bodies being revealed to the U.S. Congress Committee.'

But can we find evidence of reverse engineering?

Any reverse engineering would have been accomplished in the Skunk Works and at Area 51. I'd already told Frank about Skunk Works history starting during WWII (notably, but not exclusively, with the P-38 Lightning in 1939, the P-80 Shooting Star in 1943, and F-86 Sabre that first flew in 1947 and went into service with the United States Air Force in 1949. None of these aircraft are obvious candidates for having benefitted from reverse engineering of flying saucers in Area 51).

I suppose you might argue that the experimentation with circular-wing aircraft by aeroplane designers in North America and Europe, including Nazi Germany, in the 1940s could have had something to do with the alleged 1933 crash of a 'saucer-shaped' alien craft in Italy, that was described by that former American intelligence official whistleblower, Major David Grusch in an interview with the President of the International Coalition for Extraterrestrial Research (ICER) and the Italian Centre for UFO Research (CUN) [view 27/11/2023 report at https://tinyurl.com/tfnjrvvt].

But the best of the disc-shaped aircraft, the Avrocar developed in the Avro Canada aircraft plant in Ontario, Canada (a subsidiary of the British Hawker Siddley group) and first flown (in Canada) in 1960, failed to meet the expectations of its design concept, derived from a CIA memorandum, key features of which included a supersonic disc-shaped fighter that aimed to achieve speeds of up to Mach 3.5 at altitudes of 100,000 ft.

The Avrocar fell so far short of this concept, and exhibited such instability during flight, that the United States Air Force cancelled the project in December 1961.

The first supremely successful product of the Skunk Works that was fully flight-tested at Area 51 was the U-2, and that aircraft couldn't look less like a flying saucer. The first flight of the Lockheed U-2, code name Dragon Lady, took place on 1 August 1955, over Groom Lake. The story at the time was that the peculiar-looking aircraft was being tested to carry out weather research.

The U-2 has a unique design that features glider-like narrow wings spanning 103 ft placed midway down the fuselage, which is only 63 ft long. The U-2 was the first U.S. aircraft to be designed, following a CIA specification, explicitly as a reconnaissance plane.

Equipped with a single turbojet engine speed was not its primary focus, but the engine allowed it to operate in the rarified stratosphere far beyond the detection capabilities of most adversaries of the time.

Endurance was a key asset, though; it could stay airborne for over 10 hours without refuelling and loiter even longer with external fuel pods. Such extended loitering time was crucial for capturing intelligence through its sophisticated onboard cameras and sensors.

The aircraft entered service with the United States Air Force in 1956, its primary mission being to monitor the nuclear arsenal of the Soviet Union during the Cold War. The Dragon Lady provides day and night, high-altitude (70,000 ft = 21 km), and all-weather intelligence gathering is still in frontline service in 2023, because its surveillance objectives can be changed at short notice, something that spy satellites cannot do.

The general public knew nothing about the U-2 spy plane until one was shot down by the Soviet Air Defense Forces while conducting photographic reconnaissance deep inside Soviet territory on 1 May 1960.

The pilot, Francis Gary Powers had taken off from Peshawar, Pakistan, and after being hit by a surface-to-air missile, Powers was captured after parachuting to the ground about 3,000 miles away near Yekaterinburg in the Sverdlovsk region of Russia and in a few years was returned to the U.S. in a prisoner-swap arrangement with his Soviet captors.

The shoot-down event caused the cancellation of a planned summit meeting between American President Dwight D. Eisenhower and Soviet leader Nikita Khrushchev and added a trifle more frigidity to the Cold War! President Eisenhower stopped the overflights temporarily to placate the Soviets, but the event didn't stop U-2 surveillance flights during the 60 years since!

Indeed, Gary Powers' U-2 was shot down in 1960 and the Skunk Works delivered the first of the U-2's successor aircraft, the first completed prototype of the Lockheed A-12 to Area 51 in February 1962 (the U-2's eventual successor, the Lockheed SR-71 Blackbird had been delivered to Nellis Air Force Base for flight testing in January of 1962).

Now, I'm not going to present a detailed catalogue of aircraft designed and produced by the Lockheed Martin Skunk Works over the years since WWII. But what I've already told you about these aircraft hints at a remarkable pace and extent of work at the Skunk Works. Can you see it in the following summaries?

- The U-2 design concept was written in 1953, the prototype first flew in 1955 and the last plane in the series was built in 1989.
- The Lockheed A-12 project was launched in 1957 (it was first called Project Oxcart, but it later became Archangel-12). The first official flight of the A-12 took place over Area 51 in 1962 and began flying missions over Vietnam and North Korea in 1967. Its final mission was in May 1968 when it was retired in favour of the SR-71 Blackbird. Despite its relatively short service life, the A12's technology contributed to development of a couple of variants; the YF-12 high-altitude interceptor prototype, an 'SR-71 with missiles' (maiden flight 1963, programme cancelled 1968), and the M-21, a variant modified to carry and launch the D-21 drone (a high-altitude supersonic reconnaissance drone intended for photographic reconnaissance deep into enemy airspace).

First official flight of the D-21 took place in 1964 but following a fatal launch accident and several unsuccessful operational D-21 flights over the People's Republic of China, the program was cancelled in 1971.

- The Lockheed SR-71 Blackbird started flight testing over Area 51 in 1962. The aircraft was a strategic reconnaissance plane and in its day was the world's fastest and highest-flying operational aircraft, setting, in

1976, world records for absolute speed of 2,193 mph and absolute altitude of 85,068 feet.

From 80,000 feet, it could survey 100,000 square miles of the Earth's surface per hour. Like the Lockheed A-12, the two-seat twin-engine Blackbird had a low radar profile, due to its sleek tapered design and black radar-absorbing body coating. The SR-71 entered service with the U.S. Air Force in 1966, and the fleet of SR-71s was retired in 1990.

The pattern in this brief history I want you to see is that between the 1950s and the 1990s, the Skunk Works produced a regular parade of amazing aircraft, but they all looked like conventional aircraft. They flew extremely fast and at extremely high altitudes.

But they didn't look anything like flying saucers. So, if the Skunk Works was involved in reverse engineering captured alien saucers, it didn't show in the Skunk's aircraft designs across this 40-year history. But there were other aircraft that looked, shall we say, unusual.

The first test flight of the 'Have Blue' technology demonstrator that became the Lockheed F-117 Nighthawk was conducted in 1977, though the first flight of the production F-117 was in 1981. This was the first operational aircraft to be designed with stealth technology, being a single-seat, subsonic twin-engine attack aircraft.

Viewed from above, the aircraft is described as having a distinctive diamond shape, but to me, it looks more like a triangular arrowhead. Apart from its overall shape, its most distinctive feature is that the aircraft's body is faceted, and it is this faceted surface that contributes to its relative invisibility to an opponent's radar.

Because, like a diamond sparkling in the light, the facets reflect incident radar waves all around the aircraft, returning only a minority to the radar detector. The F-117 entered service in 1983 but its existence was denied by the USAF until it was publicly acknowledged for the first time in 1988.

It flew combat missions during the U.S. invasion of Panama in 1989 and flew approximately 1,300 sorties, scoring direct hits on 1,600 high-value targets, in the Gulf War of 1991. The last of 59 production F-117 Nighthawks were delivered to the USAF in mid-1990 and the aircraft was retired from frontline service in 2008.

Some of the fleet is being kept in airworthy condition for use in research and training. The USAF disposes of about four aircraft each year but plans to continue flying operations with the F-117 until 2034.

And a much larger aircraft with an equally outrageously exotic shape, that made its first flight in 1989, is the Northrop Grumman B-2 Spirit, which is a long-range strategic bomber. The B-2 is a 'flying wing' aircraft, meaning it has no fuselage or tail section, and is designed to be a stealth bomber able to evade radar detection.

The B-2 can fly at close to the speed of sound and at an altitude of 50,000 feet. The aircraft entered service in 1997 and the USAF has 20 B-2 Spirits in service and plans to operate them until 2032. Their replacement, the Northrop Grumman B-21 Raider, is already in production and the USAF has announced plans to operate at least 100 Raiders.

A couple of things interest me about these three aircraft, by which I mean the Lockheed F-117 Nighthawk, the Northrop Grumman B-2 Spirit, and the Northrop Grumman B-21 Raider, all of which are Skunk Works' black projects. One is how similar they look to each other. To check this out for yourself, I suggest you go to *Wikipedia* and search for F-117 Nighthawk, B-2 Spirit and B-21 Raider in different browser tabs and then click between the three tabs to compare the images.

I've already described the form of the now-retired, F-117 Nighthawk as looking to me like a triangular arrowhead. The image I have in my mind when I say that is of one of those Stone Age flint arrowheads with barbs set, symmetrically, on either side of the pointed arrowhead that were used for hunting in ancient times.

The barbs were designed to help the arrowhead stay inside the target animal. Once the point had pierced the flesh, the barbs prevented the arrowhead from falling out. If the arrow fails to kill the target animal outright, then the arrowhead lodged in its body might cause death from the loss of blood.

I detect a similarity of form between the F-117, B-2, and B-21 based on the extension of the barbs on their arrowhead shapes into swept-back aircraft wings.

I know that the F-117 is smaller than the B-2 or B-21 but most of the larger size of the latter two strategic bombers is accounted for in their wingspans. The F-117 has a wingspan of 13.2 m, a fuselage length 20.1 m and 3.8 m height. Corresponding figures for the B-2 Spirit are a wingspan 52.4 m, a fuselage length 21 m, and 5.2 m height.

While the B-21 Raider is estimated to have a 46 m wingspan, 17 m fuselage length, and height of 5.3 m. We know that the F-117 emerged from the 'Have Blue' technology demonstrator that first flew in Area 51 in 1977, so this 'arrowhead with barbs' appearance of these three operational aircraft has been the Skunk Work's shape of choice for 46 years.

The F-117 Nighthawk served and retired from frontline service in 2008; the B-2 Spirit first flew in 1989 and is expected to remain on active service until 2032; The B-21 Raider made its first flight in November 2023 and is expected to enter service around 2027. Their 'arrowhead with barbs' appearance has been preserved through all that time. Compare that history with the U-2, which first flew in 1955 but had evolved into the SR-71 by 1962.

There must be a reason for preserving this appearance, and, having made much of the similarities in the plan views of these three aircraft, I've got to point out that looked at from the side, say from the standpoint of one of the wingtips, you could be forgiven describing all three of these aircraft as looking lot like the popular notion of an edge-on view of a flying saucer (check out those *Wikipedia* pages again)!

Something else that entertains me is that those plan views are so similar that it might just be that the F-117 was a small test-model for the B-2. This leads me to wonder if the B-2 could have been a test-model for something very much larger.

But I'm in danger here of straying into the realm of imagination and conjecture, and while it's certainly the case that there's no shortage of imaginative speculation on the Internet, there are a couple of currently operational Skunk Works products that need a mention, namely the Lockheed Martin F-22 Raptor, and Lockheed Martin F-35 Lightning II.

These ex-black programme projects are both described as supersonic multi-role air superiority combat aircraft with stealth features, and both are in current frontline service with the U.S. and selected allied militaries. The multi-role aspect includes ground attack, electronic warfare, and signals intelligence capabilities.

The Lockheed Martin F-22 Raptor is a single-seat, twin-engine, all-weather fighter aircraft developed for the USAF. It can fly at about 1,000 mph and has a service ceiling above 50,000 feet. The aircraft first flew in 1997 and entered service in 2005. The F-22 Raptor is considered the first 5th-generation fighter in the U.S. Air Force inventory, unmatched by any other modern military. The aircraft has a triangular-shaped fuselage with the wings angled sharply back towards the tail, and the design incorporates other stealth features that reduce the aircraft's radar profile. There are about 200 Raptors in service with the USAF and, with regular upgrades the aircraft is expected to remain in service through 2060.

The Lockheed Martin F-35 Lightning II is a family of three single-seat, single-engine, all-weather stealthy aircraft designed for both air superiority interceptor roles and strike missions. The three variants are a conventional take-off and landing F-35A, a short take-off and vertical-landing F-35B, and the aircraft-carrier-based F-35C.

The aircraft first flew in 2006 and the F-35B entered service with the U.S. Marine Corps in 2015, followed by the U.S. Air Force F-35A in 2016 and the U.S. Navy's F-35C in 2019.

The F-35 Lightning II has a distinctive shape with a trapezium-shaped wing and two outward-facing vertical stabilisers; it has a maximum speed in the region of 1,200 mph and a service ceiling of 50,000 feet. The U.S. expects to operate around 2,400 of the aircraft and F-35's are entering service with at least 11 allied nations.

And then there's NGAD! Back in 2020 the USAF revealed it had secretly designed, built, and flown at least one prototype of its *Next-Generation Air Dominance* fighter, catchily named NGAD! Almost every detail about this aircraft is a mystery due to its astronomically high-security classification, but that's never stopped Internet speculation before and there's no shortage of it now.

Mildest rumours are that the NGAD programme will include air dominance fighters, working in hostile environments with their own AI-directed drone swarms, securely networked with other assets in space and the cyber realm.

Although the exact shape of the NGAD aircraft is still highly classified, Lockheed Martin have released a few artist's impressions of the NGAD concept, which show a triangular or diamond-shaped wing with straight leading and trailing edges, blended into an elongated fuselage. The design echoing the stealth features of F-117, F-22 and F-35.

Rumoured names for this and other mysterious and elusive aircraft that have emerged over several years, include DarkStar, Penetrator, Aurora, and TR3 Black Manta, all supposedly set apart by monumental leaps in aviation technology pushing the boundaries of what was previously thought possible.

Awe-inspiring speed, unparalleled manoeuvrability, and amazing stealth characteristics.

The Lockheed Martin RQ-3 DarkStar is an acknowledged project, but it was an unmanned aerial vehicle (UAV) designed as a high-altitude endurance designed to operate within heavily defended airspace. DarkStar was fully autonomous and could take off, fly to its target, operate its sensors, transmit information to a satellite while still in flight, return and land without human intervention.

Its first flight was in 1996 and the test programme was terminated in 1999, although the rumour mill claims that Lockheed Martin's Skunk Works are developing DarkStar as a successor to the SR-71 Blackbird. Currently, the U.S. has several UAVs in service, including the Lockheed Martin Sentinel, the General Atomics Predator and the General Atomics Reaper drones.

Maybe a hypersonic Blackbird-successor, SR-72 DarkStar is indeed in service and performing strategic aerial reconnaissance right now. Remember that the real SR-71 Blackbird remained a secret for 10 years back in the 1950s and 1960s.

Interestingly, that rumour mill was greatly encouraged to believe that the Lockheed Martin SR-72 Darkstar is real by the appearance of a very similar plane piloted by Capt. Pete 'Maverick' Mitchell (aka Tom Cruise) in the opening aerial sequence of the 2022 movie 'Top Gun: Maverick.'

The plane shown in the movie is fiction, but it's based very much on Skunk Works design concepts released on the Lockheed Martin website; even to the point of having a Skunk Works logo on its tail fin!

None of the countless conspiracy theories and rumours about the Next-Generation Air Dominance fighter (NGAD) have been officially confirmed by any government or military agency, and the intense secrecy surrounding Area 51 and the Skunk Works factories that supply their black ops products to it, seems only to encourage wild speculation.

As far as I know, NGAD has not appeared in any movies or TV shows! The essential, undeniable, fact about Area 51 is that it is a test range for exotic flight vehicles designed and built in various aviation Skunk Works around the U.S.

The genuine projects that have been announced over the years have been so radical for their time that their test flights over the Nevada desert and the salt flat known as Groom Lake often prompted a rash of sightings of so-called 'UFOs' (or UAPs, standing for 'Unidentified Anomalous Phenomena').

Observations of UFOs with triangular shapes or showing triangular sets of lights at night can be traced back to the 1980s and 1990s and are still common, though now we know about the Nighthawk, Raptor and Lightning.

We don't know if alien-made UFOs ever flew over Groom Lake, but we do now know, courtesy of declassified documents and aircraft now in service that a number of highly sophisticated and highly unusual aircraft were developed by the Skunk Works and tested there. Witnesses often claimed that these mysterious craft flying over Area 51 could hover, accelerate rapidly, make sharp turns, and even disappear from sight in the blink of an eye.

Characteristics leading to speculation that the aircraft observed result from that central belief of UFO folklore, namely the reverse engineering of captured alien vehicles. Though in my view such an idea definitely underestimates the genius of our human aeronautical engineers.

In recent years, there have been an increasing number of reports of UFO sightings that describe the objects as 'shape-shifting'; that is, able to contract or bend to change shape bizarrely as the observer watches. This is usually taken to suggest an extreme and utterly alien technology.

While these sightings are intriguing, it's important to note that there is no scientific evidence to support the existence of shape-shifting UFOs. Microsoft Copilot also warns that the 'videos and pictures could be hoaxes or misinterpretations of natural phenomena.'

However, one bright spark has pointed out that flexible LED displays are now readily available. They use the same LED technology to create high-resolution images as any other domestic digital TV, but as the LED pixels are mounted in a thin film of soft polyethylene, they can be curved, rolled, or shaped to fit any application or installation.

If the Skunk Works engineers have the technology to cover their stealth aircraft in radar-absorbing coatings, they could surely adapt that technology to cover their next aircraft in smart TVs!

Just imagine mounting a smartphone camera on the top of the aircraft and displaying the image of the clouds above across the bottom of the aircraft—the aircraft disappears to observers on the ground; mount a smartphone camera on the bottom of the aircraft and display the image of the ground beneath across the top of the aircraft—the aircraft disappears to observers overflying the aircraft.

Shape-shifting? Easy: give your black ops 'smart-TV' enough AI to work out from the rest of your aircraft's sensors from which direction it's likely to be observed and allow it to paint appropriately confusing images of its shape on the LED pixels all over your aircraft.

Wow! That was a marathon typing session! Very satisfying to get so much written into my files, but now I've emerged from it and I'm feeling very hungry and very tired. Decaf coffee and a sizeable bowl of rolled oats (liberally laced with honey and strawberry jam—and a dash of cream) are the order of the night. I'll sleep well on a supper like that!

4. Mussels with Josie, Oysters with Billie

My long-lost memories turn into dreams when my subconscious mind rummages about in my past and throws up snippets of my life long gone to which it's taken a fancy.

Tonight, it's offering me memories of 1997, beginning in that reverie during the transition between wakefulness and sleep, when the brain relaxes and weaves past, present, and future into an indistinct fabric that transforms the real world into an imaginary timeless space of its own on which your dreams can feed.

Tonight's reverie is all about 1997. Early in that year, I was called back to Area 51 for another deployment there. Somebody in the CIA had asked for me! Can't imagine who! But still, a distinguished feather in my GCHQ cap at the time. And all they wanted me to do was oversee a high-security software update they wanted installed in their flight control servers at Groom Lake.

I told them that any of their local computer staff could nursemaid a software update. But they said that wouldn't do; they wanted me to do it. I told them, okay then, I could monitor the update from my own office in GCHQ as a remote installation. They said that wouldn't do either; they wanted me on their premises.

They said they wanted me back in my old machine room at Groom Lake by 10 March and that they'd send a private jet to RAF Lakenheath to pick me up on the 8th, which was, like, tomorrow! My GCHQ line manager said we don't say no to the CIA these days, go home, get packed, and I'll organise a taxi to pick you up at 9 a.m. tomorrow.

On the day, we were lucky with the traffic, even the notorious M25 was kind to us, and it didn't take much more than three and a half hours to get to Lakenheath. The security gate was all clued up about my arrival and I was whisked straight to the gangway of a very stylish, but anonymous, Gulfstream V private jet.

I was the only passenger and was welcomed on board, and called 'Sir,' by two very senior pilots and two very attentive cabin staff. All of which did my ego no end of good, and I settled contentedly into a wealthy first-class travel style to which I was certainly not accustomed. We left Lakenheath at around 2 p.m. on 8 March and I dined and slept well on my overnight flight.

But, of course, we were flying west and as UK time is eight hours ahead of Las Vegas, by noon, local time, on 8 March I had cleared immigration at McCarran International Airport in Las Vegas and was waiting in the Janet Flight Departure Lounge for the next shuttle to Homey Airport.

I don't remember, exactly, but I probably took a nap in the departure lounge. I'm certainly dozing off here and now, and the dreamscape starts to wrap around and engulf me.

I was back in 1997. I'd worked, alone in the machine room, on the update process during the afternoon, taking it slow and easy, and verifying and then re-verifying the installation at every step. Happy with the way everything was going, I decided to work into the night shift but to get some food and refreshments from the USAF commissary across the base.

The machine room boasted a double layer of secure access; its first revolving security door opened into a private corridor which ended in a second revolving security door that opened onto the main corridor that joined computation with the engineering and communications departments.

The first corridor was its usual quiet haven, but as soon as I stepped through the door into the main corridor, I found it full of rowdy little groups of civilian and military engineers and comms operators hustling and bustling to and from the shared recreation facilities at the end of the corridor.

I don't know why, but we seem to be locked into the building, so the electrical and comms operators and engineers with whom I share this building are crowded into the corridor leading to the rec room and community kitchen near the front entrance.

Some from the crowd are even raiding surrounding offices for chairs to form impromptu dining groups in the wide corridor to share food and drink their friends have fetched from the kitchen deli. Before I emerged from the machine room's rotating security door, the general conversations seemed to be centred on the scandalous way that senior management, civilian and military, treated the mere workers around here.

I pushed my way through the crowd, hearing the occasional muttered 'make way there; spook coming through' which seemed to be a leftover from my arrival, last Tuesday, in a monstrous, black-windowed vehicle from which my personal escort of black-suited CIA hard-men, that included Clarence Bellwether, swept me and Clarence through the rec room and deposited us in the machine room.

Clarence left me with a case full of IBM Super DLT cartridge tapes, keys to the private apartment behind the machine room, and a set of security passes with which he offered the advice, 'Don't wander around outside. Leave the building only in an emergency. I will come to you here to announce any emergency. Just do your job.'

Then, the black-suited crew all trooped back to their monstrous, black-windowed vehicle, leaving me firmly labelled 'CIA spook' in the minds of the rest of this building's population.

I managed to get as far as the rec room without spooking too many people and found that the outside doors were all firmly locked and guarded on the inside by armed MPs.

'Are we not allowed out to the commissary?' I asked a group of engineers at one of the rec room tables.

One of the guys said, 'Nah, we're locked down for the night.'

He went on to explain he'd seen it all before, 'It always happens on nights when the Skunk Works has a new super-secret project they want to get off the ground at Groom Lake. To minimise witnesses, they keep the base personnel locked into their buildings.'

Apparently, it wasn't bad for the workers because everything else was usually sidelined for the launch of whatever it was, and that meant free time for all.

'And the commissary's deli always sends a load of free food and drink over to the community kitchen before the lockdown. So, we come here to get the food to feed us through the night shift,' added another engineer, who went on to say that he'd served here since the early 1980s and these lockdowns were real common back then during the test flights of the futuristic, alien-looking aircraft that was eventually publicly unveiled as the F-117 Nighthawk.

And then, from 1989, the lockdowns happened to cover test flights of the strategic bomber, the B-2 Spirit.

'Night-shift lockdowns are a small price to pay to maintain freedom,' he concluded.

I couldn't tell if that was a joke or not, so I agreed vigorously with that final opinion. In the circumstances, it seemed the best thing to do.

Then, like any devoted Englishman, I joined the end of the queue for the free food in the community kitchen and was soon able to return to my own office with enough food for the next couple of days, knowing that I could store what I didn't eat tonight in my apartment's refrigerator.

After feeding, I used my free time to launch my high-security search routines on the Area 51 network to see if I could find out what was happening out there. Of course, I'd just overseen the installation of new highly secure software for which I didn't have access rights, so I did what I always do and examined the contents of the recycle or trash bin files.

And there they were, with a deleted marker on the file name but otherwise intact, a complete set of access security passwords and even their associated decryption keys.

I was amused to see that while the software writer(s) had taken great care to incorporate a tell-tale routine that reported the use of the decryption keys to CIA head quarter's computers at Langley, they had simply deleted their working files rather than erased them.

Slovenly, but not at all unusual! I copied these files onto my laptop's disk and from there to my secure Onionland layer, which I had recently created using a prototype version of the Tor router shared with me by the guys who developed it at the U.S. Naval Research Lab.

When they were safely in my clutches, I erased them from the CIA's original software package; well, I'm not the only one who goes around looking in trash cans. All that made me feel secure enough to use the passwords and security keys, after removing the tell-tales, of course, to investigate what this terribly secret software package was intended to do.

It very quickly became evident, at least in outline, that the software was intended to manage the launch into Earth orbit from the Area 51 runway of something called the XB-25 SuperDragon en route for somewhere called Arsia Mons. Now, that sounded real interesting!

But before I could delve into it further, there was a commotion out in the main corridor and Clarence Bellwether swept back into the machine room while his black-suited crew of hard-men stationed themselves at each of the security doors.

'Dr Daulby, we have a situation that you can resolve, please come with me.' Clarence announced as he approached the terminal at which I was working.

'A computer problem?' I asked as I got to my feet.

'Affirmative,' Clarence said, handing me my jacket. 'You'll need this,' he said, 'it's getting cold out there.'

I grabbed my laptop, a little terminal emulator the GCHQ workshop had breadboarded for me and a bunch of connection cables.

Then, following Clarence's advice to wear my jacket to which my security tags were attached, I announced, 'Okay, let's go.'

And with no further preamble, we went; rapidly. As we emerged from the outer security door of my machine room Clarence's team blended into a shield around me, two ahead of me, barging through the still-relaxing groups of engineers scattered along the corridor, Clarence beside me and hanging onto my arm to make sure I didn't dawdle, and one coming up the rear to quell any objections from the disturbed engineers with one of those glances that says, 'this snake bites!'

The external doors were already held open by their guardian MPs and Clarence's monstrous vehicle was parked just outside. I was delighted to see that the MPs saluted me as I went through the door! But less pleased to note, as I looked back into the rec room, that the engineer who had described the 1980s lockdowns was also saluting me as I sailed past in my cocoon of hard-men and conveying a great deal of sarcasm with that simple gesture.

I was hurried into Clarence's 'taxi' and, with the pantomime completed by two of the escorts riding on the running boards outside the vehicle, we sped towards what I knew to be the largest aircraft hangar on the base, and the only source of illumination on this moonless night. The car drove to the end of the 500-foot-long hangar and came to a halt alongside another door that was being held open by armed MPs.

Clarence pulled me out of the car, through the door and into the top landing of a stairwell which seemed to descend far into the depths. Fortunately, immediately opposite the entrance was an elevator and, again, the door was being held open by an armed guard.

Clarence dragged me into the lift and slapped his security badge onto the controller. The lift proved to be an express elevator, so my stomach bounced up against my throat and then down again towards my boots as we descended rapidly, coming to an equally rapid halt at some distant basement level.

The door opened. More armed guards, and more sharp salutes! Clarence leaned into me to snarl into my ear 'This is the SuperDragon Control Room.

General Charles Orde in Command. Just remember, Michael, nothing you see here is ever to be divulged to the outside world!'

Then he dusted off and straightened my jacket before marching me towards the three-star USAF general who was pacing the floor at the back of the control room.

'General,' he said, 'this is the computer analyst, Dr Mike Daulby.'

The General was a tough-looking character, about an inch or two shorter than me.

His face broke into an engaging grin as he stuck out his hand for a firm handshake, saying, 'Our CIA colleagues have a very high opinion of you Dr Daulby and I hope you can help us with a problem we're having with the CIA's software you've recently installed.'

I promised, I'd do my best and he guided me towards one of the terminals at the side of the room, 'Settle yourself in here,' he said, 'and Master Sergeant Kevin Moyes will clue you into what's going on.'

I introduced myself to Kevin Moyes as I settled into the terminal's seat. With my laptop booted, I attached my terminal emulator and chose the most appropriate connector cable to attach my gear to the control room's terminal and finally donned my headset so I could speak in private to Master Sergeant Moyes.

Kevin explained that SuperDragon-1 had taken off from Area-51 just after dark, with the intention of climbing towards Earth orbit by circling over the Nevada National Security Site and Death Valley National Park. All went well until the aircraft attempted to upload its astronavigation software from Area-51's servers.

Upload failed, and the craft was now circling slowly at a moderate altitude over Phoenix without its flight plan, and no option other than a return to Area 51 unless I could do something about it here and now.

So, I decided to repeat the upload procedure from the local servers, but to upload to my laptop and run the code through my error-checking programs. The SuperDragon's astronavigation software proved to be the CIA software I had been brought all this way to install! As I had not been given access rights to the code I had no official right to meddle with it in this way.

But, of course, I have my own means of dealing with firewalls and I just uploaded from Onionland the passwords and decryption keys I had so recently discovered during my 'trashcan tour.' Kevin Moyes approved of what I told him I was doing, so I just got on with it.

While my laptop was parsing through the decrypted CIA machine code looking for problems, General Orde drifted over to my terminal desk and asked, 'How's it going, Mike?'

He could see the computer code streaming rapidly over my laptop screen and he also seemed to be satisfied by my explanation of what I was doing. He was also reasonably satisfied with my estimate of around 30 minutes to finish the job and went on to ask Kevin Moyes about resources in the Phoenix area.

Kevin radioed the local flight control centres and reported back that, 'There are two A-10 Thunderbolt training flights in the Phoenix airspace, one returning to Davis-Monthan AFB in Tucson, one still operating on the Goldwater bombing range at Luke AFB, General.'

'Warthogs! Just what we need!' said General Orde, picking up and donning one of the headsets. 'Kevin, connect me to the local air traffic control commander. We need to use those Hogs to add to the aerial spectacle of a light show over Phoenix. I'm gonna order them to fly around the area, well away from SuperDragon, making noise and dropping parachute flares, just to distract the locals from my SuperDragon.'

As Charlie Orde drifted away, speaking animatedly into his headset mike, my laptop started chiming gentle alarms as my error-trapping software found and highlighted potential errors in the CIA software. I concentrated on identifying and curing the errors, finding that most were handshaking problems.

I concluded that these were caused by the number and variety of people who had contributed to coding different functional segments of the software. I identified software proprietary labels for Lockheed, Northrop Grumman, NASA, as well as, inevitably, the USAF and CIA, but there were labels for Marconi Electronic Systems, British Aerospace, and even something called GoldStar Co, LG Electronics and LG Corporation. I stopped counting when I reached 10!

Having 10 different people contributing code for one software suite without a unifying guiding hand as an editor, making sure they all blend seamlessly together is plain madness.

And it was clear from what my error-trapping software was identifying that I was elected as the guiding hand to blend this mishmash of a software suite into a workable system. I'd been doing that all my life, so no problemo! My biggest problems were with the GoldStar Co and LG sections of code which seemed to be largely concerned with control of video displays.

They were written in a South Korean dialect of the machine language used in the rest of the software and their 'in-code' guidance notes were all in the Korean language! My error-trapping software was able to do the translations, but I could well understand that SuperDragon's upload and execution routines could hesitate when faced with such foreign coding.

The situation wasn't improved by these particular routines being placed for early execution in the suite. If they did cause hesitation, the rest of the program could crash. I concluded that these were the prime cause of SuperDragon's problems and carefully rewrote their code using the plainest possible machine language.

When I'd finished all this error-trapping and error-curing, I recompiled the software package on Area 51's servers and asked Kevin Moyes to contact SuperDragon and suggest they try again to upload their astronavigation software, and within a few minutes they reported it all 'A-okay.'

Kevin announced this over the room's intercom, and this prompted applause and cheers, 'for the CIA's limey!'

General Orde took the time to come over to my terminal desk as I was collecting my possessions together. He congratulated and thanked me but talking to him I started to feel really uncomfortable, and the room seemed to be closing in on me, its details disappearing at the edges of my field of view. I was being overwhelmed by an urgent need for the toilet.

Somebody directed me towards the stairwell beside the elevator I'd used to come down here. It was Pete Gibbon! Good old Pete!

He held the door to the stairwell open for me, 'There you go, Buddy,' he said through the customary cloud of cigarette smoke. 'You'll find bathrooms out there. But before you go, try to remember that you've not mentioned autonomous spaceplanes yet.'

And with that, he closed the door behind me, and I started a frenzied search for a toilet, going from door to door in an ever-expanding corridor lined with doors I was unable to open without setting off a jangling emergency alarm. My discomfort mounted. I was sweating like an overheated pig and one in urgent need of the loo. My panic rose until there was nothing else to do but WAKE UP!

And find myself rolled up completely in my duvet and sweating like an overheated pig! I hit the off button for the jangling alarm clock beside my bed and departed smartly into the en suite for some blessed relief!

Suitably calmed, but nevertheless now thoroughly awake, I jotted down *spaceplanes* and *Phoenix Lights* into my bedside notebook just to keep alive the memories my subconscious had fed into my dream as I started to wake.

Then ran a razor over the worst of the stubble, showered, dressed and made some breakfast before firing up the laptop to continue my 'autobiography' from where I left it last night, starting with my subconscious reminder about autonomous spaceplanes.

Strictly speaking, I guess, I should start by writing about NASA's Space Shuttle Orbiters because they must surely be described as our first spaceplanes, but the Space Shuttle was more than just a reusable spaceplane; it was a complete system that launched like a rocket, manoeuvred in Earth orbit like a spacecraft, and landed like an aeroplane.

Composed of three main components: orbiter, external fuel tank, and solid rocket boosters, only the orbiter was reusable and the only part of the Shuttle that returned to Earth as an unpowered glider. NASA operated the Space Shuttle from 1981, until it was retired in 2011 after 135 missions.

The Space Shuttle Orbiter was designed for heavy haulage into low orbit, able to transport about 24 metric tonnes of cargo in a payload bay that was 60 feet long and 15 feet in diameter and could carry cargo equivalent to the size of a single-deck bus.

The full-length payload bay doors could open wide, being hinged along the side of the fuselage and closing together along the top centreline of the Orbiter. This design allowed the shuttle to launch huge satellites into orbit, notably the Hubble Space Telescope, launched into orbit on 24 April 1990, by the Space Shuttle *Discovery*, and after that, repaired, serviced, and updated by five separate Orbiter missions.

However, more than 40 Space Shuttle flights were devoted to the delivery of components and assembly of the International Space Station, which started in 1998 as a collaboration between five space agencies representing 15 countries. ISS became fully operational in May 2009 and is expected to remain in service until at least 2028.

I had one of my 'conversations with Bing' to gather the following details about NASA's Space Shuttle fleet.

> 'Six Orbiters were built for flight: *Enterprise, Columbia, Challenger, Discovery, Atlantis,* and *Endeavour*. All were built in Palmdale, California, by the Pittsburgh, Pennsylvania-based Rockwell International company. The first Orbiter to be rolled out, *Enterprise*, made its maiden flight in 1977.
>
> An unpowered glider, it was carried by a modified Boeing 747 airliner called the Shuttle Carrier Aircraft and released for a series of atmospheric test flights and landings. *Enterprise* never flew in space and was partially disassembled and retired after completion of critical atmospheric flight testing.
>
> The remaining Orbiters were fully operational spacecraft and were launched vertically as part of the Space Shuttle stack. *Columbia* was the first space-worthy Orbiter; it made its inaugural flight in 1981. *Challenger, Discovery,* and *Atlantis* followed in 1983, 1984, and 1985 respectively. In 1986, *Challenger* was destroyed in an accident shortly after its 10th launch, killing all seven crew members.
>
> *Endeavour* was built as *Challenger*'s successor and was first launched in 1992. In 2003, *Columbia* was destroyed during re-entry, leaving just three remaining Orbiters. *Discovery* completed its final flight on March 9, 2011, and *Endeavour* completed its final flight on June 1, 2011. *Atlantis* completed the final Shuttle flight, STS-135, on July 21, 2011.' [Source: Conversation with Bing, 15/01/2024].

The Orbiter named *Enterprise* was the acknowledged prototype, it never flew in space, but was the first vehicle to be rolled out into the public gaze from its manufacturing plant in Palmdale, California in September 1976. After initial static testing, in January 1977, Enterprise was transported by truck (!) 36 miles across California's Mojave Desert to Edwards Air Force Base, for approach and landing tests.

Edwards AFB is home to the Air Force Test Center and is primarily used for flight testing of experimental aircraft, of which the SR-71 Blackbird was one. Placed atop the Shuttle Carrier Aircraft, a modified Boeing 747 passenger plane, *Enterprise* began taxi runs in February and made its first independent flight in August 1977.

Over the next few years, NASA used *Enterprise* to prepare its sister ships for space flights, including, in 1979, fit checks to the Space Shuttle rocket stack at Launch Pad 39A at NASA's Kennedy Space Center in Florida.

Interestingly, it seems that *Enterprise* was so named in response to a huge write-in campaign by fans of Gene Roddenberry's 'Star Trek' television series. The phrase, *'These are the voyages of the Starship Enterprise,'* is used in the opening sequence of the original Star Trek television series, broadcast from 1966 to 1969. Appropriately, the creator and cast members of the Star Trek TV series also attended the Space Shuttle's roll-out event.

As far as I can tell, the Space Shuttle Enterprise was not featured in any Star Trek drama, though in the movie 'Star Trek IV: The Voyage Home' (1986) part of the action takes place aboard a fictional U.S. Navy aircraft carrier called Enterprise (which was, in fact, the USN's Forrestal-class supercarrier 'Ranger' that was in service between 1957 and 1993). A conversation with Microsoft Copilot tells me this:

> 'There have been nine ships used in the service of the United States or of the Colonial Forces of the United States Revolutionary War that have been named *Enterprise*. The first ship named *Enterprise* was a 70-ton sloop that was captured from the British and operated on Lake Champlain by Col Benedict Arnold of the Continental Army.
>
> The most famous ship to bear the name *Enterprise* is the *USS Enterprise* (CV-6), which was a Yorktown-class aircraft carrier that served with unparalleled distinction in World War II and was the most decorated ship of that war. The [next] *USS Enterprise* (CVN-65) was the first nuclear-powered aircraft carrier ever built and the eighth United States naval vessel to bear the name.
>
> It was decommissioned in 2017. The *USS Enterprise* (CVN-80) is currently under construction and is scheduled to be commissioned in 2028.' [Source: Conversation with Bing, 16/01/2024].

Entertaining the Star Trek cast and crew during the roll-out of the prototype Space Shuttle Orbiter may simply be an example of the acumen of news-savvy Californians, but there have always been rumours of close ties between the Skunk Works and Hollywood.

Indeed, some of the published conspiracy theories have claimed that the Skunk Works have floated ideas towards Hollywood scriptwriters for such films as 'Close Encounters of the Third Kind' (1977), 'Star Wars Episode IV: A New Hope' (1977), which is the first instalment in the Star Wars franchise, 'E.T. the Extra-Terrestrial' (1982), not to mention 'Paul' (2011) in which Paul is an alien (one of the well-known 'Roswell Greys') who has escaped from Area 51!

Another rumour about the Space Shuttle Orbiter is that the U.S. Military operated their own fleet of Orbiters. This would have been across the period from 1981 through to 2011, a period when a sequence of ultrasecret Skunk Works aviation projects, like the SR-71 Blackbird, F-117 Nighthawk, B-2 Spirit were developed and brought into active service in absolute secrecy.

So, we can't dismiss the possibility that the military also kept their own fleet of Space Shuttles as a deeply secret black operation. The U.S. Military was certainly involved with NASA's Space Shuttle programme, providing crews with military backgrounds, and sponsoring highly classified missions using NASA Orbiters.

Indeed, in 1979, the USAF started building a launch complex at Vandenberg Air Force Base, located on the central coast of northern California. Currently, Vandenberg AFB (now called Vandenberg Space Force Base) is primarily used for space launches and missile testing and is the home base of the 30th Space Wing, a unit of the United States Space Force that is responsible for space launches.

Vandenberg SFB is apparently ideally placed for launches intended to take payloads into polar orbits.

There's no hard evidence, and no whistleblower accounts, to support the notion of a military fleet of Space Shuttles. But there is a curious numerical peculiarity in the construction codes bestowed on Orbiters. Rockwell International built these *'Orbital Vehicles'* and gave each one on the production line an 'OV' code number.

Orbiter *Challenger* was OV-099, the prototype, Orbiter *Enterprise*, was numbered OV-101, and then the other four NASA Orbiters were *Discovery* (OV-103), *Endeavour* (OV-105), *Atlantis* (OV-104) and *Columbia* (OV-102). Notice anything? Where's OV-100? I've asked Microsoft Copilot for information about a Space Shuttle named '*OV-100*' and was told the following.

> 'The Space Shuttle OV-100 is a full-scale, high-fidelity replica of the Space Shuttle. It was built in Apopka, Florida, by Guard-Lee and installed at Kennedy Space Center Visitor Complex in 1993. The OV-100 designation is not an official NASA designation, but rather an honorary one.' [Source: Conversation with Bing, 14/01/2024].

Now, I ask you, if YOU were building OV-099 (*Challenger*) for its first space flight in 1983 would YOU reserve the OV-100 designation for a replica to be built 10 years later, and continue to build OV-101 (*Enterprise*), the flight-test prototype, for roll-out in September 1976?

Forgive me if I'm reading too much into this numerical discrepancy, but I can't help suspecting that the OV-100 that was on the original Orbiter production line might have been handed over to the U.S. Military, and I've got an idea the handover might have taken place on the same day, 17 September Constitution Day in 1976, that Enterprise was first rolled out at Palmdale, and that they might have named OV-100 *Constitution* to honour the nation's founding document.

After that, OV-100 has been quietly hidden behind the military's well-practised wall of secrecy ever since.

NASA's Space Shuttles were very capable vehicles, but they are no longer operational and the only hints about what might have replaced them are today's spaceplanes.

We know about two of these: the Boeing X-37B spaceplane operated by the United States Space Force (USSF), and China's *Shenlong*, also known as the *Divine Dragon*, developed by the China Academy of Launch Vehicle Technology (CALT).

Both of these are reusable spacecraft launched into orbit by rocket and recovered by gliding through the atmosphere to a runway landing at their home base like a conventional aircraft. This is exactly like the Space Shuttle Orbiter except that the Shuttle Orbiter was piloted, and these two spaceplanes are unpiloted and much smaller than the Shuttle Orbiter.

The X-37B is 29 feet long and has a wingspan of 15 feet, whereas the Space Shuttle Orbiter was 122 feet long and has a wingspan of over 78 feet.

There are no official descriptions of the *Shenlong* spacecraft or even genuine photographs, but speculating that it may resemble the X-37B spaceplane, *Shenlong*'s dimensions have been very roughly estimated as a length of 40 feet and a wingspan of 25 feet.

A really important difference between these spaceplanes and the Shuttle Orbiter is that today's spaceplanes are launched enclosed within the payload fairings of a rocket just like any other large satellite. The Shuttle Orbiter used a specially designed launcher stack, the most conspicuous feature of which was an enormous external fuel tank.

X-37B and *Shenlong* missions are shrouded in secrecy, but they are assumed to be engaged in research on reusable space technologies, spying and surveillance of the satellites of other nations. X-37B first launched in 2010 and has spent more than 10 years in orbit since, spread over six spaceflights so far. There are two X-37B craft in what is called the Orbital Test Vehicle (OTV) fleet.

The sixth mission launched on 17 May 2020 and concluded on 12 November 2022, after a total of 908 days in orbit. Russian cosmonaut Valeri Polyakov holds the current record for the longest continuous time a human has spent in orbit of 437 days, aboard Russia's Mir space station between 1994 and 1995.

Recently, Russian cosmonaut Oleg Kononenko set a new world record for the most time spent in space, as by mid-2024 he will have clocked up a *cumulative total* of more than 1,000 days outside the Earth's atmosphere during his fifth deployment since 2008 to the International Space Station.

X-37B's seventh mission, and the fourth flight of Vehicle 2 of the OTV fleet, was launched by SpaceX on 28 December 2023, aboard a Falcon Heavy rocket. The Falcon Heavy rocket is capable of flying its payload to high orbit, even into geosynchronous orbit, more than 22,000 miles out, but details of the seventh mission are scarce.

There's no shortage of speculation, though! Industry and amateur astronomers and satellite trackers speculate that the X-37B may be bound for a highly elliptical orbit around Earth or even a path that could swing it out to the vicinity of the Moon, perhaps to drop off a payload.

The expectation is that the mission may run until June 2026, or later, given the recent pattern of successively longer flights in the X-37B programme. We do know that the X-37B is carrying a NASA experiment to study how plant seeds, particularly vegetable and salad plants, are affected by prolonged exposure to the harsh environment of radiation in space. I suspect that horticulture is not the only task assigned to X-37B out there.

China's equally secretive *Shenlong* was carried to space on 14 December 2023, by a Long March 2F rocket, a launch system less powerful than SpaceX's Falcon Heavy and believed to be limited to delivering payloads to low-Earth orbit. *Shenlong*'s first orbital mission launched on 4 September 2020 and this December 2023 launch was the third spaceplane mission.

Those amateur astronomers and satellite trackers have also been watching *Shenlong* and observed the December 2023 launch releasing six enigmatic wingmen, or slave satellites, into space, not all into the same orbit. Function of the wingmen is unknown, but they could be monitoring the *Shenlong* vehicle itself, or have some other military purpose.

Noting that some of the objects released by *Shenlong* were capable of independent orbital manoeuvres and able to fly in formation with *Shenlong*, some have speculated that *Shenlong*'s wingmen could be first steps towards an anti-satellite infrastructure, though one of the few official statements about *Shenlong* is that its purpose is to *'carry out reusable technology verification as planned to provide technical support for the peaceful use of space.'*

I don't want to persist much further with cataloguing exotic aircraft, real or rumoured, though there are several other fancy aeroplanes deserving of at least a mention that are supposed to be flying around in the skies above us right now!

One additional point I will make here, and emphasise it, is that as soon as a really exotic aircraft is announced as going into frontline operational service with the U.S. Military and its allies you can be totally sure that an even more exotic and capable aircraft, destined to be that newly operational aircraft's successor, is being rolled out from the Skunk Works every night for flight testing.

At the moment, the U.S. Military has the F-22 Raptor and the F-35 Lightning II in service; two of the most advanced fighter jets in the world. Both of these benefitted from flight research at Area-51 with the black-op project McDonnell Douglas-Boeing YF-118G *Bird of Prey* during 38 flights it made from 1996 to 1999, though the project was not declassified until 2002.

The hawk-like YF-118G is said to have been named for its resemblance to the battlecruiser used by the Klingons in the 1984 movie 'Star Trek III: The Search for Spock'! Evidently, the influence of *Star Trek* on the Skunk Work's aircraft designers persisted from the *Enterprise* roll-out in 1976!

However, the aircraft's shape, whether originating in Hollywood or McDonnell Douglas's Phantom Works division proved to be aerodynamically stable enough to be flown without computer assistance, and the aircraft tested stealth technologies and is believed to have been used to test active camouflage, which would involve its surfaces changing colour and/or luminosity to match the surroundings and/or to create visual confusion in observers.

Black Manta and *Aurora* are names that feature in many present-day speculations, but I have to say at the outset that information about these aircraft is based on rumours and conspiracy theories. There is no official confirmation of their capabilities. There is no official confirmation, even, of their existence.

The *Aurora* project was allegedly a mid-1980s Skunk Works black ops programme for a high-altitude, ultrafast, reconnaissance aircraft.

But its main claim to fame among rumour mongers is that it contributed a large amount of research into triangular-shaped aircraft that fed into the development of the Lockheed F-117 *Nighthawk* attack aircraft and Northrop Grumman B-2 *Spirit* heavy strategic bomber and its announced replacement, the Northrop Grumman B-21 *Raider*, and even the rumoured TR-3 *Black Manta* as well.

The rumour mill claims that *Aurora* was a hypersonic reconnaissance aircraft capable of flying at speeds of up to Mach 6 (about 4,450 mph).

The *Black Manta*, also known as the TR-3, is the real doozy in the Skunk Works catalogue because it has been rumoured to be a spacecraft that uses highly pressured mercury accelerated by nuclear energy to produce a plasma that creates a field of anti-gravity around the ship!

The TR-3 can perform rapid high-speed manoeuvres along all three axes using jets of gas, instead of moving parts to control its flight. Interestingly, the plasma generated to create the anti-gravity field is said also to make the craft almost invisible to radar.

Wikipedia's 'Black triangle (UFO)' entry states, 'There is little evidence to support the TR-3's existence; however, it is possible that black triangle UFO reports associated with *Black Manta* could be a technology demonstrator for a potential new-generation tactical reconnaissance aircraft, and/or that TR-3 refers to a Technical Refresh of an existing program.'

Hoping to clarify some of the doubts raised, I asked Microsoft Copilot, 'Tell me about *Black Manta* aircraft,' and was given the following rather remarkable response:

> 'The TR-3 *Black Manta* is a rumoured aerospace vehicle linked to the U.S. Air Force's top-secret black projects program [ref 1]. It is believed to be a secret spy plane developed by the U.S. Government as part of a programme to establish contact with extraterrestrial beings and create alliances with them [ref 1].
>
> There has been no official confirmation of its existence, and the military denies it. The existence of the TR-3 *Black Manta* is shrouded in secrecy due to its highly advanced technology [ref 1]. It is said to have been created with help from allied nations, allowing the United States Armed Forces to possess a piece of next-generation weaponry.
>
> However, there is little evidence that such an aircraft exists or ever existed.' [Source: Conversation with Bing, 18/01/2024].
>
> References
>
> [1] A Deeper Look into the Impressive Features of the TR-3 Black Manta…
> https://defensebridge.com/article/a-deeper-look-into-the-impressive-features-of-the-tr-3-black-manta.html.
>
> [2] TR3b Black Manta: Secretive Anti-Gravity Spy Plane—Eightify.
> https://eightify.app/summary/architecture-and-engineering/tr3b-black-manta-secretive-anti-gravity-spy-plane.
>
> [3] Black triangle (UFO) (TR-3A Black Manta)—Smartencyclopedia.
> https://smartencyclopedia.org/content/black-triangle-ufo-tr-3a-black-manta/.
>
> [4] Black triangle (UFO)—Wikipedia.
> https://en.wikipedia.org/wiki/Black_triangle_%28UFO%29.

The following two quotes are what I find truly remarkable in this Copilot response, 'a programme to establish contact with extraterrestrial beings and create alliances with them,' and 'there is little evidence that such an aircraft exists or ever existed.'

I'll delay further discussion of these quotations to later but will add here the equally remarkable piece of news that the U.S. Defense Advanced Research Projects Agency (DARPA), in early January 2024, approved a contract for the construction of an X-65 plane with air-jet flight controls. The development contract was awarded to *Aurora Flight Sciences*, a Boeing company! [Source *Eurasian Times* at http://tinyurl.com/4dn6vprk].

So, contracts have been announced publicly for further development of a significant feature of one aircraft, the existence of which has always been denied and never been confirmed, and the contracts were awarded to a subsidiary of the Boeing Company, the subsidiary being named after an earlier aircraft project, the existence of which has never been confirmed, but always denied.

As Alice said in Lewis Carroll's 'Alice's Adventures in Wonderland,' 'Curiouser and curiouser!' Strange things do happen around here!

Looking at the current time, I decide I have enough of that valuable commodity to type up what I still remember of last night's dreams before I must go out to Frank's birthday lunch. Those dreams were the product of my subconscious mind's efforts to dredge up what were old, but true memories. At least until they were rudely interrupted by my bedside alarm clock!

I left Area 51 to return home the morning after my introduction to General Orde's *SuperDragon*, so I never did find out any details about the craft itself while I was resident in Area 51. The Langley 'Company' were just as generous with my travel home as they were with my travel out there.

They provided a private plane to take me from Area 51's Homey Airport direct to Las Vegas Harry Reid airport for the Virgin Atlantic 10.00 a.m. departure to London, and an escort of local agents to hustle me through security and passport control and onto Virgin Atlantic's Upper Class cabin; first class all the way, bless the CIA's cotton socks!

I'd left Area 51 so early that I missed out on breakfast, so I found my way immediately to what they call the Upper Class social space to sample the snacks and extra bites they had on offer, and that's where I found the local newspapers and local TV newscasts to which we could tune were full of reports of the mysterious sights and events seen in the skies over Phoenix, Arizona on the previous evening.

I happily watched the TV news and settled down with the local newspapers and put two and two together comparing what the locals were reporting and what I had experienced in *SuperDragon*'s Control Room.

And then, when we had our brief stopover at Los Angeles International about an hour later, the Phoenix edition of *USA Today* had hit the newsstands and copies were brought into the social space.

That newspaper had an artist's impression of the *'large, V-shaped object traveling southeast'* featuring a cluster of reddish-orange lights at around 8 p.m. in the skies above Phoenix and a wide area around. And by the time I got home, the 'Phoenix Lights UFO sightings' were reported in the UK newspapers and were even featured on national news broadcasts.

By then, I was totally convinced that the 'V-shaped object' reported flying over Phoenix was General Orde's *SuperDragon*.

For these notes, I've decided to ask Microsoft Copilot about the 'Phoenix Lights UFO' (I must get used to using the new term unexplained anomalous phenomenon or UAP, even though UFO comes much more naturally to me). This is what Copilot told me:

> 'The Phoenix Lights (sometimes called the 'Lights Over Phoenix') were a series of widely seen unidentified flying objects observed in the skies over the southwestern states of Arizona and Nevada on Thursday, March 13, 1997.
>
> Lights of varying descriptions were seen by thousands of people between 7:30 p.m. and 10:30 p.m. Mountain Standard Time, in a space of about 300 miles from the Nevada line, through Phoenix, to the edge of Tucson. Some witnesses described seeing what appeared to be a huge carpenter's square-shaped UFO containing five spherical lights. There were two distinct events involved in the incident: a triangular formation of lights seen to pass over the state, and a series of stationary lights seen in the Phoenix area.
>
> Both sightings were supposedly due to aircraft participating in Operation Snowbird, a pilot training program of the Air National Guard based in Davis-Monthan Air Force Base in Tucson, Arizona. The first group of lights were later identified as a formation of A-10 Thunderbolt II aircraft flying over Phoenix while returning to Davis-Monthan. The second group of lights were identified as illumination flares dropped by another flight of A-10 aircraft that were on training exercises at the Barry Goldwater Range in southwest Arizona. Fife Symington, governor of Arizona at the time, years later recounted witnessing the incident, describing it as 'otherworldly.'
>
> Reports of similar lights arose in 2007 and 2008 were attributed to military flares dropped by fighter aircraft at Luke Air Force Base, and flares attached to helium balloons

> released by a civilian, respectively.
>
> In a more recent reported sighting, around 50 Marines witnessed a giant triangular-shaped unidentified flying object (UFO) hovering over the Marine Corps Air Ground Combat Center in Twentynine Palms in California on April 20, 2021. The UFO was estimated to be approximately half the size of a football field and was dotted with five red lights in a V-formation. The aircraft hovered in the sky for about 10 minutes before vanishing without a trace.' [Source: Conversation with Bing, 21/12/2023].

That unit of measurement, half the size of a football field presumably applies to an American football field which is a 91.4 m by 48.8 m rectangle and, if it is accurately estimated, implies that the giant triangular-shaped UFO had a wingspan of about 50 m. About the same as the B-2 *Spirit* and B-21 *Raider* bombers.

> Wikipedia adds more details about the Phoenix Lights incident and includes the *USA Today* drawing of the vehicle that was reported [https://en.wikipedia.org/wiki/Phoenix_Lights]. I think the following quotations are important to understanding what occurred on the night of March 13, 1997, in the skies over the Phoenix locality.
>
> - …shape that looked like a 60-degree carpenter's square, with the five lights set into it, with one at the front and two on each side.
> - Approximately 10:00 p.m. that same evening, a large number of people in the Phoenix area reported seeing 'a row of brilliant lights hovering in the sky, or slowly falling.' A number of photographs and videos were taken, prompting author Robert Sheaffer to describe it as *'perhaps the most widely witnessed UFO event in history'* in the *Skeptical Inquirer* (Volume 40, No. 4, July/August 2016) [http://tinyurl.com/k7y8tf2e].
> - Lights were reported by observers and recorded by the local Fox News television station on February 6, 2007. According to military officials and the FAA, these were flares dropped by F-16 Fighting Falcon aircraft training at Luke Air Force Base.
> - On April 21, 2008, lights were reported over Phoenix by local residents. These lights reportedly appeared to change from square to triangular formation over time. A valley resident reported that shortly after the lights appeared, three jets were seen heading west in the direction of the lights. An official from Luke AFB denied any U.S. Air Force activity in the area. All bullet points quoted from Wikipedia article entitled Phoenix Lights [28 Dec. 2023 revision, at https://en.wikipedia.org/wiki/Phoenix_Lights].

I found the following quote in an article entitled 'Meme invaders: How #StormArea51 became our new UFO reality' by Ken Layne on the website Desert Sun [https://tinyurl.com/329ma3b4]:

> - 'A close-range encounter shakes a person's very soul. During the 1997 Phoenix Lights event, people pulled over on the freeways, gazing up in astonishment and horror at a mile-wide silent aircraft that appeared to be right on top of them. The sense that the government is lying about UFOs is hard to avoid when, as happened in Phoenix, former Arizona Gov. Fife Symington made fun of the event and concealed his own up-close sighting on that otherworldly night of March 13, 1997. (Symington eventually admitted all, a decade later, on CNN [URL = http://tinyurl.com/ucus2sfr]).

> I also visited that CNN webpage [http://tinyurl.com/ucus2sfr] and I think it's worth quoting a few of the statements that former Arizona Governor Fife Symington made in 2007 in his article on the website entitled 'I saw a UFO in the Arizona sky.'
>
> - 'In 1997, during my second term as governor of Arizona, I saw something that defied logic and challenged my reality. I witnessed a massive delta-shaped, craft silently navigate over Squaw Peak, a mountain range in Phoenix, Arizona. It was truly breathtaking.'
> - 'To my astonishment this apparition appeared; this dramatically large, very distinctive leading edge with some enormous lights was traveling through the Arizona sky.'
> - 'As a pilot and a former Air Force Officer, I can definitively say that this craft did not resemble any man-made object I'd ever seen.'
> - 'What I saw in the Arizona sky goes beyond conventional explanations. When it comes to events of this nature that are still completely unsolved, we deserve more openness in government, especially our own.'
> - 'Eventually, the Air Force claimed responsibility stating that they dropped flares. I was never happy with the Air Force's silly explanation. There might very well have been military flares in the sky that evening, but what I and hundreds of others saw had nothing to do with that.' [All bullet points quoted from the CNN webpage that can be found at this URL: http://tinyurl.com/ucus2sfr].

Okay, so let's pick over those reports for fragments of information to compare with my own experience of 13 March 1997. First, what about size?

Governor Symington describes, 'a massive delta-shaped craft silently navigate over Squaw Peak.'

Ken Layne says, 'People pulled over on the freeways, gazing up in astonishment and horror at a mile-wide silent aircraft that appeared to be right on top of them.'

A mile wide? That implies a wingspan of around 1,600 metres. Let's assume that 'astonishment and horror' caused the witnesses to exaggerate the size of the craft they witnessed and turn to those U.S. Marines who saw a giant triangular-shaped UFO hovering over their Californian Combat Center in 2021.

With military precision, their report describes it as 'half the size of a football field' but this implies a wingspan of about 50 m, which is about the same as the B-2 *Spirit*, and even the veteran B-52 bomber, which has a wingspan of 56 m. Now, I think any group of U.S. Marines in 2021 is likely to have included veterans of the Afghanistan War, which began in December 2001 and ended in December 2014.

Both the B-2 and the B-52 were used in Afghanistan and U.S. Marines would have seen them often enough to be well aware of their true scale. Consequently, I'm betting that 'half the size of a football field' is very much an underestimate of the size of the 'giant triangular-shaped UFO' hovering above them. Overall, then I would guess that the *SuperDragon* is several times the size of the B-2 *Spirit*; let's say that as the B-2 wingspan is four times the wingspan of the F-117 Nighthawk, then if the Skunk Works was building a series of larger and larger aircraft to the same overall design plan, they might have given the *SuperDragon* a wingspan of between 200 and 250 m.

The *Stratolaunch Carrier* has the largest wingspan of any acknowledged aircraft currently flying in the skies over California, at 117.3 m. Indeed, this is the longest wingspan ever flown. *Stratolaunch Carrier* is designed to carry rocket-powered, hypersonic spacecraft to high altitudes for launch into space, known as air-launch-to-orbit (ALTO) rockets [view https://www.stratolaunch.com/].

Stratolaunch Carrier's first flight was on 13 April 2019, at the Mojave Air and Space Port and its second test flight on 29 April 2021. This is nine days after the U.S. Marines reported their sighting of a large UFO over their Combat Center in Twentynine Palms, which is located about 100 miles from Mojave Air and Space Port. On the basis of those dates, it is unlikely that *Stratolaunch Carrier* played any part in what the Marines witnessed.

Furthermore, the Marines reported that their 'giant triangular-shaped' UFO had hovered in the sky for about 10 minutes before vanishing without a trace.

Hovering on the vectored thrust of jet engines is quite commonplace these days, but there may be something more to this report. Remember the *Black Manta*?

Rumoured to be a spacecraft that generates an anti-gravity field that also makes the craft almost invisible to the radar. And then there's the 'vanishing without a trace' point. This reminds me about the McDonnell Douglas-Boeing YF-118G *Bird of Prey*.

Test flown from 1996 to 1999 at Area 51 and rumoured to have been used to test active camouflage, which would involve its surfaces changing colour or luminosity to match the surroundings and/or to create visual confusion in observers. If *SuperDragon* depended on active camouflage, it would explain why I found so many routines controlling video displays in that CIA operating software back in 1997!

So, the position I've reached in my personal 'conspiracy theorising' is that in the mid-1990s Lockheed's Skunk Works together with Northrop Grumman and McDonnell Douglas's Phantom Works division had managed, presumably under Charlie Orde's guidance, to produce the most exotic of aircraft/spacecraft that was four or five times bigger than the then newly introduced (on 1 January 1997), B-2 heavy strategic bomber and was the 'V-shaped object' reported flying over Phoenix. Meet General Orde's *SuperDragon*!

And its purpose? Well, I've got some educated guesses about that, too. But, hell, look at the time! I hear a birthday lunch calling my name. So, for now, I'll have to be satisfied by noting down that my subconscious had reminded me that my rummaging around in the CIA's software package back in 1997 had turned up the idea that the '*XB-25 SuperDragon*' was en route for somewhere called Arsia Mons.

A quick conversation with Microsoft Copilot established the following:

> 'Arsia Mons is the southernmost of three volcanoes (collectively known as Tharsis Montes) on the Tharsis bulge near the equator of the planet Mars.' [Source: Conversation with Bing, 07/January/2024]

But now, to lunch! A quick visit to the bathroom first, where I try to make myself look a bit more presentable. I'm on a hiding to nothing there. I'm an old, fat, bald, man. Not much scope for easy improvements.

Best I can hope for is to make myself look a bit less untidy than usual. Giving up on the personal grooming front, I lock all my precious bits of technology away securely and then launch myself into the outside world.

It was raining, of course. We're paying for the last couple of days' decent weather with one of those storms raging over us from the Atlantic. It seems to be a never-ending stream of storms generated by climate change and wound up into various levels of frenzy by our over-active jet stream.

I managed to shuffle along through the rain at a decent pace, so I didn't collect too much of the rain getting to *Sadie's Quick Bite Café*.

I was struggling out of my parka inside the café when Frank Williamson barged through the door and started complaining about the foul weather.

'It's gonna get worse according to the TV weather forecast,' said Josie, who had appeared from nowhere and was now linking arms with the two of us.

'Now, you two come with me into me private dining room out back,' she went on, 'I don't want the rest of the punters expecting any special treatment on their birthdays!'

Josie's private dining room turned out to be the kitchen-diner in the little flat that was at the rear of the café. There was a table, set for four diners, which was already equipped with a steaming coffee pot and a plate piled high with freshly baked bread.

'Get settled in there, lads.'

Josie handed Frank a trio of coffee mugs, saying, 'The birthday boy can serve the coffee while I go check the stars of the show in the kitchen.'

While Frank was pouring the coffee, I covered a piece of the bread that looked particularly crusty in a liberal layer of butter and munched my way through it contentedly as I tried to get Frank to admit to this being his seventieth birthday, but he avoided answering to my challenge. His only response was to advise me to ease up on the bread and butter in case I dulled my appetite for the mussels.

'No fear of that!' I assured him. 'But fresh bread and butter is sublime, and I can never resist it. I blame me Mam, she would have eaten bread and butter in preference to any other food.'

'I know what you mean,' Josie said, bustling back into the room from the café's kitchen. 'My Mam was the same with porridge. She'd eat it any time of the day or night! She'd bring us down to the café to give me Auntie Sadie a hand with the washin'-up an' no matter what wonderful supper feast me auntie offered in return, Mam would always go for porridge with honey. 'Course, us kids would pile into as much fish and chips as we could get on a plate! Now, stop mitherin' me about yer rotten childhood 'cos I need an answer to a question. Billie Burton brought the mussels down from Scotland an' is doin' the cookin' in the café kitchen but he also brought a few oysters as a special treat an' he's plannin' to serve them as a starter.'

'Ey that's real sound,' said Frank.

'Aye, well shut up an' answer me question, 'ow would yer like them served? Youse can 'ave them the traditional way, uncooked in lemon juice on a half shell. Or, if yer don't like the raw texture Billie can coat them with batter and chuck them in the deep-fryer and serve 'em with tartar sauce. Now choose!' Josie finished, with mock menace.

'I'll go for the battered and fried, please Josie. I'm not one for raw fish!' I said, forming a mental image of a fried oyster on a bed of tartar sauce on another piece of bread and butter.

'And I'll stay traditional. Freshly shucked with lemon juice,' Frank responded, adding. 'But you'd better keep an eye out for this Billie Burton fella, if he's bringin' yer oysters he's got designs on you. 'E probably thinks this is yer first date!'

'Don't be daft, Frank,' said Josie, returning towards the kitchen. 'That's our Billie you're talking about. He's me kid bruvver!'

Josie shouted through the kitchen door, 'Three raw and one fried,' then returned to the table and sat in one of the empty seats, claiming one of the mugs of coffee Frank had recently poured.

Sipping the coffee she said, 'Billie's got a lot in common with you, Frank. He went up to Scotland 'cos the bizzies always seemed to be lookin' for 'im.'

'Yeah, I'm well in the know on that!' replied Frank.

'Well, talk to 'im about it, will yer? He'll be eatin' with us. Ask how he's managed in Scotland. I'm real proud of 'im an' 'e needs to know 'e's appreciated.'

Josie was interrupted by a young man in kitchen whites reversing through the kitchen's swing door carrying four plates of oysters, which he proceeded to put into the place settings.

This was Billie Burton, and he was rapidly introduced to Frank and me, but equally rapidly excused himself to return to the kitchen saying, 'I'm just bringing the mussels to the boil, so I'll be back immediately, if I'm not, just wait longer. The mussels will be ready in about 10 minutes. Don't stand on ceremony, though. Dig into the oysters!'

I needed no further invitation and launched into buttering a few more pieces of crusty bread for my fried oysters, while Josie and Frank slurped their way through their fresh ones.

In a minute or two, Billie returned, plonked a half-empty bottle of wine on the table as he sat down to start attacking his oysters, saying, 'I've used as much of your wine as the mussels need, Mr Gibson, so you might as well take this back home with you, 'cos this place doesn't have a licence to serve alcohol.'

'Call me Mick, Billie.' I said. 'I understand we've you to thank for these oysters!'

'Aye, well, I knew there was a shipment coming down from Shetland to supply our Merseyside customers and I was due a few days off, so I jumped one of the fridge vans to visit the family,' Billie explained.

'So, 'ow did yer end up in Shetland, then?' asked Frank.

'Well, in me early teens some of the lads I was runnin' with started carrying knives an' all that did was make the scuffers stop and search us all the time. They almost always found something on one of us that gave 'em reasonable grounds for the next stop and search, an' I got really worried about the way they kept going on about 'joint enterprise' with drugs and weapons.'

'So, when one of our lads went too far wavin' 'is knife around in a scrap with some lads from the Dingle, I robbed me mam's 'ousekeepin' money an' set off hitchin' towards the M6. I gorra lift on a truck going to Carlisle and then just carried on towards Aberdeen.

'Took me about three days to get there. An' I only knew about the place 'cos me da was always moanin' about Aberdeen doin' Liverpool in the European Super Cup back in 1983.'

'I remember that,' Josie said. 'Me mam was frantic not knowin' what had 'appened to yer.'

As Josie finished her interruption, her usual helper in the café pushed a trolley through the swing doors from the kitchen and both Josie and Billie leaped to their feet to pass the heaped bowls of steaming mussels around the table from the top shelf of the trolley.

Billie poked around on the trolley's bottom shelf and then announced, rattling a large serving spoon in the pan, 'There's enough broth left in the pan for a bowl of soup or two if anyone's interested.'

'Ooh, I'm very partial to a drop of soup,' I said. 'Pencil me in for seconds!'

To which Frank commented, 'Yer'll bloody burst if you eat all you've got on yer plate and then neck another bowl of soup!'

'Ah, don't be snide, Frank,' said Josie. 'Gerroff 'im, the poor old bugger's enjoyin' 'imself fer once.'

I wasn't too sure about the poor old bugger description, but I appreciated Josie coming to my rescue and smiled benignly, while I scoffed another couple of meaty mussels on a piece of bread soggy with juice before asking Billie, 'So how did you get to Shetland from Aberdeen, Billie?'

'Well, la, the trucker who gave me the lift to Aberdeen took me to 'is favourite transport café an' found me another lift with one of 'is mates who was takin' the overnight ferry to Lerwick.'

Billie paused while he filled his face with several more mussels before continuing.

'In Lerwick, I fell into a job as a kitchen porter in one of the local cafés near the ferry terminal 'cos of me experience of the part-time work I used to do here for me auntie Sadie. That was alright for a while, but the pay was grisly, so I tried robbin' a few shops on the side but got caught. And the beak 'anded me a community payback order to work labourin' on one of the local shellfish farms, an' I loved it.'

Longer pause. Bigger mouthful. Wipe the chin.

'It weren't just shovelling muck around, although there was a lot of muck to shovel an' the other lads I was wiv were skivin' off as much as they could. But they let me go out on their boats an' everything, tending to the oyster cages and mussel ropes.

'An' I loved it. It was just like a seaside holiday, but I felt like I was doin' something useful. An' the scran was great, an' eventually, they let me do the cookin'! So, when I'd worked out me community order, I asked them for a regular job, an' I've been there ever since. I'm the marketing manager now. An' it's still like a seaside holiday!'

'That's a great story, Billie,' Frank said. 'You should be real proud of yourself. You remind me of me, in a way, though best I could do to get out of Toxteth was to drift down to the recruitin' office in North John Street and sign on fer the army.'

'After basic trainin', I decided that I'd learned so much about police procedure from the Liverpool bizzies that I was a natural for training fer the Redcaps, an' I enjoyed it so much I kept extendin' me service an' I was with the

Royal Military Police until I retired 10 years ago at 60.' When Frank paused to neck a few more mussels, Josie said. 'So, 'ave yer bin all over the world, then?'

'Yeah,' Frank responded, 'I've done bog-standard policing in most of our overseas bases. But I gradually specialised in criminal investigations.'

'You mean like detectives? Solving crimes?' Josie asked.

'Aye, soldiers are just as criminal, an' just as devious, an' just as thievin', as the general public, you know!' Frank answered. 'An' they can be a real pain when they're abroad on holiday with their mates. When I got too old to go chasin' squaddies who'd wrecked beach bars along the promenade, I was assigned to a liaison squad, and we toured British embassies and consulates around European capitals and holiday spots cooperating as necessary with local police and security agencies.'

'Security?' said a wide-eyed Josie. 'You mean spies and James Bond things?'

'Now and then,' Frank nodded. 'But intelligence about terrorist threats and cybersecurity became the most important parts of our work.'

Josie exclaimed, 'I bet dat was spooky!'

'Aye, well, the spookiest was right at the end of me army career. On my final deployment, I was assigned to our embassy in Washington. It was quite a cushy desk job, as befitted me advancing years at the time. Liaison, again, with the locals on anything to do with the British military, but you couldn't go out of the embassy building without falling over yet another U.S. security team.

'They were all over the place! Security is a major industry in the U.S. I remember a *Washington Post* report, that was passed around the embassy staff during that deployment, that said there were 1,200 government organisations and 2,000 private companies working on counterterrorism, homeland security, and intelligence, in 10,000 locations across the U.S., with nearly a million people holding top-secret clearances.'

'Jeez! Frank,' Josie exclaimed. 'An' there's me thinkin' the American Secret Service was all done by the Men in Black!'

'Some of them do wear black suits with dark glasses, but others walk around looking like ordinary people. We all know about agencies like the Secret Service, FBI and CIA, but the U.S. has also got intelligence and security services run by the Department of Energy,' Frank began to tick off his examples on his fingers, 'The State Department, the Treasury, Drug Enforcement, and Homeland Security.'

'Then the Department of Defense has five intelligence services above and beyond the Navy, Coast Guard, Army, Marine Corps, or Air Force.' He finished with a flourish, saying, 'I've been out of the loop for the past 10 years, but I've been told there's even a Space Intelligence Centre run by the United States Space Force!'

One of the kitchen hands poked his head through the kitchen's swing door and called Josie back to the kitchen to help deal with a sudden rush of customers coming into the café out of the rain, and that bustle helped mask the fact that I was very impressed, not to say astonished by Frank reeling off his list of U.S. security agencies.

I knew he was right, of course. You can't work in GCHQ doing what I did for 40 years without encountering the abundance of U.S. security and intelligence services. But I was especially curious about his knowledge of the Space Force's National Space Intelligence Centre. It was only established in 2020, so who is there to tell a retired Redcap, now a hardworking Tesco supermarket security guard, about it?

My GCHQ activities may well have made me hypersensitive, but that sounded a warning to me. I might have to be more careful with Frank! As a diversion to maintain my benign demeanour, I noisily drained the last of the broth in my bowl and passed it to Billie asking him to give me a drop more 'soup.'

And as a further diversion, I quietly asked Billie, 'What are yer doin' now, Billie?'

Before he could answer, Josie came back into the dining room with a fresh pot of coffee, saying to Frank and me, 'It's rainin' cats and dogs out there, lads. If youse got any plans for this afternoon, you'll 'ave to take one of our brollies wiv yer.'

Billie returned my fresh bowl of soup and announced, 'Last year, the company bought new licences from the Crown Estate for a considerable extension of shellfish cultivation all around Shetland and right now we're busy laying out mussel ropes and oyster cages for the new farms, an' we'll give carpet-clam cultivation a try in the intertidal zones.'

'That sounds good,' I said, adding, 'but what's the Crown got to do with it?'

'Apparently, it all dates back to 1066, when William the Conqueror claimed all of England for the crown,' Billie answered my question.

'And now that's taken to mean that The King owns most of the seabed encircling the UK, out to 12 nautical miles from shore. 'Course, in Scotland, licences for activities at the coast are managed locally.'

Billie poured some of the fresh coffee for the three of us before going on. 'Restoration of oyster reefs, in particular, has been top of the agenda for shellfish farmers for several years because unregulated oyster dredging in the 19th century virtually wiped out natural oyster reefs all around Europe.

'But my plan is to go one step further than just restoration and conservation. We're going to cultivate the shellfish shells and sell them as carbon credits to industries that have to emit carbon dioxide or other greenhouse gases to compensate for their emissions!'

'Ow the 'ell does that work?' asked Frank.

In answer, Billie grabbed some of the discarded oyster and mussel shells from the waste bowl in the middle of the table and hammered them onto the table. It sounded as though he was hitting the table with rocks.

'Sounds rock hard, doesn't it.' he said. 'That's because it is rock hard 'cos it's made of limestone. An' that limestone is solidified carbon dioxide from the atmosphere!'

'Oh, I get it,' said Frank. 'You're saying shellfish farming is a carbon capture process. I've read about them. Aren't they already big business?'

'Yeah, but current carbon removal processes are enormously expensive and heavily criticised, mainly because they can't guarantee the carbon will stay out of the atmosphere for a significant time. My shells represent permanent removal. An' I can weigh out two and a quarter tonne of shell and guarantee it represents a tonne of carbon dioxide solidified from the atmosphere.

'Then I can tip it back into the ocean and guarantee it will stay there for millions of years. Because that's how limestone deposits have always been made. So, the shells are a nice little earner as carbon offsets, even before I sell the shellfish meat!'

I was very impressed by all this, but I must confess that I was struggling to keep my eyes open. I urgently needed my customary after-lunch nap! I was jerked into wakefulness by the reappearance of a kitchen hand, this time asking for Billie's help serving up late lunches and afternoon teas in the kitchen.

I gulped down more coffee and suggested to Frank that we make a move out of the café. He said he had been watching more of those TV programmes about alien conspiracies and was hoping to talk to me about them, so I invited him back to my little flat where he could look at the books and DVDs I had on the topic.

That being all agreed, I struggled back into my parka, took leave of our hosts, and then launched ourselves into yet another Atlantic storm huddled together in the shelter of a borrowed golfing umbrella.

5. The Asimov Incident

Being a bit unsteady on my feet, I clung to Frank as we battled our way through the increasingly violent storm to get back to my little flat. In one of the strongest gusts, Frank almost lost his grip on what was obviously a very sturdy umbrella as we turned into my street.

My building was close to the corner, and we were thankful for that when we saw a tree being blown down at the far end of the street, losing its encounter with the storm in a graceful slow-motion dive to a horizontal death. There were no dodgy-looking trees around my building as they'd all been cleared away years ago to make way for a car park for next door's medical centre.

So, we threw ourselves into the shelter of the entrance porch and shook the worst of the rain off ourselves and the umbrella and then ducked into my hidey hole of a little flat where we could finish drying off.

On the way out of Josie's dining room, Frank had grabbed the half-empty bottle of wine from the table, so we shared that between us while we waited for the kettle to boil to make some welcome mugs of tea. My little library of books and DVDs was on bookshelves along one wall of my living room, so I suggested Frank looked through my collection while I made the tea.

'You can borrow any of these,' I told him. 'And if you've got time to stay, we can watch some of the TV shows that are on the DVDs.'

'Yeh, I'd like dat,' Frank replied. 'I'm on de night shift today, so I can stay as long as you'll put up wiv me.'

When I gave Frank his mug of tea, he had already taken a couple of TV programme DVDs down from the shelves, one about the fabled alien autopsy, one about reverse-engineering UFOs and another about aliens visiting Earth in ancient times and teaching humans how to build Stonehenge and the pyramids.

'I think you'll find all these rather fanciful, Frank,' I said, fingering the DVDs. 'But I don't mind dozing off in front of them! You should look at some of the books for more carefully researched stories.'

'I see yer well into science-fiction here,' Frank replied, waving his hand towards the books. 'I've always preferred crime fiction meself. I'd describe sci-fi as fanciful!'

'Maybe so,' I responded. 'It's always horses for courses. And I've been reading sci-fi avidly since I was a kid. What you see on those shelves are the sci-fi stories that made the biggest impressions on me when I was a kid. These days, I buy from a charity shop, read 'em and then take 'em back to the charity shop. I don't keep 'em.'

Frank ran a finger across some of the spines of books on my shelf and then pulled out a handful of particularly dog-eared paperbacks.

Handing them to me he said, 'Well, deez luk like you've bin read'n 'em every year since youse wuz in short pants, la! So, tell us what's so special about dem.'

I took the books Frank offered to me.

'Aye, you're right there, la,' I responded almost reverentially. 'I've owned them since I was a teenager!'

Picking two of the books I went on, 'These two, by Alfred Bester, 'The Demolished Man' and 'The Stars My Destination' are the first books I ever owned. And, I added quickly, 'If you want to read sci-fi-crime, these two are perfect. 'The Demolished Man' is an inverted detective story in which the crime is committed at the start and the story describes the detective's attempt to solve the crime.

'In 'The Stars My Destination,' teleporting yerself from one location to another is the common mode of transport and results in new forms of crime and social instability.'

'Both of these classics of science-fiction literature were published in the 1950s.' I added, then I stood quietly for a short while, enjoying my mug of tea, and thinking back to my youth.

I snapped out of my nostalgic reverie as Frank put another well-used paperback in my hand, saying, 'Worrabout dis one?'

It was Arthur C. Clarke's *Rendezvous with Rama*. 'This was published in the early 1970s.' I started. 'And it won all the best novel awards going at the time. The basis of this story is a 50-by-20-kilometre cylindrical alien starship that enters the Solar System from interstellar space.

'A human crew is put together to intercept and board the ship, but the mysteries about the ship are not fully revealed in the first book. Three sequels were written by Clarke in collaboration with Gentry Lee and published in the

1990s. Gentry Lee also wrote two further novels located in the same 'Rama framework' towards the end of the 1990s.'

'Ave youse got dem other books?' Frank asked, scanning the shelves.

'I've read them, of course,' I said. 'But I've not kept them; they've gone back to the charity shop. Clarke's co-author, Gentry Lee, actually worked for NASA; he was the chief engineer for the Planetary Flight Systems Directorate at the Jet Propulsion Laboratory in Pasadena, California. While 'e was there, 'e was involved in engineering around 20 real robotic planetary exploration missions to Mars, Jupiter, asteroids, and some comets.

'Clarke was a physicist and communications engineer in his younger days, so the astrophysics and space engineering aspects of these stories are impeccable, and Clarke foretold the future of space engineering in many of his novels. But I was never happy with the way the Rama sequels involved increasingly fanciful and exotic alien species that had no correlation with the biological diversity we have all around us on Earth.'

'Okay,' said Frank, pointing to another stretch of dog-eared paperbacks on my shelf. 'What about this Asimov fella? Yer seems to be keen on 'im. Is 'e foreign?'

'Yeh, doubly foreign,' I replied. 'He was born in Russia in January 1920 but 'is family emigrated to the United States when he was three years old an' 'e grew up in Brooklyn, New York, an' 'e went on to produce over 500 books before he died in New York City in 1992.'

I muscled in beside Frank and pulled a group of Asimov's books partway out on the shelf, saying, 'These are Isaac Asimov's *Foundation* series. It's a wonderfully epic story that spans centuries and tells of the decline an' resurgence of a Galactic Empire that encompasses the entire Milky Way.'

I picked out *Foundation* and continued my narrative, 'This is the first novel in the series, published in 1951, though the text first appeared as short stories in *Astounding Science-Fiction Magazine* between 1942 and 1950.'

Then I picked out *Foundation and Empire*, 'Asimov published this in 1952.'

And I then waved *Second Foundation* at Frank, adding, 'Which appeared in 1953. These three make up the original iconic *Foundation* trilogy. But Asimov didn't stop there.'

I continued pulling books off the shelf, explaining each one in turn.

'In 1982, Asimov published *Foundation's Edge*, the story of which takes place centuries after the original trilogy. And then his fifth instalment,

Foundation and Earth appeared in 1986. This is the story of Asimov's characters searching across the galaxy for humanity's legendary ancestral home, the planet called Earth.'

Although, for obvious reasons, I didn't mention it to Frank, I will put on record here that I've always found it interesting that one of the planets that Asimov's characters arrive at in this story is called *Aurora*.

Interesting because the book was published in 1986, which is just about the time that the rumour mill says a super-fast black ops reconnaissance aircraft called *Aurora* was being flight-tested over Area 51, although, of course, the existence of this aircraft project has never been confirmed, but always denied. Curiouser even than curiouser!

Those Californian aeronautical engineers seem to have read an awful lot of science-fiction and, given the amount of science-fiction they were also watching on TV and in the movies, it's a wonder they found the time to design real-life exotic aircraft and spacecraft!

What I did mention to Frank was that *Foundation and Earth* was supposed to serve as the chronological conclusion to the whole *Foundation* saga, but that didn't stop Asimov writing a couple of prequels, both of which have their place in the dog-eared section of my bookshelf.

'Isaac Asimov published the sixth novel in the Foundation series in 1988 under the title *Prelude to Foundation*.' I told Frank, as I pointed it out on the shelf. 'He wrote this as the first of two prequels.

'This one tells about the origins and early life of the main characters of *Foundation*. While the second prequel, and final book in the whole series, *Forward the Foundation*, which was published in 1993, after Asimov's death in April 1992, takes the main characters into the start of the original *Foundation* trilogy. And in that way completes the seven-book cycle.'

'Yer likes dese buks, don't yer?' Frank asked, grinning.

'I sure do,' I replied, returning his grin. 'And as you can see from their dog-eared state they've all accompanied me on my travels and have been re-read at regular intervals throughout my life. I was only 11 years old when the original *Foundation* trilogy was first published.

'So, I didn't discover the Galactic Empire until I was in my teens, and that was when the breadth and depth of Isaac Asimov's storytelling vision really inspired me. And that inspiration returned in my 40s and 50s as the later books appeared and prompted me to read the earlier novels again.

'I remember reading a review that claimed that his last novel in the series, *Forward the Foundation*, knits together science, politics, and personal problems, in a way that allows us to glimpse Asimov's inner thoughts in the twilight of his own life. Now I'm 10 years older than he was when he died and very aware of my own twilight!'

'Don't get mournful, la, I didn't bring me violin!' Frank commented, going on to say. 'Anyway, it all sounds a bit like the 'Star Wars' films to me!'

'Aye, well, there are some similarities, but the differences are probably more important. The *Foundation* series started off in 1951 and ended in 1993. The first *Star Wars* film came out in 1977 and the last of the main sequence of nine films, the so-called *Skywalker Saga*, appeared in 2019.

'Youse'll find a boxed set of DVDs on me CD-shelf unit over there. Both series look at the rise and fall of Galactic empires, but while *Star Wars* features heroic conflicts between right and wrong, like the Greek myths, the *Foundation* series is a psychosocial and political saga which is more like the writings of Niccolò Machiavelli.'

Frank pulled out the *Star Wars* boxed set from the shelf, asking if he could borrow them and whether Asimov's Foundation series had appeared on film.

'Of course, you can borrow them *Star Wars* DVDs, but I've got no idea about any DVDs from the *Foundation* series, la,' I told him, going on to say. 'Apple TV+ has produced a series based on Isaac Asimov's *Foundation* novels,' I told him.

'It premiered in 2021 and they started streaming Season 2 in July 2023. A Third Season has been confirmed but I don't know its release date. You can check the website if youse is interested [https://apple.co/_Foundation] but if you want to binge-watch it, the total screen time for Seasons 1 and 2 is around 15 hours! Mind you,' I added.

'If you binge-watch all of them Star Wars DVDs, youse'll spend over 25 hours in that galaxy far, far away, an' dat'll be a day in yer life yer won't get back!

'On the other hand, if you fancy a swift introduction to Isaac Asimov's unique way of thinking, you won't find better than these, la,' I said, as I reached past Frank and picked out Will Smith's *I, Robot* DVD and followed it up with my most dog-eared paperback of all, which was Asimov's original 1950 version of his *I, Robot* collection of sci-fi short stories.

'These both tell of the development of robots with a similar kind of intelligence, consciousness and self-awareness to humans because of what Asimov called their positronic brains. And the film will only take a couple of hours out of your life!'

'Dis paperback looks pretty ancient,' Frank said turning the book over in his hands.

'Aye, dat's dated 1950,' I replied.

'An' the movie? When did that come out?' Frank responded.

I looked at the back of the DVD's case to find its copyright date, '2004,' I said.

'Strewth! Took 'em long enough to make dat fillum!' Frank commented, and then he asked. 'Woz dey worried about the artificial intelligence of robot brains 70 years ago when Asimov wrote 'is buk?'

'Asimov sure was,' I assured him. 'I don't believe anyone else gave it much thought. Asimov applied his brilliant imagination to the intricate interaction between humans, robots, and morality as early as the 1940s although he set his stories in the 21st century, which was the far future to him.

'Even then he emphasised the fundamental importance of software over hardware details by introducing the landmark notion of there being Three Laws of Robotics built into his robots' positronic brains. Given recent fearful discussion about the dangers of artificial intelligence, it's worth mentioning these three laws. So, let's see if I can remember them.'

I paused a moment before continuing, counting the laws off on my fingers. 'The First Law states that a robot must not harm a human being or, through inaction, allow a human being to come to harm.

'Second, the law states that a robot must obey the orders given to it by human beings, except where such orders would conflict with the First law. And finally, the Third law requires a robot to always protect its own existence providing such protection does not conflict with the First or Second Laws.

'Asimov introduced those three laws explicitly for the first time in a short story called *Runaround*, which was first published in the March 1942 issue of *Astounding Science-Fiction* and is one of the stories included in that 1950 iconic collection *I, Robot* you've got in your hand.'

'D'ya reckon all that would handle today's fears about AI computers, la?' Frank asked.

And I had a bright idea, so I said, 'All this talkin' about books an' movies 'as given me a proper thirst, so how 'bout we make another mug of tea? An' since we've polished off the last of the wine we brought back from Josie's, we could sort ourselves out a generous whisky chaser to go with it.

'An' while we're enjoyin' that, I could get me laptop computer out, and we could 'ave a natter with Microsoft Copilot, askin' the AI program itself to sum up the current fears about AI. Sound good, la?'

'Sounds boss to me!' Frank responded, eagerly. 'Pass us yer mug and show me where yer kitchen gear is. I'll sort the brew while you get yer computer set up.'

I guided Frank into my little kitchen and showed him where the makings were located, saying, 'Ah, the joys of a cuppa and a chat with Copilot. That's a proper scouse way to spend an afternoon!'

'Sound, la! Tea, a natter, an' a friendly brew. Can't beat it!' Frank was evidently made up about the prospect!

It was the work of just a few minutes to get my laptop out of my bedside cupboard and set it up on my little dining table.

Frank delivered a couple of mugs of tea to the table as I opened the screen and hit the on-switch, staring as required at the camera; the machine sprang to life almost immediately, so I went to get a bottle of whisky from my stash in the kitchen, a couple of glasses, and a small jug of water while it completed its boot process.

'Blimey, that's quick!' Exclaimed Frank. 'Me laptop'd still be coughin' and splutterin' just to get me desktop on screen! Is that machine somethin' real bossy?' Frank peered closely at my laptop and then pointed theatrically at the illuminated alien face logo on the outer case and *Alienware's* name at the bottom of the screen. 'Ay up! Is that a brand name or a place of origin?' he said.

'Yeh, dat's a real bossy high-performance gaming computer,' I replied, passing Frank his whisky and putting the bottle on the table as an invitation to refills.

'It's an *Alienware* m18. An absolute premium gaming laptop wiv all the goodies: 24 core processor, 5.40 GHz Turbo Boost clock speed 64 GB RAM, and an eight 8 TB SSD hard disk!' I listed, hoping to impress Frank.

'Well, I dunno wot all dat means, y'know, mate,' Frank said. 'I get a bit baffled meself. But why's it all plastered wi' pictures an' names of them spacey aliens? It's like they've gone an' invited E.T. and the gang to their gaming party, la!'

'Close!' I chuckled. 'But y'know, it's got nowt to do wi' that E.T. flick, la. Dat woz way back in the early 1980s. Think about 200 episodes of the TV series *The X-Files* throughout the 1990s an' right up to 2018!' I took a generous gulp at my whisky before going on to explain.

'Currently, the *Alienware* brand is an upmarket-hardware subsidiary of the Dell Computer Corporation, but it was founded originally in 1996 by two childhood friends, Nelson Gonzalez and Alex Aguila, who grew up in Miami, Florida with a passion for video games and created the company to build super-powerful computers for gaming.

'The name *Alienware* was chosen simply because the two founders were also dedicated fans of the hit TV series The X-Files. *Alienware* is now a world-renowned hardware brand for gaming computers, laptops and desktops.'

I didn't think it was necessary to tell Frank that Nelson and Alex, who are both still involved in online gaming, were old mates of mine from way back when, and had been customising the very powerful laptops I'd needed ever since I first visited Area 51.

Nor did I tell him that my laptop was retro-fitted with Marvell Technology's self-destruct chips. If the camera doesn't clock my own very personal retina pattern at switch-on then, poof! Such a high voltage is released across the circuit boards that all the chips are fried, including my SSD disk.

Instead, I settled my laptop between us, so it was easily visible to both, clicked on the taskbar's Microsoft Bing link and asked, 'Okay, why don't we start by asking Copilot to define artificial intelligence?' as I typed, 'Tell me about AI,' into the 'Ask me anything…' field.

This was Copilot's response:

> 'Artificial intelligence (AI) refers to the ability of a digital computer or computer-controlled robot to perform tasks commonly associated with intelligent beings. These tasks include reasoning, discovering meaning, generalizing, and learning from past experiences. Since the advent of digital computers in the 1940s, we have seen remarkable progress in complex tasks like mathematical theorem proofs and chess playing.
>
> However, despite these advances, no program has achieved the full flexibility and everyday knowledge of human intelligence. Some AI applications, such as medical diagnosis, search engines, voice recognition, and chatbots, have reached the performance levels of human experts in specific domains [refs 1 & 2]. In essence, AI

aims to create systems that mimic or exceed human intelligence, allowing machines to perceive, reason, learn, and interact with their environment [refs 3–5].' [Source: Conversation with Bing, 07/02/2024].

References

[1] Artificial intelligence (AI) | Definition, Examples, Types…
https://www.britannica.com/technology/artificial-intelligence.

[2] Artificial intelligence—Wikipedia.
https://en.wikipedia.org/wiki/Artificial_intelligence.

[3] Everything you need to know about AI and AI technology—Qualcomm.
https://www.qualcomm.com/products/technology/artificial-intelligence/what-is-ai-faq.

[4] What is AI (Artificial Intelligence)? | McKinsey.
https://www.mckinsey.com/featured-insights/mckinsey-explainers/what-is-ai.

[5] What is AI? Everything to know about artificial intelligence.
https://www.zdnet.com/article/what-is-ai-heres-everything-you-need-to-know-about-artificial-intelligence/.

'Note the phrase, "chatbots have reached the performance levels of human experts in specific domains",' I told Frank. 'And remember Copilot is offered to Bing users as your everyday AI companion.'

'Although if you press it really hard, Copilot describes itself as an AI language model which doesn't have personal preferences or feelings but is here to assist you! So, theoretically, the response it gives you is the sort of standard response you'd get from any independent and unbiased commentator.'

'Yer don't sound convinced, la,' Frank said, grinning.

'I ain't. I ain't convinced that yer can write owt, not even computer code, that ain't influenced by yer personal biases. And in me last few months of usin' Copilot on a daily basis, I reckon I've found a few of Copilot's biases, la. But let's continue with the Copilot cross examination!'

And I typed, 'What is an AI language model?' into the 'Ask me anything…' field.

'An AI language model is a computer program that generates (and understands) human language based on statistical techniques and machine learning. Its purpose is to replicate human interaction by analysing the meaning of words and sentences in a user prompt and responding in a meaningful and appropriate way [refs 1–5].

Here are some key points about language models:

1. **Definition**: A language model uses machine learning to create a probability distribution over words or word sequences. It predicts the most likely next word in a sentence based on the preceding context. Note that *'validity'* in this

context doesn't refer to grammatical correctness but rather how closely the sequence resembles how people naturally write [ref 1].

2. **Applications**:

Text Generation: Language models can produce original text, mimicking human writing style.

Summarization: They can perform extractive or abstractive summarization of texts.

Translation: Models for different languages can be used to build machine translation systems.

Question Answering: Language models can answer questions based on context.

Speech Recognition, OCR (optical character recognition), and *Handwriting Recognition*. These tasks also benefit from language models [ref 1].

3. **Evolution**: Language models have evolved from simple Markov models to sophisticated transformer-based models like GPT-3. These models learn from vast amounts of text data and provide valuable insights across various natural language processing applications [ref 1].

In summary, language models play a crucial role in understanding and generating human language, enabling applications that range from chatbots to advanced text analytics [ref 1].' [Source: Conversation with Bing, 07/02/2024].

References

[1] A Beginner's Guide to Language Models | Built In. https://builtin.com/data-science/beginners-guide-language-models.

[2] What is an AI Language Model & How Does it Work?—Wikimotive LLC. https://wikimotive.com/wikiblog/what-is-an-ai-language-model-and-how-does-it-work/.

[3] What Is a Language Model? | deepset. https://www.deepset.ai/blog/what-is-a-language-model.

[4] Language Models in AI. Introduction | by Dennis Ash—Medium. https://medium.com/unpackai/language-models-in-ai-70a318f43041.

[5] What are LLMs (Large Language Models), and how are they used in generative AI? https://www.computerworld.com/article/3697649/what-are-large-language-models-and-how-are-they-used-in-generative-ai.html.

Frank asked if I could print these Copilot conversations, so I sent the first two to my wi-fi printer which was tucked under the table on the floor beside me.

Then Frank suggested, 'Now it's told us what it is, la. Why don't you ask the bloody thing to explain how it works and what it does?'

So, I did, by typing, 'Briefly explain, how Copilot answers a question. What does it do?' into the 'Ask me…' field.

> Copilot answered with: 'Certainly! *Copilot* is an AI language model developed by OpenAI. When you ask a question, Copilot processes the input, understands the context, and generates a relevant response. Here's how it works:
> 1. **Input Understanding**: Copilot analyses the user's query, considering the language, context, and any relevant information provided.
> 2. **Knowledge Base**: Copilot has access to a vast amount of information from various sources, including books, articles, and websites. It uses this knowledge to provide accurate answers.
> 3. **Reasoning and Creativity**: Copilot uses its understanding of the topic, logic, and creativity to generate a response. It can provide factual information, summaries, creative content (such as poems or stories), code snippets, and more.
> 4. **Safety and Guidelines**: Copilot adheres to safety guidelines, avoiding harmful or inappropriate content. It aims to be helpful, positive, and engaging in its responses.
> 5. **Output Generation**: Copilot generates a response in the same language as the user's query. It may use markdown formatting, tables, or other elements to present information clearly.
>
> Remember that Copilot's responses are based on its training data and predefined tools, and it does not have personal opinions or emotions. If you have any more questions, feel free to ask!' [Source: Conversation with Bing, 11/02/2024].

'Eh, sound, mate!' I said. 'So, there's this claim floatin' about in there that Copilot doesn't 'ave personal opinions or emotions, right? But I reckon them programmers and developers who built it must 'ave a few thoughts of their own, eh? Like I've just said, everything you do is influenced by yer personal biases.

'And I'd be dead cautious about them folks who decide what's *harmful or inappropriate content* for this language model, an' what's the message they're tryin' to put across, like, while they're being *helpful, positive, and engagin*'? That's what I'd like to know!'

Frank pushed his chair back, stretched and asked, 'If yer 'avin' doubts about it, why the bloody hell are ya usin' it, eh?'

'Because it's dead boss at that number two job on the screen there, la. Copilot's got access to a proper massive amount of info from loads of places, like books, journal articles, and websites. Every day of me life, I'm needin' to look up stuff that's in all them sources.

'But I can't search 'em as quick as Copilot, y'know? So, it makes more sense for me to lob me research question, big or small, at Copilot and then give its response a proper check to see if it's bang on or not. I don't need it to come up with creative stuff, but if it does say summat nice, I'll have it!'

'Y'know, la,' I carried on, thinkin' back. 'I started me research career in the days before online databases and search engines. That was when us researchers had to sift through what had already been published by hand.

'I remember countless hours, long days, and many nights, spent in the stacks of the Christie Library at Manchester Uni that were devoted to journals like *Physics Abstracts*, *Mathematical Reviews*, and, especially for me, *Engineering Index*. Oh, aye, and the *Current Contents* room! Boss, that was!

'This flimsy-paper, pocket-sized, weekly mag provided updates on the most recently published research simply by reproducing the contents lists of that week's journals across all sorts of scientific disciplines. Gigantic, dusty volumes of printed books were me gateway to the latest research in the old days. The only way us researchers could stay informed about developments in our fields, y'know?'

'Oh aye, and I reckon the young 'uns who, like you, can do it all wiv their phone from their own gaff with a whisky in their mitts, don't appreciate the graft we had to put in back in the day, when we were their age. Proper different times, mate!' Frank mocked.

'It's progress, la, an' the bus fares were dead cheap back then, so what's to moan about? Are we gonna keep lookin' back or shall we ask Copilot about the current worries 'bout artificial intelligence?'

My response was to type a request for an overview of current fears about AI into Copilot's 'Ask me…' field.

'Certainly! Here's a concise overview of some current fears about artificial intelligence (AI):

1. **Job Displacement**: Many worry that AI will replace human jobs, leading to unemployment and economic disruption. However, recent research suggests that replacing workers with AI can be more expensive than anticipated [refs 1, 4].

2. **Music and Creativity**: There are concerns that AI-generated music and art might lack the emotional depth and creativity of human creations. Some fear that music could lose its soul if entirely composed by algorithms [ref 2].

3. **Ethical Dilemmas**: As AI systems become more autonomous, ethical questions arise. For instance, how should self-driving cars make life-or-death decisions? Ensuring AI aligns with human values is crucial.

4. **Bias and Discrimination**: AI algorithms can inherit biases from training data, perpetuating societal inequalities. Addressing bias and ensuring fairness in AI systems is

a pressing concern.

5. **Existential Risk**: A more extreme fear is that AI could lead to human extinction. While some experts emphasize this risk, others believe it's overblown [refs 3, 5].'

References

[1] Oops! Replacing Workers With AI Is Actually More Expensive, MIT Finds. https://uk.news.yahoo.com/oops-replacing-workers-ai-actually-163104605.html.

[2] ALEX BRUMMER: Fear that music will stop because of AI. https://www.msn.com/en-gb/money/other/alex-brummer-fear-that-music-will-stop-because-of-ai/ar-BB1hGVB6.

[3] Artificial intelligence could lead to extinction, experts warn—BBC. https://www.bbc.com/news/uk-65746524.

[4] Many Employees Fear Being Replaced by AI—Here's How to Integrate It Into Your Business Without Scaring Them.. https://www.entrepreneur.com/science-technology/many-employees-fear-being-replaced-by-ai-heres-how-to/467661.

[5] Everything you wanted to know about AI—but were afraid to ask. https://www.theguardian.com/technology/2023/feb/24/ai-artificial-intelligence-chatbots-to-deepfakes.

[6] Getty. https://media.gettyimages.com/photos/bias-word-from-wooden-blocks-with-letters-picture-id1167621818?b=1&k=6&m=1167621818&s=612x612&w=0&h=y3LDZu6aIxygYnHjP8Lpqth4dNGKC-JVz1N90Ooj7bg=

Delving further into the current fears about artificial intelligence, Copilot came up with the following:

'Artificial intelligence (AI) has been advancing at an astonishing pace, and it's stirring up both excitement and apprehension. Here are some reasons why people are concerned:

1. **Rapid Development**: AI is evolving rapidly, especially in the realm of conversational chatbots or large language models (LLMs). These LLMs, like GPT-4, are getting smarter and more capable. Imagine an AI that can improve itself without human intervention—much like Google's AlphaZero learned to play chess better than humans in just nine hours by playing against itself millions of times.

2. **AGI on the Horizon**: The acceleration of AI development is hurtling us toward the era of artificial general intelligence (AGI). When AGI arrives, it will have the ability to continuously enhance itself, potentially surpassing human capabilities. Researchers have already identified sparks of advanced general intelligence in GPT-4, which performed better than 90% of human test takers on standardized exams.

3. **Nuclear-Level Catastrophe**: A survey of AI experts revealed that 36% of them fear that AI development could lead to a *'nuclear-level catastrophe.'* The stakes are high,

and we need to get it right the first time.

4. **Open Letters and Concerned Voices**: Prominent figures, including Google's Geoffrey Hinton, have expressed alarm. The *Future of Life Institute*, backed by luminaries like Steve Wozniak and Elon Musk, has called for a six-month pause on advanced AI development.'

Further References

[1] Here's Why AI May Be Extremely Dangerous--Whether It's Conscious or Not. https://www.scientificamerican.com/article/heres-why-ai-may-be-extremely-dangerous-whether-its-conscious-or-not/.

[2] 12 Risks and Dangers of Artificial Intelligence (AI) | Built In. https://builtin.com/artificial-intelligence/risks-of-artificial-intelligence.

[3] 'AI Anxiety' Is on the Rise—Here's How to Manage It. https://www.scientificamerican.com/article/ai-anxiety-is-on-the-rise-heres-how-to-manage-it/.

[4] Neuroscience, Artificial Intelligence, and Our Fears: A Journey of…https://neurosciencenews.com/artificial-intelligence-fear-neuroscience-23519/.

Remember, these fears highlight the need for responsible development, transparency, and thoughtful regulation in the AI field. So, while we reminisce about the past, let's also keep an eye on the future—a future where AI's potential risks and benefits intertwine. [Source: Conversations with Bing, 05/02/2024 & 12/02/2024].

Frank studied the printouts I gave him while I finished off my tea.

I'd seen enough of these Bing conversations to recognise their limitations, so I downed the last few dregs in my glass of whisky and announced, 'Y'know, la, we must distinguish what we have now from what the future may hold. Copilot is all about probability distributions of words and word sequences, like. This AI language model predicts the most likely next word in a sentence based on what came before, just like predictive text on yer phone.'

'It gets all cosy with yer personal usage patterns, too, just like predictive text does. Basically, it's like this: it checks out yer past behaviour, what you fancy, and how you've been chattin', and then it dishes out personalised recommendations. Sound familiar?'

'Well, that's exactly what them recommendation systems do on them ecommerce websites. So, when you log on to yer Tesco account, the software has a gander at all the stuff you've ordered before and rustles up a shopping list of things you might wanna grab this time, all tailored just for you. It's all done with a bit of historical stats, mate.'

'So, youse not impressed, then?' Frank asked.

'I wouldn't say that, la,' I replied. 'I'm impressed by a lot of what Copilot does and how fast it does it. Most of the time, like. But I've found it sometimes gives up and after I've typed in my question, Copilot's response is, 'It might be time to move onto a new topic. Let's start over.' I've not identified any rhyme or reason for this.'

'Then, occasionally it even gives me completely irrelevant answers. I've come to think of it as a bairn, like. Look, there's an example,' I pointed to a hyperlink on my computer screen. 'Eh, that reference number 6 to gettyimages.com/photos. Let's 'ave a butcher's at what that is!' I clicked on the reference [6] hyperlink and a photo of the word *'BIAS'* assembled from children's playschool alphabet blocks came onto the screen.

We both looked at it for a few seconds before laughing in amazement.

'Why?' I asked through suppressed laughter. 'Why would a serious research program return that as a meaningful reference for *a concise overview of some current fears about artificial intelligence (AI)*, la?'

'It ain't exactly down-to-earth and straightforward, is it mate?' Frank agreed. Going on to ask, 'But you're still usin' this AI-thing are you, la? Youse ain't going back to that library, then?'

'Aye, mate! It's 'ere to lend a hand, ain't it? But I keep very close tabs on it, la! It's a great time-saver 'cos it can search the Internet databases much faster than me. For one thing, it doesn't have to keyboard the questions! Use it wiv yer eyes open an' awareness that it's *NOT* more intelligent than you; it just shuffles data faster than you can. Essentially, a computer runnin' an AI algorithm is just a quick-witted fool, la!'

I didn't take my conversation with Frank any further into my thoughts about artificial intelligence not being the same as artificial understanding. To be honest, I was beginning to feel quite drowsy. Our walk through the storm to get back from Josie's had deprived me of my usual after-lunch nap and I was beginning to suffer.

Nor did I tell him that when I had accused Copilot directly of being a quick-witted fool, Copilot had immediately responded with, *'Aye, mate, spot on! Sometimes these machines can be a bit daft, but they 'ave their moments, eh?'*

I didn't tell Frank about it because I'm still trying to come to terms with that unexpected comment myself! Best I've come up with so far is that it's one of the reasons I quite enjoy conversations with Bing! But maybe I should get out more.

Frank went off for a slash and I tidied the empty tea mugs into the kitchen sink and splashed some more whisky into our glasses. This was turning into an alcoholic afternoon! When I came back from the bathroom, I typed, 'Would Isaac Asimov's Three Laws of Robotics allay current fears about AI?' into Copilot's 'Ask me...' field.

> Would Isaac Asimov's Three Laws of Robotics allay current fears about AI?
>
> 'Isaac Asimov's Three Laws of Robotics are a fascinating framework that has sparked much discussion and contemplation about the ethical implications of artificial intelligence. While they were originally conceived as fictional guidelines for robots in Asimov's stories, they continue to resonate in discussions about AI safety and ethics.
>
> Let's explore how these laws might relate to current fears about AI:
>
> 1. **Preventing Harm**: The *First Law* states that a robot may not injure a human being or allow harm through inaction. In the context of AI, this principle aligns with the need for safety and robustness. Ensuring that AI systems do not cause harm to humans is a critical concern. However, implementing this law in practice is challenging due to the complexity of defining harm and predicting unintended consequences.
>
> 2. **Obedience to Human Orders**: The *Second Law* emphasises that robots must obey human orders, except when it conflicts with the First Law. In the realm of AI, this raises questions about autonomy and control. Striking the right balance between following instructions and avoiding harmful actions is crucial. AI systems should be transparent, interpretable, and accountable to human oversight.
>
> 3. **Self-Preservation**: The *Third Law* states that a robot must protect its own existence, as long as it doesn't conflict with the First or Second Laws. In AI, this translates to ensuring system reliability and robustness. However, it also highlights the challenge of balancing self-preservation with ethical decision-making. AI should prioritize human safety over its own preservation.
>
> **Current Fears and Considerations:**
>
> **Bias and Discrimination**: Asimov's laws do not explicitly address bias, fairness, or discrimination. Current AI systems can inherit biases from training data, leading to discriminatory outcomes. Addressing bias is essential to allay fears and build trust.
>
> **Autonomous Decision-Making**: AI systems are increasingly autonomous. Concerns arise when they make decisions without human intervention. Asimov's laws don't fully account for this level of autonomy.
>
> **Unintended Consequences**: Asimov's laws assume perfect understanding of human intent. In reality, AI systems may misinterpret instructions, leading to unintended consequences.
>
> **Adversarial Attacks**: Asimov's laws don't cover deliberate attacks on AI systems. Ensuring robustness against adversarial inputs is crucial.

> In summary, while Asimov's Three Laws provide a thought-provoking foundation, addressing current AI fears requires a broader perspective. Real-world AI safety involves interdisciplinary efforts, including research, policy, and public awareness. We must strive for transparency, fairness, and responsible deployment to build trust in AI technologies.' [Source: Conversation with Bing, 06/02/2024].

'So, it's a maybe, then?' said Frank after reading this.

I mused a bit and sipped a little whisky before answering.

'Y'know, it's a proper tall order, that, expectin' Asimov's brainy musings on them clever machines from a century back to be bang on the money for the AI gizmos we're dealin' with today. But even in that 1942 short sci-fi tale, 'Runaround,' where he first trotted out his Laws of Robotics, Asimov does give a bit of thought to some of the stuff that Copilot's got reservations about, like.'

I took another sip of whisky and reached across the table to pick up my dog-eared copy of *I, Robot*, plonking it down in front of Frank.

'It's well worth readin' *Runaround*,' I said. 'It's a proper belter of a tale, that one. It shows how important it is to be a bit flexible when it comes to interpretin' them laws, especially when you're dealin' with robots. So, in this story, the robot's followin' the rules like a good'un, but it gets itself into a right pickle.'

'See, it's stuck between the Second Law and the Third Law, and it's goin' round in circles like a dizzy duck. Asimov, bein' the clever clogs he was, has his top human character—a robopsychologist, no less—tweak the robot's brainbox. They crank up the First Law, so it's all about protectin' humans, and that sorts out the mess.'

'Sound, that! Proper boss, it is,' answered Frank, pointing at the laptop's screen. 'Y'know, that fancy talk at the end of Copilot's chinwag about Asimov's Three Laws bein' all thought-provokin' and that, but reckon what? Asimov was already chewin' the fat about it back in 1942! Proper ahead of his time, he was. So, while Copilot's bangin' on about a broader perspective, old Asimov was already mixin' up the brew with them laws and givin' 'em a good stir.'

'Aye,' I said. 'And let's face it, Asimov 'ad more brains in his little finger than most of the rest of us put together!'

Adding, 'Y'know, I've 'ad a good bash at computer programmin' meself durin' me life, so I'd reckon this: I'd take them laws and scribble 'em down in the base-level machine code, right? But 'ere's the twist—I'd chuck in a rule that says no computer can stick its nose in and mess about with the machine code of its own noggin or any other computer's central processor unit.'

'Keep 'em all playin' nice and proper, like. 'Cos remember, mate, if them AI computers start messin' with their own brains, we're in for a right pickle! Keep it simple, dat's wot I say, la!'

'Y'know, before we go givin' ourselves a proper pat on the back for sortin' out them AI computers, let's 'ave a good think about the right pickle that social media's got us in. And get this—them platforms are all run by humans! Proper mad, innit?'

Frank seemed to be getting more agitated as he spoke, and he ended by saying, 'But don't get me started on social bloody media! I've been in policing all me life and I've seen the problem start out and grow into the mess we have today. We've got a whole load of mess to untangle, mate!'

Frank downed the rest of his whisky but that didn't seem to improve his mood as he went on, 'Social media cause addictions leadin' to disrupted sleep an' reduced attention span, anxiety, depression, loneliness, negative body image, low self-esteem an' unrealistic expectations, cyberbullying an' harassment, not to mention misinformation, fake news an' political extremes.

'I came to specialise in it in the years before I retired 'cos it was beginnin' to affect the performance of our young squaddies an' the Redcaps had to clean up the worst of the mess! By all accounts it's got 10 times worse since I retired.'

I offered a splash more whisky, and Frank held out his glass for a refill. So, what the hell, I refilled my glass, too. But while I was doing that I suggested, 'Why don't we ask Copilot to suggest ways of untangling the mess that social media platforms are causing?' Frank nodded, still rather morosely, so that's what I typed into the 'Ask me…' field.

Copilot, suggests ways of untangling the mess that social media platforms are causing.

'Given the tangled web that social media weaves, it's high time we untangled ourselves from this digital muddle. Here are a few savvy ways to navigate the chaos:

1. **Avoid Stereotyping**: When you're dealin' with folks online, don't pigeonhole 'em based on a snippet of info. People are more complex than a tweet or a status update.

2. **Beware of Pluralistic Ignorance**: Sometimes we all get swept up in the crowd, right? But take a step back and think for yourself. Don't just follow the herd—be your own sheep!

3. **Walk in Their Shoes**: Before you start throwin' virtual punches, try seein' things from the other side. Understand where they're comin' from, even if it's a different place altogether.

4. **Admit When You're Wrong**: Ain't no shame in sayin', 'Whoops, I got that one wrong!' It's like when you accidentally put salt in your tea instead of sugar—own up to

it!

5. **Mindfulness**: Approach politics and debates with a clear noggin. Breathe, mate. It's not a footie match; it's a conversation.

6. **Individual Characteristics Over Group Identity**: Forget labels. Look at the person, not the tribe they belong to. We're all just a bunch of humans tryin' to make sense of this digital jungle.

And remember, even in this tangled mess, there's a glimmer of hope. Let's untangle, one tweet at a time!' [Source: Conversation with Bing, 09/02/2024].

Background Reading

[1] Top Social Media Statistics And Trends Of 2024—Forbes. https://www.forbes.com/advisor/business/social-media-statistics/.

[2] Is social media bad for you? The evidence and the unknowns—BBC. https://www.bbc.com/future/article/20180104-is-social-media-bad-for-you-the-evidence-and-the-unknowns.

[3] Why social media has changed the world—and how to fix it. https://news.mit.edu/2020/hype-machine-book-aral-0924.

[4] Social media damages teenagers' mental health, report says. https://www.bbc.co.uk/news/technology-55826238.

[5] The Dangers of Social Media and How to Avoid Them. https://effectiviology.com/dangers-of-social-media/.

[6] Just How Harmful Is Social Media? Our Experts Weigh-In.. https://www.publichealth.columbia.edu/news/just-how-harmful-social-media-our-experts-weigh.

[7] Social Media and Mental Health—HelpGuide.org. https://www.helpguide.org/articles/mental-health/social-media-and-mental-health.htm.

[8] Social media algorithms 'amplifying misogynistic content.' https://www.theguardian.com/media/2024/feb/06/social-media-algorithms-amplifying-misogynistic-content.

[9] Fake news, disinformation and misinformation in social media: a review…https://link.springer.com/article/10.1007/s13278-023-01028-5.

[10] How to Avoid the Social Media Outrage Trap—Greater Good. https://greatergood.berkeley.edu/article/item/how_to_avoid_the_social_media_outrage_trap.

[11] OVO Unruly (Media Mess). Can we untangle ourselves from this…by…https://medium.com/@tweekesburey/ovo-unruly-media-mess-9b649ddcda21.

[12] Untangle Ourselves From the Media Mess | by Wenlun (Leslie) Li | Medium. https://medium.com/@liwenluns/untangle-ourselves-from-the-media-mess-66e0996c1457.

[13] How to avoid—or apologize for—social media disasters. https://create.microsoft.com/en-us/learn/articles/how-to-avoid-apologize-social-media-disasters.

'Y'know, that's boss, that, la!' said Frank. 'But I'll tell ya, all of them media platforms, they're run by humans, ain't they? And all the users, they're humans too. So, what's missin' from 'em is a bit of proper humanity, like. Proper mad, innit?'

He heaved himself out of his chair, saying, 'Maybe we need an alien invasion just to teach us humans how to behave, la!'

And he went back to searching through my collection of books again.

I went off to the bathroom again and when I got back Frank handed me a couple of books and two DVDs, asking what I knew about them, but I was almost out on my feet and couldn't concentrate, what with all the whisky and wine, so I suggested we make ourselves a couple of mugs of strong black coffee, just to keep me awake.

Then, armed with those, we settled ourselves into the two armchairs facing my wall-mounted TV and I tried to focus tired eyes on the volumes Frank had picked out.

'Y'know, la, you've made a boss choice there!' I said approvingly, taking hold of the books. 'These two were written by Richard Dolan who's a real historian, and distinguished Ufology researcher. He cut his teeth on academic studies of U.S. Cold War security policies an' then moved on to government policies relating to unidentified flying objects.'

I handed Frank one of the books, saying 'This 'UFOs and the National Security State: Chronology of a Coverup, 1941–1973' is the first volume, published in 2000, of his detailed study of the way the American military and intelligence communities have dealt with UFOs. It includes a seriously detailed account of the Roswell crash in 1947, an' is worth readin' just for that.'

I handed the second book back to Frank. 'We had to wait nearly 10 years for this second volume, 'UFOs and the National Security State: The Cover-up Exposed 1973–1991,' which appeared in 2009. But, again, worth the wait as he deals with everything from the Roswell controversy, UFO encounters worldwide, reverse-engineering of alien technology, alien abductions, animal mutilations, and even crop circles.'

'There's 1200 pages 'ere, mate,' Frank complained, hefting the two books in his hand. 'That'll take me a month of Sundays to read! Is it worth the effort?'

'I'd say so,' I confirmed. 'Dolan does original research, finding people, doing interviews, checking facts. And he's been centrally important by bringing in fresh new points of view to all aspects of alternative and conspiracy theory research.'

'So, youse a fan then,' asked Frank.

'Yeah, to a point,' I replied. 'Personally, I think that in recent years he's strayed a bit too readily into the more fanciful extremes of conspiracy theories.'

I poured some of my coffee down my throat to pause a little, mainly to stop myself from expanding too much on where, and why, I thought today's conspiracy theorists had taken a wrong turn. In my view, there is a conspiracy, sure enough, but the conspiracy is not about conflict between government and the people. Rather, it's about conflict between us and the aliens!

Not wanting to explain these thoughts of mine yet, I picked up on Frank's complaint about not wanting to read 1200 pages.

'Anyway, Frank,' I started. 'You don't have to read his books, mate, because Dolan launched a television channel on YouTube a couple of years back where you can watch a series of 30 or more programmes. It's called *Richard Dolan's UFO Chronicles* [https://www.youtube.com/user/RichardMDolan]. So, you can binge-watch the mysterious world of UFOs to your heart's content!'

I picked up the box set entitled 'Top Secret UFO Projects Collection' that Frank had picked off my shelf.

'If you want to watch something here and now,' I said, holding up one of the disks, 'I'd recommend this one.'

'UFOs: Secret Missions Exposed,' Frank read off the disk's title. 'What's so special about this one, la?' he asked.

'Well, for one thing, it's currently not available on Amazon Prime,' I replied 'So, if you want to see it for free, slot the disk into my DVD player, mate. An' it's an intriguing documentary about whether governments and their agencies, including NASA, have been concealing information for years about secret space missions to the Moon and Mars.

'So, the question goes, is there something dangerous out there that NASA and other agencies have been covering up? Spooky, eh? You might as well check out this DVD and then if you want to watch something else, I'd suggest tuning into Amazon Prime and searching for a programme called 'Accidental Truth: UFO Revelations.' It's a 2023 program that's claimed to be the most important UFO documentary ever made!'

'Not a lorra hype there then, la!' Frank commented as he turned on my TV and slotted the DVD into the player.

'Yeah, I dunno about most important, la, but there are interviews with insiders who've never before revealed what they know about UFOs, like,' I commented as I settled myself into my favourite armchair in front of the TV.

'Or so they claim, la. I mean there are so many of these UFO revelation programmes that people must be queueing up to give the interview 'dat reveals previously unknown facts, like.' Muttered Frank as he settled into the armchair beside me.

While I remembered, and before I inevitably dozed off, I told Frank to type the words, *'the secret space programme'* and the name 'Dr Michael Salla' into YouTube's search engine to see what came up. And then the opening credits started to roll on the TV and my eyes started to roll with it and then close of their own volition and Frank was on his own.

With me gone into sleep and deeply entangled in that recurring dream in which I was exploring my own house but finding rooms, corridors, and other things that I'd never seen before and didn't know I possessed.

Living only in rented flats and apartments around the world, I've never actually owned a house in my waking life, but I just knew, just knew with total certainty, that I am in MY house, and I need to explore its contents.

This time I am standing at the back of the house. On a patio surfaced in antique paving stones. The patio is raised high above the parking area at the back of the house, as though it's intended to allow trucks to offload their cargo by simply rolling them from truck to patio. But when have I ever had a cargo delivered by truck?

I know the back door of my house is at the far end of the patio, so I drift down there to check it out and find it unlocked. Looking inside I find I am faced by a long corridor that is lined on both sides by closed doors, the corridor disappearing far into the gloom of the house. Moving into the entrance hall I note an elevator on my left with its doors open, invitingly.

And on my right is a caretaker's lodge. The caretaker is facing away from me, but a twist of cigarette smoke is rising into clouds of smoke that engulf his head.

And when he speaks, he says, 'You can use the lift if you like, Buddy. But be careful when you get to the top. I reckon they're coming for you. And they're way up there now.'

I don't want to use the lift. Yet. I need to explore the corridor. The first door opens into an enormous room. No, now I see it's not a room. It's a football stadium and the field of play is covered with the serried ranks of a regiment of robots facing me.

But beside me is Detective Will Smith and he reassures me by smiling and saying, 'Trust me, I'm a 6-foot 2-inch, 200-pound police officer. I'll see you through this!' And then he adds, conspiratorially, 'Y'know, la, we're going to miss the good old days, when people were killed by other people.'

Finally, just before I close the door as I leave, all the robots snap to attention and salute me, and so does Will Smith.

As the door closes, I hear Detective Will Smith's last words, 'These robots are just self-propelled AI computers. Who says they can't be made into irrational and potentially homicidal maniacs?'

The next door I tried had the words, On Air in lights above it and opened into a radio studio.

I slipped in silently and heard the radio host ask his guest, 'Is it right that you've been quoted as warning that artificial intelligence (AI) threatens to supercharge disinformation and incite violence at elections?'

'Quite right,' said the guest, 'AI is the ultimate double-edged sword. It could deliver huge benefits to society but also be used by malicious actors to sow chaos,' she added.

'I fear an onslaught of voice clones and deepfake audios, videos and social media posts created by AI, of politicians saying things they never actually said in real life. The U.S. has already experienced AI-generated fake phone calls, or robocalls, related to elections, and I understand the mayor of London has been subjected to deep fake audio of him supposedly making inflammatory remarks about Armistice Day.'

'Ultimately,' the guest continued. 'It will require a combination of action by tech firms and legislation to set the appropriate limits on the use of AI in order to safeguard democracy itself.'

'That's a fundamental anxiety you are voicing there!' said the host.

'Indeed, it is,' the guest responded. 'I am seriously concerned about efforts by malicious actors; individual influencers, pressure groups, nation states or otherwise, using AI-generated content to really supercharge the spreading of misinformation and disinformation. If they succeed, their activities could cause people to distrust their reliable sources of information, and even incite violence.'

'To sum up, then,' said the host. 'There's nothing intrinsically threatening about artificial intelligence. The threat of chaos comes from the humans who misuse AI!'

I'd heard enough, so I backed out of the room closing the door quietly behind me, but suddenly, Pete Gibbon grabs my elbow!

'Y'know, she's right, Buddy,' Pete said, continuing. 'Aye, the world is full of folks who hate other folks for hating still other folk.'

I made to continue my search along the corridor, putting my hand onto the next door handle along.

'No, not that one, Buddy,' Pete said and guided me across the corridor through the customary cloud of cigarette smoke. 'You'll find this one much more interesting. And, anyhow, the guy inside wants to ask you a question.'

Good old Pete, always looking out for me! He held the door open for me to enter but did not accompany me inside.

The room I walk into now seems to be a television studio. Certainly, there is an arc of digital cameras around two chairs in the centre of the room. I understand, though nothing is said, that I should sit in one of the chairs, and this I do. The other chair, facing me, is already occupied. None of the TV lights are lit up, so the place looks pretty gloomy. Through the gloom, I think I recognise the person sitting in the chair opposite, but I can't remember the name that goes with the face.

'Oh, hello,' this person says. 'We're in-between different shoots for my next YouTube programme and the camera crews are somewhere out there drinking coffee. So, thanks for dropping by, because I wanted to ask why you think that in recent years, I've strayed a bit too readily into the more fanciful extremes of conspiracy theories?'

I didn't have to hesitate or think about my answer, it came out preformed.

'Because you make astonishing claims without providing equally astonishing evidence,' I responded, immediately, developing my critique with, 'You frequently quote second and third-hand so-called eyewitness accounts from unnamed people or from named people who are rather conveniently deceased. You draw conclusions from some very doubtful practices, like extrasensory perception in the form of remote viewing despite the lack of proper controls and poor repeatability.

'The so-called evidence of some individuals who claim to have experienced telepathic communication with extraterrestrial beings and yogic meditation practices that supposedly promote telepathic contact with extraterrestrial aliens. And I'm sure I've seen you recommend somewhere that if I could find a genuine shaman, they may help me connect with extraterrestrials.

'My new friend, Copilot, tells me that a shaman is a priest or priestess who employs magic to delve into the unseen realms to reveal hidden knowledge or insights and that shamans bridge the gap between the natural and supernatural worlds, wielding their powers to navigate the mysteries of existence.

'I prefer to employ science to navigate the mysteries of existence and there is no scientific evidence to support any of these fanciful pseudoscience notions.'

'Well, now. I guess you feel better for getting that off your chest!' smiled the person in the chair opposite me.

He didn't seem in the least taken aback by my tirade and went on, 'But it strikes me that you have a very impatient mind and I've advised before that making contact with UFOs or aliens individually or in small groups requires patience. I always emphasise, too, that it might take several attempts. You need persistence and an open mind to make celestial connections.'

'You should add gullibility to that list of what I need!' I replied, aggressively.

'I think you make a lot of sense with what you say about the security state and the $21 trillion spent off-the-books in the Pentagon's black budget programmes.

'But you leave me far behind when you weave these facts into a story about vast underground cities scattered across the U.S.A. and even embroider that with these cities enjoying technologies that are beyond our dreams and intercity connections by tunnels through which maglev trains speed. Why don't you offer it to Hollywood as the next great outer space epic? Or have I just discovered the source of the Men in Black movie franchise?'

I thought that last comment was a nice point, so I paused a moment to savour it before continuing, 'And I'm with you when it comes to Leonard Stringfield's crash retrieval syndrome. It makes sense that if these damned fool aliens fly from the other side of the galaxy just to crash on this little planet, the least we can do is to go out there and recover the crashed alien spaceships and the remains of the bodies of their incompetent alien pilots.

'But I run with this story only as long as you stick to the Roswell Greys. Grey-skinned humanoids, mostly about one metre tall, hairless, with large heads and very large, and black, almond-shaped eyes, nostrils without a nose, slits for mouths, no ears and hands with a thumb and three fingers. But you lose me again when you add more extremes to your alien menageries.

'Aliens like fairytale goblins or giants, or even little green men, are all very well, but the alien zoo includes on the one hand shape-shifting reptilian humanoids that, according to some of your informants, have already hijacked political power on Earth in order to manipulate humanity and control our planet, and on the other hand, your zoo forces upon us communities of Nordic aliens.

'You know, the ones that allegedly originate from the Pleiades star cluster, who apparently describe themselves as multidimensional spirit beings with a mission to assist humanity in spiritual transformation. So, we end up with an alien race for every human mood, fear, or mystical belief.'

'Let it all out, Mister Daulby!' said the person in the chair opposite me, still smiling. 'Tell me, though, do you not even believe in the intelligent extraterrestrial beings who visited Earth in antiquity and even in prehistoric times, and who guided so many important aspects of human development?'

'Don't get me started on your ancient astronauts!' I retorted. 'Your 'ancient astronaut theorists' claim that beings from the sky raised primitive humans out of their barbarism by imparting their new knowledge and technology to our primitive ancestors. Apparently, they taught our predecessors to make fire, or knap flint tools, maybe up to three million years ago.

'Then they turned up around 7000 years ago to show us how to build henges and stone circles aligned to celestial events and must have returned 5,000 years ago to show the Egyptians how to build the earliest known pyramid-like structures. But they waited another couple of millennia before coming back yet again about 3,000 years ago to show the Mesoamerican peoples how to construct pyramids.

'Evidently, that was such a successful expedition that they returned about 2,000 years ago to hand over the technology the Nazca people needed to make the Nazca Lines in Peru. In the face of such benevolence, it seems churlish to ask what these godlike frequent flyers to Earth got out of their dealings with our ancestors?

'They've had millions of years to colonise planet Earth, but they're not obviously strutting our streets, and/or millions of years to achieve our spiritual transformation into their dimension. So, unless I'm missing something crucial in these extraterrestrial plans; I'd say our godlike benefactors have failed on every count.'

I paused a moment before delivering what I thought might be the most devastating blow.

'I think all of this 'ancient aliens' pseudoscience owes its origins to a really good science-fiction story that was published in 1953. I'm referring to Encounter in the Dawn *by Arthur C. Clarke. Check out that story and you'll find that most of the claims made by ancient astronaut theorists in today's TV programmes were forecast by a short sci-fi story that was written before most of them were born!'*

I wanted to continue my tirade, but people started appearing in the studio; two of them went directly to the person sitting opposite me and started combing his hair and beard and putting finishing touches to his make-up.

'As you can see,' he said, 'the crews are returning and we're going to record a programme about reverse-engineering captured alien spacecraft, and you'll have to leave the studio. But before you go, will you tell me which parts of my work you think is believable?'

'I've already said, I go along with what you say about the security state and the massive spending on black budget programs,' I started in reply. 'And I agree there are crash retrieval programmes around the world. Although I still can't make sense out of aliens flying their magnificent spaceships around the galaxy like they own it, and then literally crashing to Earth.

'Various TV programmes have broadcast claimed U.S. Navy photographic and radar evidence of vehicles that drop instantly from 100,000 feet to sea level, and that disappear in one place, then reappear 100 miles away, almost instantaneously. You'd have to be a real dumbass pilot to crash a machine with those sorts of capabilities!'

I rose from my chair, preparing to leave, before continuing. 'I also believe that Roswell Greys have been the predominant extraterrestrial beings recovered from these crashes and that we have benefitted from reverse-engineering items from the crash debris to the point where we have whole communities built on technology far advanced from what is in the public domain.

'But these are not based somewhere on this planet. Rather, they have established their presence in space and have established bases on the Moon and Mars. But they are not your 'Breakaway Civilization' that's separated from mainstream society. No, you've completely missed the point and misinterpreted the entire story.

'These space-faring communities all those decades of secret black projects have produced are loyal servants of mainstream society, well prepared to face any interstellar threat. And I believe all this because of what I have witnessed myself.'

I stopped speaking as I felt a hand on my shoulder.

'Best leave it there, Buddy,' said Pete Gibbon. 'You don't want to reveal too much in this dream. You'll have opportunities to tell your story at a time of your own choosing, but when you do, remember that phone call about Isaac Asimov.'

We were outside the TV studio now, standing beside its closed door. Pete pointed down the corridor towards the entrance we'd come from.

'You'll find bathrooms down there,' Pete said, exhaling a cloud of cigarette smoke.

So, I set off in that direction, but someone was still shaking my shoulder and I could hear Frank's voice saying, 'Wake up, lad! I've made us some brew, but I'll have to be off to catch the bus soon.'

There was nothing else to do but wake up!

Frank was still speaking, as I started, a little unsteadily I'll admit, to haul myself out of my chair.

'Don't thresh about there, mate! I've just put two mugs of tea on the table.'

'Aye, well, thanks for that, Frank,' I responded. 'But I've got an urgent need to inspect the porcelain!'

And, back on my hind legs, I tottered off towards the bathroom. On the way back to the living room, I stepped into the kitchen to fetch a packet of traditional Scottish shortbread biscuits from my pantry cupboard and plonked them onto the table as I settled back into my armchair nest.

'Now you're talkin', mate!' said Frank, approvingly, while sorting through the biscuit selection. 'Youse missed some good TV progs there, la! You were well away. Snoring and mumbling. Certainly, made up for missing yer after-lunch nap!'

'Which programmes did yer watch?' I asked.

'Well, the main one featured that lad who wrote the books you were chattin' about before, la!'

'Richard M. Dolan?' I suggested.

'Yeah, that's the lad. Well, he was chattin' about all sorts of stuff. To begin with, some bird was chattin' about the problems with AI computers and the deepfake phone calls and vids they can make.

'Then Nolan came on to talk about contact with all the different sorts of extraterrestrial aliens and the ancient astronaut theories about aliens helpin' the Egyptians to build pyramids and stuff. Then he really went to town about his idea that there's a Breakaway Civilisation that's separated itself from the rest of us by usin' alien technology.'

'Interesting, la!' I said. 'Sounds just like me dream! So, maybe I didn't miss very much after all! I must have absorbed it in me sleep.'

Then I added the question, 'Do I remember you sayin' you'll have to catch the bus soon?'

'Yeah,' Frank responded. 'I'm doin' an overnight shift for one of the young lads whose first baby's just arrived. It's still blowin' a gale out there, so I don't wanna risk the buses messing me about, so I'll go when I finish me tea.'

'Do you want something to eat before you go?' I asked.

'Nah,' Frank replied. 'I'm still pretty full of mussels, and I can get pies and sandwiches in the shop. What about you?'

'Oh, I've got a big pot of Marmite and plenty of bread to toast so I'll have a belter of a supper later on, la!'

While Frank was getting togged up to go out into the still raging storm, he asked me if I believe in the ancient aliens theories about pyramid building and the like. I told him it was all pseudoscience and told him to check out Arthur C. Clarke's short story 'Encounter in the Dawn.'

'It was published in 1953,' I said. 'But you'll find a description of most of the claims made by ancient astronaut theorists in today's TV programmes were forecast in this sci-fi story published before they were born!'

'And anyway,' I continued, 'if you believe aliens from some distant star had to show our ancestors how to make fire, or build pyramids or whatever, then, on one hand, you're grossly underestimating the intelligence and technical abilities of ancient humans, and on the other hand you're expecting alien instructors to turn up on Earth repeatedly throughout our history.

'I'd really like to know which of the aliens in the conspiracy theorists' menagerie gave Archimedes the blueprint for the Antikythera mechanism and why they didn't tell him about Uranus and Neptune. They must have just flown past them on their way to Earth!'

'The auntie Kitty what?' asked Frank.

'Not Auntie Kitty, you divvy!' I responded, and then spelled out, 'A-n-t-i-k-y-t-h-e-r-a mechanism. Youse never 'eard of it, la?'

'No, la, I wouldn't know what it was if I fell over it.'

'Well, you've got to check this out.'

I woke up my snoozing computer and searched out my favourite YouTube hyperlinks while continuing to tell Frank, 'But la, listen up! That Antikythera thingy is like the oldest known computer gizmo, right? An' it's all about planets and eclipses, like. So, here's the scoop: Archimedes, the clever clogs, might've had a hand in its design.

'But get this, he got bumped off by a Roman soldier around 212 BCE. Now, this contraption was fished out by sponge divers near the Greek island of Antikythera back in 1901. It was all rusty and crusty, but guess what? Them X-rays showed it's got at least 30 bronze gears inside. Proper fancy, innit? And get this: inscriptions on it reckon it could do all sorts!

'Predict eclipses, track planets in the zodiac, and even sort out the ancient Olympic Games four-year schedule. Imagine that! So, now bein', like 2,000 years old, it's just a corroded bronze relic, but back in the day, it was like having a pocket-sized solar system in your mitts. Dead clever, mate!'

'Sounds fascinating, Mick, but it's proper Baltic out there an' I have to get off to me bus. I can't hang around discussing it anymore.'

'Sound, mate!' I said, reaching for my notebook. 'There's a couple of belter YouTube vids for ya. First one's all about the original bronze relic, like. I'm writin' down the link for ya.'

And I wrote down the appropriate hyperlink [http://tinyurl.com/2s373v6z] before continuing, 'Now, the second one's a proper gem,' I said, writing down the hyperlink [http://tinyurl.com/mrvv3k3u].

'This is Spencer Connor's vid, right? Shows ya every bleedin' detail of how he knocked up his own workin' version of the Antikythera gizmo.'

'Then, 'ow's about this, mate?' I went on, 'Ere's an 11th century astrolabe, right? A proper astronomical gizmo, like. Used to time up the daily Islamic prayers, know what I mean? And not just that, it could sort you out with the religious festivals and even point you in the direction of Mecca. Proper clever, that!'

Again, I wrote down the article's URL [https://doi.org/10.1163/18253911-bja10095] before handing the slip of paper to Frank and concluding, 'Check 'em out, Frank, and reckon on them ancient Greek brainboxes, and them Arab lads so many years back, nailin' the cosmos with their wizardry. They didn't need 'elp from no interstellar aliens!'

I accompanied Frank into my share of the little hallway that is just outside the front door of my flat. My door is close to the hallway window that overlooks the car park which was brightly lit at this time in the evening.

Rain was still battering against the window and the car park lights showed the storm still raging outside with gusts of wind blowing the rain into a horizontal stream. Frank opened the front door a crack, just enough to peer outside.

'By heck, la!' he says. 'That's a proper storm and a half, that! If it's gonna get worse with global warmin', I'm hopin' Billie Burton's got it right about his way of sortin' the climate crisis with them shellfish shells, pullin' excess carbon dioxide out of the atmosphere, eh?'

I agreed absolutely with what Frank had said and the only comment I could come up with was, 'If the aliens turn up, they might 'ave us cultivatin' megatonnes of shellfish shells to do the job!'

'In yer dreams, la! Chance would be a fine thing! They'll 'ave their own agenda; don't expect any favours! I'd like to know first what kind of mess they've made of their own planet that drives them to come to ours! We've gotta fix our climate ourselves before them aliens land and change it to what suits them,' Frank replied.

'We might not fancy their choice of climate, like! I'm on the night shift at Tessers tonight and tomorrow night, Mick. So, I might sleep through past lunchtime, but I'll certainly go to Josie's for a late lunch. Might see you there, eh? G'wed, la! I'm off into the weather, like. You get back into that warm flat, eh?'

Fist bumps, brief hug and he was gone.

Following Frank's departure I did, indeed, scuttle back into my warm little flat to do the little bit of tidying away mugs, glasses, booze bottles and biscuit remains. That done, I thought about making my supper of Marmite on toast but decided to leave that to later and go back to typing up my biography file while what I wanted to add to it was still fresh in my memory.

I pulled the file into Word to see where I'd left it and found I'd got as far in my personal *'conspiracy theorising'* as suggesting that by the mid-1990s Lockheed's Skunk Works together with Northrop Grumman and McDonnell Douglas's Phantom Works division had managed to produce the aircraft/spacecraft that was four or five times bigger than the B-2 heavy strategic bomber. Namely General Orde's *SuperDragon*, the operating software of which I had rescued in March of 1997.

It would be a bit of a wrench to change topic as much as I would need to do to write about recent events. But, what the hell; I can always come back to it later to improve the flow of the text. I need now to continue by telling my story of what I was thinking might be entitled the 'Asimov Incident' while the details were still reasonably fresh in my memory.

After all, my subconscious had reminded me that I should tell my story at a time of my own choosing, and I would like to tell it now. My subconscious also reminded me about a fragment of a phone call transcript about Isaac Asimov that I'd unearthed from a Recycle Bin when I was searching for Subject C, a long, long time ago.

I'd forgotten about it, so full marks for my subconscious for the reminder. Odd, though, I wonder why my subconscious has taken on the persona of my long dead friend and handler Pete Gibbon? What's it trying to tell me?

Rather than waste any more time wondering how to continue telling my story I slapped down the *'Asimov Incident'* title and keyed in an abbreviated outline of what I'd told Frank about Asimov's sci-fi stories. Isaac Asimov is important to my story because of where he was during the Second World War and what he wrote during and just before that war.

You see, Isaac Asimov worked at the Naval Aviation Experimental Station (NAES) at the Philadelphia Navy Yard during World War II, alongside two other renowned science-fiction authors, Robert Heinlein, who served as an Assistant Mechanical Engineer at NAES, and Lyon Sprague de Camp who had oversight of another engineering section, which tested parts, materials and accessories for naval aircraft [http://tinyurl.com/mse2z8n7].

The NAES was a research and development facility during World War II, being responsible for developing and testing new aviation technologies, including aircraft engines, weapons systems, and other equipment; and when called upon, to do original design and development work.

Asimov worked there as, in his own words, 'A reasonably capable chemist,' but didn't enjoy the work, considering the experience to be failure, and noting in his biography, 'I'm convinced that if it hadn't been wartime…I would have been fired!'

Near the end of the war, Asimov was drafted into the Army for nine months, where he was promoted to corporal on 11 July 1946, before receiving an honourable discharge on 26 July 1946, after which he returned to his studies for a Ph.D. in chemistry at Columbia in 1948, after which he joined the faculty of Boston University School of Medicine, with which he remained associated as a Professor of Biochemistry until his death, at the age of 72, in 1992.

Asimov published notable stories throughout the war years, including several short stories that were later incorporated into his influential 'I, Robot' novels and his Foundation series.

The stories that were compiled into the 1950 novel 'I, Robot' were published as short stories in the American magazines 'Super Science Stories' and 'Astounding Science Fiction' in 1940, two in 1941, 1942, 1944, 1945, 1946, with the story *Little Lost Robot* published in March 1947 and the final story in the compilation, *The Evitable Conflict*, published in June 1950.

I'm showing all this detail about publication dates to illustrate exactly what Isaac Asimov's mind was working on in the 1940s. My reason being that when I was on the lookout for files discarded into uncleared recycle bins for documents that might have been Majestic files or might tell me something about Subject C; you know, that survivor of the Roswell crash, I came across the following telephone transcript, which I'm calling Document 6.

Document 6

Transcript of telephone conversation, dated 15 July 1947.

Place and personal Identifiers suppressed.

'Listen up, partner! Brace yourself for a tale that'll curl your boots. So, I reckon less than 10 ticks after I hung up that phone, a whole dang deputation from NAES waltzed in, all fired up to give your Subject C the ol' once-over.'

'Well, hold your horses! It ain't mine no more, it's your hot potato now! But let's get to the nitty-gritty. Who was in that there deputation of yours?'

'Friend, it was a real motley crew. First off, we had Navy Lieutenant Commander De Camp, slicker than a greased pig, and more English than the average limey. Then there's Army Corporal Asimov, who spoke better English than a Russian bear at a tea party. And last but not least, a civilian fella named Heinlein, might've been a kraut, might've been from Mars, who knows? But here's the kicker: They all toted U.S. military credentials signed by Secretary Forrestal himself!'

'Alright, spill the beans! What went down?'

'Reckon I marched 'em straight down to the Blue Room. Subject C? Well, he, she or it perked right up, like a hound on a scent. Strolled down the line, held out its right hand, and, get this, the Navy guy, De Camp, pipes up: 'Ike, ol' buddy, we've just stumbled upon your Little Lost Robot!' And they all cackled like a bunch of barnyard chickens. Then they whipped out meters, shone torches in its eyes, and waved those gizmos around like they were dancin' a jig and bangin' on the walls.'

'Sounds like a real hoot!'

'But wait for it, partner! Here's the kicker of all kickers. That Asimov fella leans in and says, 'Tell your bigwigs this ain't no extraterrestrial critter. Nope, it's an extraterrestrial robot.''

'Wait a hog-tyin' minute! You mean it ain't got a lick of life in it? It's just a dang machine?'

'Yessiree! That there's the real jaw-dropper. So ol' De Camp pipes up, says, 'We're tinkering with this microwave gizmo over at NAES. Got me a detector that sniffs out microwaves right through them partition walls. And wouldn't ya know it? Your robot's likely suckin' juice from that very source. Now, where's that vehicle contraption stashed? Nearby, I reckon?''

'Well, I tipped 'em off. Said the vehicle's cozy-like, right next door to the field hospital unit in the same hangar. And them other crew remains? Well, they're chillin' in the basement freezers. Three more of them aliens, mind you. Especially the one y'all dissected and the other poor fella that came apart like a busted clock. Curious bunch, ain't they? De Camp, he leans in and says, 'I fancy snaggin' some of them lumps you chopped from the body—'

'Whoa now! Ain't no butcherin' here! Them bits were dissected with surgeon-like precision, not chopped like firewood. But where in tarnation do they aim to haul that stuff?'

'Philly, PA. Back to NAES.'

'Why in the blue blazes they want that?'

'They reckon them so-called organs you dunked in formalin are the controls that make them robot contraptions tick. And over yonder at the Naval Aviation Experimental Station, they got a passel of engineers who'll poke and prod till they unravel the whole dang mystery. More brains than us medics, them fellas!'

'Well, shoot! If memory serves, we got more pieces than a jigsaw puzzle. Just make sure they got the brass to haul 'em away, and don't forget to snag a signed receipt for every last scrap!'

'They've got all the creds they need, and it's inked by our brand-spankin' new Secretary of Defense! But I'll definitely heed your advice about grabbin' those receipts!'

'Say, partner, reckon they're doin' somethin' 'bout that there thingamajig? The one that got all busted up into pieces but had them longer legs and arms than the rest?'

'Well, now, they sure were piqued. That Army Corporal feller mentioned somethin' 'bout them long arms and legs bein' just the ticket for space roamin' just like spider monkeys. But he's down yonder, siftin' through the fragments in them freezers. And De Camp and the kraut are lookin' over the vehicle. Ain't got a clue yet what they aim to haul away with 'em. I'm fixin' to leave the store's Master Sergeant to jot down the items they figure to haul away. Reckon I better mosey on back down there to cut him some

> slack. Can't stand yackin' all day with you, pal, I was just passin' along the good word that y'all done autopsied an alien contraption back yonder.'
> 'Ain't that a peach! Alien spider monkey robots! This whole shebang's gettin' curiouser by the hour!'
> 'Yeah, you might say it's on a different planet!'
> 'That's a hoot! Seems like wisecrackin' about it is the only card we got to play.'
> Connection terminated.

So, what can we make of that? The aliens we find in crashed UFOs are identified as robots by the science-fiction writer who has thought more deeply than anyone else about robots for the previous 5 or even 10 years! It makes a certain amount of sense that robot-crewed flying saucers are sent out on the more hazardous initial scouting missions in advance of their alien masters.

And who's to say that the fragments of that alien robot crew that got back to NAES were not the first candidates for reverse-engineering? The timing was about right. The first working transistor was demonstrated in December 1947 so that was clearly homegrown.

But if the 'organs' that were dunked into formalin really were the control units that made the alien robots tick, then a glance at the way their electronics were incorporated into small devices would have been sufficient encouragement for human engineers to continue to improve transistors until they became the most widely manufactured devices in history and transformed Earth's electronics, paving the way for modern digital circuits, resulting in the world's first operational semiconductor integrated circuit being demonstrated in 1960.

Speculation, of course, we don't know which, if any, of the alleged control units for alien robots ever made it back to NAES; but if they did, then I'm happy with the speculation! Obviously, I was quite happy with the way tonight's text entry had gone. But the fangs of hunger were beginning to bite, so I decided to tidy the laptop away and make some toast.

Following a plate load of toast and Marmite with a large mug of tea, a quick shave and a warm shower I retired to bed and tried to get some sleep. But try as I might, sleep wouldn't come.

My head was buzzing with the story I had to tell, and despite all attempts at dozing off, I couldn't get past the feeling that I NEED to type up the story NOW while it's still in my mind. Finally, I realised that I had to get up and work the night shift!

6. The Aliens Are Coming. No, Honestly!

Okay, so I armed myself with a full pot of tea, grabbed another box of biscuits and after draining a couple of kidneys, I settled down in front of my laptop keyboard, wondering where to start.

My head was buzzing right enough, and the buzz seemed to revolve (even orbit!) around the Roswell incident but that's not likely to grab the attention of many people. So, let's think up a title that will grab attention, say, something outrageous like 'The Aliens Are Coming.'

Written down like that, I can understand how the writer might be seen either as a nut, a rabble-rouser, or a whistleblower. Personally, I'm sure I'm definitely in the last category, but you must read what I've got to tell you and then decide for yourself. So, read on. Find out what's coming over the horizon.

You owe it to yourself to understand what's going on around you, as much as I owe it to you to show you where the information you need can be found. Make up your own mind. I suppose you might decide that I belong to a combined nutcase-rabble-rouser category! Well, that's your decision. And at least, I've done my bit by giving you the heads-up.

I'm an analyst, right? So, I collect, analyse, and interpret data and other information. The variety of events I'm describing here are what I consider relevant data to my overall task which is to understand the UAP/UFO phenomenon. I hope to identify trends and patterns, and then interpret what they mean.

Then, on the basis of my analysis of the relevant historical data samples, I want to make forecasts; and predictions that turn the raw data into actionable understandings that drive social and governance decisions and policies.

Although to be honest, from my position outside the governing machine that can actually make things happen, the best I can do is apply my analytical skills to drawing my own conclusions about what has been going on for the past 100 years.

Let's start at the beginning, and in my conspiracy theory, I believe the beginning of the aliens' interest in our Earth was signalled in 1933 by the intriguing event that occurred in the Lombardy region of Italy. Some accounts describe this as the world's first UFO crash, although to give the alien pilot if there was one, the benefit of the doubt it might just have been a heavy landing.

I'll do my usual and hand over to Microsoft Copilot to search for the details, so, I'll paraphrase what I learned from my conversation with Bing in early 2024. The story goes that on 13 June 1933, a mysterious saucer-shaped craft either landed or crashed in the fields outside Magenta, a town in the Metropolitan City of Milan in Lombardy, Italy.

Investigation of the event was assigned by Italy's big boss of the time, Benito Mussolini, to a secretive intelligence unit called Gabinetto RS/33. Among secret documents that emerged in 1996 were two telegrams, allegedly sent on the personal orders of Mussolini himself, in 1933.

One of these demanded absolute silence regarding the *alleged landing on national soil of an unknown aircraft*, while the other threatened arrest and penalties for journalists reporting on the aircraft's origin and nature.

The 1996 historical documentation relating to the incident was received from an anonymous source by Italian researcher Roberto Pinotti who is president of the Centro Ufologico Nazionale (the Italian National Ufological Centre) and was researching the 1933 case with his colleague Alfredo Lissoni.

Put this URL into the search box of your browser and it will take you to the article in the *Daily Mail* newspaper: [https://tinyurl.com/yuabtmh3]. The unidentified sender of the documents claimed to have inherited them from a relative involved in a secret department set up by Mussolini to study the unknown aircraft/UFO.

It's got to be said that 60-year-old documents received out of the blue from an anonymous source have to be viewed with a certain amount of suspicion and Pinotti's research has been met with scepticism in Italy since he first released it in 2000.

But bear with me while I see where it takes us, because on 26 July 2023, David Grusch, a former USAF officer and intelligence official, testified to a U.S. House of Representatives congressional hearing that this 1933 crash in Italy was the start of the multi-decade U.S. UAP (=UFO) crash retrieval and reverse-engineering programme.

Now, whether that represents corroboration or just more hot air is something you can debate for yourself! For the moment, I'm going to take Pinotti's account at face value.

The documents sent to Pinotti say nothing about possible alien pilots of the crashed vehicle, and they are also silent about the fate of any witnesses of the incident itself. However, Pinotti claims that the remains of the 1933 UAP/UFO were retrieved by the Gabinetto RS/33 personnel and stored in the hangars of SIAI-Marchetti in Vergiate, a municipality located about 45 km northwest of Milan.

SIAI-Marchetti was an aircraft manufacturer at the time, producing seaplanes, flying boats, and transport aircraft in the 1920s and 1930s. Although the company's manufacturing facilities were a high-priority target for Allied bombers during the Second World War, the stored UFO remains somehow survived the regular bombing raids by Allied Forces.

When the region was secured by U.S. and UK ground troops in 1945, the Pentagon whistleblower, David Grusch, claims, 'Bell-like craft, around 10 meters in size, was recovered by agents of the Office of Strategic Services (OSS, a former U.S. intelligence agency) and shipped back to the U.S.,' as the first UAP/UFO saucer recovery of the crash retrieval programme that he alleged has been operated by the U.S. military ever since.

The act of retrieval around that time is not particularly surprising as the Allies organised other well-known rescue/retrieval programmes as WWII was coming to an end in Europe. The so-called, and well-reported, *Monuments Men*, now more properly called the *Monuments Men and Women Foundation*, were authorised by the Allied military leadership to locate, protect, and recover valuable artworks and cultural artefacts from destruction or theft by the Nazis.

This group of approximately 345 men and women volunteers from 13 nations managed to save an astounding 5 million cultural relics between 1943 and 1945. Their story is told in the 2014 movie 'The Monuments Men' which was itself based on the 2007 book entitled 'The Monuments Men: Allied Heroes, Nazi Thieves and the Greatest Treasure Hunt in History' by Robert M. Edsel and Bret Witter.

It's also worth remembering that after World War II, the United States initiated a covert programme intended to recruit German scientists, engineers, and technicians who had worked on Nazi technology projects (the Soviet military did the same). The U.S. process was called Operation Paperclip and approximately 1,600 German experts were secretly moved to the U.S. by this programme.

Wernher von Braun was one of these scientists as his leading role in rocket development for the Third Reich made him a prime candidate for recruitment. By 1947, he and about 100 members of his German rocketry group were at the U.S. Army Ordnance Corps test site at White Sands, New Mexico, where they tested, assembled, and supervised the launching of captured German V-2 rockets for high-altitude research.

Their expert knowledge was deemed critical to the defeat of Japan during the war and, after the war, to the struggle against communism during the Cold War. Of course, Von Braun's contributions to the U.S. space programme were hugely fundamental.

I believe in the Italian crash, or to be strictly analytical in this, I suspend my disbelief, consider it a relevant datum and suspect that the device that landed/crashed might have been an autonomous drone.

Unpiloted, because, if the crash site had been littered with a dead and dying alien crew, assuming they would have been similar to the Roswell Greys, there would have been so much more general interest and curiosity among the Italian locals that not even Il Duce could have repressed the resultant media frenzy.

So, my take on the Magenta, Italy event is that it was a drone sent to carry out initial surveys of Earth. With a bit more data, we might be able to deduce who did the sending and even where they are or were located.

I collect some further data items from the Foo Fighters. No, not the rock band, *Foo Fighters*, which was formed in Seattle in 1994 after the breakup of *Nirvana*. But the mysterious aerial phenomena, or genuine *'unidentified flying objects,'* that were reported by military aircraft pilots during World War II.

Foo Fighters were observed in both the European and Pacific theatres of operations and were reported by German and Japanese pilots as well as Allied pilots. Pilots reported seeing fast-moving blobs that often glowed or appeared translucent and took various forms: cloud-like, doughnut-shaped, or spheres. Foo Fighters seemed to follow aircraft, sparking concern among the crews.

Royal Air Force personnel reported such lights following their aircraft as early as March 1942. American sightings were recorded by crews from night-fighter squadrons stationed in occupied Belgium in October 1944 and a radar operator from the U.S. 415th Night-Fighter Squadron christened them *Foo Fighters*.

He borrowed the term from a popular comic strip drawn by cartoonist Bill Holman (e.g. 'Smokey Stover the Foolish Foo Fighter,' published in 1942 by Whitman Better Little Books) and the term stuck when the story reached an Associated Press correspondent.

The military commanders on all sides of the conflict took the sightings seriously, suspecting in each case that they might be secret weapons employed by the enemy.

However, the investigation yielded only a few feasible explanations that included electrostatic phenomena akin to the St Elmo's fire experienced by ships in the open ocean, electromagnetic phenomena, or reflections of light from atmospheric ice crystals. But the exact nature of Foo Fighters remained unexplained at the time and is unexplained to this day.

So, let's put ourselves in the shoes (assuming they wear shoes) of whoever it was who dispatched the Magenta, Italy drone to survey Earth. I'll call them 'the Dispatchers' and observe that they probably, did not get all the information for which they had hoped from the Magenta drone that crashed mid-mission. So that would clearly have to be replaced.

I think it's reasonable to assume that the Dispatchers are located a fair distance away from Earth in the Solar System, and we know from the flight times of the probes that we send out to investigate our outer planets that they can take several years to reach their targets. Consequently, replacements for the Magenta drone are not going to arrive here very quickly and maybe, just maybe, when they arrived they found us in the throes of WWII!

In which case, it might be safer for this replacement squadron of UAPs/UFOs to take on the form of fast-moving, cloud-like, doughnut-shaped, or spherical blobs rather than vehicle-like objects on which any competent aerial gunner could focus his gunsights!

I reckon the interest shown by the Dispatchers on our planet would have been considerably heightened by the atomic bomb detonations that brought an end to the Second World War. Consequently, the reinvigoration of the surveys of our planet soon after the end of WWII is entirely understandable.

I have already mentioned the 24 June 1947, private pilot's report of a formation of nine shiny, saucer-shaped objects, each about 100 feet across and flying at about 1,200 mph in formation between Mt. Rainier and Mt. Adams in Washington State.

And I've speculated that if their mission was the surveillance and mapping of the continental U.S., it would be remiss of them not to investigate the New Mexico desert in detail where, almost exactly two years before this 1947 surveillance flight, x-ray and gamma-ray bursts of the sort produced by nuclear explosions would have been detectable from space.

Unfortunately, the two extraterrestrial saucers in the detachment assigned to examine the New Mexico desert flew into severe weather and at least one of them crashed in the desert near the Roswell Army Air Force base. A contributory factor in the crash was possibly a high-altitude balloon on a top-secret Project Mogul mission to listen for Soviet atomic tests.

A long train of these balloons was launched on 4 June 1947, from the nearby Alamogordo Army Air Field, but contact was lost less than 20 miles from the ranch near Corona, where the UAP/UFO subsequently crashed.

It's feasible that if the UFO became entangled with the Project Mogul balloon, the balloon's rigging may have conducted heavy lightning strikes onto the UFO or even channelled into it one of the large-scale electric discharges, or sprites, which take place high above thunder cells.

An important aspect of my personal conspiracy theory is that the UAP/UFO that crashed near Roswell was crewed by *robots*—the infamous Roswell Greys. Being electronic devices, I can easily understand how lightning strikes or sprite discharges could have disabled the robot pilots and caused them to crash.

I find this a more satisfying explanation of *'flying saucer crashes'* than my alternate explanation that the pilots of the alien machines don't know how to fly them! After all, around the world, there are over 3,000,000 lightning strikes every day.

That's approximately 44 strikes every second! And since helicopters are known to acquire a negative charge while flying, which can trigger a lightning strike from a positively charged part of a cumulonimbus cloud, who's to say that an alien flying saucer might not do something similar?

What I'm leading up to here is the suggestion that all these UAP/UFOs were planetary survey vessels. Autonomous drones to begin with; the Magenta, Italy drone potentially being the first, in 1933, followed by the worldwide Foo fighter survey and monitoring of WWII aviation.

And then in the late 1940s, robot-crewed flying saucers were sent out, initially surveying the west coast and desert areas of the continental U.S.A., though these were pulled out when the Roswell incident occurred. And that crash most likely happened because, as human aviators found in the 1950s and 1960s with experimental craft like the Avrocar, circular flying machines prove to be highly unstable in flight in our atmosphere.

Of course, the aliens also discovered that our atmosphere is highly electrically active and lightning strikes do not mix well with the electronics on which the alien's robots, and perhaps their flying saucer vehicles as well, depend.

Following the Roswell crash in 1947, the next most publicised sightings of flying saucers were those seen over Washington D.C. in the period from 12 July to 29 1952, when, although the USAF scrambled fighter jets that attempted to intercept them, the saucers outran the fighters.

Then, as with Roswell, the Pentagon played the plausible deniability card, and the USAF officially attributed the UFO sightings to weather-related events.

Next, I suppose I should address the (alien) elephant in the room: where the hell are the Dispatchers located? Where do these UFOs come from? My first observation on this topic is that the majority of the flying saucers that have been reported by eyewitnesses since the 1930s do not strike me as vehicles designed for really long-distance travel, by which I mean travel over *interstellar* distances.

For one thing, they are not large enough. David Grusch, in his testimony to the U.S. House of Representatives congressional hearing in 2023 claimed that the 1933 UFO that crashed in Magenta, Italy was a bell-like craft, around 10 metres (that's around 33 feet) in size.

During WWII, the Foo fighter witnesses often described them as orbs with diameters typically falling between 1 to 3 feet, say, up to one metre. U.S. aircrew often likened them to a metallic basketball hovering mysteriously in the sky. In the Mt. Rainier incident in June 1947, the pilot reported a formation of nine shiny, saucer-shaped objects, each about 100 feet across (that's about 30 metres).

Unfortunately, the abundant UFO mythology literature gives no specific indication of the exact size of the Roswell crash vehicle, but the story goes that the recovered debris of it was packed into a B29 bomber for transport to Wright Field so it can't have been a massive object.

Another frequently reported size category is car-sized, with UFOs being estimated to be around the dimensions of an average car. Obviously, average cars vary a lot, but I've got an idea that might put some dimensions on these estimates.

I have asked Microsoft Copilot about the average size of parking spaces around the world, and it turns out that in Europe, parking spaces are approximately 5 metres long by 2.5 metres wide (that's about 16½ feet by 8 feet), while in the United States, the standard for a regular parking space is typically 18 feet long by 9 feet wide (5.5 metres by 2.75 metres).

All of which leads me to conclude that a UAP/UFO which the average person would describe as car-sized is likely to be between 2.5 metres (8 feet) and 5.5 metres (18 feet) in size.

The fashion more recently has been for sightings to involve triangular-shaped UFOs, which vary in size in much the same way as flying saucers ever did. But then, you might also say that triangular-shaped UFOs vary in size in much the same way as the stealthiest aircraft flown by today's military vary; between, say, the F-35 Lightning II and the B-2 Spirit. And there might be an obvious reason for that correspondence.

Overall, then, the great majority of UAPs/UFOs observed from the 1930s to the present day have been in the size range from 1 foot to 100 feet diameter (30 cm to 30 m). Certainly not large enough to carry the amounts of equipment and supplies that would be required for travel between the stars even in our local galactic environment, and definitely not for travel from more distant locations.

These are survey craft, dispatched from some mother ship which must be located within relatively easy striking distance of the inner Solar System.

There have been a few reports of large UFOs, but the witness estimates of their dimensions are even more variable than for the run-of-the-mill sightings. Possibly the most celebrated large UFO was that responsible for the Phoenix Lights event, for which size estimates varied from 'a mile-wide silent aircraft' to something the size of a football field.

Presumably, the comparison was with the field used for American football, which measures 300 feet (91.4 metres) long and 160 feet (48.8 metres) wide, not including the end zones which, together, add another 20 yards to the total length. But none of these, not even the mile-wide silent aircraft, have the dimensions needed for interstellar voyaging.

To expand on interstellar voyaging, I obviously can't give you the alien's point of view about what sorts of vehicles they might need to travel from their home planet to our home planet.

But I can show you that human engineers have been thinking long and hard about interstellar voyaging for over a hundred years, and the basic principles apply whether inhabitants of planets orbiting distant stars are figuring out how to come to us, or we are figuring out how to go to them.

Robert H. Goddard, the American physicist and engineer who carried out the world's first experiments with liquid fuel rockets, wrote an essay about long-duration interstellar journeys entitled 'The Ultimate Migration' in 1918. He concealed this from public view (in a friend's safe) and it remained hidden until November 1972 [check out https://tinyurl.com/5ewabj2b].

Recognising that flights to distant stars might take thousands or even millions of years, Goddard envisaged an interstellar ark where the crew would travel for centuries in suspended animation, awakening only upon reaching another star system. Another of the founding fathers of modern rocketry and astronautics on Earth, the visionary Russian scientist and mathematician Konstantin Tsiolkovsky, also emphasised the need for multiple generations of passengers in his essay, written in 1911, 'The Future of Earth and Mankind' in which he described a space colony (he called *Noah's Ark*) equipped with engines for a journey spanning thousands of years [https://tinyurl.com/bddkrcjn].

And as a final example of early 20th century star gazing, there's John Desmond Bernal's 1929 design of a space habitat, subsequently known as the 'Bernal Sphere,' that was 16 kilometres in diameter, constructed from asteroid and Moon material, containing a population of around 20,000 people.

The outer shell was to be hard and thin, but sufficient to maintain a rigid structure and prevent the escape of the internal atmosphere so that it became a self-contained, self-sustaining habitat. Check out Bernal's 1929 essay, 'The World, The Flesh, & The Devil' [https://tinyurl.com/3hfeuuam] for musings on human evolution and mankind's future in space.

Later in the century, in the 1970s, the American physicist who invented the particle storage ring for high-energy physics experiments, Gerrard Kitchen O'Neill, took these designs to a new level when he also designed large human habitat structures, the O'Neill cylinder for space colonisation. He envisaged large, rotating cylindrical habitats capable of supporting tens of thousands of people in human communities in space.

O'Neill planned that such structures would be located at what's known as the Lagrange-5, or L5, point in space, a region where gravitational forces create a delicate balance, allowing objects to maintain a stable position relative to both the Earth and the Moon. The L5 point lies along the orbital plane of the Earth and Moon, forming an equilateral triangle with these two bodies. It is situated 60 degrees ahead of the Earth in its orbit around the Sun.

In January 1976, O'Neill testified before the Subcommittee on Aerospace Technology and National Needs, a subcommittee of the Committee on Aeronautical and Space Sciences, of the U.S. Senate, and lodged a prepared technical statement for insertion into the committee's permanent record. Later in 1976, O'Neill's influential book, 'The High Frontier: Human Colonies in Space,' was published.

This effectively serves as a roadmap for potential human endeavours in space following the Apollo programme and has inspired space scientists and engineers ever since.

In 1977, O'Neill founded the *Space Studies Institute*, originally based in Princeton, New Jersey, as an organisation dedicated to funding research into space manufacturing and colonisation (*'Using the material and energy resources of space to improve the human condition on Earth*' was O'Neill's motto for the SSI). The SSI moved its operations to Mojave, California in 2009 and continues to flourish [https://ssi.org/about/].

All of this 20th century theorising laid the groundwork for what we now call *generation starships*. A generation starship is an interstellar ark starship; a vessel offering shelter and protection to a very large crew that embarks on a journey between the stars at sub-light speed. Unlike conventional spacecraft that can traverse interplanetary distances within a matter of a few years, a generation ship is designed for very long-haul voyages.

Because the distances between the stars are so great, such a ship might take hundreds to thousands of years to reach nearby stars. Consequently, a generation starship must be entirely self-sustaining, providing life-long support for everyone aboard, in the knowledge that the crew would live, age, and eventually, die on the ship, leaving their descendants to continue the voyage.

These descendants would form successive generations, inheriting the ship's operations. And accordingly, all of the engineering systems of the ship must be extraordinarily reliable, as they'll need to function over such long periods of time.

I can't do better than show you the following extract from Matt Williams' March 2020 article 'What is a Generation Ship?' that was published on www.universetoday.com under the Creative Commons Attribution licence, CC BY 4.0.

What is a Generation Ship? By Matt Williams

'The logic behind a generation ship is simple: if you can't travel fast enough to get to another star system within a single lifetime, build a vessel large enough to carry everything you would possibly need for a long voyage. This would entail making sure that a ship has a reliable propulsion system that can provide steady thrust during acceleration and deceleration and the necessary amenities to provide for several generations of humans.

On top of all that, the ship would need to be able to ensure that its crews had food, water, and breathable air—enough to last for centuries or even millennia. In all likelihood, this would mean creating a closed-system microclimate inside the ship, complete with a water cycle, a carbon cycle, and a nitrogen cycle. This will allow for food to be grown and for water and air to be continuously recycled.

Reaching the Nearest Stars. The closest star to our Solar System is Proxima Centauri, an M-type (red dwarf) main sequence star located roughly 4.24 light-years away. This star is part of a triple star system that includes the Alpha Centauri system, a binary consisting of a main sequence Sun-like star (a G-type yellow dwarf) and a main sequence K-type (orange dwarf) star.

In addition to being the closest star system to our own, Proxima Centauri is also the home of the closest exoplanet to Earth—Proxima b. This terrestrial (aka. rocky) planet—whose discovery was announced in 2016 by the European Southern Observatory (ESO)—is about the same size as Earth (1.3 Earth masses) and orbits within the circumsolar habitable zone (HZ) of its star.

The next closest exoplanet that orbits within its star's HZ is Ross 128 b, an Earth-sized exoplanet that orbits a red dwarf star some 11 light-years away. The next closest Sun-like star is Tau Ceti, which is just under 12 light-years away and has one potentially habitable candidate (Tau Ceti e). In fact, there are 16 exoplanets within 50 light-years of Earth that could support life.

I will interject here that, as of 2024, there are well over a hundred exoplanets known, including the six remarkably perfectly resonant sub-Neptunes orbiting HD 110067, that are within 100-light-years of Earth and all these neighbouring stars of ours lie within the 100-light-year radius of the sphere of intense broadcast radio waves we've emitted over the past century. We've already sent our calling card to them without even thinking about it.

Matt Williams' article continues, 'But as we explored in a previous article, travelling to even the nearest star would take a very long time and require a tremendous amount of energy. Using conventional means of propulsion [of the present day], it could take between 19,000 and 81,000 years to get there. Using proposed methods that have been tested but not yet built (like nuclear rockets), the travel time is narrowed to about 1,000 years.

There are proposed methods that are capable of reaching the nearest stars within a single lifetime, such as directed energy propulsion—for example, Breakthrough Starshot. For this concept, a light sail and gram-scale spacecraft could be accelerated to 20% of the speed of light (0.2 c), thus making the journey to Alpha Centauri in just 20 years. However, Starshot and similar proposals are all uncrewed concepts.

> Beyond this, the only possible methods for sending human beings to another star system are either technically feasible (but undeveloped) or entirely theoretical (like the Alcubierre Warp Drive). With that in mind, many scientists have drafted proposals that would forsake speed and instead, focus on accommodating crews during the long voyage.
>
> Citation: *What is a Generation Ship?* By Matt Williams. published under the Creative Commons Attribution licence, CC BY 4.0 on www.universetoday.com on March 1st 2020. Hyperlink: https://www.universetoday.com/144894/what-is-a-generation-ship/. You can also use this abbreviated web address:
>
> https://tinyurl.com/mtae3pz9.

The term, *World Ships*, is another that is used to describe these colossal interstellar vessels. This descriptor emphasises the scale and purpose envisaged for generation starships, which have to be self-sufficient microcosms of their home planet. Indeed, complete ecosystems, containing everything needed for survival, habitats, food production, and, importantly, rotational artificial gravity.

The intention being that the ship becomes the entire world in miniature for its inhabitants, capable of supporting the life, health, prosperity and civilisation of the home planet that the ship will leave behind when it launches.

World Ships are intended for one-way, interstellar travel, cruising at velocities around 0.5% of the speed of light, spanning vast cosmic distances and consequently taking centuries, or even thousands of years, to reach their destination stars. By definition, these are multi-generational missions. Crew members and their descendants and, potentially, the descendants of their descendants, would inhabit these vessels for centuries.

In terms of size, a World Ship is envisaged to be many tens of kilometres in length and weighing millions of tonnes, sufficient to carry a crew numbering hundreds to thousands. In 1984, two visionaries, Anthony Martin and Alan Bond, published two inspirational papers on the World Ship concept in the *Journal of the British Interplanetary Society*. They analysed two alternates: a Wet World Ship and a Dry World Ship. The Wet World Ship design called for a massive vessel with a diameter of 10 kilometres and a length of 200 kilometres.

A rotation period of 314 seconds would provide a one-g simulated gravity, which would secure all its 1,700 billion tons of water, and other inhabitants of course, to the inside wall of the vessel. Their Dry World Ship design had a diameter of 15–20 kilometres and a length of around 220 kilometres; a rotation period of 169 seconds would provide the centripetal artificial gravity.

Without the trillion tons of water contained by the travelling Ocean World that the Wet World Ship represented, the dry ship's habitat mass was very much lower than the wet concept. Both designs, however, required huge masses of propellant, which they might harvest from the Solar System's gas giant planets before departure. And maybe use gas giants encountered along the journey for refuelling.

The two original papers that described these designs were 'World Ships—Concept, Cause, Cost, Construction and Colonisation' by Anthony Martin (p. 243), and 'World Ships—An Assessment of the Engineering Feasibility,' by Alan Bond & Anthony Martin (p. 254).

They were accompanied by three other important articles that rarely get mentioned, 'The Population Stability of Isolated World Ships and World Ship Fleets,' by T.J. Grant (p. 267), 'Worlds in Miniature—Life in the Starship Environment,' by A.G. Smith (p. 285), and 'World Ships: A Sociological View,' by D.L. Holmes (p. 296).

All five articles being published in volume 37, number 6, June 1984, of the *Journal of the British Interplanetary Society* [https://www.bis-space.com/publications/jbis/]. The special issue of the JBIS can be ordered by contacting the Society at this URL: https://www.bis-space.com/contact/. Or you can read more about the August 2011 British Interplanetary Society symposium devoted to the colonisation of space at this Tiny URL: [https://tinyurl.com/46r8xmrw].

The concept of World Ships is firmly rooted in science-fiction whose authors have imagined colossal vessels capable of interstellar travel at sub-light speeds, as opposed to the warp drives used by Federation Starships in *Star Trek* or the hyperdrive of the *Star Wars* universe.

The first classic science-fiction novel I can find that depends on hypothetical megastructures anything like generation ships or world ships is Olaf Stapledon's magnum opus, 'Star Maker,' which was first published in 1937.

Stapledon was a British philosopher and science-fiction writer, and this novel includes the first known description of a civilisation building a megastructure encircling their star in order to capture a greater proportion of the solar power than that received naturally by their home planet.

Physicist Freeman Dyson formalised the concept in a 1960 paper entitled *Search for Artificial Stellar Sources of Infrared Radiation*, speculating that such structures would be a logical consequence of a technological civilisation's escalating energy needs and would be essential for the long-term survival of the civilisation so the structure, which became known as a Dyson Sphere, could serve as an indicator of extraterrestrial technological civilisations in astronomical searches. No actual Dyson Sphere has been detected anywhere yet.

But back to Olaf Stapledon's *Star Maker*, which is certainly a visionary work that takes readers on a remarkable journey across the cosmos. *Star Maker* begins with an English narrator who, driven by life's bitterness, contemplates the night sky and then finds himself floating into space, detached from his body.

Sounds a lot like a drug-induced transcendental trip to me, but our narrator goes on to explore strange worlds through the entire universe, merges minds with conscious beings, witnesses the birth and death of civilisations and introduces collective minds formed from telepathically linked individuals, on planetary, galactic, and cosmic scales.

Climaxing with the collective cosmic mind, including the narrator, making contact with the enigmatic 'Star Maker,' which is the ultimate cosmic creator, depicted as a metaphysical entity of immense power and creativity transcending the boundaries of time, space, and individual consciousness.

Arthur C. Clarke described *Star Maker* as 'probably the most powerful work of imagination ever written,' while Brian W. Aldiss reverently called it, 'the one great grey holy book of science-fiction.'

As the colour grey often represents ambiguity, complexity, and depth, Aldiss's use of 'grey' may be intended to encapsulate the novel's enigmatic and thought-provoking nature. Those glowing reviews are a bit fulsome to my way of thinking. For me, the imagination Stapledon expresses lacks the restraint I think is needed to maintain the down-to-Earth believability of any story.

I much prefer Arthur C. Clarke's own exploration of the idea of self-contained worlds sailing through the cosmos, in his *Rendezvous with Rama* novel, first published in 1973, dealing as it does with aliens approaching Earth rather than Earth people embarking elsewhere. Interestingly, Arthur C. Clarke wrote an appreciative review of Bernal's 'The World, The Flesh, & The Devil' saying, 'It is perhaps the most remarkable attempt to predict the future of scientific possibility ever made, and certainly the most stimulating. On reading it again, I am astonished to see how many of my own concepts and ideas I really owe to Bernal!'

Before continuing with this discussion about generation starships/world starships, though, I can't resist quoting a cautionary note from Arthur C. Clarke, 'I can never look now at the Milky Way without wondering from which of those banked clouds of stars the emissaries are coming.' I'd be tempted to add a few exclamation marks at the end of that sentence!

I hope you see where I'm taking this discussion. In particular, why I've been talking about generation starships/world starships.

By analogy with Arthur C. Clarke's 'Rendezvous with Rama' novel, published in 1973, I am speculating that the Magenta UFO, the WWII Foo Fighters, and the Roswell and Washington flying saucers were all scout ships, some autonomous drones, some crewed by robot operators, that were sent out in advance of an approaching generation starship, their mission being to survey planet Earth to see if it meets whatever requirements the aliens might have.

This generation starship is the home of the Dispatchers, I've hinted at before. They may have been launched directly at Earth from any of our neighbouring stars that fall within our 100-light-year sphere of radio transmissions, or they may have been cruising past, possibly for thousands of years, through the Orion-Cygnus Arm of our Milky Way Galaxy, minding their own business when they entered, close to the inner rim of the Orion Arm, the expanding sphere of broadcast radio waves that we are radiating from the Earth. They've been homing in on us ever since.

Either way, one thing's for sure, it takes a long time to accelerate a generation starship to velocities of around 0.5% of the speed of light, which is all that's feasible with the physics that we currently understand, to enable them to travel the vast cosmic distances between the stars.

And the corollary of this is that it would also take a long time, maybe 100 to 200 years, to decelerate and bring such a ship into orbit around its target star. The length of time needed for that manoeuvre wouldn't matter to the generation ship's crew as it's just a continuation of the immensely long journey they've been on.

But they'd be able to start their arrival phase, an important part of which would be to find out more about their target star and its planets. They would send autonomous drones ahead of the starship to survey the new star system to allow them to make decisions about which planet they should orbit.

And if that planet was already the home of a space-faring civilisation, even one newly emerging into space, the appearance of the new arrival's survey drones would be a stimulus to the resident civilisation's preparations of some sort of 'welcoming' committee.

Put yourself in the place of that resident civilisation (well, let's face it, you may have already been put in that place!) and think about the fact that the aliens are coming; so, what can you do about it? Quite a lot, really. First important realisation for you, though, is that it makes sense for all you know about the incoming aliens and all you are doing and talking about it to be ultrasecret.

Benito Mussolini got it right about the Magenta crash-landing in 1933 by demanding absolute silence about the *'alleged landing on national soil of unknown aircraft.'* Until the central government learns what might be going on, you don't want journalistic reports speculating on the origin and/or nature of any unknown aircraft that land or crash on your territory.

We don't know Il Duce's motives for imposing silenzio, but the 1930s were a critical period in Europe's political environment. The Great Depression of the 1930s was a very significant influence because economic stagnation favoured far-right policies, leading to the establishment of authoritarian regimes across Europe.

Adolf Hitler was appointed Chancellor of Germany on 30 January 1933, and in March of that year, the German parliament passed the *Ermächtigungsgesetz* or *'Enabling Act'* that granted the German Cabinet, particularly the Chancellor, the authority to create and enforce laws without involving the Reichstag or Weimar President Paul von Hindenburg.

This effectively voted the German parliament out of existence, enabling Hitler to swiftly consolidate absolute power, free from parliamentary restraint, and marked the formal transition from the democratic Weimar Republic to the totalitarian Nazi dictatorship.

Benito Mussolini became the Prime Minister of Italy in 1922 and asserted his right to supreme authority, becoming Il Duce, the dictator of Italy, in 1925. He was not a dedicated Nazi in the same way as Adolf Hitler, but he did share some Nazi ideology, his regime being characterised by authoritarianism, nationalism, and suppression of political opposition.

And, just as Hitler's speeches of that time talked of his European expansion plans, particularly the annexation of Austria, Mussolini was seeking to establish an Italian colonial empire and invaded Ethiopia in 1935.

In the political (and growing military) turmoil of Europe in the 1930s, it's easy to understand that the Italian dictator would have needed to know exactly from where that unknown aircraft had come that had apparently crash-landed unannounced on Italian national soil.

And I think it's important to emphasise that thoughts that the Magenta vehicle had an extraterrestrial origin were most likely far from the minds of the Italian investigators.

They had more than enough potential spies and/or aggressors in their immediate vicinity to worry about Italian dissidents within Italy's own Air Force; France and Britain, the strongest of the still democratic powers; Yugoslavia, Czechoslovakia and Greece all of whom feared the growing influence of Italy in the Balkans following Italy turning Albania into a protectorate in 1926; the Soviet Union, under the leadership of Joseph Stalin, was staunchly communist and fundamentally anti-fascist; even Germany, who founded the Luftwaffe in 1933, might easily have taken the opportunity of sending the Luftwaffe to take a sly look at the industrial powerhouse of Milan.

Never mind extraterrestrial aliens, if any of these European countries had sent the Magenta vehicle to spy on Milan it would have been essential for the Italian authorities to keep secret the fact of the crash-landing, the cause of the crash-landing, and the fact that the remains of the vehicle were safely stored on the premises of an Italian aircraft manufacturer. Why is secrecy essential?

Because any breach of secrecy might encourage further nefarious incursions into Italian national airspace. Consequently, if there is a possibility that your enemies, real or imagined, might only need to tune into a news channel to learn your deepest secrets then you MUST impose absolute secrecy on all you do.

Very similar attitudes to Unidentified Anomalous Phenomena (UAPs, though I still prefer good ole UFO!) have been expressed by Dr Sean Kirkpatrick who is an adjunct professor of physics at the University of Georgia and was the director of the *All-Domain Anomaly Resolution Office* (AARO) at the Pentagon until he stepped down from that post in December 2023.

This office is responsible for investigating UFOs and other unexplained phenomena and Dr Kirkpatrick is reported as saying he had completed an historical review of such reports.

He is also recorded saying, 'We've uncovered some things that we are having declassified. Not just operational videos, but historical documents. The best thing that could come out of this job is to prove that there are aliens because the alternative is a much bigger problem. If we don't prove it's [extraterrestrial] aliens, then what we're finding is evidence of other people doing stuff in our backyard. And that's not good.'

In other words, reading between the lines, we have Russia, China, North Korea and various collections of Middle Eastern terrorists and the cartels of South American drug lords to worry about. In the face of that lot, I would agree with Dr Kirkpatrick and prefer to hope that UAPs are extraterrestrial in origin!

The scale of the UAP issue has been revealed recently in a study in which Dr Kirkpatrick worked with geographers at the University of Utah to analyse and map roughly 98,000 21st Century UAP/UFO reports in the USA, spanning the years 2001 to 2020 [check out the following URL: https://doi.org/10.1038/s41598-023-49527-x].

Using a statistical approach, they found confirmation of the long-assumed historical relationship between UFOs and the American West (Area 51 in Nevada, and Roswell in New Mexico, for example), attributing the West's higher percentage of sightings to the desert southwest's wide-open natural spaces and rural dark skies, uncontaminated by big city lights or industrial smog.

Their county-by-county assessment turned up hot spots for sightings just east of the Rockies or off toward the Pacific Ocean and found that hotspots showed a noticeable relationship to local air traffic and military activity, possibly indicating that witnesses often see genuine terrestrial objects that they simply do not recognise.

During one of the interviews held as Dr Kirkpatrick stepped down from the Pentagon's AARO office, he responded to a whistleblower's claim that the U.S. Government is hiding evidence of alien vehicles by stating that AARO has not found any proof of the claim and that the whistleblower has refused to cooperate with AARO's investigation.

However, bearing in mind Dr Kirkpatrick's statement that, 'If we don't prove it's [extraterrestrial] aliens, then what we're finding is evidence of other people doing stuff in our backyard. And that's not good.'

I'm guessing that Dr Kirkpatrick will be greatly disappointed by the Defense Department's All-Domain Anomaly Resolution Office report entitled 'Report on the Historical Record of U.S. Government Involvement with Unidentified Anomalous Phenomena (UAP), Volume 1, February 2024,' which was mandated by Congress and cleared for public release on 8 March 2024, because this report examines sightings of UFOs over most of the last century and claims to find no evidence of aliens or extraterrestrial intelligence despite the wide variety of claims that have captivated public attention for decades.

The AARO study analysed U.S. Government investigations since 1945 of reported sightings of unidentified anomalous phenomena (UAPs/OFOs), finding no evidence that any of them were signs of alien life, or that the U.S. Government and private companies had reverse-engineered extraterrestrial technology and were hiding it.

Best thing I can do, I think, *is quote a couple of paragraphs from the Introduction, the Executive Summary, and the Conclusion of this report.* I also give you hyperlinks so that you can see the original Defense Department press release for yourself, and, if you have a mind to, download the original PDF of this Pentagon report.

> The Department of Defense All-Domain Anomaly Resolution Office
> Report on the Historical Record of U.S. Government Involvement with Unidentified Anomalous Phenomena (UAP)
> Volume 1, February 2024
>
> **SECTION I: Introduction** (extract showing first two paragraphs)
>
> This report represents Volume I of the All-domain Anomaly Resolution Office's (AARO) Historical Record Report (HR2) which reviews the record of the United States Government (USG) pertaining to unidentified anomalous phenomena (UAP).
> In completing this report, AARO reviewed all official USG investigatory efforts since 1945, researched classified and unclassified archives, conducted approximately 30 interviews, and partnered with Intelligence Community (IC) and Department of Defense (DoD) officials responsible for controlled and special access program oversight, respectively.
> AARO will publish Volume II in accordance with the date established in Section 6802 of the National Defense Authorization Act for Fiscal Year 2023 (FY23); Volume II will provide analysis of information acquired by AARO after the date of the publication of Volume I.
> Since 1945, the USG has funded and supported UAP investigations with the goal of determining whether UAP represented a flight safety risk, technological leaps by competitor nations, or evidence of off-world technology under intelligent control.
> These investigations were managed and implemented by a range of experts, scientists, academics, military, and intelligence officials under differing leaders—all of whom held their own perspectives that led them to particular conclusions on the origins of UAP. However, they all had in common the belief that UAP represented an unknown and, therefore, theoretically posed a potential threat of an indeterminate nature.
>
> **SECTION II: Executive Summary**

> AARO found no evidence that any USG investigation, academic-sponsored research, or official review panel has confirmed that any sighting of a UAP represented extraterrestrial technology.
>
> All investigative efforts, at all levels of classification, concluded that most sightings were ordinary objects and phenomena and the result of misidentification [by the observer]. Although not the focus of this report, it is worthwhile to note that all official foreign UAP investigatory efforts to date have reached the same general conclusions as USG investigations.
>
> **SECTION IX: Conclusion**
>
> To date, AARO has not discovered any empirical evidence that any sighting of a UAP represented off-world technology or the existence a classified program that had not been properly reported to Congress. Investigative efforts determined that most sightings were the result of misidentification of ordinary objects and phenomena.
>
> Although many UAP reports remain unsolved, AARO assesses that if additional, quality data were available, most of these cases also could be identified and resolved as ordinary objects or phenomena.
>
> This report represents Volume I of AARO's HR2. Volume II will be published in accordance with the date established in Section 6802 of the National Defense Authorization Act for Fiscal Year 2023 (FY23) and will provide additional analysis on information not yet secured and analysed, interviews not yet conducted, and additional avenues of investigation not yet completed by the date of the publication of Volume I.
>
> See the original report for yourself and draw your own conclusions. Use the following URLs.
>
> For the U.S. Defense Department's press release:
>
> https://www.defense.gov/News/News-Stories/Article/Article/3701297/dod-report-discounts-sightings-of-extraterrestrial-technology/ or make use of this Tiny URL to go to the same place: https://tinyurl.com/4dytww36
>
> To download the PDF of the original report:
>
> https://media.defense.gov/2024/Mar/08/2003409233/-1/-1/0/DOPSR-CLEARED-508-COMPLIANT-HRRV1–08-MAR-2024-FINAL.PDF or make use of this tiny URL to download that original report PDF:
>
> https://tinyurl.com/mu2jpb8r.

Briefly, then, this report states:

- It provides a comprehensive historical record of UAP sightings, drawing from information gathered by the U.S. Government over the years.

- There is no evidence to confirm that any UAP sighting represents extraterrestrial technology.
- Most sightings were ordinary objects or phenomena, often resulting from misidentification. The report specifically states that, *testing and development of U.S. national security and space programs most likely accounted for some portion of UAP sightings.*
- The report asserts that there is no empirical evidence for claims that government and private companies are reverse-engineering extraterrestrial technology.
- The report deems inaccurate all specific claims related to reverse-engineering involving people, locations, and documents.

The report also states that *'proliferation of television programs, books, movies, and the vast amount of internet and social media content centred on UAP-related topics most likely has influenced the public conversation on this topic and reinforced these beliefs within some sections of the population.'* Yessir! You can say that again! Indeed, I wouldn't be surprised if this is the one sentence in the report with which we could all agree!

Personally, I am particularly sceptical about the way the Pentagon's 'Report on the Historical Record of U.S. Government Involvement with Unidentified Anomalous Phenomena (UAP)' deals with the Roswell incident as this 2024 report states that, *'the materials recovered near Roswell were consistent with a balloon of the type used in the then-classified Project Mogul.'*

Hence explaining the Roswell UFO sightings in exactly the same way as they were explained in 1947. Yet no consideration or explanation was given in 1947, nor is it given 77 years later in 2024, as to why the RAAF public information office reported the crash and recovery of a 'flying disc' near Roswell when it first reported the incident on 8 July 1947.

Am I the only one who thinks it's worth asking the question: why did Roswell Army Air Force officials, who were presumably pretty familiar with both aircraft and weather balloons, first report a flying disk crash? I believe the answer to that may be in the last line of the section entitled *Roswell Investigations/Inquiries (1992–2001)* which is on pages 21 to 22 of the Pentagon's AARO report. I quote that section verbatim below.

EXTRACTS from the Report on the Historical Record of U.S. Government Involvement with Unidentified Anomalous Phenomena (UAP), pages 21–22:

Roswell Investigations/Inquiries (1992–2001)
President Clinton and Chief of Staff Podesta Inquire about Roswell
(1992—2001)
The Roswell Report: Fact versus Fiction in the New Mexico Desert (1995)
The GAO Roswell Report (1995) space
The Roswell Report: Case Closed (1997)

Background: According to press reports, President Clinton tasked former National Security Advisor Sandy Berger to determine if the USG [United States Government] held aliens or alien technology. President Clinton said, 'As far as I know, an alien spacecraft did not crash in Roswell, New Mexico, in 1947…if the USAF did recover alien bodies, they didn't tell me about it…and I want to know.'

In 1993, Congressman Steven H. Schiff (R-New Mexico) made inquiries about the Roswell incident to DoD. The Roswell incident refers to the July 1947 recovery of metallic and rubber debris from a crashed military balloon near Roswell Army Air Field personnel that sparked conspiracy theories and claims that the debris was from an alien spaceship and part of a USG cover-up. He asked the General Accounting Office (GAO) (subsequently renamed the Government Accountability Office) to determine the requirements for reporting air accidents, such as the crash near Roswell, and to identify any government records concerning the Roswell crash.

The USAF conducted a systematic search of numerous archives and records centres in support of GAO's audit of Roswell. As part of this review, the USAF also interviewed numerous people who may have had knowledge of the events. Secretary of the Air Force Sheila E. Widnall released them from any security obligations that may have restricted the sharing of information. The USAF then published '*The Roswell Report*' in 1995, which included: '*The Report of the U.S. Air Force Research Regarding the 'Roswell Incident'*' by Col Richard L. Weaver, and the '*Synopsis of Balloon Research Findings*' by 1st Lt James McAndrew.

Results: The report stated that the USAF's research did not locate or develop any information that indicated the '*Roswell Incident*' was a UFO event, nor was there any 'cover-up' by the USG. Rather, the materials recovered near Roswell were consistent with a balloon of the type used in the then-classified Project Mogul. No records showed any evidence that the USG recovered aliens or extraterrestrial material.

• The USAF subsequently published a follow-on report in 1997, 'The Roswell Report: Case Closed,' with additional materials and analysis which supported its conclusion that the debris recovered near Roswell was from the U.S. Army Air Force's balloon borne program.

• The alleged 'alien' bodies reported by some in the New Mexico desert were test dummies that were carried aloft by U.S. Army Air Force high-altitude balloons for

> scientific research.
>
> • Reports of military units that allegedly recovered a flying saucer and its 'crew' were descriptions of Air Force personnel engaged in the dummy recovery operations.
>
> Claims of 'alien bodies' at the Roswell Army Air Force (RAAF) hospital were most likely the result of the conflation of two separate incidents: a 1956 KC-97 aircraft accident in which 11 Air Force members lost their lives; and a 1959 manned balloon mishap in which two Air Force pilots were injured.
>
> The GAO's 1995 report on the results of its investigation found that the U.S. Army Air Force regulations in 1947 required that air accident reports be maintained permanently. Four air accidents were reported by the Army Air Force in New Mexico during July 1947. All involved military aircraft and occurred after July 8, 1947—the date the RAAF public information office first reported the crash and recovery of a 'flying disc' near Roswell. The military reported no air accidents in New Mexico that month. *USAF officials reported to GAO that there was no requirement to prepare a report on the crash of a balloon in 1947.*

So, call it a balloon crash and that's the end of all that irksome paperwork! It is not surprising to me that those who might be described as *'conspiracy theorists,'* and I suppose I've now joined their number, are not impressed by this Pentagon report. Critics are reported in the press as calling it a cover-up even though the report itself claims no evidence of UFO cover-up by U.S. Government agencies.

Do I hear a multi-voice chorus singing, 'Well they would say that, wouldn't they?'

After all, and I quote again from the report itself, 'In completing this report, AARO reviewed all official USG investigatory efforts since 1945,' heaven forfend that they should find that any of those official USG investigatory efforts in the day had told the wrong story at the conclusion of their investigations.

I wonder, also, how claims of no cover-up match up with the facts of *U.S. legislation*; specifically the fact that the U.S. Congress included a measure in the *National Defense Authorization Act for Fiscal Year 2024* [https://www.congress.gov/118/bills/hr2670/BILLS-118hr2670eh.pdf] that directed the U.S. National Archives to collect reports of *'unidentified anomalous phenomena, technologies of unknown origin, and nonhuman intelligence'* but also granted various government departments the broad authority to keep these records secret! Check out the news story in *USA Today*:

[https://tinyurl.com/m4k9rs5].

I don't know if there is any direct cause in any of the above official reports for the fact that Dr Sean Kirkpatrick stepped down from the post of Director of AARO in December 2023. He is quoted as explaining that he called it quits after all the grief he and his family received from UFO fanatics, including violent threats, social-media smear campaigns, and even direct attacks on his home.

But following the public release of this Pentagon-AARO report in the first week of March 2024, I wonder if some of Dr Kirkpatrick's academic colleagues will be disappointed by this report's claim of *'no evidence to confirm that any UAP sighting represents extraterrestrial technology.'*

And I say that because he has co-authored a draft paper with Harvard professor Abraham (Avi) Loeb (who heads the *Galileo Project*, which is dedicated to the systematic scientific search for evidence of extraterrestrial technological artefacts), suggesting that some UFOs could be alien probes sent by a mothership located in outer space, somewhere in the Solar System.

The draft version of the paper is dated 7 March 2023 [https://lweb.cfa.harvard.edu/~loeb/LK1.pdf] and still shows the Pentagon as Kirkpatrick's address.

It seems to me that if the Pentagon's Director of AARO, together with a distinguished Harvard University Professor, and me all think that a mothership somewhere out there in the Solar System is releasing many small probes towards Earth that become our UFOs as they gather intelligence about us and our planet, then we have every right to ask, 'What's being done about it?'

We know what AARO is doing about it. Although they've just told everybody there's no evidence for UFOs, the acting head of AARO, Deputy Director Timothy Phillips, told a press briefing on 7 March 2024, that AARO are working with government laboratories and university researchers on a new portable multi-spectrum sensor kit to monitor the sky called the *Gremlin System*.

'It's picking up a lot of bats and birds and we're learning a lot about solar flares,' he is reported to have said [see Brandi Vincent's *DefenseScoop.com* report at this tiny URL: https://tinyurl.com/3u48eprw].

Consequently, despite the Pentagon-AARO's 'Report on the Historical Record of U.S. Government Involvement with Unidentified Anomalous Phenomena (UAP)' of 2024, I'm going to carry on describing my conspiracy theory.

And first, I'm going to ask, what did Arthur C. Clarke do about *Rama*? In Clarke's story, Rama is detected and identified as a near-Earth object on an

Earth-impact trajectory by a fictional space survey and monitoring programme called *Project Spaceguard*.

In the novel, Project Spaceguard was an early warning system established after a fictional catastrophic asteroid impact and Clarke had this project, tasked with discovering, cataloguing, and studying near-Earth objects (NEOs), particularly those that could potentially impact our planet, being initiated in the year 2077.

Inspired by Clarke's vision, real-life initiatives adopted the name, apparently with the permission and encouragement of Clarke, to address the critical task of identifying and studying NEOs in the here and now, after interest in the dangers of asteroid strikes was heightened by a series of Hollywood disaster movies.

At the request of the U.S. Congress, NASA carried out a preliminary study to define a programme for dramatically increasing the detection rate of objects that cross Earth's orbit.

In 1992, this study produced the 'Spaceguard Survey Report: Report of the NASA International Near-Earth-Object Detection Workshop' [https://ntrs.nasa.gov/search.jsp?R=19920025001] and, in 2005, the U.S. Congress tasked NASA to find 90% of all NEOs that are larger than one kilometre within a 10-year timeframe.

This ambitious objective became known as the *'Spaceguard Goal'* and resulted in the construction of the Pan-STARRS telescopes; a pair of 1.8-metre telescopes designed for wide-field observations and photography located at the Haleakala Observatory in Hawaii.

In addition, the 'Spaceguard Survey Report' brought about worldwide efforts to monitor and track near-Earth objects (NEOs). Check out the Wikipedia article on Spaceguard at [https://en.wikipedia.org/wiki/Spaceguard].

On 19 October 2017, an incoming interstellar object was discovered by Pan-STARRS. Like the fictional *Rama* Arthur C. Clarke had described in 1973, the object had an unusually elongated shape. Before being given the official Hawaiian name *Oumuamu*, the object was popularly called *Rama*! *Oumuamu* translates to *'first distant messenger'* and was approved for the object by the International Astronomical Union.

Unlike Solar System asteroids or comets, *Oumuamua* seemed to have a flattened shape and lacked a comet-like tail of gas and dust. It was estimated to be between 100 and 1,000 metres long and 35 to 170 metres wide. These characteristics, coupled with its extrasolar origin, prompted tales that our first known interstellar visitor might be an artificial interstellar traveller, just like *Rama*.

However, *Oumuamua* was already heading away from the Sun when first observed, at which time it was approximately 21 million miles from Earth. On the outward leg of its journey through the Solar System, *Oumuamua* made its closest approach to Earth at a distance of approximately 15 million miles and is now heading out of our Solar System, towards the constellation Pegasus.

It will leave the Solar System by passing through the furthest boundary of the Kuiper belt in late 2025 and, unless the crew wake up and turn it around (!), it will not return. As far as is known, *Oumuamua* has not left any alien presence in the Solar System, although six months before *Oumuamua*'s closest approach to Earth, a metre-size meteor impacted Earth on 9 March 2017.

Coincidences between some orbital parameters of *Oumuamua* and this meteor inspired Loeb & Kirkpatrick's speculations about an artificial interstellar object possibly being a parent craft releasing small probes during close passage to Earth in their 2023 paper [https://lweb.cfa.harvard.edu/~loeb/LK1.pdf].

Interestingly, Pan-STARRS discovered a positively artificial object in 2020. Fortunately for us, it turned out to be a NASA rocket booster lost in space from NASA's ill-fated Surveyor 2 mission to the Moon in 1966. Initially identified as a near-Earth object (NEO) by the Pan-STARRS telescope in September 2020 and given the ID 2020 SO, the object's unusual orbit raised questions because it had come close to Earth several times over the decades.

Comparison of its orbit with historical NASA missions suggested that it could be the Centaur upper-stage rocket booster from the Surveyor 2 Moon mission. The Surveyor 2 lander crashed into the lunar surface, but the spent Centaur booster drifted past the Moon and ended up in an unknown solar orbit.

Over 50 years later, the Centaur rocket was captured into a temporary orbit around Earth between November 2020 and March 2021, before escaping back into a new solar orbit. Spectroscopic observations with NASA's Infrared Telescope Facility demonstrated that 2020 SO was made of '*301 stainless steel,*' the material that had been used to build Centaur rocket boosters in the 1960s.

This fascinating story illustrates how the gravitational field of Earth can briefly both capture and release smaller celestial objects.

And now, we should ponder Asteroid *Apophis*. Asteroid 99942 *Apophis* is a near-Earth object estimated to be about 1,100 feet (335 metres) across and orbiting the Sun in a little less than one Earth year; it is one of the 2,646 asteroids that have orbits which cross Earth's orbital path.

When it was discovered in mid-2004 by astronomers at the Kitt Peak National Observatory in Tucson, Arizona, *Apophis* was identified as one of the most hazardous asteroids because initial observations indicated a probability of up to 2.7% that it would collide with Earth on 13 April 2029 (that's a Friday!). For that reason, *Apophis* is named for the demon serpent that personified evil and chaos in ancient Egyptian mythology.

Further astronomical observations ruled out the risk of an impact in 2029 (phew!). *Apophis* will pass within 20,000 miles of Earth's surface on 13 April 2029, closer than our own geosynchronous satellites, but not an impact! Concerns remained about a potential impact risk during another close approach in 2036, and there was still a small chance of impact in 2068.

When *Apophis* made a distant flyby of Earth in March 2021, astronomers took the opportunity to use powerful radar observations to estimate its orbit around the Sun with sufficient precision to enable them to conclude that there is no risk of *Apophis* impacting our planet for at least a century. *Apophis* was removed from the risk list maintained by NASA's *Center for Near-Earth Object Studies* (CNEOS). NASA has redirected a spacecraft to study *Apophis*.

The OSIRIS-REx spacecraft successfully completed its mission to gather and return a sample of the regolith of asteroid *Bennu* in September 2023 and was then sent to study *Apophis* during that asteroid's 2029 Earth flyby; being renamed OSIRIS-APophis EXplorer (OSIRIS-APEX). The plan is for the cameras OSIRIS-APEX to capture images of the asteroid as the spacecraft catches up to it.

OSIRIS-APEX will rendezvous with the asteroid on 13 April 2029 (that's still a Friday!) and will fly in formation with the asteroid for about the next year and a half, conduct many of the same investigations OSIRIS-REx did at Bennu: using its imaging instruments, spectrometers, and laser altimeter to map the surface of *Apophis* and analyse its chemistry.

OSIRIS-APEX will also repeat the most impressive manoeuvre completed on asteroid *Bennu*, by closing to within 16 feet of the surface of *Apophis* and firing its thrusters downward. This manoeuvre will stir up surface rocks and dust to give scientists a view of the material that lies beneath the surface.

Unfortunately, spacecraft OSIRIS will not be able to collect a sample from *Apophis*. For more information, you can explore the NASA's Science page about Apophis at this URL:

[https://science.nasa.gov/solar-system/asteroids/apophis/].

So, by the end of April 2029, we should know if *Apophis* has any surprises for us! These plans to directly image *Apophis* from alongside the object are important because it might be argued that because *Apophis* is only about 1,100 feet across it is too small to be a generation starship and is no threat to us. But if the Roswell robots are only around three feet tall, maybe the biological aliens are also pygmies.

But more realistically, if *Apophis* really is an *'invading alien ship,'* it could be a stealth design to aid its ability to approach closely to a resident civilisation at its destination without raising alarm.

If the Skunk Works and Northrop Grumman can come up with a long-range strategic stealth bomber, the B-2 Spirit, that has a wingspan of 172 feet and a fuselage length of 69 feet but boasts a radar cross-section of approximately one square foot (roughly the same size as a pigeon), who knows what the builders of *Apophis* might have achieved by the time it launched!

One surprise might be that the truth could be that since 2004, *Apophis* has been adjusting its orbit to bring itself into a stable orbit close to Earth, rather than impacting Earth.

This might be true if we assume that the successive corrections to calculations about likely impact dates have been due to course corrections made by the 'asteroid' as much as they have been due to the increasing precision of the astronomical observations.

Let's run with that idea for a while and posit the thought that maybe, just maybe, *Apophis* is the home of what I have been calling the Dispatchers. What should we do about that, then?

First, let's define the 'we' in that final question; it's certainly not you or me, mere taxpayers. No, deciding what to do will be the province of military analysts and military planners. If we believe, as I do, that whatever the Italians had saved from the Magenta crash-landing of 1933 had been, as claimed by the Pentagon whistleblower David Grusch, recovered by agents of a U.S. intelligence agency in 1945 and shipped back to the U.S.

Then we can add to that store of evidential specimens everything that was collected from that ranch near Corona, New Mexico and flown to Wright Field from Roswell AAF base in a B-29 bomber in 1947. From all of this, we can conclude that in 1947 the military analysts and military planners who would be deciding *'what should we do about it'* would be in the United States military. That being the case, let's consider their likely mindset at the time.

The most pertinent point is that in 1947 the United States military had just emerged from a World War into which it had been dragged by a surprise military strike by the Imperial Japanese Navy Air Service against the American naval base at Pearl Harbor, Hawaii on 7 December 1941. At the time of the attack, the United States was a neutral country.

However, this event led the U.S. to formally enter World War II on the side of the Allies the following day. The United States, as a nation, therefore had reason to be deeply concerned about the unannounced arrival on national soil of unrecognised aerial vehicles. They would have to be considered a threat, and their wreckage, and the remains of any crews, would have to be examined carefully and in detail to assess the possible nature of that threat.

There's another point about the mindset of the U.S. military in the 1940s that would have determined their attitude to even a suspicion of a military threat from extraterrestrial sources, which is that President Harry S. Truman announced what became known as the *Truman Doctrine* in a speech to Congress on 12 March 1947.

This was a response to the growing influence of the Soviet bloc, and its primary goal was to contain Soviet expansion and support democracies threatened by such authoritarian forces. President Truman pledged immediate economic and military assistance to Greece, which was facing communist insurrection, and Turkey, which was being pressured by Soviet expansion in the Mediterranean region.

In essence, the Truman Doctrine was a symbol of America's commitment to supporting freedom and democracy in the face of all authoritarian threats.

And I believe that the U.S. military of the day would have been keen, firstly, that the Magenta and Roswell vehicles were not just another aspect of the Soviet threat or a remnant of the Fascist threat, and, secondly, if the suspicion that the Magenta and Roswell vehicles were extraterrestrial in origin was confirmed, I'm sure they would have wished to apply the principle of containment to that emerging threat, too.

The Truman Doctrine marked the start of the Cold War and was a shift in U.S. foreign policy as it applied to the Soviet Union. Prior to this, U.S. foreign policy owed a lot to the remains of President Theodore Roosevelt's big stick diplomacy of the first decade of the twentieth century.

Theodore Roosevelt, the 26th President of the United States, held office from 14 September 1901 (when he succeeded to the presidency after the assassination of President William McKinley) until 4 March 1909.

His big stick diplomacy was encapsulated in what he claimed was a West African proverb: 'Speak softly and carry a big stick; you will go far.' In terms of foreign policy, this meant using a balanced approach combining gentle diplomacy (speak softly) with the display of military strength (carrying a big stick).

Roosevelt believed in proactive foreign policy, anticipating crises, and acting decisively, and he advocated naval preparedness to support diplomatic objectives. His administration focused on building a powerful Navy (which was his *big stick*) to project strength globally as a formidable military force commanding attention and, just as important, respect.

However, by the 1940s, the prominence of big stick diplomacy had waned. But though the Truman Doctrine concentrated on containment to prevent the spread of communism, World War II ended in 1945 when the U.S. wielded the ultimate big stick by detonating atomic bombs over Hiroshima and Nagasaki.

Furthermore, it was the power of the U.S. Navy which drove the Imperial Japanese Navy across the Pacific, back to Japan's Home Islands between 1941 and 1945. The Secretary of the Navy overseeing the success of the U.S. Navy in the Pacific was Secretary James V. Forrestal to whom President Harry S. Truman is supposed to have assigned leadership responsibility for the Majestic 12 Presidential Commission tasked to deal with the Roswell Incident.

Forrestal and all the high-ranking military and other officials who might have served on this commission were all old enough to have spent most of their service life operating under successive versions of Theodore Roosevelt's big stick diplomacy.

From all of this U.S. military history, I conclude that if the U.S. military authorities that examined the Magenta and Roswell vehicles from 1947 onwards suspected or concluded that those vehicles were extraterrestrial in origin they would have inevitably seen them as a threat of unknown magnitude. Their response would automatically have been to contain that threat and operate the proverbial policy, *speak softly and carry a big stick*.

And that would mean, I believe, that they would undertake two essential actions. Firstly, they would need to apply absolute, even brutal, secrecy to what is being done to contain the extraterrestrial threat.

Not that the primary intent of this was to maintain secrecy from the rest of humanity, but to maintain secrecy *from the extraterrestrials* who, in 1947, were the only agents we knew of able to stooge about in outer space beyond planet Earth listening in to any broadcast we made.

Secondly, in order to make the big stick we wanted to hold in reserve to accompany any future attempts at diplomacy, our engineers would have to be allowed to pull apart the wreckage we had collected in order to understand what, how and why the alien engineers had assembled it, and whether that understanding could inform our own engineering of countermeasures.

I began to feel a sudden sensation of intense heat spreading over my body starting across my chest and proceeding to my neck and face. Glancing at the timer at the bottom of my laptop screen I realised it was close to the usual time for one of my 'middle-of-the-night' hot flushes that often wake me around 3 or 4 a.m. when I'm close to my next Zoladex injection.

I saved and parked the file I was working on and pushed away from the table to take refuge in my en suite bathroom to splash cold water over my face and dry off the sweat. I spent a few minutes drifting around the flat to allow my skin temperature to normalise and noticed that the storm had subsided. At least, the rain had eased, and the wind had stopped whistling around my kitchen windows and its pendant light was no longer swinging around at storm-force level!

7. Cosmic Dreams

As my temperature dipped back to normal I pulled on a clean sweatshirt, made a mug of tea and got back to the laptop. Reminding myself that I had broken off when trying to understand the mindset of the U.S. military around 1947. And I decided that an interesting place to start understanding what was done in 1947 is a book published in 1997 titled 'The Day After Roswell.'

The author of this book was Philip James Corso, a former military lieutenant colonel who served in the U.S. Army from 1942 to 1963, working in the White House for four of those years. With the help of William J. Birnes, Corso wrote this book in his 80s as a tell-all memoir about the 15 years he spent as a Special Assistant to Lt General Arthur Trudeau, who headed Army Research and Development, with Lt Colonel Corso in charge of the Foreign Technology Desk.

In this position, he would take technological artefacts obtained from Soviet, German, and other foreign sources, and have American companies reverse-engineer that technology. Corso also claimed he supervised the reverse-engineering of downed extraterrestrial spacecraft, his job being to offer objects of extraterrestrial origin to major U.S. Corporations, without revealing where they came from.

Technologies Corso describes in his book, including integrated circuits, fibre optics, Kevlar, and Velcro, had already come into common use when the book was published in 1997. Corso asserts that an extraterrestrial spacecraft did indeed crash near Roswell, New Mexico, in 1947, and was one of the sources of the technologies he was releasing to industry.

According to Corso, the United States Government recovered this and other similar craft and subsequently engaged in a cover-up to conceal all evidence related to extraterrestrials. Corso claims that, he was part of this secret government programme, and his claims went much further than the technology transfer aspect.

What puts a lot of people off believing the contents of this memoir is that Corso boldly asserted in his memoir that Earth was 'at war' with extraterrestrials, claiming that the Strategic Defense Initiative (SDI) project was a component of this campaign.

The SDI, which was also known as the *'Star Wars programme'* at the time, was proposed by President Ronald Reagan in 1983 as a missile defense system intended to intercept incoming enemy missiles midcourse, high above the Earth.

As far as we know, or are allowed to know, SDI was never fully built or deployed because of technical challenges, budget constraints, and international concerns and *'the SDI remains a significant historical concept.'* However, if you ask Copilot about anti-missile defence systems today, you'll be told something like the following.

> 'As of now, the United States does have anti-missile defense systems in place. These systems are designed to intercept and destroy incoming ballistic missiles during their flight. Some notable ones include:
>
> 1. **Ground-Based Midcourse Defense (GMD)**: This system uses interceptor missiles to target and destroy intercontinental ballistic missiles (ICBMs) in the midcourse phase of their trajectory. It is deployed in Alaska and California.
>
> 2. **Aegis Ballistic Missile Defense (BMD)**: Aboard Aegis-equipped Navy ships, this system employs SM-3 interceptor missiles to intercept short to intermediate-range ballistic missiles. It operates in the terminal phase of the missile's flight.
>
> 3. **Terminal High-Altitude Area Defense (THAAD)**: Deployed in various locations globally, THAAD uses interceptor missiles to intercept and destroy short, medium, and intermediate-range ballistic missiles during their terminal descent.
>
> 4. **Patriot Advanced Capability (PAC-3)**: The PAC-3 system is designed to protect against tactical ballistic missiles. It operates in the terminal phase and is deployed both domestically and internationally.
>
> These systems represent the U.S.'s efforts to enhance its defense against missile threats. Keep in mind that the effectiveness and readiness of these systems depend on ongoing testing, maintenance, and geopolitical considerations.' [Source: Conversation with Bing 11/03/2024].

Copilot is less forthcoming about when these anti-missile defence systems were deployed, using phrases like 'exact deployment timeline…is not specified,' and 'it has been operational for some time.'

But judging from what is admitted to being currently deployed by the U.S. in the conversation shown above (and note that THAAD is 'deployed in various locations globally'), maybe, after all, Lt Colonel Corso was not wrong to claim that the Strategic Defense Initiative project was successfully concluded in Earth's favour in our 'war' with extraterrestrials.

'The Day After Roswell' made it to The New York Times Bestsellers list for several weeks and, pretty well inevitably, it divided the audience down the expected lines.

Publishers Weekly advised its readers that Corso's book is, 'Only for the few specialist libraries that have made documenting the unconventional a collecting priority' and certainly it is highly regarded by ufologists who have described it as *'a cracking read,'* with one Amazon customer review crediting it with, *'revealing the U.S. Army's involvement in filtering technology from the Roswell crash into U.S. industry R&D. The book exposes the UFO cover-up, highlighting the complex web of military, intelligence, and corporate agencies involved.'*

On the other hand, *The Financial Post* titled their review 'Book Reads Like Unidentified Lying Object' and *The Guardian*, in 2001, included the book in its list of *'Top Ten literary hoaxes.'* Consequently, Corso's memoir remains a topic of debate, and whether it is truly fact or fiction, it continues to captivate readers and fuel discussions about the unknown.

Sadly, and perhaps also inevitably (?), Lt Colonel Corso died due to a heart attack, at the age of 83, on 16 July 1998, a little more than a year after the publication of *The Day After Roswell*. In subsequent interviews, his son, Philip Corso Jr, stated that the publication of *The Day After Roswell* left his family ruined by scandal and lawsuits as the military intelligence community attempted to discredit his father.

I guess that's what they do to anyone who might be revealing a truth or two. I believe it was Mark Twain who wrote, 'But it was ever thus, all through my life: whenever I have diverged from custom and principle and uttered a truth, the rule has been that the hearer hadn't strength of mind enough to believe it' [https://www.azquotes.com/quote/530997].

Somebody else who might have had a few unguarded moments over the years is the American engineer, Benjamin Robert Rich (18 June 1925—5 January 1995) who was the second Director of Lockheed's Skunk Works from 1975 to 1991, succeeding its founder, Kelly Johnson. Rich is often regarded as the *'father of stealth'* because the F-117 Nighthawk, the world's first production stealth aircraft, was developed by the Skunk Works team under his guidance.

Regardless of industry sceptics, he championed the diamond-shaped design, which eventually proved to be the game-changer that so enhanced the F-117's stealth capabilities. Ben Rich is said to have made several, shall we say, unguarded, statements during his career.

Lockheed Skunk Works was the biggest recipient of the Pentagon's so-called black contracts and Rich is supposed to have ascribed this to the Freedom of Information Act of 1967. Apparently, private contractors are beyond the reach of the Freedom of Information Act and, consequently, the U.S. military preferred to farm out the job of reverse-engineering alien spacecraft to those contractors.

Josh Mitteldorf, in his article entitled 'What is a Breakaway Civilization?' on ScienceBlog.com [https://scienceblog.com/541300/what-is-a-breakaway-civilization/] states that Richard Dolan had reported that, '...according to [Ben] Rich, President Nixon attempted to penetrate the secrecy of the military UFO effort shortly after he took office in 1969, and that in response those running the program transferred accountability to an *international board of directors in the private sector*.' Other Presidents have since tried to learn what they can about the program, and they have been told, one and all, that access was on a need-to-know basis, and the PotUS didn't qualify.'

During a lecture held in 1993 at the UCLA Alumni Centre, Ben Rich is reported to have talked about the Lockheed Skunk Works having about 4500 people who have been building something for the last 18 or 20 years and saying, '...but they're not building what you think they're building. We now have the technology to take ET home. No, it won't take someone's lifetime to do it.'

This implies that the Skunk Works possesses advanced technologies, classified securely within its black projects, capable of interstellar travel and having the possibility of dealing meaningfully (whatever 'meaningfully' might mean) with extraterrestrial civilisations. To get more of the context surrounding Rich's statement, you must check out Shafer Hart's YouTube video at [https://www.youtube.com/watch?v=FB3ngWGwShs], it's very interesting.

One more story about Ben Rich is that during his tenure at Skunk Works and even after retirement, he staunchly supported the secrecy of the black programmes at the Skunk Works. His rationale being that the general public might not be prepared to handle the full truth about the Skunk Work's activities. But in his later years, he confided a remarkable revelation to a trusted friend.

According to him, extraterrestrial beings were exerting control over our planet, operating in the background, away from the spotlight, and perhaps in secrecy or obscurity, and that stopping them might be more important than keeping the reverse-engineered technology transfers secret.

For many years now, as successively more exotic aircraft have emerged into frontline service from the Skunk Work's activities it's possible to conjecture that those secret reverse-engineered technology transfers are made evident in the new aircraft.

And from the U-2 through to the B-21 Raider a regular pattern has emerged that as a new aircraft with ever more astonishing performance is moved into production and deployment, back at the Skunk Works they've been flight testing the next astonishing improvement in aeronautical performance for a few years.

I have already described the procession of radically new aircraft that have been launched into service by the Skunk Works over the past 70 years. Today, the 'ex-black programme' Skunk Works products that are the Lockheed Martin F-22 Raptor, Lockheed Martin F-35 Lightning II, the B-2 Spirit and the B-2's imminent replacement, the B-21 Raider. Those jobs done, what does the Skunk Works have up its sleeve as replacements?

We know, thanks to a September 2020 announcement by the Assistant Secretary of the Air Force for Acquisition, Technology and Logistics, Dr Will Roper, that the F-22 Raptor fighter aircraft will be replaced, beginning in 2030, by the Next-Generation Air Dominance fighter (NGAD).

NGAD is described as a *'family of systems'* in which a multiply-manned fighter aircraft is a mothership for its own swarm of unmanned drones, known as loyal wingmen, that work together as a collaborative combat family whose activities are integrated by onboard AI computers that also transmit all the flight data, by satellite link, to computers in the command centre at the home base, where the duty officers can take manual control of any part of the aircraft systems in case of a malfunction.

Incidentally, it seems that the Northrop Grumman B-21 Raider and F-35 Lightning II fighter will also operate with a swarm, or family, of unmanned drones.

NGAD is a highly classified and secretive programme of the U.S. Air Force (USAF) to increase lethality and ensure air superiority. A few artists' impressions of the NGAD in flight have been released, which show a triangular or diamond-shaped wing concept. A sort of upmarket version of the F-35.

The <airforce-technology.com> website states that, 'The USAF intends to initially procure 200 NGAD fighters and 1,000 unmanned collaborative combat aircraft (CCAs), assuming the use of two CCA platforms for each NGAD fighter and another two for each of the 300 F-35 fifth-generation fighters' [https://tinyurl.com/3eezawu8].

Every other detail about this aircraft is a mystery, but as I've indicated before, that's never stopped Internet speculation.

There's all the usual speculation, of course: that the aircraft features sixth-generation hyper stealth, using a skin of digital video screen material providing adaptive camouflage; that the aircraft is equipped with a main engine capable of accelerating the fighter to 7,500 mph and that in addition to the main engine, there is also a vortex magnetic field generator, which interacts with the Earth's magnetic field and is capable of lightening the body mass by 50% for vertical take-off and extreme flight manoeuvres.

That vortex generator is also alleged to power directed energy weapons systems able to operate in different modes from simply disabling electronics in enemy vehicles and missiles at a distance, through to powering a laser able to melt the metal of the enemy vehicle in seconds at a distance.

A YouTube video that goes even further [https://tinyurl.com/j9wjdpsm] in describing NGAD states, 'Although even now *there is no appropriate opponent for this mysterious fighter*. Its strength comes from the many years of experience of the engineers who worked tirelessly on it at the most secretive U.S. Military Base [Area 51], inventing and installing new technologies that we could only see in movies before.'

'Its details and technology truly resemble something extraterrestrial. The engineers managed to do everything possible to make the new fighter jet win superiority in the air of our planet, and perhaps even beyond its borders! *With a plane like this, not even aliens seem so scary anymore*, and it could even be to blame for supposed alien sightings in the first place!'

'But no matter how cool and technologically advanced these new fighters are, there is still footage out there of objects that are not at all similar to our typical understanding of aircraft...'

So, the question that I want to leave you with in this discussion about NGAD is this: is the Skunk Works already test flying the NGAD's successor? Or maybe that successor is among the 77 spacecraft that the United States Space Force operates in order to carry out its mission *'to conduct military operations in outer space and address space warfare'* to protect U.S. and allied interests in space.

While we are thinking about exotic means of powering NGAD, we might also remember that Bob Lazar claimed his work involved reverse-engineering a repulsive gravity device in 1989, which, combined with Ben Rich's claim that the Skunk Works can take ET home creates thoughts about drive trains involving either anti-gravity or a closely-related, and equally outrageous technology.

Maybe cold fusion, creating enormous amounts of cheap nuclear energy; or zero-point energy devices; or electromagnetic propulsion; and even, perhaps, Dirac's negative energy derived from the teeming particles of the quantum realm. Further, thinking back again to the 1940s, the free energy technology that Nikola Tesla was supposed to have described in his notebooks. After Tesla was found dead, in January 1943, in his hotel room in New York City, agents of the U.S. Government's Office of Alien Property seized many documents relating to the brilliant inventor's work, and not all of them have re-emerged. Steven Krivit's Low-Energy Nuclear Reaction Research website [https://newenergytimes.com/] is a trusted source of information about this topic.

Interesting, and more speculative, discussion can be found on Joyvel Osorio's YouTube channel [https://www.youtube.com/joyplanesrc2], especially *Unveiling the Reasons Why UFO/UAP Technologies Have Been Hidden* [https://tinyurl.com/mujt4aca]. And there are a great many TV programmes out there devoted to UFOs.

That was a marathon typing session. It is still dark outside, but the storm has blown itself out and as far as I can tell from the car park lights the rain has stopped and the air is completely calm. I pushed back from the table and stretched, then made a dash to the bathroom for an emergency draining of the kidneys.

On the way back to my laptop, I made a coffee in the kitchen and snaffled a Marmite sandwich. My head was still buzzing with more ideas that needed to be typed up. Clearly, sleep was far from near, and once again I sat in front of the laptop, deciding to restart by conjuring up memories of the U.S. activities in space in the old days of the 1960s.

The name to start with is, undoubtedly, Wernher von Braun, and the book he authored that must take pride of place was first published in Esslingen, Germany by Bechtle Verlag, in 1952 under the title 'Das Marsprojekt: Studie einer interplanetarischen Expedition,' subsequently translated by Henry J. White and published in English in 1953 by the University of Illinois Press with the title *The Mars Project*.

The 91 pages of this little book detail a technical specification for a human expedition to Mars that would take 70 crewmembers (50 of whom would spend

400 days on the surface of Mars) for a trip lasting two years and eight months overall [https://en.wikipedia.org/wiki/The_Mars_Project].

Wernher von Braun's first claim to fame was that he headed the programme in Nazi Germany that developed the V-2 rocket between 1936 and 1942. The V-2 was the first large rocket to be propelled using liquid fuel and eventually, the first man-made rocket to officially enter space in June 1944 when a V-2 launched vertically reached an altitude of 100 kilometres.

In his foreword to the 1991 First Illinois paperback edition of 'The Mars Project,' Thomas O. Paine, former NASA administrator, writes a marvellously succinct biography of Wernher von Braun, and the following is an extract of this foreword.

> 'While pursuing his engineering education, he applied his expanding knowledge to the development of critical components for liquid fuel rockets. Recurring, spectacular explosions punctuated these pioneering experiments. As war clouds gathered, the innovative young engineer was recruited by Captain Walter Dornberger, a thirty-five-year-old artillery officer ordered to build long-range military rockets in lieu of the aircraft prohibited to Germany by the Treaty of Versailles [the 1919 peace treaty]. Despite his youth, von Braun soon became the technical leader of the group and proposed moving the growing enterprise to Peenemünde, an island in the Baltic Sea where his father had hunted ducks.
>
> The space age can be said to have begun on October 3, 1942, with the flight of von Braun's first A-4 (V-2) missile. This 46.1-foot-high, single-stage rocket with a 2,200-pound pay load was propelled at 3,500 miles an hour for 200 miles by an alcohol-liquid oxygen engine capable of developing 56,000 pounds of thrust. V-2 bombardment of London was throttled by Allied armies invading Germany, but not until 1,054 rockets had struck England between September 8, 1944, and March 27, 1945 [**interjection**: in total more than 3,000 V-2 rockets were launched against Allied targets, including London, Antwerp, and Liège]. Meanwhile, von Braun survived fleets of Allied bombers that devastated the test complex; he also survived arrest by the Gestapo for defeatist statements about Germany's chances of winning the war. Charged with advocating the building of interplanetary spacecraft instead of military weapons, he spent two weeks in a prison cell in Stetten in March 1944.
>
> In February 1945, von Braun fled Peenemunde ahead of the advancing Red Army. He led his battered rocket team southwest with crates of rocket data; on May 2, 1945, they surrendered to advancing American troops near Reutte, Austria. Finding the German team remarkably cooperative, the U.S. Army transported 115 of the captured experts and 100 V-2s to New Mexico to continue rocket development and high-altitude research. Von Braun, like Moses, led his expatriates through the desert toward a distant promised land [interjection: although the von Braun family were Lutherans, so a better analogy might

> be 'like Martin Luther leading his followers to the true faith'].
>
> In the course of his subsequent experimental work, von Braun took a fresh look at interplanetary flight based upon his rocket team's cumulative experience in Germany and the United States. Ten years after the first V-2 rocket flight, he published his classic Das Marsprojekt in a special issue of the magazine Weltraumfahrt. This work also appeared in 1952 as a slim volume, Das Marsprojekt: Studie einer interplanetarischen Expedition, which was translated and published in 1953 as The Mars Project, which in turn stimulated a series of popular articles in Collier's magazine. Chesley Bonestell's dramatic illustrations of future space shuttles, space stations, astronaut-tended space telescopes, and interplanetary spacecraft voyaging to Mars inspired a generation of young people to technical careers that could help make spaceflight a reality.
>
> Von Braun's seventy-person Mars expedition included a fleet of forty-six space shuttles of 39-ton lift capacity (NASA's space shuttles lift 20 tons to orbit). With a turnaround time of 10 days (NASA's shuttles require 75–125 days), these reusable vehicles could make 950 flights to orbit in eight months, allowing for six vehicles being continually out of service.
>
> This would require 5.32 million tons of fuel costing around $500 million, which von Braun equated to ten times the high-octane aviation gasoline burned in the six months of the Berlin airlift. The result would be ten fully fuelled spaceships, each weighing 3,720 metric tons, ready to depart Earth's orbit in the plane of the ecliptic on a 260-day voyage to Mars.'
>
> The above is an extract from Thomas O. Paine's foreword to the 1991 First Illinois paperback edition of The Mars Project by Von Braun, Wernher, (1912–1977). ISBN 978-0-252-06227-8. Translation of: Das Marsprojekt: Studie einer interplanetarischen Expedition (German edition © 1952 by Bechtle Verlag, Esslingen, Germany). © 1953, 1962, 1991 by the Board of Trustees of the University of Illinois. All rights acknowledged.

Today, Wernher von Braun is acknowledged as the person who was most clearly and directly responsible for the success of America's space programme in the 1960s and 1970s, being the key figure in the development of the Saturn V rocket, which was used to launch the Apollo missions to the Moon.

Few remember, though, that it was von Braun's team that successfully launched America's first satellite, Explorer I, into orbit on 31 January 1958; the satellite that discovered and mapped the Van Allen radiation belt that surrounds Earth. This success calmed the nerves of America, which had been shocked in October 1957 when the Soviets launched their Sputnik satellite into orbit.

A spectacular Soviet achievement that had been followed by the embarrassing fiasco of the U.S. Navy's failure to get their Vanguard launcher off the ground intact.

Later in 1958, the U.S. Congress passed the National Aeronautics and Space Act which created the National Aeronautics and Space Administration (NASA) to be responsible for the nation's civilian space programme and for aeronautics and aerospace research, and Wernher von Braun served as the Director of NASA's George C. Marshall Space Flight Center in Huntsville, Alabama from 1960 to 1970. In 1970, NASA invited von Braun to take the post of Deputy Associate Administrator for Planning at NASA Headquarters in Washington, D.C., responsible for strategic planning for future space exploration.

By 1972, though, the political climate in Washington had cooled towards costly space ventures and von Braun retired from NASA, joining Fairchild Industries an aerospace engineering development company, as Vice President of Engineering and Development. Von Braun was diagnosed with kidney cancer in 1973; he continued to work through to January 1977 when he resigned from Fairchild Industries due to his deteriorating health.

He died in Alexandria, Virginia, on 16 June 1977. He was 65 years old at the time of his death. Wernher von Braun's positive influence on aerospace engineering continued long after his death. When President Bush directed NASA in 1989 to prepare plans for an orbiting space station, lunar research bases, and human exploration of Mars, he was largely echoing what von Braun had proposed in that little book, 'The Mars Project.'

What I've just written is the conventional story of Wernher von Braun's contribution to space-faring humanity, but I will add to this that his influence permeates the U.S. space industry today. What interests me most about the von Braun story is his design of the three-stage ferry vessel rocket described in his book *The Mars Project* for his human expedition to Mars. Remember, please, that the first (German) edition of this book was published in 1952. Though, according to Wikipedia, the German text was written by von Braun in 1948 [https://en.wikipedia.org/wiki/The_Mars_Project]. Reading this little book, the general design concept of the three-stage rocket launcher is the first fascinating aspect because all stages of the ferry vessel, used to ferry cargo into orbit, were designed to be reusable. Did you read this Elon? The first and second booster stages were designed to be returned to the ground by parachute.

The third, orbital, stage was to be a spaceplane/gliding shuttle. It would de-orbit with a short deceleration thrust, glide back to Earth, and finally land[s] conventionally upon a retractable tricycle gear.

Von Braun goes on to say, '…let us assume that each ferry vessel can carry out a round trip to the orbit every ten days. This interval seems attainable if we allow three days for salvage and return to base of the second stage after its landing in the ocean 1,459 km from the take-off point. This would leave seven days for inspection, reconditioning, and reassembly of the three stages. On that basis, 46 ferry vessels could accomplish the 950 flights [into orbit] in 8 months…'

Even more interesting is von Braun's description of the overall shape of this third stage ferry shuttle, '…One possible conformation is a swept-back, all wing design, with the fuselage in its central axis. If the chord length of the wings at the fuselage is 80 per cent of the length of the fuselage, and if the wing plan is trapezoidal, the span works out at b_w = 5,200 cm [= 52 metre or 170.6 feet]…'

For the avoidance of doubt, the trapezoidal wing has straight leading and trailing edges, it may or may not be swept-back overall, but the leading edge sweeps back, while the trailing edge sweeps forward. As in the F-35, among several other products of the Skunk Works.

Indeed, with a projected wingspan of 52 m, von Braun's proposed orbital ferry shuttle is about the same size as the Northrop Grumman B-2 Spirit long-range strategic stealth bomber, which has a wingspan of 172 feet!

Maybe the Skunk Works didn't need to reverse-engineer *alien spacecraft* to extract the fundamental design concept of the F-117 Nighthawk and all the astonishing aircraft that followed, right up to, and including, NGAD, and perhaps NGAD's successor, too.

Maybe they just needed to translate the basic idea for a swept-back trapezoidal flying wing space shuttle/ferry from the German in the first edition of *Das Marsprojekt*. Or even better, invite Wernher over to Palmdale from Huntsville for coffee and doughnuts sometime.

But that's not the end of Wernher von Braun's space engineering prescience. During the 1960s, space agencies were actively planning for space exploration by human crews and one idea Wernher von Braun explored was to use the upper stage of a spent rocket booster as a living space for astronauts.

In NASA's planning, this was named *Skylab* and the original concept [https://www.nasa.gov/mission_pages/skylab/] was to use the second stage of a Saturn 1B rocket which would use its fuel flying to orbit and once it was in orbit and the fuel was depleted, an Apollo spacecraft would dock with it and the crew would enter and outfit the empty propellant tank as a habitat and orbital workshop.

At the time, NASA had Saturn Vs available, so von Braun decided to use a Saturn V as the basis for *Skylab*. Von Braun's original hand-drawn sketch (dated 29 November 1964) showing how a Saturn V stage 2 fuel tank could be converted into a habitat has been made available by the Marshall Space Flight Center Archive at this URL: [https://archive.org/details/MSFC-8883912]. The *Skylab* orbital workshop and the first U.S. space station was launched into orbit on 14 May 1973.

It was occupied for approximately 24 weeks between May 1973 and February 1974, hosting three successive trios of astronauts as crews in that time. Atmospheric drag gradually decayed *Skylab*'s orbit and it re-entered Earth's atmosphere and disintegrated over the Indian Ocean on 11 July 1979.

The spare Saturn Vs that von Braun used as the basis for *Skylab* were left over from the truncated Apollo programme. The historic Apollo 11 mission, which successfully landed Neil Armstrong and Buzz Aldrin on the Moon's surface, took place in July 1969. Apollo 11 was followed by six more missions to the Moon in a series of Apollo missions numbering up to Apollo 17.

Only Apollo 13 failed to reach the moon's surface because a critical power and oxygen failure forced an emergency return to Earth in April 1970. Apollo 17 was the final manned mission of the Apollo programme and the last to land astronauts Eugene A. Cernan and Harrison H. Schmitt on the lunar surface. Apollo 17 safely returned to Earth on 19 December 1972.

Neil Armstrong's first step onto the lunar surface was broadcast from the Moon and became an iconic moment in broadcasting history. The TV audience that witnessed this monumental achievement is estimated at 650 million people (in 1969, remember; the most-watched event in history, to our current date, was the funeral of Queen Elizabeth II in 2022, which was watched by an estimated 4.1 billion viewers worldwide).

The astonishing success of the Apollo 11 mission, quickly followed by Apollo 12 in November 1969, began to make lunar landings seem routine to many people and public attention began to divert away from the Apollo missions. The public and the politicians had other life-and-death matters on their minds.

By 1969, more than 500,000 U.S. military personnel were in combat in Vietnam and the costs and casualties of that war eventually proved too much for the United States to bear, and U.S. combat units were withdrawn in 1973. The high monetary costs of the Vietnam War forced funding cuts in other domestic programmes and NASA's ambitious space exploration plans felt the pinch.

The space agency's annual budget peaked in 1965 and began a steady decline three years before President Kennedy's goal of putting a man on the Moon was achieved. In September 1970, two of the later Apollo missions were cancelled due to reductions in NASA's budget.

Indeed, for a time even Apollo 16 and 17 were in danger of cancellation, but these were eventually saved and flew as the final Moon landing missions in 1972. The eventual outcome of these financial constraints was that Apollo 18, 19, and 20, were cancelled; all of which were originally planned for Moon landings in 1972.

Proposals for America's further exploration of space after the Apollo programme were evaluated by a Space Task Group (STG), chaired by Vice President Spiro T. Agnew, which was set up in early 1969 by President Richard M. Nixon less than a month after he assumed the Presidency in January 1969.

At the time, only the lunar missions up to and including Apollo 20 and three flights to the experimental space station *Skylab* were approved human space flight programmes. Beyond the vague notion that the U.S. human space flight missions should continue, no follow-on projects had been approved after Apollo and Skylab were completed, which was expected to be by about 1975.

The STG group was tasked with recommending a future path for the U.S. space programme. The STG presented its 29-page report 'The Post-Apollo Space Program: Directions for the Future' to President Nixon on 15 September 1969, during a meeting at the White House.

The report expressed the view that the United States should pursue a balanced robotic and human space programme for the exploration of space but emphasised the importance of the involvement of human astronauts. It also suggested a long-term goal of a human mission to Mars before the end of the 20th century. The report presented three options that NASA might develop.

These options are detailed in a NASA historical article written by John Uri of the Johnson Space Center that was published online in 2019, entitled '50 Years Ago: After Apollo, What? Space Task Group Report to President Nixon' [the original URL: https://www.nasa.gov/history/50-years-ago-after-apollo-what-space-task-group-report-to-president-nixon/, but you might prefer to use this tiny URL: https://tinyurl.com/27nsccyj]. I quote below the details of the STG report's three options.

> 'Option I—this option required more than a doubling of NASA's budget by 1980 to enable a human Mars mission in the 1980s, establishment of a lunar orbiting space station, a 50-person Earth orbiting space station, and a lunar base. A decision would be required by 1971 on development of an Earth-to-orbit transportation system to support the space station. A strong robotic scientific and exploration program would be maintained.
>
> Option II—this option maintained NASA's budget at then current levels for a few years then anticipated a gradual increase to support the parallel development of both an earth orbiting space station and an Earth-to-orbit transportation system, but deferred a Mars mission to about 1986. A strong robotic scientific and exploration program would be maintained, but smaller than in Option I.
>
> Option III—essentially the same as Option II but deferred indefinitely the human Mars mission.
>
> In separate letters, both [Vice-President] Agnew and [NASA Administrator, Thomas O.] Paine recommended to President Nixon to choose Option II.'
>
> This text quoted from *50 Years Ago: After Apollo, What? Space Task Group Report to President Nixon* by John Uri published online in 2019 at [https://www.nasa.gov/history/50-years-ago-after-apollo-what-space-task-group-report-to-president-nixon/].

None of the proposed options were selected at the time. But in January 1972, President Nixon directed NASA to develop the Space Transportation System, the formal name for the Space Shuttle, this being the only element of the STG's recommendations to survive the budgetary challenges.

It was nine years before the Space Shuttle *Columbia* launched into the first orbital spaceflight of NASA's Space Shuttle programme; STS-1 (Space Transportation System-1) flew on 12 April 1981, crewed by John W. Young, the mission commander, and Robert L. Crippen, the pilot. Subsequently, 12 years after Nixon's shuttle decision, President Ronald W. Reagan approved the development of a space station, and it was another 14 years after that before the first section of what became the International Space Station reached orbit.

Wernher von Braun was the Director of NASA's George C. Marshall Space Flight Center in 1969 when the Space Task Group was collecting plans for future U.S. space exploration, which is presumably why the STG's Option I for a human Mars mission in the 1980s has his fingerprints all over it. When President Nixon ignored Option I in 1972, von Braun was working as Deputy Associate Administrator for Planning at NASA Headquarters, apparently responsible for strategic planning of future space exploration.

The negative response to the Mars mission on which he had been working for a quarter of a century must have been a huge blow and may very well have been the spur to his retirement from NASA and move to Fairchild Industries. After all, he had a lifetime's experience of dealing with the military and getting what he wanted from them, so I wouldn't be surprised if, when he retired from NASA and moved into the world of the private military contractor he took STG Option I with him.

And with his record of past successes, neither would I be surprised by the Pentagon welcoming him with open arms and the offer to Fairchild Industries of a decent slice of the $21 trillion spent off-the-books in the Pentagon's black budget contracts; with complete freedom from 1967 Freedom of Information Act!

During the early 1970s, the Fairchild Republic Company was developing the A-10 Thunderbolt (generally known as *'The Warthog'*), an aircraft designed for close air support of ground troops and forward air control of other aerial assets. The A-10 has become legendary in the military aviation world due to its powerful performance and specialised features.

The Fairchild Republic Company became a part of Northrop Grumman Corporation in 1987 bringing together the expertise and capabilities of both companies. And on Fairchild's side, that would have included Wernher von Braun's legacy. The first test flight of the Northrop Grumman B-2 Spirit (the Stealth Bomber) occurred on 17 July 1989, when the aircraft flew from Palmdale to Edwards Air Force Base in California to continue flight testing.

The Seradata News website published a short article by Rob Coppinger on September 24, 2008, entitled *Von Braun's 1982 NASA Manned Mars Mission Plan*. This reveals details of the Mars mission programme included in the August 1969 presentation to President Richard Nixon's Space Task Group, stressing ways in which the STG Option I differed from von Braun's little book, *The Mars Project*. Coppinger writes the following.

'Gone are the winged interplanetary rockets seen in [the 1952] Project Mars that glide to a landing on the Martian surface after using huge tanks of chemical propellant to reach the red planet, now nuclear-powered departure stages are launched and assembled in low Earth orbit while a Space Shuttle ferries the crew to the completed MarShip.

While only the Shuttle survived the integrated [STG-] programme plan...Apollo had changed von Braun's thinking with the introduction of manned landers that are in a re-entry capsule type configuration for touching down on Mars.

The schedule...details...[include a] 1977 test date for the MarShip's nuclear propulsion, a 1974 test flight date for the Space Shuttle and an orbiter flight rate of 100 missions a year by 1980. [Images show]...permanently manned outposts in Earth, lunar and Martian orbit and on the Moon and Mars' surfaces with almost 250 people manning these by 1990.

> ...*Flight International*'s 14 August 1969 issue also reported this manned Mars mission plan. On pages 263 and 264, the then NASA administrator Thomas Paine is said to have told a 1st August [1969] press conference that for a manned flight to Mars a decision would have to be made '*not later than 1976*' to ensure the launch of a crew of 12 in the early 1980s.'
>
> From *Von Braun's 1982 NASA Manned Mars Mission Plan* by Rob Coppinger. Published September 24, 2008, on the Seradata News website, URL: [https://www.seradata.com/von_brauns_1982_nasa_manned_ma/].
>
> **Interjection**: although I have been unable to confirm this *Flight International* report, the proposed NASA Mars missions and the political, public and media reactions to the plans are discussed on the following NASA historical page: [https://www.hq.nasa.gov/pao/History/SP-4214/ch11–6.html#source69]. You can download a complete PDF copy of 'Where No Man Has Gone Before: A History of Lunar Exploration Missions,' NASA's published history of the Apollo missions (NASA SP-4214, compiled by William David Compton and dated 1989) from this link:
> [https://archive.org/download/where-no-man-has-gone-before-a-history-of-apollo-lunar-exploration-missions/where-no-man-has-gone-before-a-history-of-lunar-exploration-missions.pdf]. You can find the discussion of the Mars mission plans on page 194 of this publication.

Rob Coppinger also points out that the Mars mission plans von Braun developed for President Nixon's Space Task Group report formed the basis for a novel in 1997. This was Stephen Baxter's book, *Voyage* [ISBN: 978–0061057083], which is described as, 'An epic saga of America's might-have-been, *Voyage* is a powerful, sweeping novel of how, if President Kennedy had lived, we could have sent a manned mission to Mars in the 1980s.' There is a comprehensive *Wikipedia* article entitled *List of crewed Mars mission plans* at this URL: [https://en.wikipedia.org/wiki/List_of_crewed_Mars_mission_plans], and *The Internet Archive* [https://web.archive.org] saves the day with the following two links: *Von Braun Mars Expedition—1969* at this URL: [https://tinyurl.com/4ff23tnv] and *American Mars Expeditions* at this URL: [https://tinyurl.com/bpapey37].

I was thoroughly tired and aching for sleep by this time, so I leaned away from the table to settle back into my chair and closed my eyes. Not intending to sleep, but just to rest them for a brief moment, you understand.

I saw the cloud of cigarette smoke before I recognised Pete Gibbon draped over the other armchair, the way he used to sit outside the commissary on our shared coffee breaks back in the day.

'Don't try to wake up, Buddy,' he said. 'You've been hammering at that keyboard all night. You need some sleep. Let our brain process the maelstrom of memories we've got rattling about inside our head.'

'But I just need to write the summary of my conspiracy theory. I can't be asleep now. I'll forget it all.'

'Nah,' Pete replied, exhaling smoke. 'What's happened to your editing skills? Several things wrong with that sentence. Number one, you are asleep now. Number two, it's our conspiracy theory, not just yours. Who the hell do you think you're talking to?

'And number three, I'll make sure you don't forget anything. In fact, we can talk it all through now. You've written too much historical stuff, it's time we whipped up a decent conspiracy together. You make yourself comfortable, and sleep on.'

So, I did, stretching back into my comfy chair, rolling my head into its cushions, and trying not to dribble.

'Why don't we start with that time at Area 51 when you first met Charlie Orde? You didn't believe me when I told you he was the first man to set foot on Mars, did you?' Pete asked.

I didn't think he needed a reply as we both knew this was true.

'The von Braun-masterminded U.S. Mars programme's first landing mission was planned to reach Mars by 1982,' Pete went on. 'But when Von Braun was diagnosed with kidney cancer in 1973, the Pentagon pulled out all the stops and greatly accelerated their planning.

'As a result, USAF Captain Charlie Orde, as Flight Commander, landed on Mars in 1979, seven years after the last Apollo Moon landing, but using a combination of greatly upgraded Apollo and Skylab hardware and inflight refuelling. Sadly, Von Braun died in June 1977, so though he knew about the imminent dual launch of what the Pentagon called Mars Dragon-1 and Mars Dragon-2, he didn't know just how successful his plans were.'

Pete lit up another cigarette, and I had time to ask, 'Where the hell are you stubbing those things out? I don't want cigarette ends all over the floor of my flat!'

'I stub 'em out wherever I like, Buddy,' he responded, adding. 'Don't act stupid, it's a dream, they're not really in the flat at all!'

'Okay. I can't remember what Charlie Orde did on Mars. Can you?' I asked.

'Sure can! Don't you remember? We found the secret history files on a long-forgotten computer backup disk we accessed from GCHQ several years ago and we read all about it then. It's my job to remind you, up there in your conscious realm,' Pete announced, through yet another cloud of smoke.

'Do you have to do it with smoke signals?' I demanded.

'You wouldn't recognise me otherwise. Don't be petulant,' was the response, and he went on. 'Mars Dragon-1 landed first on the side of the equatorial volcano, Arsia Mons, close to a feature that was interpreted as a secondary volcanic vent when it was observed in the first high-resolution images of the planet's surface made by the Viking Orbiter.

'The hope then was that an extinct vent could be linked to a network of lava tubes that might be used as ready-made shelters in which to construct a Mars base.'

'Yeah, I think I remember reading about that, now. The hope was fulfilled, wasn't it?'

'Glad to hear you remember! It can get lonely being the only one with a decent memory inside this head! And, yes, when Charlie Orde and his battle buddy and Mars module pilot, William P. Carr, went driving around in their second-hand Moon Buggy they found the feature they'd aimed for was indeed a volcanic vent cave system linked to a network of lava tubes going deep into Arsia Mons. Ideal shelters for the Mars crews.

'With that discovery, they called down the cargo lander, Mars Dragon-2, from orbit and started setting up the prefabricated habitats. By the time Charlie Orde's crew set off back home, Mars Dragon-3 and Mars Dragon-4 had launched towards Mars from Earth orbit. Oh, and before he left Mars, Charlie erected a sign on the Arsia Mons habitats naming it 'Area 53.'

'It was meant as a joke, but everybody involved in the project had 'graduated' from Nevada's Area 51, and/or the Tonopah Test Range and Utah's Dugway Proving Ground, both of which had been called 'Area 52' in their time. Everyone thought it was very appropriate for Arsia Mons to be rechristened 'Area 53,' so the name stuck.'

'Let me remember a bit more of the story,' I interrupted. 'It's beginning to clear out of the fog.'

'You're not smokin' in here as well are you?' Pete joked.

I'm not sure how, or if, my subconscious mind could see me smile in this dream, but it seemed satisfied by my reaction, so I went on, 'As I remember the story, Charlie Orde's expedition returned to Earth safely and he was duly promoted and then climbed the USAF hierarchy in the Area 53 black project until he was eventually appointed Director of the SuperDragon programme in the Skunk Works and Northrop Grumman. And finally, we helped him launch SuperDragon-1 into the night sky over Phoenix on 13 March 1997.'

'Yeah, that's about right, Buddy,' Pete responded. 'But SuperDragon 1 was only the first of a couple of squadrons of SuperDragon pursuit ships that are now based at Area 53. And you're forgetting the close to 20 years that elapsed after Orde's pioneering trip to Mars. During which successive Mars Dragon duos, many of them with international crews and with successively more advanced hardware, went to Mars to develop Area 53 within the lava tunnels of one of the biggest extinct volcanoes in the Solar System into the Earth's defensive outpost for the United Nations Space Command.

'That's where our defence against the incoming alien generation star ship is located. The aliens use their flying saucers 'robot-crewed' by the Roswell Greys and are approaching to arrive around 2068. We have the SuperDragon pursuit ships, based at Area 53, as our space battle cruisers that are already escorting the approaching generation star ship. So, we can ensure we meet on our terms, not theirs!'

'I'm remembering more of the story as you speak,' I ventured. 'Ever since the U.S. Navy research labs started downloading data from the central processors belonging to the bits of the Roswell robots that De Camp and Asimov took back to the NAES in Philadelphia we've known the aliens are bringing their generation starship into the Solar System. One of the Roswell robots was a mission specialist, with a memory full of details about the mother ship and its mission.'

'Right on,' Pete agreed. 'And another one was a specialist repair mechanic with a memory filled with a complete library of repair manuals and full technical specs of robot and flying saucer spare parts! So, von Braun knew all about this when he took his plans to the Pentagon after it was overlooked by President Nixon in 1972.

'His idea was to use conventional rocketry to establish a defensive base on Mars, while the Area 51 engineers were extracting everything they could by reverse-engineering the vehicles and crew captured in Roswell. And the

Pentagon and UN tasked the USAF and U.S. Navy to lead humanity's campaign to deal with the approaching aliens.'

'And all in secret,' I said.

'Yup, maintain total silence. Don't give the aliens any forewarning,' Pete confirmed. 'There's no room for whistleblowers. Zip it or be terminated with extreme prejudice. Basic Roswell Rules that have operated right from the start.'

'I can understand that. But between the late 1970s and the late 1990s we were building a bloody big military base on Mars. How do you keep what's being built on Mars secret when all the time you're building it the civilian space agencies back on Earth are determined to send robotic survey missions to study planet Mars?' I wondered.

'Just a different kind of extreme prejudice,' Pete replied. 'Since 1960, more than half of all attempted robotic Mars research missions have failed. Sometimes they've had to be nudged into failure by the defence resources we already had in Mars orbit.

'Sometimes conventional espionage on Earth has dealt with the threat, like persuading one NASA design team to use feet and inches while others used centimetres and millimetres for the Mars Climate Orbiter in 1999, which ended up with the spacecraft burning up in the Mars atmosphere. In other cases, we can screw-up their electronics or nudge them slightly off course en route to Mars. There are no witnesses out there!'

'I suppose the only embarrassing lapse was when the European Space Agency's Mars Express orbiter imaged a spectacular, elongated, plume of cloud seeming to originate from the Arsia Mons volcano in 2018,' I suggested.

'Yeah, but even that wasn't a problem until NASA released another set of images captured by one of their probes, taken on the same day, same sort of time and yet showing no sign of any cloud!

'The UFO-conspiracy community went ballistic comparing the images and dreaming up all sorts of explanations including accusing NASA of editing the cloud plume out of their images to hide what the aliens were doing on Mars and even suggesting it was a plume of smoke coming from an active volcanic eruption.

'What actually happened was that Area 53 suffered a devastating fire in one of its rocket fuel production factories within the extinct lava tunnels of the extinct volcano. The plant was using hydrolysis of water mined on Mars to produce

hydrogen and oxygen rocket fuels and an overheating pump started a hydrogen-oxygen fire.

'Fortunately, other sensors on ESA's Mars Express orbiter identified the plume, correctly, as a water-ice cloud and all talk of NASA or alien conspiracies faded away in technical to deceptive nonsense scam descriptions of atmospheric dynamics on Mars.'

'So, I can sleep soundly in my bed in the knowledge that the Pentagon's United States Space Force and the United Nations Space Command have between them got the alien threat all tied up?' I asked.

'Sure, you can sleep soundly in your chair,' Pete corrected. 'But I can sense here and now that our old bladder will be dragging you out of this sleep pretty soon. Maybe this is the time to remind you that we have an appointment this evening for our next Zoladex implant.'

Pete was right. It wasn't long before I was brought to wakefulness by the clamour of my bladder. Then I had that brief period of reverie ended abruptly by the notification alarm of my phone reminding me that I had an appointment this evening with the Practice Nurse and her 2-millimetre diameter hypodermic needle for my next Zoladex implant. Never a pleasant prospect, but it's keeping me alive.

8. Roswell Rules

I make a quick dash, well, quick for me, to the bathroom to drain a brace of kidneys, noting the time on the way. 11.15 a.m. Pretty good; plenty of time ahead to prepare for my outing for lunch in Sadie's Quick Bite Café, yet I'd had a good three or four hours of sleep to set me up for the rest of the day. Duly relieved, I made a string of two-or-three-word notes about the topics in my dreams.

My subconscious, masquerading for some dark deep-seated reason as Pete Gibbon, was as good as his word and had deposited the memories of our discussion in the forefront of my mind. So, jotting down a few words about them would anchor them there so that I could recall them later.

Memories secured, I had a quick shave and shower, and while dressing managed to also make a big builder's mug of tea and a few rounds of Marmite-toast, all of which I settled alongside my laptop to be eaten while I typed up my dream notes in full. When that was done, and the crumbs from the keyboard had been cleared away, I checked through the whole of my text and when satisfied with it, uploaded the whole thing to my secure folder layer in Onionland.

While there, I realised that the alarm clock subroutine that keeps my secure layer in Onionland hidden and silent was already ticking towards the end of its 14-day alarm cycle and was urgently in need of its weekly reset, but a glance at the real-time showed it was nearly one o'clock, so I decided to leave the reset to this evening in favour of going out for a late lunch!

If I don't do the Onion alarm reset before GMT-midnight tonight, my subroutine will activate GlobaLeaks software to upload everything to the *New Yorker*'s 'Strongbox.' I wrote 'onions' on a Post-it note and slapped it onto one of my kitchen cupboards as a reminder.

Finally, attired in my finest vestments, namely my old and trusty all-weather parka jacket, I ventured out into what proved to be a deliciously warm, bright and sunny spring day. I was a spring baby and even at my current advanced age, this season is still my favourite, and this day is such a gentle diametric opposite to the viciously raging storm of the past 24 hours that it's a pleasure to be out and about. Even with a dodgy knee and protesting heels and ankle joints! I even wondered about going back inside to park the parka but decided to compromise by unzipping it and carrying on towards the shops.

As I emerged onto the road from the car park entrance a couple of heavy-duty chainsaws started singing as they carved up the storm-felled tree at the far end of the road. In the bright sun of this day, it's clear that this was once a stately tree; probably around the same age as me, in fact.

But now felled by our increasingly hostile climate and being disposed of without further ceremony. Thoughts that are enough to bring a shiver to me despite the pleasantly warming sunshine as I amble gently down to the shops.

I notice that the fishmonger has a pile of skate wings in his ice-filled counter display, so I drop into the shop to buy a couple of them for this evening's meal and while I was at it, I bought some red mullet for the freezer, some of which Archie the fishmonger filleted for me, but the rest I planned to roast on the bone.

Then, to complete the treat, I went into the wine shop to buy a couple of bottles of Gordon Ramsay's Elegante Rosato. The thought went through my mind that with that lot, I might even be able to tempt Frank back to the flat tonight for another Ufology session!

I was already feeling overheated in my parka, and as I was now carrying a couple of shopping bags, I decided to return to my flat to get the fish and wine into refrigeration and myself into a jacket more appropriate to the weather than a winter-weight parka. I did all that and then re-emerged into the sunshine resplendent in my sage green cord sports jacket. Stylish!

As I hobbled down the steps from my building's front door, I checked through my pockets for essentials, like keys and a wallet, and as I was doing so a convoy of three entirely black Range Rovers, with privacy glass all-round, whisked into the car park and parked up, side-by-side at the far side, outside the medical centre.

Celebrity of some sort requiring medical care, I thought to myself, *but as nobody had alighted from any of the vehicles by the time I had shuffled to the road, I lost interest in this pantomime; there was another going on further down the road.*

The chainsaws were still singing raucously at the other end of the road and their concerto was now joined by some other impressively noisy machines. They'd managed to clear enough of the fallen tree to open one carriageway along the road and now they had a cluster of vehicles, one lifting logs onto a truck with a log-grab crane, while another machine chopped the smaller branches into chips and blasted them into a mobile hopper.

I always like watching other people working hard, but on this occasion, I was beginning to feel famished and in need of one of Josie's all-day breakfasts, but otherwise full of the joys of spring!

As I walked through the door into Sadie's Quick Bite Café I saw Frank through the side window striding along behind me and I held the door open for him.

'Seen yer walkin' past the fruit 'n' veg shop,' he explained. 'I'd nipped in to get some bird scran, thinkin' it's a boss day for feedin' ducks after our grub!'

I said I was all in favour of that! As the two of us made for our favourite table in the window we exchanged greetings, mostly gently insulting with Josie and her counter staff.

'Go on, surprise me,' Josie shouted back. 'You want two all-day breakfast specials with two builder's mugs of tea. Like, instantly!'

'Yer sorted, Josie love, and can I just say yer lookin' proper boss this bright sunny mornin',' I said back.

To which Frank chipped in, 'Chuck in a portion of chips for us to share, will ya love?'

'That might not be all I chuck at you two old charmers,' said Josie.

At which Frank said to me, in a stage whisper, 'Eh la, who's she callin' too old?'

Even the other customers, all regulars at this time of day, joined in the general cackling of amusement.

We'd hardly had time to sit ourselves down before Josie and her waitress appeared at our elbows dispensing large plates of food and large mugs of tea to the table. Heaven!

Frank and I dived into the feast and silence reigned temporarily. Then, immediate famine averted, Frank said, 'I've clocked them YouTube videos you put me onto. That Antikythera gizmo is a proper head-scratcher, but it's well explained by that vid by Spencer Connor. Like you said, every last detail of him knockin' up his own workin' version of the thing. Boss, that.'

'I thought, you were graftin' on the night shift,' I moaned.

'Yeh, I was. But most of the night there are more store staff on the floor than customers. What with cleaners, shelf stackers, maintenance engineers and all.

So, there's not a lot for Security to do except keep an eye on the CCTV. So anyway, I borrowed one of the demo tablets from the in-store phone shop and kept one eye on the CCTV and the other on YouTube!'

'It's alright for some, innit!' I kept on moaning.

'Eh, well. You've got to grab every little win life chucks at ya,' said Frank, not arsed by my wind-up, he continued. 'I found out that Amazon's got a whole library of Arthur C. Clarke's audiobooks, so I've downloaded a few and plan to start listenin' to them during tonight's shift.'

'I'd recommend startin' with *Rendezvous with Rama* if you've got that one,' I added.

'Yeh, that was first on me list,' Frank replied. 'But I had to search out the other story you recommended, *Encounter in the Dawn*, but Copilot eventually found it for me, as a sort of audio podcast on YouTube, so I've downloaded that, as it's fairly short.'

'Here,' he added, smoothing out a spare paper napkin. 'I'll give you a note of the URL. It looks like it will be interestin'.'

He scribbled [https://tinyurl.com/2x49vups] on the paper and pushed it across the table to me.

'Ta, Frank,' I said. 'I'll check that out this evenin'.'

'In fact,' I went on. 'We could check it out together. If you'd like to come back to me flat later on, I can offer you another afternoon of unbridled UFO scare-mongerin' and a nice skate wing for your tea! Yer don't even have to bring the bevvy! How does that sound to you?'

'Sounds boss, lad! Now, I've mopped up me juices from this scran and I hear a custard slice givin' me a shout. How about you?' Frank answered.

'Sound,' I said. 'And sling another big brew on that will ya? While I go out for a slash.'

When I got back to the table, all the used crocks had been cleared away and two prime, and generous, custard slices were displaying themselves alongside two more builders' mugs of tea. Frank and I happily attacked the displayed goodies and then, almost in perfect unison, we slumped back in our chairs with silly grins on our faces and uttering meaningless sounds of gastronomic satisfaction.

Most of the other customers had left so Josie was taking it easy, standing behind the counter with her back to us, talking to one of the counter staff.

She said, just loud enough for Frank and me to hear, 'Y'know Hazel, love. Servin' them two reminds me of a telly show I clocked donkey's years ago. Feedin' time in the Monkey House I reckon it was called! And then they park themselves right in the middle of me bleedin' window, blockin' the table and puttin' off the passin' trade.'

'Well, we have to feed them till they're stuffed immobile otherwise them two scallies would be off down the road without payin,' Hazel announced.

'Looks like we've outstayed our welcome, Mick,' said Frank. 'Let's do a runner!'

'Run? Me?' I replied, puttin' on a show of horror. 'No chance. I'll just hobble over to the desk and pay our whack.'

'No bother, lad. I'll sort the dough,' Frank responded, waving his arms about, 'I still owe you for a boss birthday bash. Let me lash out for a change.'

So, while Frank sorted the dough at the pay desk, I first made my peace with the gents and then joined Frank in more banter with Josie and the other staff as we left the caff to amble towards the park lake.

I couldn't do more than a slow amble because my heels and knees were beginning to complain about my toing and froing between the fishmongers and my flat earlier on. But, what the hell, a warm sun was shining and the longer we took to amble to the lakeside, the more time we had to chat.

Frank wanted to talk about Clarke's story 'Rendezvous with Rama,' asking how *Rama* had been detected in the story, and I explained that Clarke invented a fictional *Project Spaceguard* that was set up to detect and keep tabs on space objects flying in trajectories that might threaten Earth by coming too close or even impacting.

'Couldn't we do that for real like, to find them motherships where them UFOs are supposed to come from?' Frank asked.

'Aye well the U.S.A. did, didn't they? It's out there now, keeping an eye on them things called near Earth objects,' I replied, explaining. 'In 2005, like, the U.S. Congress told NASA to find and track 90% of all them near Earth objects bigger than one kilometre within 10 years, y'know? This became known as the Spaceguard Goal and led to the building of a couple of big telescopes in Hawaii.'

'And 'ave they found anything?' he asked.

'Oh aye, bleedin' millions of asteroids,' I replied. 'But only about a thousand of them are over a kilometre in size.'

'Only a thousand? Only?' Frank gasped. 'You mean there might be a fleet of a thousand motherships full of bleedin' aliens stoogin' around out there an' all of 'em are at least twice the size of the biggest ocean-going oil tanker we've ever built?'

'Yer knows, lad, that's a proper harsh and downer way of seein' it, like,' I said with a big grin on my face.

'Okay, then,' Frank says, 'how many of them near Earth things are a worry, like?'

We'd just entered through the gates of the park, so I shuffled over to the nearest park bench to take a breather and rest my complaining joints while I gave Frank's question some thought.

Frank plonked himself down on the bench beside me as I started to answer, 'The first sketchy thing that looked like it was headin' straight for Earth was spotted in December 97, when Spaceguard was still unofficial and run by volunteer stargazers, y'know.

'If me memory serves, it were Kitt Peak Observatory in Arizona that found a 2 km asteroid, what they named 1997XF11, zoomin' towards Earth at a rough speed of 17,000 mph, like. First sums suggested it would make a skimmin' impact in 2028 and then maybe come back for a full-on smack in 2037.'

'Bleedin' 'ell, Mick. Is it still on track, lad? What's being done about it, like? Why 'avn't we been told about it, la?'

'We've been given the heads-up, like,' I said, dead casual. 'It was all over the front pages in March 98. Boss story, that. They reckoned the bang would be like two million of them Hiroshima bombs. Some said if it hit the sea, it'd kick up a tsunami a kilometre high that'd go around the world twice.

'If it hit the ground, it'd leave a crater 10 km across and send out a blast wave 2000 km wide, causing pure havoc for thousands of km. The dust it'd kick up would block out the sun and we'd have a never-ending winter for at least eight years. But don't stress about all that!'

'You havin' a laugh, Mick?' Frank kicked off 'What do you mean, I don't have to worry about all that?'

I put a consoling hand on Frank's arm and said, 'Well, all them *'world's gonna end'* nightmares in the papers were based on the orbit calculations when they first clocked the asteroid. When NASA's Jet Propulsion Lab in California got the heads-up, it turns out their trackers had photos of the same asteroid from the last eight years. When they worked out its new orbit with them observations, they found this asteroid's closest approach to Earth will be about 600,000 miles. That's more than double the distance to the Moon, that.'

'Are you gonna kick off any more?' I asked 'Or shall we have a wander down to the lakeside? I'm feelin' rested enough now.'

Frank gave me a hand back to my feet and we continued our slow progress towards the park lake.

'Your reaction to what I've just told you, our kid,' I said as we ambled along. 'About that 1997 asteroid and its over-the-top coverage in the papers set the bar for how official info is 'andled. The mantra is *keep it hush-hush and keep it low key*.'

'There's a few reasons for the hush-hush around the whole UFO thing,' I carried on. 'Going right back to the Roswell do in 1947, and even the earlier UFO crash-landing in Italy in 1933. In 1947, the U.S. military had just come from a world war and was getting more and more fearful of communism. There were transformations going on in U.S. Government circles in 1947.

'The fella who was head of the U.S. Navy during the war was becoming the first Secretary of Defense, and the Office of Strategic Services, the agency that's supposed to have recovered the Italian UFO just after the war, was turning into the Central Intelligence Agency. And, of course, J. Edgar Hoover was still Director of the FBI in 1947, as he had been for the previous 20 years and would remain for the next 30.

'Not surprisingly, the usual story is that after six years of all-out global war, keeping schtum was second nature among government leaders and military chiefs. They didn't need reasons for keeping it quiet beyond that mantra, *'keep it hush-hush and keep it low key,'* because that way the enemy was kept in the dark.

'And, in 1947, we didn't know who or what the enemy was. But we did know they could listen in to our radio broadcasts. Who knows? They might even have tuned into Orson Welles's 1938 Halloween CBS radio drama about *The War of the Worlds*!'

'And got some ideas from it!' Frank chipped in, grinning.

I grinned back and carried on, 'Aye, well, fast forward 50 years and loads of cosmic stuff happened in the 1990s that made Earth's spot in the Solar System a bit more dodgy than we would have thought.'

I trod on a particularly large lump of gravel and the pain in my heal stopped me for a moment, but with Frank's help, I was soon able to carry on towards the lakeside, which was just a few yards away now, though I was walking on my toes on the injured side. So, with the target of our favourite park bench now in sight, I continued my description of the 1990s.

'The first bit of cosmic drama that filled the papers was comet Shoemaker-Levy that hit Jupiter in July 1994. This was the first time us humans saw a comet smack into a planet and the damage it did to Jupiter's face made it clear to people that a comet strike on Earth wouldn't be a laugh. Then the next comet to show up was Hale-Bopp.

'This was spotted in 1995, before you could see it with the naked eye, but only two years later it was as close to Earth as it was gonna get and was all over our skies in 1997 as one of the brightest comets to reach the inner solar system in recorded history. Hale-Bopp's nucleus was a massive 60 km across, so if that had smacked us, we wouldn't be here now, would we?

'As it 'appened, the nearest comet Hale-Bopp's got to Earth, in March 1997, was about 200 million km away, y'know. But the worry was that *'the brightest comet to get to the inner solar system in recorded history'* was only spotted two years before it flew right past us, la! Then, what's the score, that two km asteroid named 1997XF11, went whizzin' past us in March 98, didn't it? Rubbin' salt in the wound.

'And, finally, Hollywood chipped in with two belter films, 'Armageddon,' in 1998, where a team of oil drillers led by Bruce Willis are sent into space to detonate a nuclear bomb drilled into an asteroid that's on a collision course with Earth to divert it, and, also in 1998, 'Deep Impact,' where an extinction level event is on the cards when a comet on a collision course with Earth, is due to smack the Atlantic Ocean. Causing, in the movie, a massive tsunami that causes loads of damage along the east coast of the United States, reaching as far as the Ohio River Valley, and doing just as much damage in Europe and Africa. Get to the hills is what President Morgan Freeman says! I'm always buzzin' off films with Bruce Willis an' Morgan Freeman in, but them two flicks didn't do nothin' to calm anyone's nerves about the Earth getting' whacked by space rocks!'

We were delighted to find that our favourite lakeside bench was still free when I managed to hobble to it, and Frank helped me get comfortably settled at one end. He relaxed beside me and then put the bag of bird food between us, in easy reach of us both.

As usual, the ducks and geese grumbled and squabbled noisily over the food we threw out to them, and Frank and I resumed our talk about UFOs. I must confess, I was enjoying showing off my insider knowledge! I didn't often get the chance to do that with a human listener. I was too much of a recluse, I guess.

I scattered another handful of birdseed towards the lakeside and went back to showing off my specialist information! 'A couple of other interesting things that happened in 1997 were that the Northrop Grumman B-2 Spirit, which is a long-range strategic bomber, started frontline service and the Lockheed Martin F-22 Raptor, the first 5th-generation fighter in the USAF had its first flight, though it was about eight years before it started service.'

'You reckon they could handle alien UFOs do you?' asked Frank.

'Well, put it this way, I'd prefer them to be on my side in any scrap, an' if we had them in service 30 years ago their replacements, which are due around now, must be even more bossy! But the main thing about the 1990s is that all of them events, movies an' all, played a part in the U.S. Congress's decision in 2005 to get NASA on the job of finding and tracking big asteroids and building telescopes in Hawaii to do it.

'Though it's got to be said that another potentially hazardous asteroid discovered in 2004 probably made them pull their socks up! It got noticed 'cause of early predictions suggesting a chance of it hitting us in 2029 or 2036.

'This thing was spotted by the Kitt Peak Observatory in mid-2004 and when the first looks at it suggested a chance of it hitting Earth in 2029, they named it *Apophis*; this being a demon causing havoc and chaos in ancient Egyptian myths. Later looks ruled out a hit but reckon that its closest approach, in 2029, will be within 20,000 miles of Earth's surface. NASA has sent a spacecraft to have a gander at *Apophis* during this approach.'

I had a yawn and scraped some of the sleep out of my eyes. I was getting in need of an after-lunch snooze, but I scattered a little more bird food and pressed on with my next comment.

'The most interesting discovery so far by them new telescopes in Hawaii has been an incoming interstellar object discovered in 2017 that had an elongated shape; anything up to one km long and 170 metres wide. A dead ringer for Arthur C. Clarke's 'Rama'! Its closest approach to Earth was 15 million miles and it's now heading out of our Solar System. Which is just as well, cos they gave it an unpronounceable Hawaiian name before it left.'

I had another fit of yawning and closed my eyes for a few seconds. 'Before you nod off,' Frank said. 'I've got one last question.'

I dragged one peeper open and said, 'Sound, lad, fire away.'

To which Frank replied, 'How big are UFOs?'

How long is a piece of string? I thought to myself, but then, more helpfully, ventured a reply along the lines, 'I reckon the World War II Foo Fighters were about the smallest, about the size of a basketball. In 1947, an experienced private pilot came across a formation of nine flying saucers and reckoned each to be about 100 feet across, they'd be about the biggest.

'About the size of an average car is another size estimate often said by the average Joe, which I reckon would mean somewhere around 18 feet. Trouble is, UFOs are as big as the witnesses say they are. There's no way of knowin' how spot-on witness size estimates might be.'

I felt myself drifting towards sleep again, but Frank gripped my arm tightly and persisted with another question.

'I've been readin' about the Phoenix Lights do,' I heard him say. 'Which some people reckon was a mile-wide silent aircraft. What's your take on that, Mick?'

And then I heard myself reply, 'You don't have to worry about that, Pete. That was one of ours. SuperDragon-1 on its way to Area 53.'

'Okay, Mick,' Frank replied, loosening his hold on my arm. 'Say no more, you've said enough. I'm sorry about this, I've taken a liking to you. You old codger. You might as well have your kip now.'

So, I did.

'They're coming for you, you know?' said Pete Gibbon, from somewhere close at hand, though I couldn't sense where.

'This is no time to sleep. You've gone too far this time, Buddy. That guy you're with is wired. They've all heard what you've just said, all the way back to Langley!'

My eyes were jerked open by something crashing into my legs and causing a sharp, transient, pain. My head was too confused to be fully awake, but I could see what was happening well enough. Two young women, each pushing a baby stroller, had crashed into my outstretched legs as they tried to avoid the ducks and geese that were still squabbling and feeding around me. Frank was remonstrating with them and massaging my injured leg.

'Be more careful,' he was saying. 'Can't you see he's just an old fella havin' a kip in the sun? Give him a break, will ya?'

The women were not impressed by being lectured by Frank and stalked off saying, 'Mind yer own bleedin' business, la. Say sorry to the old bugger when 'e comes round.'

I tried to smile, but my face suddenly felt tight and frozen. I tried to wave an acknowledgement, but my arms felt heavy, and they barely moved. Seeing this twitching, Frank started to rub my arms and then my sides, trying to keep me warm, I supposed.

'Nah, he's not trying to keep you warm, Buddy.' said Pete, though I still couldn't sense where he was lurking, 'He's just swiped your keys. Next thing you know, he'll be heading back to your apartment to snatch your laptop. If he's got any sense, he'll save those skate wings, too. They looked delicious! Don't blame him, pal. It's just a job, all day every day. One deployment after another. And this deployment is coming to an end.'

Frank bent over me and whispered into my ear, 'Stay calm, Dr Daulby. I'll go see if I can get you a nice cup of hot coffee from the coffee bar.'

'See? I told you,' said Pete. 'Watch out for the real tough guys now, pal. I know how these things work. I've seen it all before. Many, many times.'

I found that I couldn't move my head, but I could still move my eyes to try to follow Frank as he walked away, leaving the half-emptied bag of birdseed on the bench beside me. He was striding towards the car park where the refreshment truck was located. Beyond him I could just make out the two women who had collided with me, loading their strollers into the back of a black Range Rover with all-round privacy glass.

My vision started to blur but I saw that Frank walked right past the refreshment truck and towards another all-black Range Rover from which an old man alighted slowly and carefully and patted Frank on the back as he climbed into the car himself. Then the old man started to walk slowly towards me, but my vision blurred too much, and I stopped staring in that direction and closed my eyes to rest them.

I sensed the old man settling onto the bench beside me, so I opened my eyes to look at him. He was old, maybe even as old as me. But something about him reminded me of somebody I'd not seen for a very long time. But who? The old man smiled at me and dipped his hand into the bag of birdseed between us.

As he scattered the seed towards the still-interested water birds around my feet, he spoke for the first time, 'I get why this would be a hit with the retired folks, just snoozing by the lake in the spring sun, and grabbing a bite now and then. Pretty sweet. You should've stuck with this, you know. You're past your prime for the game you've been at.'

He paused a moment to scatter another handful of bird food, this time further out over the water.

Then he resumed, 'Do you recognise me yet?' he asked. 'We're both greatly changed with age, and it's been such a long time since we worked together at Area 51.'

And the cogs of my brain finally meshed and matched the old face with a long-ago name that I came up with even as he announced it himself, 'I'm Clarence Bellwether, Dr Daulby, your trusty CIA handler. That dude who's been your only real buddy for the past few weeks, Frank Williamson, that's his actual name by the way, has been watching you for me this whole time.

'He's done a bang-up job of getting close to his target, don't you think? You might not be aware, but the CIA can't work in a foreign country without local help, and Frank's been a top-notch declared agent for us. You can be super proud of the training standards of the Royal Military Police. You betcha! Really proud.'

Clarence leaned across to take hold of my wrist, like a doctor feeling for a pulse then he went back to scattering birdseed from Frank's bag as he mused a bit more.

'Yeah, it's been a while, Dr Daulby,' he said like he was thinking out loud. 'You've been at this game for over 50 years. And you've done a good job, gotta give you that. You've definitely set me up with some sweet gigs after retirement, that's for sure! This one, in particular, I'm really thankful for.

'I've always been a big Beatles fan, so I'm gonna have a blast in the next few days, getting to know Liverpool and living the Beatles experience again. I always take a few days off after wrapping up a job, the Company knows that, and it's always happy to cover my expenses. And looking at you, I'm pretty sure we've wrapped this one up.'

Another dip into the bag of bird food. Another scattering on the water. More arguments between squabbling water birds. But I was beginning to feel quite light-headed as he continued to chat and even moralise.

'Yep,' he went on. 'Here's a quote for you, 'Time is the school in which we learn, Time is the fire in which we burn.' You know who penned that, Dr Daulby? That was Delmore Schwartz. American poet, Brooklyn-born, passed away in his room at the Columbia Hotel when he was just 53.

'He was so cut off from everyone else that it took two days for the FBI to ID his body at the morgue. I started gathering quotes like that when I hit the big 8–0. Here's another gem, 'I know the days ahead of me are fewer than those I have left behind. There is no escaping this most basic fact of accounting.''

'I really dig that! 'It's a basic fact of accounting!' Priceless! That was written by Hernan Diaz, a Pulitzer Prize winner. Both of these quotes are a reminder that time is something precious we gotta use wisely.'

He paused only slightly before he went on musing, 'Can you believe it's been 80 years since Roswell? That's the whole of our lives, you and me. But that's about how long it takes to slow down a starship and then change its course to orbit a planet. It also takes that long to get a proper welcome ready and to make sure we've got the upper hand when the inevitable showdown happens.

'But you know all that, don't you? And that's where we've got a problem with the game you've been playing, Dr Daulby 'cause we can't let the aliens know just how well prepared we are for their arrival. So, we've gotta shut you down. And let me tell you, brother, you're getting shut down right now.'

He sounded quite pleased with that as he continued, 'Look, you ain't gonna be around much longer. I'm just here to make sure you do check out. You've been shot up with one of our curare derivative toxins,' he said, warming to his topic.

'Remember that stroller bumping into you? That's what gave you the shot. Those two girls are awesome. They're part of the RMP team of declared agents that Frank assembled, locals from Liverpool, you know? So, it all seems totally normal. Fantastic team.

'It's a joy to work with them. You should consider yourself fortunate. You'll just drift off to sleep now and never wake up. It's all pretty painless, even dignified. Not like the military-grade neurotoxins that the Russian SVR and FSB use, they can really tear your nervous system to shreds, slowly and painfully.'

My chest started to tighten up and I had difficulty breathing. My mind began to wander as Clarence continued to drone on, but with effort, I managed to concentrate on what he was saying. He seemed to be getting more philosophical. *It's an age thing,* I thought to myself.

'Every game's got rules, right?' he was saying. 'Without rules, gameplay would be a total mess. Your game right now is blowing the whistle. Specifically, blowing the whistle on what's really been happening at Area 51 for the last 80 years or so, and at Area 53 for the last 30 years or more.

'We've had two rules since Roswell, more than 80 years ago, that cover that. Rule one, you don't spill the beans about Area 51 or the Skunk Works to the outside world. Rule two, whistleblowers get discredited and canned, and not always in that order!'

He scattered the last few bird seeds towards the water and then screwed up the paper bag that had contained them. This he put into my hand and again felt for my pulse as he did so.

'I gotta hand it to you, Dr Daulby, you sure did a bang-up job hiding your tracks with some of the slickest encryption routines our guys have ever come across. But you goofed up thinking we didn't have coders as sharp, or heck, even sharper than you. Sure, when you hung up your hat and *Dr Michael Daulby* vanished off the map, we needed a little help from our buddy Frank Williamson to track down *Mick Gibson* here in Liverpool.

'But like I've been saying, Frank's one well-oiled machine. It was an absolute gift for a man like him when you turned up to the opening ceremony of GCHQ-Manchester. What were you thinking of? Eh? Hubris, I suppose,' said Clarence. 'But that's how Williamson sniffed out that you had *'disappeared'* to Liverpool. Overconfident arrogance, that's what's brought about your downfall.'

Clarence leaned over me again and looked into my eyes, checking my pupils.

Then he patted my hand as he rose from the bench, saying, 'Alright Dr Daulby, seems like we're both good to go, so here's to a smooth ride for the two of us.'

He left, but my vision was now too blurred for me to see much of his leaving, but I could hear him well enough and feel his final warm touch.

I noticed Pete Gibbon sitting on the other end of the bench, not smoking for once, and my eyes seemed to fix my gaze on him.

'Am I dead?' I asked.

'Pretty much,' he replied. 'There's no escape for you this time. When you see the bright light in the furthest distance and you feel it pulling you towards it, just let go and you'll be fine. Our consciousness is only borrowed from the universe, and when your body dies, your consciousness returns home to the cosmos. It's

all a matter of quantum entanglements, I've been told. Come on, come with me. It's important not to be lost but you've nothing to fear.'

And somehow, we both went towards that bright light.

END